DATE DUE

Dogged Persistence

The unread story is not a story; it is little black marks on wood pulp. The reader, reading it, makes it live: a live thing, a story.

Ursula K. LeGuin

Kevin J. Anderson

Dogged Persistence

Kevin J. Anderson

With an Introduction by
Kristine Kathryn Rusch

Golden Gryphon Press
2001

"Canals in the Sand," first published in *War of the Worlds: Global Dispatches*, edited by Kevin J. Anderson, Bantam Spectra, 1996.

"Dogged Persistence," first published in *The Magazine of Fantasy and Science Fiction*, September 1992.

"Drumbeats," copyright © 1994 by Kevin J. Anderson and Neil Peart. First published in *Shock Rock II*, edited by Jeff Gelb, Pocket Books, 1994.

"Dune: A Whisper of Caladan Seas," copyright © 1999 by Brian Herbert and Kevin J. Anderson. First published in *Amazing Stories*, Summer 1999.

"Entropy Ranch," first published in *Starshore*, Winter 1990.

"Final Performance," first published in *The Magazine of Fantasy and Science Fiction*, January 1985.

"Fondest of Memories," first published in *Full Spectrum 3*, edited by Lou Aronica, Amy Stout, and Betsy Mitchell, Doubleday Foundation, 1991.

"The Ghost of Christmas Always," first published in *Pulphouse*, December 31, 1991.

"Human, Martian—One, Two, Three," first published in *Full Spectrum 4*, edited by Lou Aronica, Amy Stout, and Betsy Mitchell, Bantam Spectra, 1993.

"Much at Stake," first published in *The Ultimate Dracula*, edited by Byron Preiss, David Kellor, and Megan Miller, Dell, 1991.

"Music Played on the Strings of Time," first published in *Analog*, January 1993.

"New Recruits," first published in *Weirdbook*, no. 25, 1990.

"The Old Man and the Cherry Tree," first published in *Grue*, no. 3, 1986.

"Prisoner of War," first published in *The Outer Limits: Armageddon Dreams*, edited by Kevin J. Anderson, BSV Publishing, 2000.

"Reflections in a Magnetic Mirror," copyright © 1988 by Kevin J. Anderson and Doug Beason. First published in *Full Spectrum*, edited by Lou Aronica and Shawna McCarthy, Bantam Spectra, 1988.

"Scientific Romance," first published in *The UFO Files*, edited by Ed Gorman and Martin H. Greenberg, DAW, 1998.

"Sea Dreams," copyright © 1995 by Kevin J. Anderson and Rebecca Moesta. First published in *Peter S. Beagle's Immortal Unicorn*, edited by Peter S. Beagle, Janet Berliner, and Martin H. Greenberg, HarperPrism, 1995.

"Tide Pools," first published in *Analog*, December 1993.

Copyright © 2001 by Kevin J. Anderson
Introduction © 2001 by Kristine Kathryn Rusch

Edited by Marty Halpern

LIBRARY OF CONGRESS CATALOGUING-IN-PUBLICATION DATA
Anderson, Kevin J., 1962—
    Dogged Persistence / by Kevin J. Anderson ;
    with an introduction by Kristine Kathryn Rusch. — 1st ed.
        p.   cm.
    ISBN 1-930846-03-7 (hardcover : alk. paper)
        1. Science fiction, American.   I. Title.

PS3551.N37442D6   2001
813'.54—dc21   00-053576

Printed in the United States of America.

First Edition

Contents

This collection is for REBECCA,
the love of my life,
who will always be part of every sentence I write

Acknowledgments

Since this collection spans more than a decade, it is impossible to thank every influence and every editor who helped shape the stories. My gratitude goes to my various collaborators—Doug Beason, Brian Herbert, Neil Peart—for their contributions, as well as the dozens of small-press publishers who let me occasionally see my work get into print even as the rejection slips piled up.

I especially appreciate the time and dedication my editor, Marty Halpern, put into making this collection as perfect as possible, with an attention to detail that would have driven other people insane. Gary Turner at Golden Gryphon Press has faith in these stories and I appreciate being included among his ambitious and impressive line of books.

And finally, my applause for Dave Dorman—thanks for so many great covers!

Introduction

KEVIN J. ANDERSON IS ONE OF THE MOST DRIVEN people I've ever met—which isn't to say he's not talented—he is—but drive is probably his most defining feature. To most Talented Authors, people who wait for the muse to strike and who write maybe one short story a year, "drive" is a dirty word. They lack it, and because they lack it, they believe someone with drive is somehow cheating the system and denying them their great opportunities by filling "limited publishing slots" and "writing junk."

These Talented Authors get a lot of press. Whining, it seems, appeals to reporters. (I can say that. I used to be one. Whining, however, did not appeal to me.) Talented Authors also get forums at writer's conferences where they make speeches disparaging bestsellers and complaining about the thousand ways literature is dying.

Actually, literature is doing very well. More books are being published today than ever before, and many of them are extremely good. The books we all read in college—those famous old classics—were the bestsellers of their day. Art requires an audience. Without an audience, a writer's voice never gets heard. Without an audience and a faithful following, a writer cannot be remembered.

Who has the better chance of being read fifty years from now:

A Talented Author who writes (and publishes) one short story a year or Kevin J. Anderson?

Well, that's a no-brainer. Kevin J. Anderson, of course.

And that's because Kevin is driven.

I noticed Kevin's drive the day I met him. I've known Kevin longer than anyone else in the publishing industry (although Stanley Schmidt, the editor of *Analog,* has been reading Kevin's fiction longer than I have; Stan remembers Kevin's first submission to the magazine when Kevin was *eleven years old*). I met Kevin in college. I was an elderly twenty and he was eighteen. We signed up for the same creative writing seminar at the University of Wisconsin, Madison.

Kevin claims he noticed me early on because I was the only other person in the class who wrote science fiction. That observation means it took him weeks to figure out who I was. Understandable for a Tuesday/Thursday class where everyone sat around a U-shaped block of tables, and no one had to speak if she didn't want to. I sat at the very back of the U, as far from the professor as I could get. (It had taken all the guts I had to sign up for that class, and I was convinced I wouldn't be allowed in.) Kevin, on the other hand, sat to the right of the professor—the immediate right. I noticed Kevin the very first day because he made a scene.

I'm used to Kevin's scenes now. They're always interesting and always justified, and I always learn from them. But this was the very first one I'd witnessed and I was shocked (and quietly intrigued).

The professor, a fairly young man, introduced himself, and proceeded to give us a speech. He told us we had to turn in one short story during the semester and that he would not grade it for grammar or spelling. "That's what Strunk and White is for," he said. Then he turned the class over to us.

Kevin raised his hand. He was still a gawky teenager. He hadn't hit his full growth yet. He was in that weed stage, the one most boys hit which leaves them too skinny and looking like they might break in a strong wind.

"What have you published?" he asked in a voice that clearly hadn't finished changing.

"Excuse me?" the professor replied.

"You're teaching a creative writing class, aren't you?" Kevin said. "I want to know your credentials."

The professor smiled condescendingly. "I got my M.F.A. from Yale in Creative Writing."

"No," Kevin said. "I want to know what you've *published*."

"Well," the professor said, "I've had a short story in the *Kenyon Review*."

In those days, the *Kenyon Review* paid in copies. It had prestige in literary circles, but only about 200 people read the magazine.

"The *Kenyon Review*?" Kevin snorted—and I mean snorted (I think this is the first time I ever heard anyone make this sound appropriately in a conversation)—and said, "I've published over one hundred short stories and have been paid for all of them. I should be teaching this class."

I have no idea what the professor said in response. I really don't remember. All I remember doing was staring at Kevin, this gangly Wisconsin boy whose voice was still nasal, and realizing that he had published. I felt like he had found the Holy Grail.

And he had. He was right. *He* should have been teaching that class, not some M.F.A. who had no idea what made a good short story. I knew it from the moment Kevin spoke. I stayed in the class for two reasons: I got college credit for writing that I would be doing anyway and I got to learn from Kevin J. Anderson.

Kevin taught me a lot of things. He taught me how to mail my stories. (No kidding. I had no idea there was a system to it.) He taught me that rejection was part of the business. And he taught me how to focus my own drive so that I could pursue writing as a career.

I taught him how to use a computer. Somehow, I don't think that's a fair trade-off.

You see, to this day, Kevin still out drives me. (Not on the road. I won't get into his car. That's another, longer story—funny, but not appropriate for this slim volume. Suffice to say it has to do with my memories of Kevin learning how to drive. Sometimes having old friends is a disadvantage.) He works harder than anyone I know, and he cares about that work. He is always looking for the most efficient way for his determination to help his writing. (I think that's the scientist in him. I didn't tell you he double-majored in Physics and Astronomy with a minor in Russian History, did I? He did that because he wanted to be a science fiction writer when he grew up.)

I'm still learning from him.

But I didn't just learn business and drive. In the early days, I learned how to use detail from reading Kevin's work. And as time went on, I learned how to incorporate science into my fiction so that my science fiction was more realistic.

In the early years of our writing, our work fed off each other's.

His novel *Resurrection, Inc.* influenced my short story, "Stained Black," which then influenced his novel (soon to be released) *Hopscotch.* We sometimes used the same settings. We stole from each other. And we've used each other shamelessly in our work.

His short story, "Dogged Persistence," is set at my house, or what was my house in 1992. I had to work hard at not mentioning that when I wrote the story's introduction for *The Magazine of Fantasy and Science Fiction* (which I was editing at the time) because I wanted this strong story to stand on its own, which it did.

"The Old Man and the Cherry Tree" was written when we were both watching *Shogun,* the miniseries, on television. I was the one who took the Japanese history class (or maybe I took it first), but he was the one who used the information in a story—one that got picked up for a best of the year collection.

"The Ghost of Christmas Always" is the best of the many Christmas stories that Kevin wrote when he used to come to our holiday gatherings in Oregon. We read stories out loud before a fireplace on Christmas Eve, a Victorian tradition that we had made our own. Appropriately, Kevin wrote a Christmas story about the quintessential Victorian, Charles Dickens. And it's a damn fine writing story as well.

I adored that story from the moment I heard Kevin read it, but my husband Dean Wesley Smith didn't remember it. The room was hot that night (the fire was really stoked) and Dean, who'd been working twenty-hour days starting up a publishing company, fell asleep. He was sitting beside Kevin, and snored (literally) through the entire event. Kevin kept blithely reading, unconcerned. I'd've at least elbowed Dean and asked him to move.

Later, when Kevin mailed the story to the magazine Dean was editing, *Pulphouse,* Dean asked me why he didn't remember the story. I reminded him that he'd slept through that particular Christmas Eve. So Dean read the story for the very first time, pronounced it the best thing Kevin had ever done, and promptly bought it for the magazine.

You'll find only a fraction of Kevin's writing in here, from "Final Performance," the first story Kevin sold to *F&SF* back when we were both college students (and had no idea that I would be editing the magazine ten years later), to more recent work like "Prisoner of War."

"Prisoner of War," by the way, is a sequel to one of Harlan Ellison's most famous works. Harlan gave Kevin permission to do the story. Kevin often gets ideas like this and then, using that all-powerful chutzpah and drive, actually asks folks to work with him.

Now, I'd known Harlan for years and I would never have thought of asking him if I could write a sequel to one of his stories. Kevin, who had only met Harlan once or twice, just called and asked. The day after Kevin called, I was at Harlan's house.

"Do you know this Kevin Anderson?" Harlan said to me.

"He's one of my closest friends," I said. "I've known him since college."

"Is he a good guy?"

Well, the answer was obvious, of course. If I didn't think Kevin was a good guy, we wouldn't be friends. But I must admit, for a split second, I debated about telling Harlan about the stupid fight Kevin and I got into when we were finishing *Afterimage* or the sneaky way Kevin used to make his younger sister cry or the day Kevin and I scared an elderly lady in the pasta section of an upscale grocery store by brainstorming the best way to poison an entire town.

But I behaved myself. I didn't tell Harlan any of that stuff. Instead, I said, "There's none better."

And that is the absolute truth.

So when you hear some Talented Author disparage bestselling writers, remember a few things. Bestsellers, like Kevin, got where they are because they write more than anyone else, because they are talented, and because they care so much they're willing to do anything for their art.

Including work at it.

—Kristine Kathryn Rusch
August 2000

The Writer's Words about the Artist's Art

*M*ANY OF MY READERS WILL RECOGNIZE THE WORK of Dave Dorman from his excellent cover art for all fourteen books in the *Young Jedi Knights* series. Dave is, in my opinion, the very best of all the Star Wars artists, and he has also done outstanding work for Aliens, Batman, Indiana Jones, and Predator. His original work grabs your eyes and won't let go, and Dave laments that most of his fans seem to know him only for his media-related work.

Gee, that sounds familiar. . . .

Dave Dorman was my obvious first choice to paint the cover for this collection. As you can see, he has a startling technique with a wide range of colors and shadows, fluid movement, and razor-sharp details. He has created a haunting, unified painting that isn't just a handful of spot illustrations for various stories in this collection; instead, he has chosen to develop a work of art that tells its own story, culling some of the primary thematic ideas I've used. You can see more of his work on his web site, www. dormanart. com, and in his book, *Star Wars: The Art of Dave Dorman* (FPG, ISBN 1-887569-37-5, $24.95).

I hope you can judge a book by its cover . . . because this cover is *good*.

—Kevin J. Anderson
August 2000

Dogged Persistence

Introduction to
Fondest of Memories

Several years after a painful marriage break-up, I discovered that, over time, my subconscious had been erasing many of the bad parts of the relationship and tinting the fond memories with a rosy glow.

It seems that everyone tends to edit their memories of lost loved ones, emphasizing the admirable qualities and the good times to heroic proportions, while obliviously erasing the unpleasant aspects.

If a character had the chance to bring his lost wife back, through the miracles of cloning and memory transference, would he be satisfied with the real *person . . . or would he choose to make a few changes to match his altered memory of her?*

What would you do?

Fondest of Memories

HE STARS IN THE BOWSHOCK ARE BLUESHIFTED AS the ship soars onward. With each passing moment, the difference between my age and Erica's becomes smaller. Her newborn/reborn body, still on Earth, continues its second life as I grow farther away in distance, but closer in time.

I lean back in the comfortable captain's lounge. The ship runs by itself, and I am its lone crewmember. Time passes much swifter for me, thanks to relativistic effects. But it still seems like an eternity until I can return home, until I can have Erica back the way she was.

This is my favorite memory of her, the one I recorded first:

Erica and I had met hiking in the back country. Both of us enjoyed the isolation, to get away from the gleaming cities. We introduced ourselves during the long walk, and two weeks later we arranged to meet again, to go rafting down the river.

The current was languid and warm at the heart of summer. Erica brought her own inflatable raft, and we laughed, so caught up with seeing each other again that we forgot to bring along the auto-inflator pump. Embarrassed at our mistake, we took turns using our own lungs to inflate the large raft as we knelt in the

3

rocks and sand of the bank. Red-faced and puffing, we thought the situation seemed ludicrous at the time, but it forged a golden thread in our relationship.

"I'm glad you're not upset about it," Erica said.

I shrugged and said exactly the right thing. "The point, my dear, is to spend time with you. It doesn't particularly matter what we're doing."

Our embarrassment was strained further when we saw that we hadn't brought the oars either. We got into the raft and pushed ourselves into the current, kicking with our feet, paddling with our hands, using our rubber sandals to move us toward the center of the river.

We spent hours that day, floating under the sun, talking to each other. We ate bread and cheese from the cool-pack nestled between us; we drank cans of cheap beer. When we got too hot, we would roll over the flexible side of the raft into the river, splash around until we were cooled, and then crawl back in again.

Once I swam up to Erica and, on impulse, slid my hand against the bumps of her spine and pulled her close for a stolen kiss. She let it last a full second longer than I had expected, and time seemed to stop as we hung there in the warm current, buoyant, as if in a place without gravity.

Neither of us worried about how sunburned we were getting. I paid altogether too much attention to how beautiful the diamonds of drying water were as they shone on her skin. . . .

Of all the scenes I relived for the recorders, that is my favorite memory of her.

I had already seen the explosion of the lunar passenger shuttle on the news before the authorities tracked me down. I watched the rough picture on screen as the craft took off from the crater floor and headed back on its two-day journey to Earth orbit. At the extreme range of the lunar base cameras, the liquid fuel tanks erupted, turning the shuttle into a cloud of dissipating wreckage and scintillating chunks of ice and frozen air. The image was streaked with pops of video static because the news crews had enlarged it so much.

Erica had been on that shuttle. The irony was, she had gone to the moon base for its bimonthly safety check. Erica had gone to inspect the underground tunnels, the above-surface domes, making sure the wall plates and life-support systems would keep the base inhabitants safe for another couple of months.

No doubt Erica had been perfectly relaxed, thinking her job

done, as she departed the gravity sphere of the Moon. Someone else had seen to the safety of the transport shuttle. . . .

I got rid of the Transport officials and their preprogrammed sympathy as quickly as their protocol would allow. I stared at the wall, at the home Erica and I had made for ourselves over the years. The lights turned into garish flares through the distorted lens of my tears.

I went into our bathroom and picked up a hairbrush Erica had forgotten to pack. I held it in my hand and stared at it, at the few strands of golden hair trapped by the bristles. She was gone. They would never bring back any sort of remains. A few strands of hair, like golden threads, were all I had left of her.

The first time I went to her apartment, Erica didn't think I was watching as she primped in front of the mirror, using her brush with a snap of her wrist, before she came back out to meet me. I had dressed in my finest clothes.

Erica had the music turned low, candles lit. She normally didn't cook, but had studied food-preparation tapes to get everything just right. That she would do that for me impressed me more than the food ever would.

She made me sit down and accept her attentions as she served salad in a transparent bowl, as she ladled steamed broccoli (which I don't even like) onto the plate, and then bronze-colored chicken breasts. She poured us each a glass of frigid burgundy in a chilled goblet, and we proposed a silent toast, smiling.

"Everything perfect?" Erica asked.

I made an "umming" satisfied sound and said, without thinking, "Well, burgundy isn't really supposed to be chilled. You serve it at room temperature."

Her reaction shocked me. She seemed devastated. My one thoughtless comment had destroyed all of her preparations. I hadn't realized how fragile she was.

"But it doesn't matter—" I tried to say, but Erica stood up so quickly from the table that her chair wobbled, and she—

NO. I rewound and edited that from the memory recorder. A trivial detail, not worth condemning to permanent archive. A simple thing. Fingering the controls, I deleted my tactless comment, ran back to a few moments earlier.

I closed my eyes, focusing on my imagination. This would be better for Erica.

YES. She had kept the burgundy at room temperature after all; we ate artichokes instead (which I do like). The meal went perfectly. We ended up smiling and holding hands across the table, in the light from the candle flame.

The man from the clone-bank sealed Erica's golden hairs in a sterile, transparent envelope. "No need to worry, sir. This is quite sufficient. I expect no problems at all." He tucked the envelope away. "I am indeed sorry about what happened to your wife, but we can fix that now."

I sat back in their self-adjusting chair and tried to feign a relaxed appearance. I felt so empty, so desperate. Part of this seemed completely wrong, but it also seemed the only thing to do.

The man from the clone-bank—I can't recall his name now—sensed my hesitation. He was a professional, accustomed to nervous people like me. He had a thin, clipped accent, not identifiable as any particular foreign language, but the inflections sounded too *processed,* as if he had learned to speak through language implants.

"You have been through our counseling sessions, have you not?" he said. His eyes did not waver as they looked at mine; they appeared too small for his face. "You understand that we will use information from these hairs to fertilize a donor egg. The resulting child will be the genetic equivalent of your wife."

He held up one finger; the nails were neatly manicured. "However, she will be a newborn baby. The body will be the same, but the age difference, some thirty years now—"

"I'm taking the star-freighter option," I interrupted.

This caused the man's eyebrows to raise. "Most people do not. While they can bring themselves to do the actual cloning, they are not willing to abandon their friends, their lives."

"Erica counts more than any of that," I said.

The man from the clone-bank smiled again. "We can help you choose an appropriate star-route with the relativistic difference you desire. When you return, your wife will look exactly as you remember her, the same appearance and the same age. But the memories, ah, the memories . . ."

I looked the other way. I didn't want to hear about this part. I had been avoiding it. Those memories were lost, and I would never truly have the same Erica with the same past.

But the man from the clone-bank waited and then said, as if sharing a secret, "For that, we have a way."

Reliving these memories, focusing my mind to resurrect every last detail and bring it into the recorders, is the kindest form of pain imaginable.

Of course, I deleted all memory of my affair entirely. It's gone. It never happened, as far as the new Erica is concerned. I saw no need to put her through that kind of pain twice.

I realized, even while I was doing it, that I didn't want her to be unaware of my dissatisfaction, the reasons that drove me to seek companionship and understanding other than her own. Though the affair tore apart many of those precious threads that bound us together, if Erica had been able to *learn* from it, she could have understood more of the things that I needed, the things I found missing between the two of us.

And so, when I rewrote my memories I retained some of the minor quarrels and resentments we had toward each other. But instead, I rationalized a way for her to recognize her inadequacies before it became too late. Erica saw what she was doing, how her work shut me out, how she paid too little attention to me—and now, in my imagination, I rebuilt some of those events.

This time, she fixed things between us in the ways I wish she had done before. This time, as I recalled it for permanent record, instead of her red-faced and tear-stained expression, instead of her anguished screaming at me for what I had done to *her* . . . this time, still with tears in her eyes, she bowed her head a little, apologized, and said she did indeed love me.

The man from the clone-bank made sure I understood the apparatus before he left me alone in the room with my thoughts and memories. The mesh-net of contact electrodes, the soothing subliminal music in the background, the warm lights and gentle air currents were all designed to lull me into a semihypnotic trance so I could recall everything for Erica.

"The memories we record are extraordinarily vivid," the man said. "We take everything. Our lives are more than just grand events, but a sum of little details as well.

"We have a frame-of-reference processor that can shift the viewpoint of everything it records. When you recall something that happened between you and your wife, you naturally remember it through your own eyes, through your own filters of perception. With the frame-of-reference parallax, we can change that, adapt it, so that when we implant those memories into the clone, she will recall them as if she had experienced them herself. In such a way, you can indeed share everything you remember together. She will be your wife once more."

The man's voice tightened as he looked at me. His mouth curled into a button of fleshy lips. "Please attempt to remember as many details as possible, even the most trivial things. Summon them up and record them. The more input we have, the more exact will be the re-creation of your wife."

They scheduled me for eleven sessions, and I began the task with relish, because I wanted to relive every single one of my precious moments with Erica.

Our biggest fight, the one I regret the most, came when — after months of subtle hints that I carefully ignored — Erica finally approached me and asked me if I wanted to have children. The tone of her voice and the way she acted made it obvious how badly she wanted them herself.

I had heard about the "biological clock," how many of my acquaintances had suddenly and irrationally decided to toss away their careers and have families instead. Erica and I had just moved into a large home of our own. We were moving up in the world. We had everything we wanted. Erica's sudden request took me by surprise.

She routinely accepted more inspection jobs than she could handle; her job already kept us apart more than I wanted. She was always off on the lunar shuttle, or checking the trans-Channel tunnel, or the Bering Straits bridge. Adding a child to the equation (or more than one, from the way she presented the question) would swallow up what little private time remained to us.

I didn't feel either of us had the time or the energy to be good parents, and I knew how children could be ruined by parents who had come to resent their existence. I told Erica that we were not in a position to be good parents and therefore, for the sake of our potential child, we should not become parents at all.

This devastated her. She refused to make love to me for weeks. She moped around, saying little to me. The whole thing soured our relationship. It seemed almost a relief when job duties called her to the moon for a routine inspection tour, her last.

Now the most important thing was just to have Erica back.

So, as I recalled our discussions and my persuasive arguments, instead of Erica acting childishly and refusing to see reason, I altered the memories again, making her think for a long while about what I had said. Then finally, with dejection but genuine understanding, she nodded and agreed.

"You're right," she told me. "It was just a nice thought. I don't want to have children after all."

I was happy with the new memory. It would make things stronger between us.

I sit at the helm of my ship and think of Erica as the stars rush by. The chronometer continues to reel off two sets of numbers: my subjective time inside the captain's cabin, and Earth-normal time, which flies by as the ship streams toward its destination. Before long, I can turn the ship around and begin my swift journey back to Earth.

Three decades will have passed by the time I return. I have put all our income into trust, and the star-freight company has deferred my salary into interest-bearing accounts with a regular stipend paid to the clone-bank to prepare Erica's clone.

When I arrive home, she will be the same age, the same appearance . . . the same *person* who was lost to me. I lean back and smile again. I picture Erica coming to greet me at the starport. I can't wait to see her again.

She will be just the way I remember her.

Inntroduction to
Music Played on the Strings of Time

The tiniest of circumstances, the most trivial of decisions, could have ripple-effect consequences for our lives—but then, we'd never know it, would we?

If you had just stomped on the brakes half a second faster, you would have avoided the fender bender that gave you whiplash which cost thousands of dollars in insurance. If you hadn't chosen that particular moment to run to the grocery store, you would have gotten the phone call that you'd won the radio station's grand prize contest. If you had chosen to stay home and read instead of going off to the coffee shop, you might not have bumped into the person who would turn out to be the love of your life. . . .

Who can say?

Back in high school, I read Ray Bradbury's classic short story, "A Sound of Thunder," in which he portrays time and destiny as an easily unraveled web, where the untimely death of a mere butterfly back in the age of dinosaurs is enough to alter all of human history.

In this story and the next, I developed a company—Alternitech— that allows prospectors to hop to adjacent and subtly different time-lines in search of differences, advantages, that can be brought back home and exploited. Not time travel, and a little more developed (I think) than the TV show Sliders, which came out a few years after I had published the first of these stories in Analog. I eventually intend to write other Alternitech stories, because I feel I still have plenty of room to explore around the basic idea.

Music Played on the Strings of Time

*H*E ARRIVED, HOPING TO FIND A NEW LENNON, OR A Jimi Hendrix. Or an alternate universe where the Beatles had never broken up.

As the air ceased shimmering around him, Jeremy staggered; with his head pounding, he sucked in a deep breath. His employers at Alternitech always made him empty his lungs before stepping through the portal. The company had strict rules limiting the amount of nonreturnable mass shuttled across timelines, even down to the air molecules. Take nothing tangible; leave behind as little as possible.

The air here smelled good, though; it tasted the same as in his own universe.

He snatched a glance around himself, making sure no one had seen him appear. It had rained recently, and the ground was still wet. Everything about this new reality appeared the same, but each timeline had its subtle differences.

Jeremy Cardiff simply needed to find the useful ones.

The Pacific Bell logo on the phone booth had the familiar design, but with a forest-green background color instead of bright blue. He had always found a phone booth in the same spot, no matter which alternate reality he visited. Some things must be immutable in the Grand Scheme.

Jeremy reached into the pocket of his jacket and withdrew the ring of keys. One of them usually worked on the phone's coin compartment, but he also had a screwdriver and a small pry bar. His girlfriend Holly had never approved of stealing, but Jeremy had no choice—in order to spend money in this universe, he had to get it from somewhere *here*, since he could leave none of his own behind.

The third key worked, and the coin compartment popped open, spilling handfuls of quarters, nickels, and dimes—Mercury dimes, he noticed; apparently they had never gotten around to using the Roosevelt version. He scooped the coins out of the phone booth and sealed them in a pouch he took from his pack. Never get anything mixed up, the cardinal rule.

Time to go searching. Jeremy picked up the phone book dangling from a cable in the booth and flipped through the yellow pages, hunting for the nearest music store.

Before he had left his own timeline that morning, everything had happened with maddening familiarity:

"Your briefing, Mr. Cardiff," the woman in her white lab coat had said. The opalescent *Alternitech: Entertainment Division* logo shone garish on her lapel, but she seemed proud of it. Her eyebrows were shaved; her hair close-cropped and perfectly in place; her face never showed any expression. This time Jeremy saw she was attractive; he had not noticed before. Every other time he had been too preoccupied with Holly to pay attention to anyone else.

"You tell me the same thing every trip," Jeremy said to the Alternitech woman, shuffling his feet. He felt the butterflies gnawing at his stomach. He just wanted to get on with it.

"A reminder never hurts," she said, handing him the customized high-speed tape dubber. It had eight different settings to accommodate the types of music cassettes most often found in near-adjacent timelines.

At least the woman had stopped giving him the "time is like a rope with many possible strands" part of the speech. Jeremy was allowed only into universes where he himself did not exist at that moment; it had something to do with exclusions and quantum principles. He chose never to stray far from his own portion of the timestream, stepping over to adjacent threads, places where reality had changed in subtle ways that might lead to big payoffs in his own reality.

Other divisions of Alternitech sent people hunting for elusive cures to cancer or AIDS, but they had been by and large unsuccessful. A cure for cancer would change history too much, spin a timeline both farther and further away from their own, and thus make it harder to reach.

'Ghost music,' on the other hand, was easy to find. Jeremy wanted to find new work by Hendrix or Jim Morrison, Stevie Ray Vaughan or Kurt Cobain, a timeline where these musicians had somehow escaped freak accidents or avoided suicide.

"Do you have everything now?" the woman asked him.

"All set." Jeremy stuffed the tape dubber in his shoulder pack. "I've got my money bag, a snack, some blank tapes, and even a bottle to piss in if I can't hold it." Sometimes the precautions seemed ridiculous, but he wasn't here to question the rules. Alternitech would deduct from his own commission the transport cost for every gram of mass differential.

"You have five hours until you return here," she said. The portal opened, shimmering inside its chrome framework. "I trust that will be enough time for you to search."

"I've never needed more than two hours, even if I have to walk to the mall."

She ignored that. He was disrupting her memorized speech. "You are entitled to your commission on whatever new music you locate, but according to our contract we retain all rights and royalties." She smiled. Her lips looked as if they had leaped off the screen from the *Rocky Horror Picture Show*.

"Of course," he said. Jeremy had already learned that once, with his first big payoff, finding three new albums by Buddy Holly. He had actually been looking in the Hs because of Holly's name, and he had been so surprised upon finding this new music that he had almost forgotten what to do. Almost. He had coasted on that triumph for a year, but he had found nothing new in a long time. He felt the anticipation building each time, wondering what he might find.

Exhaling the air in his lungs, Jeremy went sailing into the timestream.

Shopping malls had to be the most ubiquitous structures in creation. Jeremy had never encountered a timeline where the mall did not exist.

Inside the music store, Jeremy scouted down the aisles. The new releases displayed the appropriate Big Hits; a familiar Top 40 single played on the store's stereo system. The important changes would be subtler, difficult to find.

He checked under the Beatles first. At other times he had found strange but useless anomalies—a version of *Abbey Road* that did not include "Maxwell's Silver Hammer," a copy of the "White Album" that actually listed the songs on the back, a release of *Yesterday and Today* that had retained the disgusting butcher cover censored in the U.S. But since he could not take anything physical back with him, cover variations were worthless. In this store, however, everything looked the way it should have.

Disappointed, he next tried Elvis, the Doors, Led Zeppelin, John Lennon—those would net him the most commission if he brought an undiscovered treasure back.

He might as well have stayed home.

With a sigh, he finally searched for Harry Chapin and Jim Croce, Holly's favorites. New songs by these two wouldn't sell well back in his own timeline, but he always checked, for her. He stopped himself—it didn't matter anymore. Who gave a damn for Holly? But he looked anyway.

He thought of Chapin, killed in a car accident . . . his Volkswagen smashed under a truck, wasn't it? And Jim Croce, dead in a plane crash at age thirty, two weeks after his song "Time in a Bottle" had been a theme in a TV movie: *She Lives,* one of those countless "my lover is dying of a terminal disease" films of the early '70s. Jeremy considered the song sappy and sentimental; Holly insisted it wasn't.

"You know, if it were me saving time in a bottle," he had said to her, "I could think of a lot better things to do with it. Like find more time for my own music."

He knew just how to push Holly's buttons. After one fight, he had left a box on her doorstep in which she could keep "all those wishes and dreams that would never come true." He had intended it to be ironic; she had called it cruel.

He and Holly had such different needs that they clashed often during the two years they had been together, coming close and drawing apart. He decided it was probably over now for good. Jeremy had his music, his need to write songs and work toward breaking into the business. Holly, though, just wanted to hang out with him, wasting hours in conversation that had no topic and no purpose. She said it brought them closer together; he resented her for draining away time that he could have used for composing.

In the house he kept his own sound mixer, a MIDI sequencer, synthesizers, music editing programs, a set of panel speakers mounted on marble blocks, and an amp that could lift the house two inches off its foundation if he cranked up the volume. He had all the gadgetry; he studied the hits; he tried to come up with a sure-fire blockbuster. Listening to all the crap on the radio, he just couldn't see that his own stuff was any worse.

He just needed a lucky break: you had to know a name, get under the right label, and somebody would *make* your song a hit, crowbar you to the top of the charts. Otherwise, music people tossed unsolicited demo tapes out the window. Reject. Sorry, kid.

But Jeremy planned to get in through the side door, to make a name for himself by bringing 'ghost music' back to his own time-line and taking credit for it. Then the studio execs would be ready to listen to his stuff. . . .

But it wouldn't happen here, not in this timeline, not in this music store. Jeremy sighed. No Beatles, not even any new Chapin. He flicked his gaze down to Croce.

Holly disagreed with Jeremy's approach to songwriting. She worked as a nurse and sometimes treated him like a patient with psychological problems. Therapy. Pop psychology. "You can't just find a formula and imitate it. You need the depth, the emotion. And you can only get that by drawing it from yourself, by being brave enough to look deep. But you're afraid to. You need to have something inside yourself before you can share it with anyone else."

But he knew Holly must be wrong. What did a *nurse* know about music? He played in bars on weekends, drawing a few crowds. Holly herself came to watch, sitting at a table near the stage and mouthing the words to his own lyrics that no one else recognized. Somebody would notice him. One of his songs would catch on. He needed some more practice and then a foot in the right door.

Startled, he found five different cassettes with Jim Croce's name on the side. In his own timeline, Croce had made only two albums, and most of those cuts had been compiled into varied "Greatest Hits" collections. After a moment of excitement—Jeremy always felt his skin crawl at finding an obvious change—he picked up the cassettes, glancing at the titles, reading the package copy.

In this reality, Croce's plane had never crashed. In the late '70s he had changed his style dramatically, but the cassettes didn't seem to be big successes. Croce had gone for dance music, funky r&b, with more and more desperate attempts at reaching the Top

40 again. Songs like "The Return of Leroy Brown" were sure danger signs of waning creativity. On his last album Croce had not even written his own material, instead doing covers of old hits. When Jeremy found "Time in a Bottle: Disco Remix" he couldn't stop from chuckling.

Personal zingers aside, the alternate Jim Croce would have little commercial value for Alternitech back in his own timeline. And Holly would hate him for bringing this stuff back, for spoiling the memories. That would be too petty. He couldn't do that to her.

Not knowing quite why he didn't want to rub her face in it, he decided against the cassettes. Alternitech wouldn't be impressed anyway, and it would be a poor shadow to those new Buddy Holly tapes he had found. Better to leave old Jim dead in his plane crash. Jeremy shook his head, feeling pleased about doing his good deed for the day.

Then he noticed another tape shelved under "Misc. C." It bore his own name: JEREMY CARDIFF—*This One's for Holly.*

He paid for the cassette by stacking up the quarters from the phone booth, one dollar at a time. The clerk looked at him strangely for paying in coins, but Jeremy was already tearing the cellophane wrapping from the tape case. The blurb sticker said "Contains the SMASH hit *For Holly!*" Promo material tended to exaggerate the magnitude of any song's success, but he felt enthralled that something of his had actually been called a hit.

By the time he emerged into the scattered crowds wandering the mall walkways, Jeremy had popped the cassette into his player. He sat down in one of the mall lounge areas, closed his eyes next to a trickling fountain, and listened.

Jeremy recognized the first two cuts as variations—sophistications, actually—on songs he had already written. The third cut was one he had just begun in his own timeline. He felt a sense of unreality drifting over him, euphoria at having achieved his dream. In at least one timeline he had succeeded. He wondered what his alternate self was doing now, how he was planning to follow up a successful first album—

Then the other part of it struck him with a force great enough that he sat bolt upright on the padded bench. He shut off the player. He was not allowed to enter another timeline where he himself still existed. Exclusion principles. The Jeremy Cardiff in this reality—the one who had been a hit musician—must be dead!

He checked the copyright date on the cassette liner. Last year. His counterpart must have died not long ago.

Jeremy had never dared to check before, had never been interested to find out what altered circumstances had erased his own existence in these other timelines. But here he had achieved his goals, his dreams — what had happened to him? Another point- less plane crash like Jim Croce's?

Jeremy checked the timer that would send him back through the portal to Alternitech. He had three hours to find out.

"But can you tell me how he died?" Jeremy tried to keep his voice calm on the telephone. The music company réceptionist had kept him on hold long enough that he had already needed to plunk four more quarters into the pay slot.

"Self-inflicted," she said. Music company receptionists must go to school to learn that perfect 'go screw yourself' attitude, he thought. "You know, the old couldn't-handle-success story."

Jeremy's heart caught in his throat. *Self-inflicted?* "Don't you have any other information? Please, this is important."

"Look," she answered, clearly impatient now, "he took sleeping pills, or shot himself in the head. I can't remember. Jeremy Cardiff had one hit, he made a little money, now he's dead. So what? The price of gas hasn't changed."

Jeremy swallowed as he hung up on her. "No, I don't suppose it has."

While waiting for a bus, Jeremy used the high-speed tape dubber to copy *This One's for Holly* onto a blank cassette from his own timeline, one he could take back with him. He would have to discard the original before he returned through the portal. The sky overhead was gray, as if preparing to rain again.

He listened to the rest of the tape after he had found a seat on the bus. He munched on a granola bar from his pack, careful to stow the empty wrapper back in the zipper compartment.

As the songs played, the initial astonishment wore off, and he began to hear his music with a fresh ear, like a listener would. Sadly enough, he was forced to admit that the songs seemed rather empty, the "oooh, baby, baby, yeah!" kind he had always scorned. Had he been too close to them? How could he have missed it? None of them had any punch.

Until the last song, "For Holly," which stood head and shoul- ders above the rest of the cuts. This had been the reason for the album. This had been the demo somebody had noticed.

He couldn't put his finger on the difference here—the music, the quality of his singing voice, the words? The pain sounded real. Somehow, it combined into a punch of emotion the others had lacked. He rewound the tape and listened to the song again.

When the bus stopped, he got out. The library was three blocks away.

He flipped through eighteen back issues of *Rolling Stone* until he found his own obituary. It occupied a quarter of a page, showing the cover of his album and his photograph. Jeremy felt an eerie chill seeing his own face stare at him from a photo he did not remember ever having taken.

The uncredited obituary stated the facts and little else. It carried the distinct flavor of an "also ran" notice. Jeremy Cardiff had had one hit, which reached number twenty-three on the charts. He had been unhappy with his modest success, ended up washing down a bottle of sleeping pills with a pint of Jack Daniels. He would be sorely missed, but by whom it did not say.

"That's it?" He blinked up from the pages of the magazine, looking at the other people around in the library. No one noticed him, no one knew who he was. "That's all?"

He left his original cassette on the table in the library, hoping that someone would pick it up and listen to it.

During their last fight, Holly had said, "I hope you do become famous. I really do. Because I love you." Her voice was low with an undertone of exhausted anger, as it always was after the shouting stopped and they had both gone to their separate corners. "But you won't make room in your life for anything else. It doesn't have to be that way."

She tugged her blond hair behind her ears, keeping it out of the way. Faint mascara tracks marked her tears. Few people even recognized that Holly wore makeup, but Jeremy knew she spent half an hour each morning carefully constructing that impression.

"You'll never understand it," Jeremy said. He had tried to explain it over and over to her, but still she refused to give him the space, to let him have the time and energy he needed to devote to creating music. Instead, she was like a sponge, demanding his devotion, wrestling his attention to her own personal needs instead of to his composing.

"This isn't just a job like being an auto mechanic—" *or a nurse,* he did not add, "I really have the power to move people. I can send out a message that could make everyone think. But I have to take time to get it just right. I can't just drop what I'm working on whenever you're feeling insecure." The anger crept into his voice once more.

But Holly was having none of it. Quietly, she picked up her purse and went to the door. "Take all the time you need. Follow your yellow-brick road. I don't want to be the one responsible for you not achieving your dream."

He couldn't think of anything to say in response before she closed the door behind herself. He stood alone in his studio with the tall speakers, the amp, the MIDI equipment, and all his unfinished music. The house was very quiet.

He listened to his copy of the tape as he made his way back to where the return portal would open for him. He treasured the song "For Holly." *Would I want to go through time with you? Are you the one?*

What if he had given up everything with Holly for a chance that was ultimately a flop? What if practice and brute strength and determination were not enough? That was the way to *manufacture* songs, like the empty derivative stuff on the rest of his album. Listeners could see right through that facade. He could never send a message to the world if he had nothing to say.

As he walked along the road, Jeremy removed the last quarters from his money pouch. Since he couldn't take them with him, he tossed the quarters in one big handful into a puddle in the gutter. Like a wishing well—but he no longer had any idea what to wish for.

He needed the substance inside himself before he could put it into the songs, but he had tried to bypass that part, to skip an important step. Sorry, no shortcuts allowed. Holly was right. With a sinking feeling he knew it would be a hell of a lot more difficult.

As he stood in position and waited, Jeremy listened to the last song on the tape one more time. He had managed the true inspiration once, and he could do it again. He could use "For Holly" as a model—and it would be a great gift for her. He must swallow his pride, tell her he had been stubborn.

His chronometer showed only a minute or so before he would return to Alternitech. The executives would be upset when he returned empty-handed again. But Jeremy felt eager now, ready to start a new timeline of his own. He would scrap the empty songs he was working on and spend the time he needed; he would get some studio to listen to "For Holly." Maybe Holly would even want to help him; he had never let her actually help him before.

Jeremy froze with his hand on the cassette player. He was not, after all, returning empty-handed. He had his own music—and the contract stated that any songs he found in alternate realities belonged to Alternitech/Entertainment. Everything. The whole copyright, hook, line, and sinker. He had signed it, knowing full well what it contained. If he tried to cross them, they would press the legal buttons and swallow him up.

He could not let that happen to a song like this. He had only one choice, and there was no use crying about it—Alternitech would deduct for the mass differential of a fallen teardrop left behind. He felt his throat trembling as he pushed the button.

The cassette made a thin whimper as it zipped through the high-speed dubber, sending his music back into nothingness, erasing it forever.

Even if he could remember the tune, the words, he could not copy the emotion that had made the song so powerful. Such things could not be imitated; they had to be felt. He didn't want to end up with a minor hit he could not repeat. He had to learn how to *do* it, not how to copy it.

The air shimmered in front of him, opening into a brief doorway back home. His chest felt like lead, but he exhaled, pushing the foreign air out of his lungs. Shifting his pack on his shoulder, he stepped into the portal.

Reality changed subtly around him. It was all right, though. He had new inspiration, new work to do. He opened his eyes in his own timeline.

It might not be the same cut he had heard on his own tape, but it would be different from his other attempts. His focus would be different. He had a song to write, for Holly.

Introduction to
Tide Pools

Another Alternitech story.

From a news program, I learned about "orphan diseases," often fatal illnesses that are perfectly treatable . . . but because these diseases affect so few people, the pharmaceutical companies do not find it cost-effective to manufacture the necessary medications that will save people's lives, nor will insurance companies cover the treatment. I found this appalling (but then, anyone who has had the misfortune of dealing frequently with the U.S. healthcare system will have plenty of opportunities to use the word "appalling").

Searching for medical cures seemed another likely possibility in which the Alternitech Corporation would engage, and so I created a second timeline prospector.

Tide Pools

THE RETURN PORTAL FORMED IN THE AIR LIKE razor blades slashing through clear ice. Andrea stepped across the threshold, her mixed elation and disappointment so overwhelming that she barely noticed the skin-fizzing sensation of hopping back home from an adjacent timeline.

"I got something!" she called, unslinging the backpack from her shoulder. "How about a miracle cure for multiple sclerosis, anybody?" It wasn't what she had hoped to find, but she had to make it look good.

In the receiving room of Alternitech, portals and complex control panels surrounded her. At her announcement, technicians and other cure hunters began to pay attention. "How much follow-up do we need?" asked the chubby man in the operating booth.

"Not necessary—I got all the right data." Andrea brushed a hand through her short, sweat-rimed dark hair, feeling her cheeks grow warm.

Cure hunters like herself dreamed of such unlikely chances. Peeping into parallel timelines, digging through other-universe medical libraries, Andrea searched for effective treatments that doctors in her own timeline had somehow missed.

Who would have thought that a drug used for skin disorders

would be amazingly effective against MS? When injected into the spinal columns of those suffering from the disease, the drug dissolved the small white plaques covering nerve sheaths.

No one in her own timeline *had* thought of it, but in an adjacent universe, a doctor had stumbled upon the treatment and published it to high acclaim. Alternitech would profit greatly from the discovery, and so would mankind.

The man in the operating booth spoke into his intercom, summoning verification reps to paw through her data. Other cure hunters applauded Andrea as they waited for their own gates to open. She surrendered her backpack and its contents to the security guard.

It was phenomenally expensive to haul foreign mass from other timelines. Hunters like Andrea recorded pertinent data onto the diskettes or videotapes they carried with them. Apparently, there was no cost to transfer *information* between timelines, though Andrea supposed the entropy specialists would probably come up with something sooner or later.

After the announcement of her discovery, the reporters would come, the television interviewers, the applause from the public, the heartfelt thank-you letters from MS patients given sudden new hope for their conditions. She allowed herself to revel in the times she made a find like this.

Andrea also felt a disappointment inside, despite the rewarding rush of success. After all, she had not been *looking* for a cure for MS. She had failed in her primary mission.

The problem gnawing at her was whether or not she should tell Everett. He was the one who had everything at stake.

Home at last, Andrea entered through the front door, propping it open to let in the fresh breeze. Sunlight gushed through the bay windows, warming the sunken living room.

Everett straightened from his work by the laser generator. "Andrea? Is that you?" She stood in full view, and he was staring directly at her. His eyesight grew worse every day.

"Expecting someone else to barge in and blow you a kiss?" she asked.

"I expected you home hours ago. Wait, I have to start all this up again!" He held up his hands, then felt his way around the equipment, squinting at it, careful not to stumble. "I have a surprise. Where are you? Come into the foyer—I've set that up as prime focus."

Andrea smiled to see him looking so earnest, so bustling. This was much better than the phase of moping he had gone through a month earlier. She went where he directed her and looked around the walls. Tiny faceted mirrors were mounted at strategic points around the room.

"Ta da!" Everett switched on his laser projector, and a 3–D holo sculpture congealed around her like a spider web of light, a kaleidoscope of rainbows. Each line was split, not quite resolved, so that it was really dozens of layered images overlapping each other, partially unfocused with chromatic aberration. His grids were out of phase, and she doubted Everett even knew it.

"My masterpiece," he said. "I wanted to leave something impressive behind. I call it *Timelines*. It's for you, Andrea."

Everett was looking at her with a childish expression of delight and anticipation. His gaze was slightly off.

Timelines. She looked at the fuzzed edges of the light threads, the overlapping images that were almost but not exactly like each other. Perhaps it wasn't just some jittering lack of surety caused by Everett's fading eyesight and his trembling hands; timelines nearly overlapping but subtly different. He *must* have done it on purpose; she had to believe that, or else his failure would tear her heart apart. "I think it's beautiful, Everett. I don't know how you managed it."

He lowered his head to cover his smile. She almost expected him to say "Awww, shucks." Instead, he found a soft futon and sat down. "I was going to have it done by your birthday, but now everything takes me so damned long." He sighed. "Are you going to stay home with me tonight, or are you going back to Alternitech?"

Watching Everett made her wince, and she closed her eyes momentarily. What good was a multiple sclerosis cure for him? She had failed him at the time he needed her most. She had to keep searching.

Heidegger's Syndrome. The disease selectively attacked the myelin sheaths around the optic nerve, then chewed away at the medulla oblongata, deteriorating the nerves that controlled breathing and heartbeat. After a slow descent into blindness, Everett would one day just find himself without a heartbeat, then fall over and die. Andrea dreaded the morning she would wake up to find him cold in the bed beside her. She could not prevent it in any way.

Andrea stared at Everett in the living room. The solution was painful and obvious. But Alternitech had flatly denied her permission to hunt among the timelines for a cure.

She walked up behind Everett, threw her arms around his waist, then pressed her cheek against his shoulder blades. The tapestry of light glittered around them, defeating even the sunlight. *Timelines.*

"It's your best work, Everett," she said. "I love it."

Andrea fidgeted in the university office of a man she had never met. In the halls of the Neurological Wing of the Deudakis Medical Research Facility, she could hear annoying sounds of construction, hammers and saws and power drills. She'd had to weave her way around scaffolding and construction barricades to reach Dr. Benjamin Stendahl's office. The hall lights flickered, but remained on.

She looked at her watch again, sat down in the only uncluttered chair, then stood up once more. Stendahl's computer sat on a corner of his desk, glowing with a garish screen saver of multi-colored lines. She ran her fingertips along the spines of the journals on his bookshelves, stacks of dusty manuscripts, technical papers held together with old rubber bands; one band at the top of the pile had snapped, splaying curled printouts.

A man stepped into the office breathing heavily and mumbling to himself. He came to a full stop as he saw her. His eyebrows were like fluffy gray feathers mounted on his forehead. "Oh! I forgot." He dropped a bulging briefcase atop the stacked books on his desk. "You're here to talk to me about Heidegger's Syndrome — your husband, right? Well, there's nothing I can do for him. You realize how rare the disease is? Only eight people a year are diagnosed with it in all of North America."

Andrea thrust her chin forward. "I've read all your papers. Looks like you were making good progress toward a cure. Why did you stop work on it?"

"Simple answer — no more money. That's the rotten part. Heidegger's isn't really an insidious bastard like cancer or AIDS. Given some research data, I could do a lot. But our rhesus monkeys were rerouted and never arrived. I could afford only one grad student, but she got married and moved to Ohio. I couldn't get her replaced before the end of the fiscal year, when my funding went away."

Stendahl sat behind his desk, jiggling the mouse so that the screen saver dissolved to display a master menu. "I think 'orphan disease' is the colorful term they have for it. With research dollars so scarce, who wants to waste time coming up with a cure for something nobody cares about?"

"I care about it," she said. "Eight people a year care about it, and so do their families, and everybody they know."

Stendahl looked at her with sympathy in his big, dark eyes. "Look, millions of people get cancer, leukemia, cystic fibrosis. Heidegger's just doesn't cut it. The disease was a medical curiosity when it was first reported, little more."

Andrea stared at the journals on his shelves. Pounding hammers from the hallway punctuated her sentence. "And now?"

He shrugged again. "I'm working on other things."

Andrea wanted to spend her every waking hour hunting alternate timelines for a cure, but she also needed to be with Everett. Each day was like Russian roulette with him, never knowing which heartbeat might be his last.

Seagulls wheeled overhead, tiny checkmarks that screamed against the booming rush of the Pacific. The ocean and the huge sky above made the universe seem oppressive in its grandeur. Headlands sprawled out in muted browns and grayish greens to the shore, where a string of tide pools dotted the wave-chewed rock like diamonds on a necklace. Barefoot and in cut-off shorts, Andrea and Everett picked their way among the rocks.

Andrea took sandwiches out of the pack, and they split a bottle of beer. Everett squatted beside one of the pools and dangled his fingers into the water, startling two crabs that ducked for cover beneath the rocks. He squinted to make out details. Eyeglasses would not help him; Heidegger's was not a problem of focus, but of the optic nerve itself.

The tide pools were colorful, filled with life, a microcosm of unfurled pale-green anemones, tiny fish, and shells. Snails worked their tedious way across the rock surface, finding rich patches of algae. Everett tossed a rock, watching the ripples spread to the boundaries of the tide pool, but constrained by the walls so that it could not affect the other tide pools.

"Each one is like its own universe," he said. "Full of life, nearly identical to the others, but different. I'm like an anemone in a tide pool, stuck to the bottom, waving my fronds in the hope that I'll catch something, but ultimately trapped right where I am. You, on the other hand, are more like one of those rock crabs. With Alternitech, you can scuttle over the wall and get to other tide pools, go see new places, look at what they've got, and maybe take something back with you."

Andrea didn't know what to say. She did indeed have the flashy, high-paying career. Who could imagine a world where a "research librarian" was considered a glamorous profession? Andrea was constantly being interviewed, receiving awards and applause. She had loved it—until the search had become personal, and desperate, and she had failed.

"I'm still looking for something to help you. I'll find it. Don't worry."

A wave curled against an outcropping partly out to sea, dashing spray into the air like tiny crystal droplets. Two gulls swooped down, then wheeled high overhead.

"Why help me when you can help thousands?" Everett said. His voice held a strong resignation that had emerged from his initial depression.

"As if one cure precludes another!" Andrea scowled. "Why do we pit the two types of research against each other, as if they were our only two choices? The government spends more money maintaining *flower gardens* around monuments than they do on Heidegger's research—why does one bit of science have to siphon money from other science, rather than something else? Everything isn't equal." She looked down, though she knew he couldn't see her face anyway. "Besides, if I find something, I'll just tell Alternitech that I found it by accident while doing other research. They can't prove otherwise."

Everett smiled, like a parent watching a child deliver promises with false bravado, then he reached for his sandwich. She watched him squint until he found it.

She swallowed a large bite. "We should get back. I can go out hunting at least two more times today."

Everett's face was a plain mask of disappointment, but he said nothing.

In her long search, most of the alternate universes appeared identical. Digging into the medical research libraries, sometimes she discovered even less progress on Heidegger's Syndrome, or none at all. Twice, she found minimal successes beyond her own timeline, but nothing worth bringing back. With a run of unlikely bad luck such as Stendahl's, it seemed obvious that in some other timeline he would have received his rhesus monkeys, his grad student would have stayed an extra six months.

Throughout her search, she also had to find enough other tidbits to keep Alternitech happy. They had told her not to waste time hunting a cure for an orphan disease, yet they were delighted when she found a way to artificially change eye color from blue to brown and back again. Plenty of cosmetic and commercial applications, they said. Their priorities made her sick.

She had lost count of the timelines by now. On each mission, Andrea went directly to a university's medical library and buried herself in Stendahl's publications, checking to see if he had anything new to offer. This time, according to the library, Stendahl had completed his experiments, but his crucial summary papers were "in press," which meant they were not yet published and would be available only in his office.

Andrea hurried along the dim corridor. So far, every timeline had the same chaotic construction in the west wing of the building. Perhaps chaos itself was the only constant among the timelines. Yellow barrier tape blocked off corridors, light fixtures lay on the floor, the sounds of hammers and power saws echoed in the halls. Andrea passed a pile of newly-cut boards, ducked under a scaffold holding drip-splotched cans of paint. She hadn't yet been able to determine if they were building something up or tearing something down.

Stendahl's door was closed. Taped to the wall beside his office hung a handwritten note giving an address where to send Get Well cards. Under that, she read a newspaper clipping that described how Benjamin Stendahl had broken his leg after stumbling in a construction area, and that he was not expected to return to teach classes for the remainder of the semester.

Stendahl's door would be locked, but all cure hunters kept lock-picking tools in their packs. If this timeline had some crucial information for Everett, she would take whatever measures were necessary. As she worked at fumbling the slim tools into the door's keyslot, construction noises drowned out the sounds of her hidden efforts. But she kept looking over her shoulder. She was not very good at this.

Wrapping her sweaty palm around the knob, Andrea finally opened the door. She ducked inside and closed it behind her, flicking the light switch.

Stendahl's abandoned office smelled oppressive and long-empty, though he had been in the hospital for only a week. She switched on the computer, letting it boot up as she scanned the bookshelves. She did not have much time to find what she needed, and Stendahl's cluttered organization made the task more difficult.

She saw the title on the fresh manuscript lying on top of one pile, then found a folder filled with memos, his hand-jotted records of the experiments, raw data. She flipped through the pages. At the end of his summary Stendahl even suggested a few treatment methods.

She glanced at her wristwatch, trying to determine how soon the Alternitech portal would come back for her. She could use her camera to photograph each page of the hardcopy summary report, but this was raw data — files and files of it — experimental records, which suggested follow-up tests. It would be laborious and time-consuming to copy all of it. More time than she had. But she could store everything onto one of her diskettes — if she could find the right files on Stendahl's computer.

Andrea went to the computer, glancing at the menu and searching for any Heidegger files. As she feared, Stendahl had imposed little organization in his filing system. Some of the file-names contained the word "Heidegger," but when she called them up, they were mere memos requesting supplies. Stendahl had named seven of the files REPORT1, REPORT2 . . . each taking up significant disk space. She checked the file-creation dates, then called up the most recent, but it had nothing to do with Heidegger research.

Out in the hallway, the construction workers used something that sounded like a jackhammer on the walls. Andrea tried to ignore the racket and concentrate on her work.

Finally, when she pulled up REPORT5, the words described all his tests, all his results, all his suggestions. Jackpot!

Excitement and anxiety growing within her, Andrea checked her watch again. She unzipped her pack and pulled out the various blank diskettes from her own universe. She pulled a disk out of its plastic sleeve and tried to slide it into the drive.

It was an eighth of an inch too wide. But she had other formats, other sizes to accommodate slight differences among the timelines. She tried another from her stack.

She finally found a diskette that fit. Stendahl's drive began formatting it. Alternitech experts had always been able to decode her diskettes, no matter how subtly different their computers might be. Of course, the techs might not help if she brought back something she had been instructed not to look for. She might have to call in all of the favors she had earned in her years working for Alternitech.

The disk finished formatting. It would take a few moments to copy the files. She didn't have much time; the portal would come back for her soon.

At the far end of the hall, one of the construction workers cursed as the jackhammer noise changed with an abrupt clank.

All the lights in the building went out.

Stendahl's office filled with blackness. The computer died. Andrea's hopes died with it.

By flashlight, she photographed as many pages of the draft manuscripts as she could. Working backward, Andrea snapped each image of conclusions, then the experimental method, and finally began plowing through all the raw data. She stared at her chronometer, watching the time tick down.

Alternitech's machinery cast her across the parallel universes at random like a fishhook in the water. Now that she had found a timeline that offered hope for a Heidegger's cure, chances were very slim that she would ever find herself back *here*. Frantic, she kept photographing the data, hoping that her flashlight provided enough illumination for the pictures to turn out.

Finally, when she could not wait a second longer, Andrea clicked one more photograph, then ran out of Stendahl's office, leaving the papers scattered all around. Glowing green EXIT signs shone in the darkness. She heard voices calling, complaining about the power outage. By the bobbing light in her hand, Andrea ran through the halls, dodging construction barricades. She had to get back to the portal.

A gruff voice yelled for her to bring the flashlight over so they could find the circuit panel, but she ignored it. She nearly tripped over a pile of pipes against one wall, but she caught her balance. Reaching the secluded stairwell, Andrea stumbled into the shadows just as the Alternitech portal slashed through the air.

Clutching her precious data, Andrea fell across the sea of timelines.

"Well," Stendahl said, raising his bushy eyebrows, "that's the good news." Andrea suddenly felt her stomach turn into ice.

He folded his hands on his desk and leaned toward her. Around him, she could see photocopies of the article and notes she had taken from the alternate universe. Stendahl had studied them, marked them with a red pen. She spotted several pieces of data circled, a few with exclamation points beside them. Andrea feared that she had not managed to include the *one page* that contained crucial measurements or descriptions of the one round of tests that would have allowed Stendahl to create a treatment for Heidegger's. It would all be lost.

Alternitech management had not been pleased with Andrea when she had returned with information on Heidegger's Syndrome, information she had been specifically told not to seek out. They had suspended her, until they received a phone call from an angry senator whose daughter was even now being treated for multiple sclerosis—using the prescription Andrea had brought back. The phone call seemed like a miracle cure to her situation.

Now, Everett was the only one who had something to lose.

Andrea met Dr. Stendahl's gaze. "What is it?" she said, her voice hoarse. "What's the bad news?"

"I've confirmed—er, I mean I *agree* with my own conclusions." He forced a wry smile. "This research does indeed suggest a treatment regimen that could offer hope for people diagnosed with Heidegger's Syndrome. But—"

Andrea flinched, but she didn't dare say anything else.

Stendahl looked away. "As with so many other ailments, beginning the treatment at the onset of the disease holds the key to the cure. If we could have started this right when your husband's eyesight was affected, when the disease was still confined to the optic nerve, we might have had a chance. He could have suffered a loss of eyesight, but the disease itself would be eradicated."

His feathery eyebrows rode up his forehead. "In your husband's case, the disease has already migrated to the medulla oblongata. The damage is already being done to the crucial nerves that govern involuntary functions such as heartbeat and respiration. This treatment itself purges the disease, but at the cost of destroying the nerves that are affected—somewhat like amputation."

Andrea took a long, shuddering breath. "Obviously, we can't do that in Everett's case. Not anymore." She felt a dry whispering sound in her ear, as of her own ragged hope draining away.

Stendahl was lousy at sounding optimistic. "From now on, anyone else diagnosed with Heidegger's will have a chance. You've saved those eight people a year you were so concerned about. No one else would have funded my research. You have that to show for your efforts, if nothing else."

Andrea found she couldn't listen any more.

Mist generators sent a cool fog toward the ceiling of the room, making the bright green and red laser beams stand out. Everett had been furiously working on another sculpture, fine-tuning it and trying to finish while he could still function. He had cranked up the laser intensity to the maximum safe level, just so he could discern the beams with his failing eyesight.

With the rest of the house darkened and only a few stars visible out the window, Andrea lay next to him on the floor, looking up at the laser tracery.

Everett spoke in the darkness. "There was a poet during the Boer War who said to live every day as if it were your last, for one day you're sure to be right."

"When did you start reading poetry?" Andrea said, trying to change the subject.

"I've had a lot of time to do things while you were off at Alternitech." He sighed. "But I'm glad you found the cure anyway."

"You're still going to die!" Andrea snapped. Her failure seemed like fluttering wings around her head.

"We're all going to die," he countered. "But you've given a longer life to the other people who get the same stupid disease I did." He took a long breath. "I came to terms with this illness a long time ago. *You're* the one who needs to accept it."

"I had to try," she mumbled. But she began to wonder if her obsession to find a cure, her need not to fail at the task she had set for herself, was actually more for herself instead of Everett.

"I know you did," he said. "Thank you for trying, Andrea. But all those days you were gone hunting . . . I would rather have gone to the mountains with you, done a few more bed and breakfasts up the coast." Everett's words stung.

"There are plenty of other versions of *me* in other universes who *will* have a long and happy life with you. In our timeline, I had an unlucky break. I got an incurable disease that nobody's ever heard of. A long life together just doesn't happen in *this* timeline, with this Everett and this Andrea."

He sat up abruptly. "We've got money saved, so why don't we spend it? Besides . . . you'll be getting a big life insurance check from me before long."

Andrea winced, but he gripped her hand. She thought of the hours she had lost in her desperate hunt. "I suppose I could take a leave of absence from Alternitech," she said haltingly, "especially now. It would give them time to cool off." She flashed him a smile that was at first forced, but gradually grew sincere as she thought of the things they could do together, now that all the restraints had been snipped away.

"All right," she said. "Let's go be alive together as long as we can."

Introduction to
Reflections in a Magnetic Mirror

My first collaboration with Doug Beason started out as a lark. I was working as a technical writer at the Lawrence Livermore National Laboratory, where Doug had come to spend the summer as a visiting physicist. Up to that point, I'd had a few minor short stories published, as had Doug, but neither of us had broken into any professional sales. Being two aspiring science fiction writers in the same workplace, it was a natural for us to meet.

We knocked around a few ideas and decided to write this story just when Doug was recalled to Albuquerque, where he was stationed in the U.S. Air Force. We sent partially completed drafts of the story back and forth through the mail (long before the days of compatible computer systems, so that each of us had to rekey the other's pages whenever they arrived).

This story appeared in the first volume of Bantam Books' highly respected anthology series, Full Spectrum. *Our second collaborative story, "Rescue at L5," written for a solar-sail fundraising anthology spearheaded by David Brin, later evolved into our first collaborative novel,* Lifeline. *All told so far, Doug and I have written eight novels together.*

Reflections in a Magnetic Mirror

with Doug Beason

The Church questions whether this "anomaly" is even alive. And if alive, we question whether it is intelligent. And if intelligent, we insist — *without qualification* — that it has no Soul. Man cannot create a Soul; that is for God alone.
— Cardinal Robert K. Desmond

*A*S THE DEUTERIUM PASSED THROUGH THE OPEN-ing, the discharge bombarded it from all sides. Electrons were torn from their nuclei, heating the fuelstuff in the plasma until the elementary particles fused together. The reaction sustained itself. Billionths of a second passed — an eternity to the plasma — while lasers delicately probed the inner workings of the maelstrom.

His own thought processes moving infinitely slower, Keller stood in silent awe, praying that it would *work*.

The particles bounced back and forth in the chamber, billions of times a second, unable to escape past the giant yin-yang magnets on either side of the Magnetic Mirror Fusion Facility. Long-range coulombic forces sculpted the plasma, creating swirling, complex interactions.

"And?" Keller asked.

The technician reached up to the screen directly in front of him, touching a blue icon that opened up to display two columns of numbers happily glowing green. "Everything's perfect, Gordon. Blessed be the Holy Laws of Physics."

Keller frowned at how the technician — all Californians, in fact — too often used his first name: especially in this, his moment of triumph after so long. He wanted to feel important.

In the background, filling the stuffy room with a much needed festive atmosphere, two operators hoarsely sang, "Fusion power, here we come!" to the tune of "California, Here I Come."

Then someone else called from behind another barricade of control consoles. "There it goes again!"

The singing abruptly stopped.

Keller reached forward to touch icons on the top two screens, opening up another numerical display while the second screen showed the data from varying perspectives.

"Glitches again!" the technician cursed. "But they're different from the last time."

The data repeated itself in oddly distorted cycles. The plasma seemed to be on the verge of blowing up as the instabilities on the screen grew, then decayed, as if a dancer were lightly touching the boundary of a dance-space, feeling her way. It seemed almost as if the plasma was testing its enclosure, exploring.

Keller stared at the screen, silently urging the anomalies to go away, but knowing they would not heed him. He wanted the experiment to be *over*, successfully completed at long last — he had driven so hard, worked his brain to the bone. And at thirty-three, he felt he was getting to be a little too old to be the proverbial whiz kid anymore. When they brought the MMFF online, the damned instabilities were always there . . . but they were *always* different. Whatever the hell they were. He sighed and checked different readouts. In disgust, he walked to the windowless wall, wishing he could stare through the concrete cinder blocks to where, half a block away, a gigantic vacuum chamber held the eye of the storm, a sustained fusion reaction in a plasma confined by magnetic mirrors.

"But it *does* run? It's stable?" Keller asked without turning, sounding half-defeated.

"Sure, it runs. Close enough for government work," the technician answered.

Keller placed his hands behind his back and mentally tried to think of something historic or profound to say. "Good," was all he could manage.

> This could prove to be extremely dangerous or extremely embarrassing. I don't want it to be either.
> —Confidential memo to Laboratory management, regarding the MMFF anomalies.

Keller shielded his eyes from the glaring, obnoxious lights. Three camcorders, eleven microphones, and sixty people crowded in a conference room that had been intended for forty-five, waiting for him to speak. Many of the reporters fingered their laminated temporary ID badges, looking with some concern at the dosimeters attached to them. Keller tried to kill the butterflies in his stomach. The Department of Energy bigwig on his right grinned broadly and finally removed his arm from around Keller's back. Just before entering the crowded room, the DOE man had force-fed him some coaching for the cameras. "And for God's sake, don't *mumble!*"

The official held up his hands, quieting the crowd. "If you could please hold it down, Dr. Keller can say something about the Magnetic Mirror Fusion Facility." Silence was a long moment coming, but the DOE man finally continued. "Gordon, why don't you tell us what's so special about the MMFF?"

Keller leaned forward, cleared his throat, and tried not to look at all the faces looking at him. "Well, to start with, thank you for coming. This really *is* important, I think.

"The MMFF is the simplest design of all mirror machines: as you can see from the diagrams in the press kits, it's basically a long tube with a special type of powerful magnet on each end. The magnets act like mirrors, bouncing the plasma back and forth, confining it long enough so that fusion occurs. Once our yin-yang mirrors were perfected, all we had to do was turn it on. The MMFF doesn't have a lot of the instabilities associated with other mirror devices, such as the tokamak and spheromak machines."

The DOE official cut him off, interrupting with a large grin on his face. "And best of all, this machine uses *no* dangerous heavy elements such as uranium or plutonium. We all remember Three Mile Island. But TMI—and all other commercial nuclear power plants—rely on nuclear *fission*, rather than its opposite, nuclear *fusion*. With fusion power, five gallons of seawater could provide electricity for a town the size of Livermore for a week. Once we can bring MMFF sites up commercially, it's a no-lose situation."

The DOE man clapped Keller on the shoulder, then turned back to the audience. "Dr. Keller has been assigned to continue studying the MMFF, and he will release his complete findings at the November APS meeting in New York. To reiterate, the MMFF machine you saw a few moments ago is purely a feasibility study, but a study that has achieved the breakeven point in fusion energy. The next step is a facility that can be used for the *commercial* generation of power. And I'm sure we'll be asking Dr. Keller for his advice and assistance during the next phase of the project. And on that note, allow me to introduce Dr. Zel'dovich, the director of the MMFF–2, currently in the planning stages."

Scattered applause came as Keller turned, then was ushered away from the head table and into the background. He stood and watched, feeling sheltered and hidden by the other people. The fusion facility worked, despite the unexplained glitches, and he wondered if it was all over, if he had indeed completed the purpose of his life . . . if the heaviness inside him would grow any larger. When he realized he wouldn't be missed in the conference room, Keller slipped away.

> What is Life? What is Death? For that matter, how many angels can dance on the head of a pin? You can argue yourself silly, and I don't really *care* what the answer is. Right now, I want to know what the hell we should do about that *Thing* in there!
> —Dr. F. Gordon Keller, MMFF staff meeting

Keller stared at the small radio for a long moment, but ultimately decided to keep the house silent. Though he didn't particularly want to hear the depressing sound of the rain outside, he wasn't sure he was in the mood to hear music or another human voice, either. Keller slipped into his pair of faded, threadbare old brown cords and a lightweight cotton shirt—his "around home" clothes—but he couldn't shed the thoughts of his work as easily as he shed his clothing. He heaved a sigh.

Glitches.

He placed a TV dinner with a fancy-sounding French name into the microwave, carelessly jabbing at the timer pad. They had been so *careful* designing the huge magnets, the fusion chamber, the diagnostics. What the hell was going on? The plasma theorists were just as stumped as the computational physicists to explain the anomalies.

The microwave sent rhythmic pulses of electromagnetic radiation into his food, warming it. Keller muttered to himself that he would never have received a Ph.D. in physics if he'd set up his plasma experiments the same careless way he cooked his food. But at least when he cooked a frozen dinner in the microwave oven, it left him with no surprises . . . disappointment maybe, but certainly no surprises.

The anomalies just didn't make any sense.

He decided not to switch on the lights while he ate. He sat alone in the shadows, surrounded by the gray-washed dimness of the rain-streaked windows. He stared absently at one of his son's crayon drawings attached to the refrigerator door with an old happy-face magnet. The drawing was somewhat curled around the edges and starting to yellow, but he hoped he wouldn't be able to notice that in the dim light. Three months—had it really been three months? He couldn't even remember if he had answered Shelley's letters.

It wasn't so long ago that she'd been the most important thing in his life; and when Justin was born, the little boy had taken over that special place in his heart. And what did Keller have now? The MMFF was online, and he finally had time to spend with his family . . . time that had been so precious to him, so precious that he'd put his wife and son on hold just to complete the project—but now Shelley was gone, with Justin.

Some things just went wrong—there was nothing you could do about it, no equation you could solve, nothing you could explain with a simple, clear-cut answer.

But the plasma anomalies were a *physics* problem. They were solvable—they had an answer, an explanation. And if he didn't spend too much time wallowing in self-pity, he could probably clear his head and figure out some simple thing that was causing these anomalies, these embarrassments. He had a Ph.D.—Piled Higher and Deeper, in layman's terms—which meant he was supposed to *know* something about physics.

That had been his scholarly battle cry for so long. *Get the Ph.D.* The incessant pushing, grinding out problem sets, spending long hours at the lab. It was the single most important thing in his life, with his entire world centered around that one goal: *Get the Ph.D.* He couldn't settle for anything less. And then, after actually getting the doctorate, it was as if all his personal drive had been snatched like a rug from under his feet.

He put down his fork and stared down at his wrists. Two slashes, running across the veins, had healed years ago to thin white scars, now almost invisible in the dim light by the dining room table. He'd spent so much time in the physics books that he couldn't even kill himself right; the cuts were supposed to be made *along* the vein, so that the bleeding would be more profuse. He knew that now. The shock, the jolting reality of obtaining his degree—getting what he wanted more than anything else in the world—had left him with nothing else to live for. At the time, it had seemed so coldly logical: he had achieved his one goal in life, and what else was there left to do? It sounded trivial now, but it did help explain his depression about finally completing the MMFF.

But what were the damned glitches?

Depression—it was such a nice excuse. He could still remember his mother, but at the time he had been too young to know what "cancer" was; watching her die had been a profound experience for him. One moment she had been lying on the white bed, as she had for the previous interminable weeks, connected to a wall full of electronic machines. An oscilloscope displayed patterns that showed she was alive.

Her suffering went on. The doctors all said she couldn't experience pain in her coma, but young Gordon Keller suspected otherwise. They said she couldn't feel the long, long time she spent on the machine, that it wouldn't be real to her. Keller had felt an urge to end it all for her, to *make it stop*. . . .

But then one moment the machine had changed its mind and pronounced her dead. His grandparents said that the Hand of God had reached down and taken her soul, but young Keller had seen nothing. Even now, Keller still found it difficult to understand, with the physicist in him trying to break down the entire experience into specific questions with specific answers.

What *actually* had taken place during those few seconds in the hospital room? What *actually* had been the difference between life and death? Just a tiny voltage differential across the brainpan?

He remembered the somber warnings from his electronics classes about the kid who had leaned over a bank of capacitors: a line had slipped and the capacitors had discharged across his temples. The twenty microamps had been enough to short-circuit his head, killing him. Was that all life was, an electric field skittering around the contours of your brain? Was even the template of the brain, the body, just so much extraneous mass to hold a special electric field?

He switched on the light and switched it off again.

Glitches. Anomalies.

He decided to go back to the lab.

*   *   *

Before going to the MMFF control room, Keller walked down the deserted Laboratory street past the trailers and other research buildings. Heavy equipment sat idle, sleeping, in wide roped-off lots near numerous construction sites. Keller stopped in front of the huge housing for the MMFF chamber, which rose into the darkness like an airplane hangar. Concrete walls three stories high plunged deep below ground to make the structure earthquake-safe. Girders strung with fog lights bathed the interior of the bay with an orange-yellow light. Even at this hour of the night, a dozen workers kept their vigil around the armored hull of the MMFF chamber, an airtight cylinder over a hundred feet long, layered with thick sheet metal and bristling with diagnostic instruments. The great fusion chamber throbbed and pulsed, making thunderous sounds pitched just below the level of human hearing. Inside, held captive by two of the world's largest magnets, were temperatures hotter than the sun itself, powerful enough to melt through any metal known to man. He stared for a moment, then headed to the main building.

"We've tried *everything* to get rid of them, and at times we got some responses you wouldn't believe." The technician was packing up, getting ready to go home in the darkness and the rain. "You know, Gordon," he said with a lopsided grin as he looked over the readouts displaying the glitches, "sometimes it reminds me of my wife. Like we're dealing with something that's got a mind of its own."

The technician left, calling his goodbyes into the room. The new shift of technicians mumbled about the prospect of working the next eight dead hours of the night while the rest of the world slept. Keller smiled thinly, distracted. "Yes, like it has a mind of its own." He stared at the readouts for along time, hypnotized by the wavering plots that sometimes displayed patterns, sometimes chaos.

He reached forward carefully without taking his eyes from the display screens. His fingers were shaking somewhat. Then he began to touch the controls, adjusting the laser probes. Injection on, and the m numbers ran up the scale: the plasma went through the sausage, kink, and firehose instabilities, all in sequence, all on the verge of getting out of control.

Injection off, and the sequence reversed . . . then *repeated* itself—spontaneously. Like a code. Or was it only some weird sort of resonance?

Keller drew in his breath. He sat and tried to establish a link, any link, using anharmonic modes from the RF generator. It could almost be classed as communicating.

He caught himself. Communicating?

> . . . The discovery at the MMFF facility opens wide a new door for the human race. It will force us to restructure our philosophy of the universe and life itself.
>   —Editorial, *Physical Review Letters*

The official Lab spokesman looked good on TV, perfectly groomed, selected from the vast DOE complex as *the* man to best handle the explosive publicity. The late-night talk show host nodded soberly, hanging on to every word said by the panel of distinguished experts. As Keller watched, he knew the publicity generated by the televised discussion would bring out every nut, fruitcake, and religious fundamentalist who was offended by the suggestion that *something* was happening inside the MMFF. He had already taken his phone off the hook.

The host defused an argument among the "experts" and cut right through the static: "But *has* the Fusion Facility created life? Yes or no?"

The Lab spokesman had been talking around the subject all night, and he finally looked as if he had been trapped. "We like to think of it as an unknown physical phenomenon which can spontaneously react to stimuli within correct statistical parameters."

The host rolled his eyes, and the Lab spokesman responded a little too defensively. "That is a direct quote from Dr. Keller's recently published paper in *Physical Review Letters*. I'm sure Dr. Keller could explain what he meant to say—"

"Dr. Keller is not available for comment at your lab," the host snapped.

"Ah, yes." The spokesman brought his fingertips together. "He is a very busy man, and I assure you he is doggedly working on this problem."

"I'm sure he is," said the host dryly.

"But getting back to your question, and answering quite honestly—we just don't *know* what the phenomenon is. Granted, some do claim it's alive. But a simple virus is also technically alive, too. A better question would be, does it have self-awareness? These questions just can't be answered at this time.

"But the point is that *something* is happening inside the chamber, something we can't explain. This was to be just a test run, a feasibility study to see if the MMFF would indeed perform as expected before we began full-scale tests. The experiment was originally scheduled to be shut down after three days of continuous operation, but, given the unusual anomalies, we have directed that the facility be kept running for as long as it takes us to understand what is going on."

The discussion grew more philosophical, with the Lab spokesman dancing away from pointed questioning. It went on and on, growing fuzzy like a plasma . . . until the spokesman leered out at Keller, stuck his head through the TV set, and made a grab at him. Keller tried to run but his legs were stuck in a magnetic field and he couldn't stop bouncing back and forth and back and forth and—

Keller woke with a start. He blinked his eyes and realized he had fallen asleep, probably for more hours than he had slept the entire previous night. Keller glanced up at the television and saw that the panel discussion had been replaced by the climax of an Italian-made vampire movie on *The Late Show*.

A man—obviously the hero, obviously the vampire hunter—had pinned the king vampire in his coffin just before sunset. He held a wooden stake against the vampire's chest and made ready to strike.

Keller stood up stiffly from his chair, tried to straighten his shirt but then pulled it off instead, and shuffled over to the television. On the screen, the king vampire had awakened, glaring in melodramatic horror at his victorious adversary and the wooden stake, but then a calm, beatific expression of relief passed over the vampire's face.

"You are trapped, Count!" cried the vampire killer. The actor's lips didn't quite move in tandem with the English words.

"Trapped?" whispered the vampire. "I have been trapped for uncounted centuries. Trapped as what I am, unchanging, never to see the light of day. I have lived for so long that what you do to me is an act of kindness. I can no longer endure my life." The king vampire closed his eyes again and drew a deep breath. "Kill me."

Keller flicked the switch and shut off the television. "There, you're dead."

> We do a lot of stuff here, so we always have protesters. But I'm getting tired of those nuts claiming we've got God bottled up in there. They're spooky!
>
> —Security guard, MMFF

With a sour and harried expression on his face, Keller wadded up the formal invitation and threw it at the motel room wastebasket. An invitation to speak to a Congressional hearing on the Search for Extraterrestrial Intelligence project. SETI wanted him to talk about "communicating with alien beings"—they had their gall, especially now!

He flopped back on the hard bed. It probably wouldn't be long before the reporters found him again—Livermore had only a few motels, and those were used mostly by out-of-town job interviewees and DOE contractors. Judging by the stories they ended up printing in their newspapers, the reporters never seemed to listen to his answers to their questions anyway, but they were damned persistent in trying to track him down.

He knotted his fingers in the bedspread. He could hide from the reporters, the decisions, the publicity—but he couldn't hide from the problem.

The thing in the plasma had stopped communicating. Or rather, as the careful side of him liked to point out, the plasma "wasn't spontaneously initiating any controlled instabilities" anymore. The glitches showed it was still there, still living within the fusion chamber, staring at itself in the magnetic mirror. Like Alice unable to get into Wonderland.

Keller could not fathom why the thing didn't treasure every bit of communication, why it didn't eagerly anticipate every new mathematical challenge. It was trapped within its huge chamber, unchanging, unable to come out. It had nothing to do but listen, and talk.

The Congressional invitation caught his eye. He hated to talk in front of people. Yet, it was the most logical thing in the world for SETI to ask him to speak on their behalf, since he was the only human being ever to "successfully" communicate with an alien intelligence.

But what in the hell was Keller supposed to say to the SETI people? Should he confess that he'd always thought their project was basically a waste of time and effort? Sure, he believed there were other civilizations Out There, but the nearest star was five light-years away, the nearest galaxy 2.2 *million* light-years away—as the photon flies. How in the blessed world were you supposed to hold a conversation?

If they were to receive a message from Andromeda tomorrow, it would have been sent twenty thousand centuries before *Australopithicus africanus* had just begun to make his first tool, just begun to chase woolly mammoths while wondering why it was getting so cold even in the summertime . . . and no one on Earth then had even the slightest desire to build a satellite antenna to listen for extraterrestrial signals. And if SETI were to acknowledge that message, how many millions of years in its grave would be the civilization that had initiated the conversation? It was all a matter of perspective on time.

And here he was, Dr. F. Gordon Keller, separated from an alien intelligence by only a thin wall of stainless steel, but he couldn't communicate with the thing either—and he didn't have the incredible time differential working against him. But something was very wrong with the creature in the plasma. It didn't seem to want to communicate anymore.

Then it hit him like a load of bricks falling on his head.

How many times did he have to stare at something before the obvious answer reached out and bit him on the ass? Time scales of tenths of nanoseconds were critical to a plasma: in a second, a plasma could undergo thousands of millions of interactions. A second to Keller would be *billions* of times longer to something that lived on a plasma time scale.

A strange sense of horror began to grow in the pit of his stomach, and Keller even found himself feeling sorry for the thing.

Imagine being *alone*, trapped inside the fusion chamber for what was—to the thing—an absolute eternity. Even when Keller was communicating with it, tapping icons on the touch-sensitive screen or rapidly keying in commands—centuries would have seemed to pass between each individual finger stroke. The thing had been alive and aware for a million centuries, without a break to the monotony.

Keller remembered his mother dying, in a coma "with no sense of time," connected to the life-sustaining machines as an oscilloscope displayed her life as a pattern on a screen.

Electrical patterns in a plasma. Putting it out of its misery would be like switching off a light. But he would be destroying the world's oldest living thing. He would be killing a living being.

A million centuries alone and in silence, without another living being to talk to. Something wrenched in his stomach as the implications pounded themselves home. The thing was immortal, chained to an utterly useless life, unable to die as long as the MMFF remained running.

He would be giving it peace. Something in the world deserved peace.

*   *   *

It was the dead of night, with only a skeleton crew in the control room. Nothing had changed for days. A security guard checked Keller's badge at the gate, and then another let him pass into the control room. He wasn't going to break in and shut down the experiment . . . he was going to *walk* in and shut it down. He would free the living being that had been trapped inside, bottled up for eternity by Keller's wonderful mirrors. He moved with brisk and determined steps to the MMFF control room. Every moment he delayed meant another year of suffering for the thing.

"No change, Gordon," one of the operators said, seeing him as he walked purposefully into the room.

Without acknowledging, Keller went to a vacant bank of computer screens and stared at the jagged display of glitches on one of them. Even as he stared, even as his heart beat, years were ticking away for the thing imprisoned in the chamber. It could only bounce back and forth and *exist* for millions of its years, unable to escape and see the world outside. Keller felt his eyes sting, almost with tears, at the unspeakable loneliness.

But what about himself? He'd thrown away his marriage working on this damned project, trying to push and work and *achieve* so that he could hold an accomplishment up before himself to prove that his life was worthwhile. Like his Ph.D., getting the degree for a trophy. Was he trying to commit *career* suicide this time? The MMFF success had been the pinnacle of his research, but the living thing he had created was unexpected, a blessing, a curse. Keller had hidden from the publicity, passing the responsibility to others. But no one else would see the responsibility he had now, the imperative goal to free the creature he had trapped between the magnetic mirrors. It was time for Gordon Keller to stop hiding.

Keller stared at the red switch. Emergency shutdown—the only hardwired switch in the entire computer-screen-driven control room. It would be simple. Keller held out the palm of his hand —the razor blade against his wrist, the oscilloscope in his mother's hospital room, even the stake on the movie vampire's chest.

With a quick thrust of his arm, he shut the MMFF down.

He would have more time for Shelley now, and Justin. He'd try to call her, and maybe—*maybe*—she would even admire what he had done, tell him he'd been brave. He could write a book, *Memoirs of a Modern-Day Frankenstein*. Or maybe Zel'dovich would consult him about how the next generation of fusion chambers could be built without spawning a new life form.

As it died, and before anyone could act or any alarms could sound, Keller thought he felt a tingling rush through his skin—a flash of dissipating electricity. But it was only his imagination, or just the release of some of the psychological weights on his shoulder. With a sigh, he slowly eased himself into a chair as the shouting started.

Introduction to
Entropy Ranch

Another twist on the time travel story. Instead of traveling back to distant centuries and famous historical events, what if your time machine was limited to going back only a day or so? Such a journey would not be useful for most of the classic science fiction plots — but it would be just the thing needed to fix minor disasters found on the evening news.

Who would take action in such circumstances, and why?

I should note that this story was written and published many years before two television shows with a similar premise were ever broadcast. In Seven Days, *a government project allows the heroes to go back in time one week in order to correct disasters; in* Early Edition, *the main character receives a copy of tomorrow's newspaper, which effectively gives him the chance to prevent disasters before they happen. The dedicated folks at Entropy Ranch, however, don't always get it right the first time. . . .*

In my earlier life as a technical writer, I spent a week in Dallas at the American Industrial Hygiene Association Conference — and yes, it was as exciting as it sounds. There, I had plenty of time to let my mind wander and develop the background for this story.

Entropy Ranch

Dallas Morning News, May 20—A single-engine plane collided with a DC–10 jet during takeoff from DFW airport Tuesday, killing 93 people. The pilot of the Cessna 172, Lawrence Stilwell, 42, of Dallas, apparently received conflicting instructions from the control tower and was unable to avoid the collision. The crash killed Stilwell and 92 passengers and crew on the DC–10.

<PAUSE> <REWIND> <PLAY TIMELOOP B>

Dallas Morning News, May 20—A single-engine plane narrowly missed collision with a DC–10 jet during takeoff at DFW airport Tuesday. Looking shaken, the pilot of the Cessna 172, Larry Stilwell, told reporters after the incident, "It was real close. I got clearance from the tower the same time the jet did." This is the third such near miss in four months at DFW, and the National Transportation Safety Board plans to investigate. "I paused for just a second," Stilwell said. "Somebody had put one of those religious pamphlets on my pilot seat and I took the trouble to throw it away. Maybe it was a miracle, or maybe just a coincidence. You tell me."

GREEN-UNIFORMED BELLMEN HOVERED AROUND the hotel entrance, ready to pounce on anyone carrying luggage. Jersey glanced again through the angled glass of the revolving doors. If the shuttle bus didn't come soon, he'd be late getting to the Dallas Convention Center.

He dutifully snapped open his briefcase to check the sheaves of *Grovemont Industrial Gloves* leaflets, computer printouts of permeability characteristics, and a stack of business cards held together by a red rubber band. Killing time.

Jersey withdrew the *Hi! My Name Is:* badge from the conference packet and pinned it on. They had gotten the first name wrong, again. Ed*mond* Jersey, not Ed*ward* Jersey! Why do people always assume that someone named "Ed" is a *-ward* and not a *-mond?*

It would have felt so good to shout at the convention registration clerk, but Jersey had calmed any such response before it could jump out of his mouth. Another dagger-headache threatened to take center stage in his brainpan. It was *their* mistake, not his, right? Jersey had accepted the badge in silence as he wandered off into the vast convention center crowded with other industrial hygienists, posters and exhibits.

Now, the following morning, he sat waiting in the hotel lobby. The A shuttle bus supposedly showed up every fourteen minutes, and he had been sitting there for eleven.

He dusted a comb through his thinning brown hair and adjusted his tie. Jersey still didn't feel comfortable in a suit, but he did his best to keep up the corporate image. The conference schedule had some interesting papers being presented in the third session, but Jersey would have to man the display table in the Exhibit Room. Time to pay his dues, to banter statistics, to coax new customers, and to give the good old Grovemont Gloves cheer.

He pressed his briefcase shut and stood up, brushing the seat of his pants. Better wait outside, he thought. He eased his way through the revolving door under the Hilton's wide awning. One of the green-uniformed bellmen moved toward him, but Jersey ignored him.

When the shuttle bus had missed its scheduled rounds by a full minute, Jersey scowled, but he quelled the annoyance. *It doesn't matter. Damned if I'm going to be an ulcer candidate before I turn thirty-three.*

But the conference did start promptly at eight. He looked at his watch again.

One of the fat yellow buses pulled up to the curb with a groan of brakes. Jersey hustled toward it until he saw the bright "D" in its window. Wrong shuttle. With an effort, he made his face become calm again. He wouldn't risk bringing on another dizzy spell. They had been getting worse and worse over the past month, and Jersey didn't want to look like a fool by fainting to the sidewalk in front of everyone.

The traffic light changed at the corner, and other cars came flooding past the hotel. He could hear the D bus revving up. Its doors hissed shut, like a monster gobbling prey. The muggy air smelled of oily exhaust.

Bright blue-mirrored skyscrapers clustered around the downtown, peeking over the older buildings that still remained like fossils in limestone. Across the street from the Hilton stood a three-story-high Cokesbury Bible bookstore, flanked on either side by a pawnshop and "ABC Bail Bonds—Guaranteed!" Jersey smirked. Here, in the very midriff of the Bible Belt filled with this 'holier than you-all' attitude, what God-fearing Texan could ever possibly need "Bail Bonds Guaranteed"?

Out of the corner of his eye, he saw a plump fiftyish woman. She wore a baggy print dress that obliterated all sexual details, and under one arm she carried a stack of printed leaflets. Her face bore a beatific yet militant smile that said "The Lord is my Shepherd, and don't you forget it, buster!"

Jersey looked away quickly, trying to avoid her gaze, but she came toward him anyway. At another time he might have bantered with her, but not this morning—he had to save his rhetoric for potential customers, not waste it on a salvation zombie. He made up his mind to cross the street and look in the window of the pawnshop until the bus came.

He didn't look, didn't pay attention to where he was going as he flashed a glance behind him at the woman. The street seemed clear, and he clutched his briefcase as he scuttled around and in front of the waiting D bus, directly into the path of the second bus swerving around.

Jersey turned, had time to gawk at the giant yellow-and-black wall of metal slamming into him. He felt his nerves suddenly disconnect, as if short-circuited. No pain came into his head, but he sensed dozens of bones breaking at once—his arms, his rib cage, his skull. Then his vision turned all red, as if his eyes were filling with blood from the inside.

< PAUSE > < REWIND > < PLAY TIMELOOP B >

Out of the corner of his eye, Jersey saw a plump, fiftyish woman dressed in a baggy print dress. Under one arm she carried a stack of printed leaflets.

He quickly tried to avoid her gaze, but she came stumping toward him anyway. *Oh, not this morning!* he thought, wondering if he could dodge back into the hotel. He flicked his eyes back and forth. It might be easier to go across the street, stand by the pawnshop—a good Christian lady would never choose to be seen near such a sinful establishment, would she? Jersey made up his mind instantly.

"Wait!" she called. "The world is coming to an end!"

He turned his head and quipped back, "Yes, and I have soooooo much to do before it does! Can't stand around talking!"

Hah! Got off a zinger! He snickered and skipped out into the street, directly in front of the accelerating D bus. He missed the curve, stumbled, and pinwheeled his arms, trying to back up. Jersey saw the bus driver's head turn away to chat with one of the passengers. Jersey dropped his briefcase. The giant vehicle looked like a prehistoric monster rearing up as it struck and rolled over him.

< PAUSE > < REWIND > < PLAY TIMELOOP C >

"Wait!" she called, "The world is coming to an end!"

Jersey groaned to himself. Couldn't she see that he didn't want to 'Know the Lord' at eight o'clock in the morning? He scuttled toward the street. Maybe if he cut across against the traffic, she'd give up and seek easier prey.

The street seemed clear. The D bus began to move, lurching forward as it gained momentum. The woman hurried desperately, reaching out to clutch his arm and scattering a few of her leaflets on the sidewalk.

Startled, Jersey looked at her hand on his arm and glared at her. "Do you mind?"

The woman seemed surprised at her own action and quickly released him, abashed. "I . . . I'm sorry, sir. Sometimes I get a little carried away in the service of the Lord. I just wanted to have a word with you."

"Kindly keep your words to yourself." He didn't like someone intruding upon his morning. Now he'd probably be annoyed for hours.

He stepped off the curb, almost walking into the D bus as it passed. The bus driver honked at him in annoyance, then pulled out into the traffic.

With relief, Jersey saw the A shuttle bus arrive in a hissing of air-brakes and a belch of oily smoke. The missionary woman dropped back, and he was surprised she gave up so easily.

But as he grabbed the rail of the bus, Jersey felt a painful blackness swimming up between his ears, like a crowbar on his temples. A deep-seated sickness clawed its way from his heart and his solar plexus. He thought he was going to vomit. Disorienting pain burst from all the nerve endings in his brain.

Oh, not here, not here!

He slumped and sat down heavily on the steps of the bus. His face turned a discolored white, like a melted vanilla milkshake.

"Hey man!" the bus driver said.

The missionary woman stood over him, looking astounded and concerned. She moved quickly, holding his chin, peeling the eyelids back and staring at his eyes, his pupils. She held his wrist as an expert would, taking his pulse. With the back of her hand, she felt his forehead.

Then all the pain and dizziness passed, as it usually did. The woman's appearance changed, a mask dropping back into place. She returned to her role as a formless old Bible-thumper. "There, there," she said. "Maybe you'd best just go lie down?"

Jersey thrust her away and stood up again, blinking and embarrassed. "Just moved too fast, that's all. Now please leave me alone."

She frowned, but dropped back. Jersey made his way to an empty seat. He closed his eyes and breathed deeply, in and out, in and out, as the bus pulled away from the hotel.

Jersey tugged his tie loose as he fumbled for the hotel room key in the pocket of his slacks. Thus ends another typical day at the convention. The suit jacket hanging over his arm steamed with perspiration in the afternoon heat. The Hilton had no swimming pool, only a couple of hot tubs on the roof—ninety-five frigging degrees outside, and they had a *hot tub.*

Inside, the maid had shut off the air conditioner. He tossed his jacket on the bed. Jersey rubbed his temples, feeling the aftermath of hour upon hour at the Grovemont Gloves booth. He had arranged and rearranged the colorful brochures. He plied the customers like an old carny huckster, holding forth his computer printouts of comparative permeability characteristics as if they were sacred scrolls. During a self-imposed break, Jersey wandered around the other exhibits, picking up a plethora of free pens, kitchen magnets, key chains. The spoils of war.

Jersey unbuttoned his shirt. Tonight, the conference would be having their banquet—Texas-style barbecue, of course. He could find dozens of better barbecue places up and down the street, within walking distance from the hotel. But he had come to the conference to *enjoy* himself—and everybody else would be going to the banquet.

Then he noticed the neat white envelope on the bed, propped against the pillow.

For a moment, he felt a touch of amused annoyance. Probably one of those 'thank you for staying at the Hilton' cards. He snatched up the note, then sat on the bed, puzzled.

The letterhead said simply *Entropy Ranch.* His mind pondered the ludicrous notion, as if redneck Texas ranchers concerned themselves with 'entropy.' The note was handwritten, careful and neat, and made out to him personally. The paper itself smelled of faint perfume.

> Dear Mr. Jersey,
> We would like very much for you to visit us this afternoon. We are concerned about the dizzy spell you had this morning on the bus. This is not a sales pitch—it's a personal invitation extended to you alone. Please take the time to come.

No signature. The only other thing he found in the envelope was a map.

The teeming madness of the Dallas freeway system finally fell behind, and all of Texas seemed to spread out in front of him: ranch houses; fields; the roadside dotted with mesquite, cornflowers, and occasional stands of live oak and cottonwood. He drove with one hand on the steering wheel of the rental car, one hand holding the sketched directions.

How the hell had they known? Jersey wasn't sure whether he felt more amazed or frightened. It took him nearly an hour and a half to get to the last turnoff, a thin unpaved road branching off from a county highway—unmarked, and not much different from similar roads he had been passing for a dozen miles.

The rental car trundled along the gravel, raising dust. Jersey glanced at the odometer, ticking off seven-tenths of a mile as mentioned on the map. An alfalfa field spread out on either side, heavily overgrown with weeds. The unpaved drive hooked around a slight view-blocking hill, and then Jersey saw a barbed-wire fence and an ornate wrought-iron gate. Red-brick posts flanked the gate on either side.

Down the driveway, a large, well-kept farmhouse towered like something out of a Faulkner novel. Three cottonwood trees spread voluminous boughs in a protective shell around the house.

Jersey pulled the car to a stop outside the gate. He took his keys and stepped out of the car. How did they know? Why did they pick him? What did they have in mind?

Barbed wire stretched out for half a mile in either direction, enclosing nothing of significance, as far as Jersey could see. Several signs hung from the fence, alternating between KEEP OUT and NO TRESPASSING, in a typical Texan welcome. On the iron gate a small metal plate bore only the plain engraved words: *Entropy Ranch.*

Jersey stood on the metal slats of the cattle guard under the gate and punched the intercom button mounted in one of the posts. "Excuse me? My name is Edmond Jersey. I . . . received a note."

A filtered drawling voice drifted up from the speaker, "Yes, Mr. Jersey. Please come on up to the house." The lock on the gate clicked open electronically. "You can leave your car where it's at—we're not expecting nobody else."

Feeling a bit uneasy, Jersey pushed open the gate and entered. His dress slacks were starting to get dusty. He strode up toward the house and paused, but forced himself not to turn back as the gate swung shut behind him. He wiped sweat from his forehead.

When he reached the farmhouse, Jersey noticed a thin dark-skinned woman reclining on a porch swing in the shade of the cottonwood trees. She stood up, smiling, as he approached. She wore a crisp white lab coat over worn blue jeans. She had soft, wide eyes, high cheekbones, and a hard smile. Her hair was cropped close to her head.

"Welcome, Mr. Jersey. I'm pleased to meet you after all this time. I am Lilith Semper." As she extended her hand, he noticed that she wore no rings, that her nails were clipped close to the fingertip and scrubbed clean. Her voice was cool, educated.

"You sent me an invitation and I came," he said, sounding more impatient than he wanted to. He calmed himself; he'd already had the mother of all dizzy spells today, and did not wish to experience another. "Now what's this all about?"

Lilith Semper smiled invitingly. "Step inside. We've already saved your life twice today, but we'd like to check out a few things, if you don't mind."

Before he could mutter a baffled question, she opened the front door of the farmhouse and stepped inside.

Within the house's facade stood two sets of double glass doors, behind which sprawled great banks of computers, clean white walls, and giant viewscreens the size of picture windows. Jersey counted five other technicians within sight, moving about, checking instruments.

Lilith Semper startled him by placing a hand on his elbow. "Come on inside—have a look around. This is Entropy Ranch."

Cold, dry air came out at him, heavily air conditioned to shield computer units from the humid heat. Jersey followed her across the threshold between the two doors. He stepped on a square of sticky gray material that grabbed the soles of his shoes.

"For the dust," she explained. Then, from a bin in the foyer, Lilith pulled out plastic booties—instinctively, he scanned for the Grovemont label—and slid one set over her own shoes. She reached into a locker and handed him a stiff lab coat that smelled of bleach. Jersey shrugged into the lab coat and worked the plastic coverings over his shoes. He forced himself not to say anything. She waited for him, then opened the second set of doors.

On one wall, the large viewscreen simulated a detailed sequence of an airplane collision. Most of the technicians stood by a monitor that showed three children trapped in the blazing interior of a burning house. A screen on the far wall, partially hidden behind a bank of control panels, displayed the scenario of some kind of bus accident. Near the door, a police scanner crackled and occasionally spat out a string of words. A notepad and a laser printer sat beside the scanner on the same table.

Jersey swallowed, feeling a thickness in his throat. A dull ache began to pry at his temples again. Movie special effects? No, that wasn't it. Actual film? Or detailed accident simulations . . . what kind of morbid interests did these people have?

Lilith Semper gripped his upper arm. "I know what you're going to ask, Mr. Jersey. But wait a second—let it all sink in."

He continued to stare. One of the technicians, a freckle-faced and sunburnt young man, smiled at Jersey knowingly, then turned back to the freeze-frame image of the burning house. Jersey could see the gruesome detail, the graphic portrayal of the children dying in the fire. The sunburnt technician spoke to his companions, who seemed to be pondering deeply.

"It's time travel, Mr. Jersey," Lilith leaned over and said into his ear.

Startled by her voice, it took him a moment to realize what she had said. "What?"

"We can go back and change the past, or the future, depending on how you want to look at it. As I said, we've already saved your life twice today."

She took his arm and steered him toward the back of the room. The buzzing sounds of the air exchangers began to make Jersey dizzy. "I'm sorry we have to show you like this—it'll be unpleasant, sure enough. But if I can convince you at the outset, we'll save us a lot of doubts later on."

She took him to the large screen showing the bus accident. As he looked at the image of the yellow shuttle bus, Jersey felt a chill creep inside him. It looked too familiar. He could recognize the front of the Hilton; he thought he even recognized the shadowy bus driver behind the windshield. But the mangled pedestrian under the bus tires—

"Rerun timeloop 0804 A," Lilith said to the attending technician, then turned to Jersey. "We can stop this at any time, if it disturbs you too much."

A new scene appeared, then began to move: the bus arrived, people stood in front of the Hilton. Jersey watched in horror as *he* came into view, looking around, distracted. Then the missionary woman walked up to him . . . he tried to escape across the street, and stepped in front of the bus.

Jersey did not even think to cover his eyes. "That's our original attempt. We tried to stop it from happening, but we weren't aggressive enough at first. We have to change as little as possible each time, you see."

A new tape played. Jersey appeared on the screen again, the missionary woman came, they bantered, he snickered and tried to dash across the street—and, again, the bus struck him. But Lilith froze the image on the screen before the picture could actually show his death.

"Have faith, Mr. Jersey," she said with a beatific smile, "We'll tell you everything, of course."

Jersey felt beads of sweat form on his forehead, dampening his hair. The inside of his skull began to throb. He took several deep breaths, forcing the nausea away. Not another dizzy spell. . . .

She patted him on the shoulder, failing to comfort him. "It'll be fine now. We just go back in time and do a little tweaking, here and there, to prevent such tragedies from happening."

"But . . . why?" *Stupid question!* Nothing else came to mind.

Lilith Semper looked at him with a confident smile. "Why, it's our Christian duty."

She seemed ready to defend her assertion, but Jersey refused to take his eyes from the image on the screen—the expression on his reflected face, the oncoming bus, the deadly impact hanging only a second away.

"But how can you change what's already happened? Isn't it set in stone? If time is . . ." He faltered, not sure what he wanted to say.

Lilith stiffened, and her voice carried a sudden sharp edge. "We are Baptists here, Mr. Jersey, *not* Calvinists. If you want to talk about Predestination, you'll have to find a Presbyterian." She scowled, but before Jersey could understand how he had insulted her, Lilith's expression softened again. "If you feel up to it, let me show you something, like a demonstration."

Jersey fought down his unsteadiness as she led him to the screen displaying the burning house. He could see toys littered about, a pair of bunk beds and an extra twin bed on the opposite side. One set of sheets had begun to smolder. The boy's form underneath sprawled half out on the floor, but he lay motionless. One girl retched on her knees, choking and screaming; her hair caught fire. The girl in the upper bunk lay mercifully still, apparently strangled by the thick smoke. The paint on a small blue rocking chair in the corner bubbled away from the wood.

Jersey glanced at Lilith. Her eyes glistened with tears, but her voice came out strong and angry. "Meet Tammy, Cindy, and their brother Brett. The door is locked. You see, Tammy, Cindy, and Brett forgot to come home before six this evening. They were playing down by the creek, catching crawdads and waterbugs. They lost track of time, that's all. But they . . . they came home late, and all muddy, and their daddy got angry. Ten swats for each one of them, and then to their room with no supper." She drew a deep breath, and blew it out slowly. "He locked them in while he went off to play softball.

"We don't know how the fire started yet. The children are going to be killed—they already *have* been killed—but how can we just leave them? What kind of world can let that happen?" Lilith stared at him as if demanding an answer.

"Now, by changing a few parameters, we might be able to save them. We can influence precursor events so that this tragedy *does not happen.*

"Ethically, we have to interfere as little as possible to achieve our results. We don't want to damage the future. We have developed our own rules, set ourselves a time limit of ten subjective hours to fix a disaster. You see, if we go back only an hour or two, it shouldn't set up significant ripples in future events. But the longer we wait, the greater a chance for a backlash. You must have heard plenty of stories about time-travel paradoxes."

She fell silent for a moment, almost brooding. "That means if we can't find a way to save these children soon, they're gonna die like this, in flames."

Jersey stared at the screen, mulling over Lilith's words. "What do you mean, 'subjective hours'? And how can you sit here and manipulate events—once you change something, then it never really did occur, so how can you *know* about it. I mean . . . this is confusing."

"Believe me, Mr. Jersey, all of us here have studied paradoxes until our heads spin. We're safe because we're in this place, Entropy Ranch. Within the boundaries of our fence is a sheltered area, like an island in the timestream. All timelines come here, ripple around, and move on. We can reach in, stir the waters where we like, and watch what happens."

She shrugged. "We've got operatives on the outside, like the lady who distracted you this morning. These operatives change little things, interact in tiny ways, and we observe from here. Sometimes we have to do it over and over again until we achieve what we want.

"For instance, maybe we'll have someone give the daddy a rose on his way home from work, get him in a better mood when he sees his kids getting home late and muddy. Maybe then he won't lock the door, and they'll be able to get out of there. That's the type of thing I'm talking about."

"But why did you pick me? What have I ever done for you?"

Lilith shrugged, and somehow that infuriated him. "Entropy Ranch is just starting out—we need test cases, success stories. Right now we can only respond to local accidents, whatever we pick up on the Dallas-Fort Worth police radio.

"We heard on the scanner that you were killed in an accident this morning. We thought we could fix it. We sent one of our operatives to the scene and, after three attempts, finally managed to distract you long enough so you didn't step in front of that bus. You were very persistent about being killed, Mr. Jersey."

Her eyes took on a passion. Jersey could feel her perspiration as she gripped his hand. "Think of it—we can eliminate awful fires like this, prevent plane crashes, terrorist attacks, stop all those stupid accidents that . . ." she faltered, then pushed on, "that needlessly claim so many lives. We can *do* something about it, even after it's happened.

"But we need to know the effects of what we do. We need to study you, Mr. Jersey, because after we had changed time to save your life, you suddenly collapsed on the bus. What did we do to you—have you uncovered some very peculiar side effect? We have to know before we go on. That's why we broke our secrecy and called you here."

Lilith led him away from the image of the burning house. "The techs need to get on back to work. Please come over here—I want you to meet someone." She motioned to one of the other workers.

The man was thin enough that the lab coat sagged around him like a discarded skin, but he moved with an effeminate grace. His silvery gray hair had been swirled and molded with generous amounts of hair oil. A braided bolo tie hung around his neck, secured by a garish lump of turquoise.

"This here is Dr. Barens," she introduced them, "and Mr. Edmond Jersey."

Automatically, Jersey extended his hand. Barens shook it and then took his cue, moving over to the third screen, which still showed the image of Jersey on the verge of death. "We want to check you out, Jersey. Maybe we set up some backlash when we sidestepped you from your appointed meeting with death."

Barens called up a file from the terminal. The image on the screen dissolved and returned to show Jersey climbing the steps of the shuttle bus. The missionary woman chased after him. Suddenly, the other Jersey's expression turned gray and waxen. He stumbled against the railing, sinking to the bus steps. The missionary woman hurried up, looking professional now, feeling his pulse, checking under his eyelids.

"We've never seen anything like your attack before," Barens continued. "It looks serious, and we want to check it out, to see if our tweaking caused some unexpected physical response."

Jersey chuckled a little to himself. "You're both jumping to conclusions. That was just one of my dizzy spells—I've been having them for a month. I doubt they have anything to do with your, er, activities. Not unless you've been 'rescuing' me since April."

Lilith Semper's face wore an almost comically shocked expression. Barens himself cringed, as if stunned. The noise of the air exchangers grew to a loud buzzing as Jersey felt the other techs in the room fall quiet. Some of them watched him openly; others glanced out of the corners of their eyes.

"We never did consider *that*, Lilith," Barens mumbled.

She pursed her lips and finally turned to Jersey but continued to speak to the doctor. "Then we got to find out what's wrong with him anyway. It's our Christian duty to help, remember?

"Mr. Jersey, won't you please go with Dr. Barens and give him complete details of your symptoms? He may want to do some tests after all."

Barens reacted uncertainly, but Lilith glared at him. The doctor motioned Jersey out another set of double doors into a small sitting room. Barens began to interrogate him in detail about the history and background of his dizzy spells. About halfway through the discussion, the doctor grew concerned enough to start taking notes.

Jersey fidgeted on the sofa as Barens sat in silence. The doctor got to his feet, concentrating on his notes and his thoughts. "Wait here," he said and began to walk back toward the main control room.

"Bullshit!" Jersey said, "I want to know what's going on."

"All right, come on then."

Lilith Semper watched them, hopeful. She raised her eyes, waiting for the doctor to speak. At the other viewscreen, the technicians working on the burning house scenario chattered to themselves about a possible solution. "Well?" she asked.

"His symptoms are pretty clear, but I can't tell how serious it is without different equipment." He continued, as if intentionally ignoring Jersey. "You know, I'm supposed to put in a thousand qualifiers that say 'maybe' and 'possibly' and 'some symptoms suggest'—it's standard bedside manner. But the patient never listens to them anyway, so why bother? I think it's either an aneurysm or a brain tumor, but I'd need a CAT scan to verify it. We're not set up for that kind of sophisticated test here—this isn't a medical research lab, you know."

Lilith looked stricken and turned an ashamed expression toward Jersey, but he felt too sickened himself to respond. Finally he muttered, "I've got to get out of here."

"He's right," Barens agreed, "If this has been going on for a month, then he should get himself to a hospital *soon.*"

Lilith looked around in anguish for support from the other technicians, but they rapidly turned their heads away. "We *can't* let him go. Not now!"

*   *   *

Jersey, Dr. Barens, and Lilith Semper joined the technicians in the large dining room. Stripped of their lab coats, the people took on a more relaxed air. Lilith helped some of the techs bring in empty bowls, baskets of bread, and two large pots containing green or red chili. Dr. Barens brought him a can of cold beer, and Jersey savored it.

"This *is* a dry county we're in, but somebody runs in to Dallas once a month to pick up a couple cases of Pearl." Barens sighed. "We can't be expected to sacrifice ol' demon alcohol for science or for God, you know."

Three of the places remained empty as they all sat down. "Somebody had another idea to save the children," Lilith said. "Not much time left, so they couldn't take a meal break."

She opened up the windows, and the sound of grasshoppers came from outside. Everyone sat quiet for a moment. Jersey reached for the basket of bread. Then Lilith started intoning a prayer, which grew to several minutes in length.

Jersey had little appetite. *Aneurysm. Brain tumor.* Possibly malignant—fatal. Now he felt angry and helpless, upset at the people of Entropy Ranch. He should be back in a Dallas hospital, undergoing *real* tests, seeing what the best medical techniques could do to save him. Instead, they wanted to keep him here for a couple of days—*We don't have the facilities for more than a blood test and some other high school chemistry experiments*—where he would only grow worse, hour after hour.

When Lilith Semper finished her rambling prayer, and the others had echoed "Amen," the technicians began to serve themselves, ladling out chili and breaking off chunks of bread.

"The green is hot, the red is milder," Dr. Barens said in his thin voice. Jersey took a small bowl of the red chili, sniffing it suspiciously.

"Since I already know too much for you to ever let me get out alive," Jersey said, "why don't you tell me how you managed to put this little research facility out here without anybody knowing about it."

"Oh, Mr. Jersey," Lilith said, "don't you be so melodramatic."

"Am I?"

She took a spoonful of chili and followed it with a bite of cornbread. "Entropy Ranch, this entire giant project, is funded by one of the better-known TV evangelists. Don't look so surprised. We're taking that money and turning it to the benefit of all of us, as God wants us to do. Our scientists were able to do work with a more open mind than all them party-line physicists, and they found a different way to look at relativity. You see, our people start out with the assumption that miracles *can* happen, and they look for an explanation. Most other researchers break their backs proving that things are *im*possible, not possible. Our engineers came up with a way to map the timestreams, and once you get to *seeing* something, it's a relatively simple step to manipulate it.

"So, rather than just learning from our mistakes, we can now go back and fix them in the first place. Just like we saved you this morning. Love one another, strive for peace, do unto others, and turn the other cheek. Those are all admirable goals, aren't they?"

"No other reason, huh? No profit? No glory?"

"No publicity whatsoever. Now that we have the technology, how can we *not* use it to help other people?"

Jersey ate his chili, keeping a sour expression on his face. "Well, I thank you for saving me—but if you don't mind, I'd best be saving myself. Get to a hospital, you know?"

"We're *trying*, Jersey," Dr. Barens interrupted, "but we need a little time to work out some technical difficulties."

"What's to stop me from just leaving? Are you going to force me to stay? Whatever happened to Christian charity and doing all that stuff unto others?"

Lilith sighed and met his eyes with a sympathetic expression. Barens pushed himself away from the table and went into the kitchen to get Jersey another beer.

"It's easy to get *into* the Ranch," she explained, "because all timestreams converge here. But we're reaching out, manipulating dozens of different futures that all intersect right here and then branch off in their own directions, swirling around the fenceline. At the moment, our most crucial problem is to save the children in the burning house, and we may have to try something desperate, something unorthodox." Her dark eyes went distant for a moment, then she stared back at him.

"But bear in mind that we *are* working for your best interests. Give us time to put everything straight. We can set you back down at a point in time that everybody will see as 'this afternoon.' Nobody will even notice you've been gone."

Jersey still felt indignant. "You're going to erase my memory or something?"

Lilith lowered her eyes. "We *would* like to hypnotize you for our own protection, but that needs your complete cooperation. If you choose not to cooperate, well—we are Christians, you know, and we do prefer to think the best of people."

He ate the last of his chili and concentrated wholeheartedly on finishing the beer.

"We'd like you to stay in our guest house tonight."

Jersey lay back on the unfamiliar bed, listening to it creak as he moved. He could see the oak bedposts in the moonlight that came through the window. A sluggish breeze stirred the curtain, but Jersey felt sweaty and uncomfortable. Though they had provided him with a pair of light cotton pajamas, he preferred to sleep in his own underwear.

How long did they really want to keep him there? He closed his eyes, turned his thoughts inward—he could sense the alien presence of *something* growing inside his head, like a parasite. Even if they put him back a day into the past, the tumor would still have grown a day's worth in his 'subjective' time or the aneurysm would have worsened. If he could only get to a hospital.

Outside, crickets thrummed, but otherwise the ranch seemed quiet, asleep. He got up and crept to the door, certain he would find it locked—but the door swung open, revealing the small sitting room in the guest house. No guards either. These people were absurd in their trust. Feeling exposed, he slipped back into the bedroom and pulled on his slacks, holding the car keys and coin purse in his pocket to keep them from jingling.

How could he possibly benefit by waiting? His life lay on the line, after all, not theirs. It seemed an ironic denial of their own Christian charity. They couldn't do anything for him here—they said as much. Holding him over for an extra day or two was just a stalling routine. Pointless. Maybe an extra day *would* make the difference for him in a real hospital, if things were as serious as Dr. Barens had suggested.

He buttoned his shirt and took a deep breath. What would they do if they caught him trying to escape? Not that it mattered —he had to try. He pushed open the screen door, careful not to let it slam, and stood on the porch. Just to his right, the tall white farmhouse blotted out the stars, surrounded by the black masses of giant cottonwood trees. He saw lights on inside, a thin figure silhouetted in the window; it looked like Lilith Semper, watching. But, standing in the bright room, she would not be able to see him.

He paused, listening and waiting. He expected some kind of security, but he'd seen no evidence of dogs, not even the typical ranch-hand German shepherd wandering the grounds. None of the doors were locked. *We are Christians, you know, and we prefer to think the best of people.* He wondered if they'd be interested in buying some nice swampland in Florida. . . .

Jersey began to walk down the drive, walking on the grass to avoid crunching the gravel. His heart beat heavily, and he drew air in short, quick breaths. He moved faster, but forced control on himself, making sure he didn't run in panic.

Down at the bottom of the hill, he neared the wrought-iron gate, but he stopped, suspicious. If anything, the gate might be alarmed or tied to a motion sensor. If he was going to have to climb over the wrought iron, he might just as well scramble through the barbed wire instead.

Jersey saw the outline of his rental car on the opposite side of the gate, and that reassured him. If they had truly meant to keep him trapped, they would have moved the car first thing. This was laughably easy—did they *want* him to leave?

He waded through the weedy alfalfa until he came to the barbed-wire fence. Jersey had made up his mind that he wouldn't tell anyone—explaining Entropy Ranch would be too awkward, and he did owe Lilith Semper that much, for saving his life the first time. Turn the other cheek, and all that.

With a last glance at the spectral silhouette of the ranch house, he pried the strands of barbed wire apart and, careful not to snag his slacks, he climbed through—

—and landed in the middle of the burning bedroom. Flames licked at the side of a child's rocking chair. Clotted smoke in the air blurred the outlines of a pair of bunk beds and an extra twin bed. Stunned disorientation made him lose his balance as intense heat blasted him, singeing the hair on his arms and head and scouring the insides of his nostrils. He whirled, staggered back, but the barbed-wire fence, the ranch house, all had vanished, leaving only an impenetrable bedroom wall.

How could he have fallen into a different timeline? His eyes filled with water and then, it seemed, with steam. He dropped to his knees. When he drew in a deep breath to scream, the hot air scorched his lungs.

If he died, would the people at Entropy Ranch know where to look? Would they come back to rescue him again? Then sick despair slammed into him with double force. Their ten-hour time limit to save the children had expired—Lilith Semper wouldn't look at all.

Or had they somehow *set this up* for him? Was this the "something desperate, something unorthodox" plan Lilith Semper had concocted? Because they had saved him once today, did that give them the right to throw him into this?

Jersey lurched to his feet, pawing his hands in front of him. The fire roared, blistering the air. He could smell the awful reek of incinerating wood, plastic, paint. The door would be locked; he *knew* it was locked.

And then, in deeper horror, he saw the three children. The boy Brett sprawled half out of his bed, stricken down while trying to escape. One girl lay motionless in the upper bunk; the other girl was coughing on the floor.

He would not *refuse* to help them, just to spite Lilith Semper if she was watching. Edmond Jersey could 'Do Unto Others' as well as anyone else. His anger made him want to curse Lilith, but it wasn't worth wasting precious seconds. Recklessly, he yanked at the girl on the upper bunk as he dragged the other girl to her feet. He jerked the comforters off the beds, then slapped the boy several times, rousing him from his unconsciousness.

"Come on! Come on!" He tossed the thick comforter around himself and the motionless girl. He blanketed the other two children and hustled them along with him.

Jersey's brown hair seemed to be flaking off in silky ash, and his face burned, raw. Jersey did not hesitate as he savagely kicked at the door with his heel.

The door shuddered in its frame, and he stepped back to kick again. He felt something crack in his leg, but wood splintered around the doorknob. He struck at the door one last time, and the wood around the lock bolt shattered to pieces. The door swung open to another sequence of the inferno.

The hallway looked alien, filled with a jungle of flames. Never having been in the house before, Jersey hadn't the slightest idea where he was—he couldn't even tell if they were upstairs or downstairs. They could never get out that way.

He didn't blink, but lowered his head and pulled the comforter around him as a shield. "Out! We have to get out!" Jersey held tightly to Brett and the girl Tammy as Cindy choked and cried. She sobbed and almost fell to her knees again, but he jabbed her in the ribs and shouted harshly. "Dammit! Cry later!"

He pulled them back into the room. Opening the door had been a mistake. *Stupid, Jersey!* On the opposite wall of the bedroom, a small window stood partially covered by the frame of the bunk bed. That would have to do. He hoped they weren't on the second floor.

He had to let go of the children. Cindy managed to stay on her feet, but the other two children slid to their knees, choking. Jersey burned his hands as he picked up the small rocking chair, but he smashed it through the window. A crossdraft roared through the room, sucking heat along with it.

Jersey heard noises outside—axes splintering wood, shattering glass. He pushed Brett toward the window blindly. The boy crawled over the frame, cutting himself on the glass but seemed not to notice. Jersey turned to drag Tammy to the window without watching Brett disappear.

He had to wrestle the girl up to the sill. She squirmed, just moving and not cooperating. On the floor behind him, Cindy continued to cry. He could hear her even over the roar of the fire.

Tammy fell to the ground. Jersey saw a glimpse of Brett managing to crawl away across the lawn.

Then he saw moving figures, like monsters from outer space. Echoes of stray thoughts ricocheted through his head. *Is my life flashing before me?* After he had broken open the door, the heat in the room had grown ten times worse. The comforter on his back burst into flames. He could not breathe at all anymore. He needed oxygen, but he felt his lungs burn. He couldn't see anything right.

But he still needed to get Cindy out the window. Jersey could barely move—every step pushed the hot wind against his face. His feet seemed like someone else's appendages. The girl was hot to the touch, but his fingers were beyond feeling. She seemed incredibly light, like a rag doll he tossed out the window.

He leaned through the window himself. He tried to shout for help, but his vocal cords seemed to have been turned to ash. The cold air outside felt like heaven, allowing him to breathe. But the window was too narrow. His shoulders wedged against the bunk bed frame and the side of the window. Glass cut into his arm as he pushed, but he could not fit through the window.

All right, he would just die here then. Keep Lilith Semper happy. Breathing the air and looking outside. That was a better way to go than a brain tumor anyway. He didn't want to die, but he couldn't make any more effort. He surrendered entirely to the fire and slumped forward.

Someone grabbed his arms, his shoulders, pulled him through. He screamed as the glass cut into his biceps, then in a last anguished moment, he fell into the outside early-evening air.

For a moment, Jersey blinked stinging tears out of his eyes, then barely discerned the shapes of fire trucks, people moving about, water being sprayed onto the flame-filled shell of the house. The three children lay collapsed on the ground, but they were being taken care of. They would be all right. Jersey knew he had saved them, and that filled him with an overwhelming sense of wonder.

He preferred his way to the subtle manipulation of Entropy Ranch. Jersey's breath hitched in his burning throat as he whispered, "While you were biting your nails, I was saving them!"

He collapsed and began to sob, but he could feel only the monotonous symphony of pain all over his body. But that was good. The pain meant he would survive, the pain meant that he was not burned as badly as he imagined.

". . . delirious," a voice said. Jersey's ears still rumbled from the roaring sound of fire.

"He's in shock, I think. But he'll be okay—those burns will heal."

"Better get him off to a hospital."

Jersey tried to sit up, but other hands grabbed his arms, lifting him. It hurt him deeply, but that didn't seem to matter anymore. He heard one of the girls, Tammy, begin to cry.

"Yes," he sighed, looking up and trying to see faces. Everything remained a blur, but they were taking him where he wanted to be. He had done his good deed. He had earned it. Everything would be all right now.

"Take me to a hospital . . . a hospital."

Introduction to
Dogged Persistence

*More people have read this piece than any other short story I've writ-
ten . . . but most of them don't know it.*

While doing research on nanotechnology for my novel, Assemb-
lers of Infinity, *written with Doug Beason (1993), I realized that I
could use some of the tangential information I had learned for other
ideas—different approaches to the threat or the promise of K. Eric
Drexler's* Engines of Creation.

*This story—about a family on the run, their 'immortal' dog, and
a violent conspiracy group trying to hunt them down—was originally
published in* The Magazine of Fantasy and Science Fiction. *Years
later, when Chris Carter & Co. asked me to write a third X-Files
novel, I realized that this idea seemed perfectly adaptable to a case
that might have intrigued our favorite FBI agents, Fox Mulder and
Dana Scully.*

*I incorporated most of "Dogged Persistence" into my X-Files
novel,* Antibodies, *which became an international bestseller and has
been translated into numerous languages.* Antibodies *was also the
first media tie-in novel of any kind to reach the nomination ballot
for the Bram Stoker Awards for Superior Achievement, as presented
by the Horror Writers of America.*

*Here is the original story, the streamlined version, without any
interference from too-credulous FBI agents.*

Dogged Persistence

THE DOG STOPS IN THE MIDDLE OF THE ROAD, DIS-tracted on his way to the forest. The asphalt smells damp and spicy with fallen leaves. Infrared laser-guidance posts line the shoulder at wide intervals, but most of the vehicles that travel this road are of the old kind, growling inside from hot engines, belching chemical exhaust.

The twin headlights of the approaching car look like bright coins. The image fixates him, imprinting spots on his dark-adapted eyes. The dog can hear the car dominating the night noises of insects and stirring branches. The car sounds loud. The car sounds angry.

Moving with casual ease, the dog saunters toward the shoulder. But the car arrives faster than he could ever run, squealing brakes like some death scream. He hears the thud of impact, the bright explosion of pain that suddenly vanishes. He is flying through the air toward the ditch. He smells the spray of blood from inside his own nose.

Knowing he must hide, the dog hauls himself into the brambles, under a barbed-wire fence, to the dense foliage.

Car doors slam, running feet, the babble of voices: "Shit! That was no deer—that was a dog! A big black Lab!" "Where'd he go?"

"Shit, must have crawled off to die." "Look at all the blood—and look what he did to your car!"

The dog has found a safe place. The human voices become fuzzy as black unawareness overcomes him. He will not move again until it is finished. He will be all right.

Inside his body, millions upon millions of nanomachines begin to repair the damage, cell by cell, rebuilding the entire dog. The night insects resume their music in the forest.

Patrice went to the window and watched her son bounce a tennis ball against the shed. Each impact sounded like gunshots aimed at her. She cringed. Judd didn't know any better; he remembered none of what had happened so long ago. Sixteen should have been a magic age for him, when teenage concerns achieved universal importance. In all those years, she had never let Judd come into contact with other people, much less those his own age.

She opened the screen door and stepped onto the porch, taking care to keep the worried expression off her face. Judd would consider the concern normal for her anyway.

The gray Oregon cloudcover had broken for its daily hour of sunshine. The meadow looked fresh from the previous night's rain. The patter of raindrops had sounded like creeping footsteps outside the window, and Patrice had lain awake for hours, staring at the ceiling. Now the tall pines and aspens cast morning shadows across the dirt road that led from the highway to her sheltered house.

Judd smacked the tennis ball too hard and it sailed off to the driveway, struck a stone, and bounced into the meadow. With a shout of anger, Judd hurled his tennis racket after it. Impulsive— he became more like his father every day.

"Judd!" she called, quelling most of the scolding tone. He fetched the racket and plodded toward her. He had been restless for the last two days. "What's wrong with you?"

Judd averted his eyes, turned instead to squint where the sunshine lit the dense pines. Far away, she could hear the deep hum of a hovertruck hauling logs down the highway.

"Pancake," he finally answered. "He didn't come back yesterday, and I haven't seen him all morning."

Now Patrice understood, and she felt the relief wash inside of her. For a moment, she was afraid he might have seen some stranger or heard something about them on the news. "Your dog'll be all right. Just wait and see."

"But what if he's dying in a ditch somewhere?" She could see tears on the edges of Judd's eyes. He fought hard against crying. "What if he's in a fur trap, or got shot by a hunter?"

Patrice shook her head. "I'm not worried about him. He'll come home safe and sound. He always does."

Once again Patrice felt the shudder. *Yes, he always does.*

Fifteen years before, Patrice—she had gone by the name of Trish, then—had thought the world was golden. She had been married to Jerry for four years. In that time, he had doubled his salary through patents and bonuses from enhanced silicon-chip development at the DyMar Laboratories.

Their one-year-old son sat in diapers in the middle of the hardwood floor, spinning around. He had deactivated his holographic cartoon companions and played with the dog instead. The boy knew "Ma" and "Da" and attempted to say "Pancake," though the dog's name came out more like a strangled "gaaaakk!"

Trish and Jerry chuckled together as they watched the black Labrador play with Jody. She did not start calling the baby Judd until after they had fled. Pancake romped back and forth with paws slipping on the polished floor. Jody squealed with delight. Pancake woofed and circled the baby, who tried to spin on his diapers on the floor.

"Pancake's like a puppy again," Trish said, smiling. She had owned the dog for nine years already, all through college and in her four years with Jerry. Pancake had settled into a middle-aged routine of sleeping most of the time, except for a lot of slobbering and tail wagging to greet them every day when they came home from work. But lately the dog had been more energetic and playful than he had been in years. "I wonder what happened to him," she said.

Jerry's grin, his short dark hair, and heavy eyebrows made him look dashing. "Maybe all those little things that make a dog feel old got fixed inside of him. The sore joints, the stiff muscles, the bad circulation. Like a million million tiny repairmen doing a renovation."

Trish sat up and pulled her hand away from him. "Did you take him into your lab again? What did you do to him?" She raised her voice, and the words came out with cold anger. "What did you do to him!"

Trish stopped and turned to see her baby boy and the dog looking at her as if she had gone insane. What business did she have yelling when they were trying to play?

Jerry looked at her, hard. He raised his eyebrows in an expression of sincerity. "I didn't do anything. Honest."

With a woof, Pancake charged at Jody again, wagging his tail and banking aside at the last instant. The holographic cartoon characters marched back into the room, dancing to a tune only they could hear. The dog trotted right through the images to the baby. "Just look at him! How can you think anything's wrong?"

But in only four years of marriage, Trish had learned one thing, and she had learned to hate it. She could always tell when Jerry was lying.

"Mom, he's back!" Judd shouted.

For a moment, Patrice reacted with alarm, thinking of the hunters, wondering who could have found them, how she might have given themselves away—but then through the open window, she could hear the dog barking. She looked up from the stove to see the black Labrador bounding out of the trees. Judd ran toward him so hard she expected him to sprawl on his face. Just what she needed, Patrice thought, he would probably break his arm. That would ruin everything. So far, she had managed to avoid all contact with doctors and any other kind of people who kept names and records.

But Judd reached the dog safely, and both tried to outdo the other's enthusiasm. Pancake barked and ran around in circles, leaping into the air. Judd threw his arms around the dog's neck and wrestled him to the ground.

According to her notes, Pancake would be twenty-four years old in a few months. Nearly twice the average life span of a dog.

Judd and Pancake raced each other back to the house. Patrice wiped her hands on a kitchen towel and came out to the porch to greet him. "I told you he'd be okay," she said.

Idiotically happy, Judd nodded and then stroked the dog.

Patrice bent over and ran her fingers through the black fur. The wedding ring, still on her finger after fifteen years alone, stood out among the dark strands. Pancake had a difficult time standing still for her, shifting on all four paws and letting his tongue loll out.

Other than mud spatters and a few cockleburs, she found nothing amiss. Not a mark on him. There never was.

She patted the dog's head, and Pancake rolled his deep brown eyes up at her. "I wish you could tell us stories," she said.

In Jerry's lab, the dog paced inside his cage. He whined twice. He obviously didn't like to be confined and he was probably confused, since Jerry had never caged him before. Pancake wagged his tail, as if hoping for a quick end to this.

Jerry paced the room, running a hand through his own dark hair, trying to kill the butterflies in his stomach. He had worked himself into self-righteous cockiness at showing the management assholes just what they had spent all their money on. Progress reports went unread, or at least not understood. Memos describing their work and its implications disappeared in the piles of paper—yes, even though Ethan and O'Hara had perfectly functioning electronic mail systems, they still insisted on old-fashioned paper memos from DyMar underlings.

He glanced at his watch. "What the hell is taking them so long?"

Beside him, Frank Peron sighed. "It's only five minutes, Jerry. You know, wait for them, but they'll never wait for you. We were lucky to get them to come down here at all."

"Considering that this breakthrough will change the universe as we know it," Jerry said, "I'd think they might want to give up a coffee break to have a look."

He couldn't take his eyes off the poster tacked up on the lab wall. It showed Albert Einstein handing a candle to someone few people would recognize by sight—K. Eric Drexler; Drexler, in turn, was extending a candle toward the viewer. *Come on, take it!* Drexler had been one of the first major visionaries behind nanotechnology some thirty years before.

It will change the universe as we know it, Jerry thought. Pancake looked expectantly at him, then sat down in the middle of his cage. "Good boy," Jerry muttered.

"They're management boobs," Frank said. "You can't expect them to understand what it is they're funding."

At that moment Mr. Ethan and Mr. O'Hara, two of the highest executives in DyMar Laboratories, entered the lab room, apologizing in unison for being late. Smiling, Jerry assured them that neither he nor Frank Peron had noticed.

"Dr. McKenzy, your memo was rather, uh, enthusiastic," Ethan said.

Beside him, O'Hara scowled and chose a different word. "Ebullient. Tossing around promises of immortality, the end to all disease, curing the handicapped, stopping aging—"

"Yes, sir, we felt we had to limit our discussions to only those topics," Jerry interrupted. He had to shock these two so thoroughly that they would be ready to question all their preconceptions. "Actually, this nanotechnology breakthrough opens the doorway to much more, such as an end to dirty industry, instantaneous fabrication of the most complex machines, new materials stronger than steel and harder than diamond. That's why so many people have been working on it for so long. We've all been racing each other because when it happens, it *happens*. And the first ones to break through are going to shake up society in ways you won't be able to imagine."

Ethan and O'Hara looked as if they had never heard so much bullshit before in their lives. *Very well,* Jerry thought, *time to haul out the big guns. Literally.*

"Watch this, please, and then we can adjourn to the conference room."

Jerry pulled out an automatic pistol from the pocket of his lab coat. He had bought it at a sporting goods store for this purpose only. No one should have been able to smuggle a gun into the lab, but security was lax. He had brought the dog in, hadn't he? He looked at Pancake.

The two executives scrambled backward, muttering outcries. Jerry didn't give them time to do anything. He was running this show. Melodramatic though it might seem, he knew it would work.

He pointed the pistol at the dog and fired two shots. One struck Pancake's ribcage; another shattered his spine. Blood flew out from the bullet holes, drenching his fur.

Pancake yelped and then sat down from the impact. He panted.

"My god!" Ethan shouted.

"McKenzy, what the hell do you think—" O'Hara cried.

"The first thing that happens," Jerry said, then repeated himself, yelling at the top of his lungs until he had their attention again. "*The first thing that happens* is that the nanomachines shut down all of the dog's pain centers."

The two executives stared wide-eyed. They were both shaking.

In his cage, Pancake looked confused with his tongue lolling out. He seemed not to notice the gaping holes in his back. After a moment, he lay down on the floor of the cage, squishing his fur in the blood still running along his sides. His eyes grew heavy, and he sank down in deep sleep, resting his head on his front paws. He took a huge breath and released it slowly.

"In a massive injury like this, the machines will place him in a recuperative coma. Already, they are scouring the damage sites, assessing the repairs that will be needed, and starting to put him together again. They can link themselves into larger assemblies to make macro repairs." Jerry knelt down on the floor beside the cage, reached his hand in to pat Pancake on the head. "His temperature is already rising from the waste heat generated by the nanomachines. Look, the blood has stopped flowing."

"The dog's dead!" O'Hara said. "The animal activists are going to crucify us!"

"Nope. By tomorrow, he'll be up and chasing jackrabbits." Jerry felt intensely pleased with himself. "I brought in my own dog so we didn't have to go through all the procurement crap to get approved experimental animals."

"You are out of a job, Dr. McKenzy!" Ethan said. His face had turned a deep red.

"I don't think so," Jerry answered, and smiled. "I'll bet you a box of dog biscuits."

The light near sunset slanted through a cut in the Oregon hills where the trees had been shaved in strips from robotic logging. The clouds had cleared again, leaving Patrice and Judd to sit by the table in the living room. The lights, sensing their presence in the household, would come on soon.

The two of them worked on a sprawling jigsaw puzzle that showed the planet Earth rising over the lunar crags, photographed from the moonbase. The blue-green sphere covered most of the table, with jagged gaps from a few continents not yet filled in.

Patrice and Judd talked little in the shared comfortable silence of two people who had had only their own company for a very long time. They could get by with partial sentences, cryptic comments, private jokes.

Judd knew why they had to hide from the outside world. Patrice had kept no secrets from him, explaining their situation in more complicated terms as the boy grew older and became able to comprehend. He had never complained. He knew no other life.

Outside, Pancake barked. He stood up on the porch and paced, letting a low growl loose in his throat.

Patrice stiffened and went to the lace curtains. Her mouth went dry. Somehow, she knew the dog was not making one of his puppy barks at a squirrel. She had owned the dog more than half her life, and she knew him better than any human being could. This was a bark of warning.

"What is it, Mom?" Judd asked. From the drawn expression on his face, she could tell he felt the fear as much as she did. She had trained him well enough.

Patrice could hear a vehicle toiling up the winding gravel drive away from the highway and toward the house.

The demonstrators outside DyMar Laboratories consisted of an odd mix of religious groups, labor union representatives, animal-rights activists, and who knew what else. Some were fruitcakes, some were violent.

Staring out the window, Jerry McKenzy didn't know how to deal with the mob. Maintenance had added steel bars in the last week. "We didn't get as much breathing space as we had counted on."

He paced in the lab office, occasionally stopping to search brainstorming files and records on his computer, even consulting disorganized handwritten notes on his desk. The actual nanotech experiments were done in clean rooms in the annex building, where Jerry himself rarely went. But with the demonstrations growing, all experiments had been shut down as the DyMar execs tried to figure out what to do. But then, they were idiots anyway.

DyMar had made a fatal error in announcing the nanotechnology breakthrough to the world. Pressed for time and knowing their research facility couldn't be the only one so close to success, DyMar had blitzed the public with premature announcements. They had taken everyone, including Jerry and his team, by surprise.

The outcry in response had been swift and frightening, much more organized and aggressive than the misguided or ineffective complaints Jerry had normally seen. The protest was organized under the aegis of a new organization called "Purity" that had burst into existence with unbelievable speed.

Peron stored his file in the computer and tapped his fingers on the keyboard. "And *you* thought we'd be the only ones to grasp the implications of nanotechnology."

"It's always nice to see that some people understand more than you give them credit for," Jerry said.

Peron tugged on his lower lip. Something had been bothering him all morning. "Did you ever hear the story about the guy who perfected a solar-power engine? Would have put the gas and electric companies out of business, would have changed the world as we know it. But he disappeared before he could disseminate his blueprints. Now, somebody with a billion dollar invention like that doesn't just drop out of sight. Do you know what I'm saying?"

Jerry scowled at him. "Oh, that's just an urban legend! Like the choking Doberman."

Peron shrugged. "Well, Drexler predicted back in 1985 that we'd have functioning nanotech within a decade—and that was thirty years ago! A dozen groups have been working, but somehow the crucial experiments fizzle at just the wrong times, the key data gets misprinted in technical journals. It's only because of your damned arrogance, Jerry, that we plowed our way around the usual scientific channels. Have you *checked* how often the most promising nanotech researchers move off to other fields of study, how often they die in accidents?"

Jerry blinked at the other man in astonishment. "Have you run a reality diagnostic on yourself recently, Frank? You're sounding paranoid."

Peron forced a laugh. "Sorry. This isn't exactly a high-security installation we're working in, you know. You smuggled your damned dog in here twice, and Pancake isn't a lap dog that'll fit in a glove compartment. And what about your gun? A chain-link fence and a couple of rent-a-cops does not make me feel safe."

As if in response, the crowds outside took up a loud chant.

Jerry sat down, and spoke in his "let's be reasonable" voice. "Frank, some bone-headed fanatic is always trying to stop progress —but it never works. Nobody can *un*discover nanotechnology." He made a raspberry sound.

Jerry spent a quarter of an hour reassuring his partner, convincing him not to worry. With dogged persistence they could get through this mess. He felt confident when they both packed up to brave the gauntlet of protesters and go home.

But he never saw Frank Peron again.

When Patrice saw the red vehicle approaching, she squinted into the sunset and made it out to be a small American truck outfitted with laser-guidance sensors, mud-spattered and identical to a million other vehicles in Oregon. She didn't recognize the silhouette of the man behind the wheel.

She didn't have time to run.

Patrice and Judd had lived in the state for nine years, at the same location for three of them. She and her son had fled to Oregon because of its track record of survivalists, of religious cults, of extremists and isolationists—all of whom knew how to be left alone. The state's rural ultra-privacy legislation forbade any release of tax documents, credit card transactions, or telephone records.

But the last time she had gone into a grocery store, she had noticed the cover of a weekly newsmagazine depicting the fenced-off and burned ruins of DyMar Laboratories. The headline advertised a fifteen-year retrospective on the disaster, bemoaning the loss of all records of such an important technological breakthrough. No doubt the story would talk about how she and her son were still missing, presumed killed by Purity extremists. The feature article probably contained pictures as well—of her, as Trish McKenzy, not Patrice Kennesy, and the boy Jody, not Judd. On impulse, she tossed the magazine into her basket.

Uneasy, she had taken her groceries and backed away from the *TV Guides* and beef jerky strips and candy bars by the register. No one, she insisted to herself, would have put it all together, would have connected all the details. Still, the clerk stared at her too intently. . . .

Now, with a grim expression on her face, Patrice stepped out on her front porch to meet the approaching stranger.

The demonstrators did not go home, not even late at night. Jerry had remained at the lab office until after ten o'clock, sending a vidmessage to Trish that he wanted to finish another simulation before locking up. People massed against the chain-link fence, shouting and chanting. They had lit bonfires.

Somehow he could not believe that anybody but the technically literate would understand how significant a breakthrough he and Frank Peron had made. This wasn't the type of thing people normally got up in arms about—it was too complicated and required too much foresight to see how the world would change, to sort the dangers from the miracles DyMar had been promising in its PR. Who was orchestrating all this?

Like Utah's cold fusion debacle from decades before, DyMar had made a lot of promises and produced nothing tangible. They were waiting for patent approval before releasing any details, but the red tape had been tangled, the patent office had lost the first two sets of applications, though the e-mail trace verified that they had been received and logged in. Lawyers did not return vidmessages. News of the 'immortal dog' had been leaked in one interview, but Jerry sure as hell was not going to shoot Pancake again in front of a TV camera just to make a point.

The dog wasn't the only one blessed with nanotechnology cell repair, though. He had seen to that himself. Nobody knew that he carried his own cell-repair machines tailored to human DNA, and it would stay that way.

Outside he heard glass breaking, the roar of the crowd. It just didn't make any sense to him. He watched out the window. Clouds had obscured most of the stars overhead, but mercury vapor lamps spilled garish light across the near-empty parking lot.

At the gate, a team of rent-a-cops paced about holding rifles ready, probably quaking in their boots. DyMar had called for backup security from the State Police, and they had been turned down. The ostensible reason was some buried statute that allowed the police to defer "internal company disputes" to private security forces. How they could consider the mob of demonstrators to be an internal company dispute, Jerry could not imagine. It felt as if somebody wanted the lab unprotected.

He heard sharp popping noises outside, and it took him a moment to realize they were gunshots. He turned to see one of the security guards fall; the others ran away as a group of people stormed through a breach in the chain-link fence. He heard more gunfire.

"This is nuts!" he said to himself, then switched off the light in his lab. No use attracting them; but they would know exactly where he was working. Jerry couldn't believe it, but he knew he had to get away immediately.

Glow from the parking lot lights mixed with the dim EXIT sign to give him enough illumination to move. He slipped out of the room and hesitated, wondering if he should call the police or the fire department. Someone smashed the front doors downstairs. He had no time.

They would ransack the place and destroy his work. Jerry tried to think if he could save anything, like in all those old movies where the mad scientist rescued his single notebook from the flames. But his work and Frank Peron's was scattered in a thousand computer files, delicate microhardware, and intangible AI simulations. Everything was backed up, with duplicates stored in various vaults. It would be safe. For now, the important thing was to escape. The mob had already killed one of the guards; Jerry had no doubt they would tear him apart.

He ran down the hall as he heard footsteps in the lobby, shouted orders, another gunshot. Jerry fled to the back stairwell, yanked open the door, and leaped down the concrete stairs three at a time, balancing himself on the railing. At the bottom, he ripped off his lab coat and left it on the landing before emerging into the administrative section of the main building.

He peeked around the door. They had not gotten this far down the halls yet, and managerial offices would not be their first target. He heard a huge roaring explosion and saw through a set of windows the annex building erupt into orange flames. Impossible! This couldn't be happening! But ignorant peasants had always stormed the doctor's castle, carrying torches.

Jerry kept close to the wall as he hurried along. The front and side doors would be out of the question. But the back had an emergency exit, a crash-out door that would also activate alarms and notify the police and fire departments. He couldn't decide if that would be good or bad.

A window shattered in one of the suites in front of him, and a puddle of flames spilled from a broken bottle. Molotov cocktail; one of the front offices—either Ethan's or O'Hara's—burst into flame.

Jerry placed his ear to the emergency exit door. He heard chaos outside, but it sounded distant. He imagined somebody stationed back here with a rifle pointed at the door, waiting for him to come running. But he had no other choice.

Jerry used his back to slam out through the door, throwing himself to the ground as he emerged. He rolled, waiting to hear gunshots strike the door, ping off the asphalt, slam into his chest. What had Pancake felt when the bullets slammed into him? He didn't know how much damage his own body could endure and still repair itself. He had never tested his limits.

But the only gunshots came from the side of the building. He heard more shouts and running people. He got up and sprinted to the corner of the building. If only he could make it to the parking lot and to his car, he could crash through the fence and drive off, get Trish and the baby, and hide in a motel for a few days until this stuff calmed down.

He let himself feel a ripple of smugness. The violence here would stun the protest movement; once the public saw them do murder and destruction like this, all sympathy for their cause would be gone. This was like mass insanity. Killing people by blowing up abortion clinics never won any support for Pro-Life groups, did it? Carlton Armstrong's bomb hadn't helped the Vietnam war protest decades before, had it?

But when Jerry saw the people attacking the DyMar building,

saw the weapons they carried and the uniform way they moved, he knew immediately that this was no mob, this was no ragtag band of second-generation hippies yanking shotguns off their mantels.

Fire from the lower level spread through the main building. More burning bottles had been tossed through downstairs windows.

With a shock he noticed a complete absence of TV crews, though they had been covering the protest since its beginning. On the parking lot near the gate, Jerry saw the sprawled uniformed bodies of two security guards. The others were probably dead somewhere along the fence line—unless they were themselves part of the assault team.

In the confusion, Jerry added an angry expression to his face and ran among the mob, working his way to the parking lot. He slipped through, shouting directions to anyone who looked his way as if to challenge him.

Once Jerry got to the cars, he ducked low, working among them. This late at night, not many vehicles remained, only his own, the guards', a handful of other cars and trucks that had either broken down, or sat with FOR SALE signs in their windshields.

He found Frank Peron's black sports car and hesitated. But Frank had left days ago! Unless he had never made it. Jerry swallowed a cold lump in his throat.

Once he got in his car, he would have to start it and drive away fast, keeping his head low to avoid gunfire. Judging from what Pancake had endured, Jerry could survive some major injuries with his nanotech healing machines, but he had no desire to test them.

He reached the passenger side of his car and fished in his pocket for the key ring. Among the shouts and burning and gunshots, the noise he made was insignificant, but still the jingle seemed too loud to him. He unlocked the door and slipped in, crawling over the passenger seat and pulling the door shut behind him. Squirming, he positioned himself behind the steering wheel, still ducking low, and took an absurd moment to strap himself in with the seatbelt. He would have to crash through the fence and he did not want to smack his head on the dashboard and knock himself senseless.

Before starting the car, he plotted his route, found a side gate with an access road that would take him off to the highway. He switched off all the automatic collision-avoidance systems, the laser-guidance options. He was going to have to drive like a stunt man. He made up his mind to plow right over anybody who stood in his way. This was life or death here. Adrenaline pounded through him. He would gain nothing by waiting.

He turned the key in the ignition.

The car bomb instantly blew him into pieces, trapping his body in the burning hulk of twisted metal. Not even his cell-repair machines could fix so much damage.

In front of Patrice's house, the man wasted no time as he ground the red vehicle to a halt. He left the engine purring, slid the door open, and stepped out.

He brought a scattershot rifle out of the front seat and leveled it at Patrice. "Ding dong, Avon calling," he said.

Patrice stood defiantly on the porch, unable to move. She felt old and weak. When Judd stepped out and stood beside her, she felt weaker still.

"Or would you rather I said 'I'm from the government, I'm here to help you'?" the man continued. He had a medium build and wore a red flannel shirt with a white T-shirt poking up to his neck. His face was bland, nondescript, showing no indications of outright evil.

Without taking his eyes from them, he reached in to the dashboard of his truck and yanked out two sheets of paper, colored computer printouts showing faces. The images were split: one side showed a photograph of her from fifteen years before, and the other image — computer enhanced — had "aged" her to approximate what she looked like now, along with a detailed personality analysis suggesting how she might normally dress. The second sheet of paper showed baby Jody and a much-less-exact extrapolation of how he would look as a sixteen-year-old boy.

"I'm convinced," the man said. "Or are you going to deny it, Mrs. McKenzy?"

For a moment, all the words backed up in her mind. She couldn't think of anything to say, couldn't think of anything worth saying. "What do you want from us?"

"What do I want?" He laughed and stepped around the door of the vehicle, still pointing the scattershot at them. "Purity's been looking a long time."

Growling, Pancake stood up and eased forward, baring his teeth. He stepped in front of Judd.

The Purity man stopped and blinked in astonishment. "Jesus,

that's the dog! The goddamned dog—it's still alive! Well, well, well!"

"Do you want money?" Patrice said. She didn't have much left, but it would stall him for a few minutes. "I have cash. It won't show up on any account record."

"This goes beyond money," he said. "We need to bring you in. Take the dog and destroy him. Then find out from you and the boy if you've kept any of Dr. McKenzy's notes, maybe some of his nanotech samples. We can't take chances with the human race."

Seeming to sense the boy was the weak link in this scenario, the Purity man aimed the scattershot at Judd's head and took a few more steps toward them. Holding the rifle with one hand, he fumbled in his pocket, withdrawing a pair of polymer handcuffs.

"Now then, Mrs. McKenzy, let's not make this difficult. I want you to cuff one of these around your wrist and the other around the boy's ankle. That'll make it impossible for you to run anywhere." He extended the handcuffs forward.

Pancake lunged. Black Labradors were not normally used as attack dogs, but Pancake must have been able to sense the fear and tension in the air. He knew this man to be an intruder, and Pancake had been with the same owner for twenty-four years.

He struck the Purity man full in the shoulders, startling him, spoiling his aim. As the scattershot dropped, the man's finger squeezed the trigger. The explosion roared through the quiet isolation far from the main road.

Instead of taking off Judd's head, the swath of silver needles spattered across the boy's chest, spraying blood behind him to the walls of the house.

Patrice screamed.

Pancake bore the man to the ground. The man thumped into the front of his vehicle, banged against the sharp laser-guidance detectors and then sprawled. He tried to fight the dog off. Pancake bit at his face, his throat.

Wailing, Patrice dropped to her knees and cradled her son's head. "Oh my god! Oh my god!"

Judd blinked his eyes. They were wide with astonishment and seemingly far away. Blood bubbled out of his mouth, and he spat it aside. "So tired." She stroked his hair.

Pancake backed away from the motionless man on the ground. Blood lay in pools from the man's torn throat.

The headlights of Patrice's carryall glared up from the wet pavement long after dark. She had switched off the old and unreliable laser-guidance systems and drove faster than safety or common sense allowed, but panic had gotten into her mind now. She kept driving, pushing her foot to the floor and wrestling with the curves of the coast road, heading north. Dark pine trees flashed by like tunnel walls on either side of her.

She had to find someplace else, to run again, to start a new life.

Pancake rested in the back of the station wagon, exhausted. Clumps of blood bristled from his fur. She hadn't taken time to clean him up. She had paused only long enough to throw all of her ready cash into the glove compartment. The Purity man's own wallet had held two hundred dollars and several cred cards under different names. . . .

Looking down at the man's body in the failing dusk light, she had noticed that the blood had stopped flowing, yet his heart continued to beat. He looked to be in a deep sleep, and his skin felt warm and feverish. She had stepped back in horror. Of course the government had nanotech healers of their own! All of Jerry's records were supposedly destroyed in the DyMar Labs disaster, but with backups and disjointed systems, no simple fire could have eliminated everything.

Now she knew why, after all these years, others had not made similar breakthroughs. Jerry had been merely the first, but other researchers were close on his heels. The sham organization of Purity, or the government, or some worldwide power consortium had kept nanotechnology to themselves, blocking or absorbing all other breakthroughs as they occurred.

This man would wake up in a day or so, and report back to his superiors. She could destroy him now, set his body on fire or squash his head with the front wheel of his own vehicle.

Instead, she siphoned all the fuel out of his truck and switched license markers. In some coast town, she would find a darkened parking lot and other unattended vehicles, and she would switch markers again. Then she would move on.

In the back seat of the carryall, Judd lay in silence, wrapped in two bloodstained blankets she had torn from the beds upstairs. His pulse was faint, his breathing shallow, but he still lived. He seemed to be in a coma.

The obstacle alarm screeched. From the trees on her right, a dog stepped into the road in front of her.

Patrice cried out, slammed the brakes and yanked the steering wheel. The dog bounded back out of sight. She swerved, nearly lost control of the car on the slick road, then regained it. Behind her, in the rear-view mirror, she saw the dark shape of the dog walk back across the road, undaunted by its close call.

She remembered one of the last conversations she had had with Jerry, after he had finally told her what he had done to Pancake and the immortality his nanotechnology had brought. Jerry had wanted to give her the same type of protection.

She blinked at him in horror when he told her he had already done it to himself. He wanted to do it to her, too.

The thought of a billion billion tiny machines crawling through her body, checking and rechecking her cell structures, seemed abominable to her. She refused to let him. Jerry would not let her ponder the question, would not let her come to grips with the idea. He wanted an answer *right then*. That was just the way Jerry McKenzy did things.

Baby Jody started to cry, awakened by their raised voices. Trish had looked up at her husband with wide eyes; she caught a faint smile on his face as Jerry glanced toward Jody's room.

"You didn't do anything to the baby, did you! What did you do to Jody?"

"Nothing!" Jerry said. He smiled. "I didn't do anything."

But she could always tell when her husband was lying.

As she drove off into the night, with her son's bleeding body in the seat behind her, Patrice prayed she was right.

Introduction to
Human, Martian—One, Two, Three

Sometimes an idea and the characters are just too big to fit into a work of short fiction. This story, originally intended to be novella-length, quickly grew into my novel, Climbing Olympus. *The original shorter version, though, was published in the fourth volume of* Full Spectrum.

The core idea came from the notion of obsolete software. A program that has not changed, that still serves its purpose exactly as it had when it came out of the box brand new, becomes completely useless as other technology changes around it.

I then wondered if there could be obsolete people *as well, and cast that idea into terraforming operations on the planet Mars. In this concept, prison camp "volunteers," surgically altered to enhance their ability to survive, are sent to tame the harsh and inhospitable Martian environment. But when they did their jobs too well, and began to change the climate so that natural humans could live there, they found themselves obsolete, no longer useful, and treated as monsters.*

ℋuman, Martian—
One, Two, Three

*I*CE, THE COLOR OF SPILLED PLATINUM ON OCHRE dust, extended in a lake outward from the breached pipeline. Lumpy white stalactites dangling from the pipe marked where reclaimed water had spewed into the thin atmosphere, froze, and then began to evaporate. Before long the solid lake would erase itself again, volatilizing into the Martian sky.

As she brought the crawler vehicle toward the pumping station, Rachel Dycek tried to assess the area of spilled ice. "Thousands of liters," she said to herself, "many thousands. A disaster."

She turned a sharp eye from the clinging scabs of ice on metal to the broken pipe itself. The thin-walled pipe was more than just breached; someone had torn it apart with a crowbar.

That almost piqued her interest. Almost. But Rachel didn't let it happen. Her successor would have to deal with this debacle. Let him show off his talents. He deserved the trouble. She no longer considered herself in charge of the Mars colony.

As she drove up, three *dva* emerged from the insulated Quonset hut beside the pumping station. The *dva*—from the Russian word for "two"—were second-stage augmented humans, surgically altered and enhanced to survive the rigors of the Martian environment. Rachel watched them approach; she recognized none of them, but she had done little hands-on work herself with the second stage. Only the first.

She parked the crawler, checked her suit's O_2 regenerator system, then cycled through the airlock.

"Commissioner Dycek!" the leading *dva* greeted her. He was a squat man covered with thick silver and black body hair, wearing loose overalls, no environment suit. Rachel looked at him clinically; she had spent a great deal of her time in UN hearings justifying every surgical change she had made to the *dva* and their more extremely modified predecessors, the *adin*.

The man's nose and ears lay flat against his head to protect against heat loss, and his nostrils were wide sinks on his face. The skin had a milky, unreal coloration from the long-chain polymers grafted into his hide. His chest ballooned to contain grossly expanded lungs.

The other two *dva*, both females also wearing padded overalls, clung beside him like superstitious children. They let the man do the talking.

"We did not expect someone of such importance to investigate our mishap," the *dva* man said. His accent was thick and exotic; from the southern Republics, Azerbaijan or Kazakhstan most likely. He shuffled his feet in the rusty sand, kicking loose fragments of rock. "You see, it is much worse than we reported in our initial transmission."

Rachel stepped forward, turning her head inside the environment suit. "What do you mean, worse? How much water was lost?"

"No, the loss is what you see here." The *dva* man gestured to the metallic sheet of ice. Wisps of steam rose from its surface. The salmon-colored sky had an olive tinge from the algal colonies that had proliferated in the atmosphere for nearly a century. Rachel saw no sign of the seasonal dust storm she knew to be on its way.

"Come with me," the man said, "we will show you what else."

As the *dva* man turned with the two women beside him, Rachel finally placed him and his ethnic group. Kazakh, from one of the abandoned villages around the dried-up Aral Sea. The Aral Sea had been one of Earth's largest fresh-water bodies until the early twentieth century, when it had been obliterated by Joseph Stalin. Trying to rework the desert landscape to fit his whim, Stalin had expended all that water to irrigate rice fields in the desert—rice, of all things!—until the Aral shoreline had retreated kilometers and kilometers inland, leaving boats high on dry land, leaving fishing villages starving and disease-ridden. The area had never recovered, and when the call went out for *dva* volunteers, many families from the Aral region had leaped at the chance to come to Mars, to make a new start. Even here on a new planet, though, they clung to their ethnic groupings.

Rachel followed the *dva* man. Her suit crinkled, unwieldy from its high internal pressure. The three *dva* led her to the area behind their hut. Part of the back wall had been knocked down and then shored up. Bright scars showed where someone had battered his way in from the outside.

Under a coating of reddish dust and tendrils of frost, two iron-hard corpses lay on the ground. Rachel bent down to look at the wide, frozen eyes, the splotched, bloodstained fur, the ragged slashed throats.

With a grim smile, Rachel could think only of how the new commissioner, Jesús Keefer, was going to have a terrible blot on his first month as her successor. So far Keefer and the UN had kept everything cordial, a comfortable transition period between two commissioners who held nothing but outward respect for each other. But Rachel had been cut out of all responsibility, with nothing to do but twiddle her thumbs in the pressurized habitation domes until the supply ship came to take her back to Earth. After she had gone, Keefer would probably find some way to connect this event with something Rachel had done during her administration. He had to keep his own record clean, after all.

"We left this other one by himself." The *dva* man took her to the far side of the Quonset hut. "We did not want him tainting the soil beside our comrades."

The third body lay sprawled, arms akimbo, head cocked against a boulder as if the *dva* survivors had tossed his body there in disgust. Inside her helmet, Rachel Dycek let out a gasp.

"*Adin*," the *dva* man said, stating the obvious. First-phase augmented human.

"I thought they were all dead by now," Rachel said.

"Not all," the *dva* man answered, gesturing with his stubby hand at the exaggerated adaptations of the *adin*. "One other escaped."

The *dva* looked human—distorted to the point of the caricatures found in Western newspapers, but human nevertheless. But the *adin*, placed on Mars in an earlier stage of the terraforming process, had endured more extreme transformational surgery. A continuous frill hooded the deep-set eyes to shelter them from cold and blowing dust; the nostrils were covered with an extra membrane to retain exhaled moisture. A second set of lungs made bulbous protrusions in the *adin*'s back, half hidden by this one's skewed position in the dust. This *adin*'s body lay naked in the freezing air.

"He came out of the darkness," the *dva* man said. The two women nodded beside him. "His comrade smashed the pipeline, and we were distracted by the screaming sound of the water. This *adin* came through the back wall of our dwelling and attacked us. He slashed the throats of our two comrades while they were still trying to wake up. We managed to club him to death."

Rachel noticed what she should have seen right away. Frozen blood trailed dark lines from the *adin*'s ears; his eyes had shattered. "Down here on the plain the air pressure must have been killing him. The *adin* were adapted for conditions much worse than this."

She heard faint sounds from the chemical O_2 regenerator system in her suit. It hissed and burbled as it made her air. She marveled at the irony of the atmosphere being too thick, the temperature too warm for the first group of Mars-adapted humans.

Rachel turned back to the lake of ice and the broken pipeline that stretched from the water-rich volcanic rocks of the Tharsis highlands. "Can you repair this yourselves?" she asked. She did not want to report back to the UN base if she didn't need to.

The *dva* man nodded as if it were a matter of pride. "We are self-sufficient here. But we hope there will be replacements for . . . for our lost comrades. We have much work to do."

Rachel made a noncommittal response. No more *dva* would be created, and both of them knew it. Though conditions on Mars remained worse than a bad day in Antarctica, tough unmodified humans would soon be making an earnest attempt at colonization, more than just the token UN base Rachel Dycek had overseen. Politics had changed, and the days of augmented humans — and their creator — were over.

"You will need to make your repairs with haste," Rachel said. "A Class-Four dust storm is on its way from the north and should arrive late today."

The *dva* women looked at her with sharp, deep-set eyes. The man nodded again and took a step backward. "Thank you, Commissioner. We already know about the storm. We can smell it in the air."

The response took her aback. Of course the *dva* would know

such things just by living closer to the Martian environment.

Rachel herself had been concerned only with how the storm would obliterate her own tracks, allowing her to disappear forever. . . .

The breached water pipeline had been a mere pretext for her to take one of the crawlers from the inflatable base. Everyone else had duties, and no one had complained when she volunteered to make the long trip. Now the *dva* would perform their repair tasks, and Commissioner Keefer would think Rachel had taken care of everything. She would be long gone before anybody suspected something might be wrong.

After cycling back through the crawler's airlock, she drove off toward the volcanic highlands and the mighty rise of Olympus Mons, leaving the *dva* behind with their spilled ice and their dead. She had no intention of ever returning to them, or to her base.

Even on the highest slopes, the Martian air tasted spoiled to Boris Tiban. His first inclination would have been to mutter a curse and spit at the ground, but he had learned decades ago never to waste valuable moisture in pointless gestures. All the *adin* had learned that in their first days on Mars.

Boris reached the opening of the cave and turned to survey the endless slope that stretched down to the horizon. The climb from the plains to the highlands had not even left him out of breath. With only a third of the gravity that his body had been born to, Mars made him feel like a superman. He belonged here at high altitudes, where he could still breathe.

Two of the other *adin* came out to greet him as he stood in the cave entrance. They appeared unkempt, inhuman—as they had been designed to look. When they saw him alone, they hesitated. Stroganov asked, "Where is Nicholas?"

"Dead. The *dva* killed him." But the cause of death had been more than the *dva*. He and Nicholas had descended too rapidly, and the atmospheric pressure had maddened him with pain. Nicholas had begun to hemorrhage before the *dva* struck their first blow.

"Oh, Boris!" Bebez said. Her words sounded too human coming from the tight, insulated lips, the flattened face.

Boris leaned against his pointed metal staff, torn from the center of a transmitting dish, and closed his eyes. *Boris Tiban.* That was what they had called him in the camps in Siberia, decades ago on Earth before his surgical transformation into *adin*.

Prior to that he had worked in the Baku oil fields near the Caspian Sea; his superiors had shown no mercy when a fire in his area caused a major explosion that destroyed a week's production of petroleum. Sentenced to Siberia, Boris Tiban had grown strong in the hellish winter wasteland, the harsh labor. And then they had snatched him away again, put him through rigorous selection procedures, made him sign forms written in English, a language he could not read, and then worked their black cyborg magic on him.

"Is Boris all right? Why doesn't he come inside?"

Boris had never heard Cora Marisov's voice in the rich atmosphere of Earth, but he imagined it had been deep and musical, not the shrill tones caused by the thin air. Cora herself must have been beautiful. She refused to leave the shadows now, especially now.

He stepped into the cave. "We destroyed one of the water pumping stations. It will do no good. Nicholas died."

Inside, the caves were comfortable, the air breathable. The dim light hid the traces of green lichen crawling over the rocks. Boris remembered how excited he had been, how all the *adin* had been, when their terraforming efforts began to show results: the lichens, the algae, the changing hue of the sky. They had worked together in selfless exertion, tearing themselves apart to terraform the planet, to make it a better place for *themselves.*

The *adin* had been the first true Martians, feeling the soil with their bare feet, breathing the razor-thin air directly into their enhanced lungs. They had set out to conquer a world, and they had succeeded — too well. Now none of them could breathe the dense air below.

Cora came out, swaying as she walked. She went to him, and he embraced her. "I am glad you came back. I was worried."

Boris could not feel the details of her body against him. The long-chain polymers lacing his skin insulated against heat loss but also deadened the nerve endings. He felt like a man in a rubber monster suit from a ridiculous twentieth-century film about Martians. But like those costumed actors, Boris Tiban was human inside. Human!

With the death of Nicholas, only five of the *adin* remained of the initial one hundred. He, and Cora, and three others.

And Cora frightened him most of all.

Through the trapezoidal windowports of the crawler, Rachel Dycek could look out at the Martian sky and see bright stars even during the daytime. Twice a day the burning dot of Phobos swam from horizon to horizon, running through its phases — full, to quarter, to crescent, to new — though they were visible only in telescopes. The other moon, Deimos, seemed nailed to the sky, hanging in nearly the same place day after day, as it slowly lost pace with the planet's rotation.

The uphill slope of Olympus Mons was shallow, taking forever to rise up from the Tharsis Plain until it pushed itself clear of the lower atmosphere. The crawler vehicle made steady progress, kilometer after kilometer.

The monotonous landscape sprawled out on all sides. Rachel felt small and insignificant, unable to believe the arrogance with which she had tried to change all this. She had been successful against a world; because of her work, adapted humans could live in the open air of Mars — but now her successors were tossing her aside as casually as if she had been the most miserable failure. That phase of the project was over, they said.

The terraforming of Mars had begun with atmospheric seeding of algae many decades before the first permanent human presence on the planet. The algae latched onto the reddish dust continually whipped into the air, gobbled the abundant carbon dioxide, photosynthesized the weak sunshine, and laid the groundwork of terrestrial ecology.

Encke Basin, in the Southern Highlands, showed the great recent scar where the united space program had diverted a near-Earth comet into Mars. The comet brought with it a huge load of water, and the heat of impact measurably (though only temporarily) raised the planet's temperature. Encke Sea had volatilized entirely within seven years, further raising the atmospheric pressure.

But the terraforming had been an enormous and unending drain on Earth's coffers, siphoning off funds and resources that — some said — might better be spent at home. Fifty years had passed, and still no humans smiled under the olive sky or romped through the rust-colored sands as the propaganda posters had promised. Popular interest in the project had dropped to its lowest point. The beginning of a worldwide recession nearly spelled the end of a resurrected fourth planet.

No wonder the Sovereign Republics looked on Rachel Dycek as a national hero. With her secret work, she had succeeded in creating a new type of human that could survive in the harsh Martian environment: double lungs, altered metabolism, insulated skin like a living protective suit.

In a surprise move, suddenly there were people living on Mars – and they were Russians, Siberians, Ukrainians! The news shocked the world and catapulted Mars back into the headlines again.

Rachel Dycek and her team came out of hiding with their rogue experiments and raised their hands to accolades. A hundred human test subjects began eking out a living on the surface of Mars, breathing the air, setting up terraforming industries, ingesting the algae and lichens and recovered water. They transmitted progress reports that the whole world watched. They were called the *adin*, the first.

After months of interrogation by outraged – or perhaps envious, Rachel thought – investigative commissions from the world scientific community, she and her team had developed a second generation of Mars-adapted humans, the *dva*, who needed less drastic changes to survive on a world growing less hostile year by year.

All the enhanced males were given vasectomies before they were shipped to Mars. Since the *adin* or *dva* were not genetically altered, any children they conceived would have been normal human babies who would die instantly upon taking their first freezing, oxygen-starved breaths.

And finally, just five years ago, a "natural" human presence had been established on the surface, living in thin-walled inflatable colonies set up in canyons protected from the harsh weather. Rachel had been given the title of commissioner of the first Mars base as a reward for her accomplishments. She had watched as her *dva* workers paved the way on the highlands, remaking the world for humans to live on unhindered.

The *dva* project no longer needed her supervision, though; and most of the *adin* had abandoned their work and died out before Rachel ever set foot on the planet. Adapted humans were a short-term phase in the terraforming scheme.

Jesús Keefer, the UN Mars Project advisor, had come to replace her. Rachel's work on Mars was finished, and she had been ordered to go home. Keefer would not want her around, and Rachel's superiors had left her no choice. They would return her to Earth a well-respected scientist and administrator. She would fill her days with celebrity banquets, lecture tours, memoirs, interviews. Charities would want her to endorse causes; corporations would want her to endorse products. Her face would appear on posters. Children would write letters to her.

It would be pathetic. Everything would remind her of how she had been retired. Obsolete. Tossed aside now that she had completed her task. But Mars was her home, her child.

The crawler toiled up the lava slope of Olympus Mons. Black lumps of ejecta thrust out like monoliths from the dust, scoured and polished into contorted shapes by the furious wind. On the sunward side of some of the rocks she could see gray-green smears of lichen, a tendril of frost. It made her heart ache.

Even in the one-third gravity her body felt old and weak. Returning to Earth—and the extra weight it would make her carry—would be hell for her.

Instead she had made up her mind to go to the highest point in the solar system, fourteen miles above the volcanic plain. *Make sure you finish up at the top,* she had always said. Olympus Mons stood proudly above most of the atmosphere, two and a half times the height of Mount Everest on Earth.

On the edge of the eighty-kilometer-wide caldera, Rachel Dycek would stand in her laboring environmental suit and look across her new world.

Already she could see the bruised color of the northern sky as the murky wall of dust stampeded toward the southern hemisphere.

The crawler itself might survive—the vehicles had been designed to be tough—but the sandstorm would obliterate all traces of *her.*

Cora Marisov remained in the shadows of the lava tubes where the *adin* lived, partly out of shyness, partly out of the revulsion she felt toward her changing body.

Fifteen years ago her eyes had been modified for the wan Martian sunlight. They had been dark eyes, beautiful, like polished ebony disks, slanted with the trace of Mongol features retained by many Siberians. Her *Martian* eyes, though, were set deep within sheltering cheekbones and brow ridges, covered with a thick mesh of lashes. She remembered her grandmother braiding her hair and singing to her, marveling at what a beautiful girl she was. Her grandmother would no doubt run away shrieking now, making the three-fingered sign of the Orthodox cross.

Cora made her way up the sloping passageway to where sunlight warmed the rocks. The wind picked up as she stepped outside. The cramps in her abdomen struck again, making her wince, but she forced herself to keep moving. She used her fingers to collect strands of algae that had clung to the flapping skimmerscreens that captured airborne tendrils. The *adin* would cook the algae down, leach out the dusts, and bake it into dense, edible wafers.

After greeting her upon returning from his raid, Boris Tiban sat brooding in silence below, basking near the volcanic vent. She thought of him as a rogue, one of the legendary Siberian bandits, or perhaps one of the exiled revolutionaries. It had taken her a long time to grow accustomed to the abomination of his body, the lumpy alien appearance, the functional adaptations tacked onto his form.

She recalled her emotions the first time they had made love, more than the usual turmoil she felt when lying with a man for the first time. This was no longer a man, but a freak, with whom she grappled in a charade of love.

He had taken her under the dim sun, inside a sheltering ring of lava rock that reminded her of a primitive temple. She lay back in the cold, red dust but could not feel the sharp rocks against her padded back. When Boris held her and caressed her and lay his body on top of her, she could enjoy little of his touch. Too much of her skin's sensitivity had been surgically blocked.

Thin wind had whistled around the rocks, but she could hear Boris's breathing, faster and faster, as he pushed into her. Her external skin may have been deadened, but she squirmed and made a small noise deep in her throat; the nerves inside had not been changed at all. They moved and grabbed at each other, making an indentation in the dust that looked afterwards as if a great struggle had occurred there.

They had nothing to worry about. The Earther doctors had made sure they were all sterile before dumping them on this planet. Sex was one of the few pleasures they could still enjoy. Cora and Boris had made love often. *What did they have to lose?* she thought bitterly.

A hundred of the *adin* had set out to establish new lives on Mars. Eight had died within the first week when their adaptations did not function as expected; more than half succumbed within the first year, unable to adapt to the harsh new environment.

As good workers, they had transmitted regular reports back to Earth, at first every day, then every week, then intermittently. With a forty-minute roundtrip transmission lag, they could transmit their report and be gone again from the station before the Earth monitors could respond. Boris had liked using the delayed messages to taunt and frustrate. The Earthers couldn't do a damned thing about it.

After three years, cocky with invulnerability, Boris had spoken to the remaining *adin*. The Earthers had abandoned them on Mars, he said, to sink or swim depending on their own resourcefulness. Earth wanted to watch a soap opera, the quaint outcasts' struggle for survival. Finally Boris transmitted an arrogant refusal to do terraforming work anymore, and then destroyed the station. He had taken the metal spire from the tip of the dish and kept it as his royal staff.

By that time, only thirty *adin* remained. They moved to higher altitudes where the climate was more comfortable, the air thinner and easier to breathe.

Within a Martian year, the first *dva* arrived. They had been planned to replace the *adin* all along. . . .

Now, her arms laden with wind-borne algae strands, Cora turned and listened to an approaching mechanical noise, tinny in the thin air. She looked down the slope and saw the human crawler in the distance, raising an orange-red cloud behind it.

Cora stumbled back down into the cave, but already the other *adin* had heard it. Boris leaped to his feet from where he had been brooding; his body glistened with diamonds of frozen vapor. He held the pointed staff in his hand and peered out the window opening. The other three *adin* hurried to him.

No one paid attention to Cora. She couldn't be much help to them right now anyway.

Cora slumped down against the rough rock wall, breathing heavily and sorting out the algae strands. She felt tears spring to the corners of her eyes as she patted her swollen belly—the last great practical joke of all.

The crawler helped Rachel choose the best course. She opted to follow a gaping chasm that spilled down the slope of Olympus Mons, possibly extending to the base of the towering cliff that lifted the volcano from the Tharsis bulge. The chasm was one of the only landmarks she found on the vast uphill plain. It suggested days long past when liquid water had spilled downhill from melting ice. Or perhaps the enormous shield volcano had simply split its seams. She knew little about geology; it was not her area of expertise. If she had been a geologist on Mars, her specialty would never have become obsolete.

Gauges showed the outside air pressure dropping as she ascended. The wind speed picked up, bringing gusts that carried enough muscle to rattle the crawler. She had been climbing for half a day. The distant sun had passed overhead and dropped to the northwestern horizon. Behind her reeled two parallel treads, marking the path of the crawler. They would be erased when the storm hit, certainly before anyone thought to come looking for her.

With a momentary twinge of guilt, Rachel hoped the *dva* at the pumping station would be all right, but she knew they had been trained—and made—to survive the weather conditions of this new transitional Mars.

Ahead Rachel saw areas that looked like ancient volcanic steam vents, lava tubes, and towering jagged teeth of black rock rotten with cavities formed by blowing dust. It looked like an extraterrestrial Stonehenge guarding a gateway to a wonderland under Mars. Long sunset shadows stretched like dark oil spilling down the slope.

And then figures stepped away from the rocks, emerging from the lava tubes. Human figures—no, not quite human. In the fading light she recognized them.

Adin.

She saw three at first, and then a fourth stepped out. This one carried a long metal staff. Her heart leaped with amazement, awe, and a little fear. Rachel's first impulse was to turn the crawler around and flee back downslope to report the presence of this encampment of rogue "Martians." What would they do to her if they caught her?

But instead she stopped and parked the vehicle, locking its treads. So what might they do, and what did it matter? She sealed the protective plates over the windowports, then stood up. The recompressed air in her suit tasted cold and metallic.

Rachel had nothing to lose, and she wanted to know how the *adin* had fared, what they had done, why they had broken off contact with Earth. At least she would know that much before she died, and it would bring closure to her work. She had to find out for herself, even if no one else would know. She was probably the only one who cared anyway.

She cycled through the door of the crawler and turned back to key the locking combination. Rachel stepped forward to meet the *adin* survivors as they bounded toward her.

The Earther inside the suit looked fragile, like eggshells strung together with spiderwebs. She would never survive ten seconds unprotected outside.

Assisted by Stroganov, Boris took the captive woman's arm

and lifted her off the ground. Her reflective suit, bloated from internal pressure, felt slick and unnatural in his grip. He noticed that the suit design had changed somewhat since he had last dealt with Earthers, when they had first deposited the *adin* on the Martian surface.

He and Stroganov carried their captive easily in the low gravity; oddly, she did not struggle. Boris set the woman down in the dimness of the lava tube and scrutinized her small body. Apparently nonplussed, she straightened herself and looked around the grotto. Through the faceplate of her helmet, Boris saw dark eyes and an angular face, salt-and-pepper hair. He discerned no expression of helplessness and fear. He found it disconcerting.

"I recognize you," the Earther woman said. Her words filtered through the speaker patch below the faceplate in crisp textbook Russian straight from Moscow schooling. "You are Boris Petrovich Tiban."

Pleased that she knew him but also angry at where she must have seen him, Boris said, "You must have been entertained by our struggle for survival on this world, while you sat warm and cozy on yours? How often do they replay my last transmission to Earth, just before I dismantled the dish?" He rang his staff on the porous lava floor for emphasis.

"No, Boris Tiban, I remember you from my selection procedures." She paused. "Let me see, Siberian labor camp, correct? You had been a worker at the Baku oil fields in Azerbaijan. Your record showed that you got into many brawls, you came to work drunk more often than not. During one shift you had an accident that started a fire in one of the refinery complexes. The resulting explosion killed two people and ruined a week's oil production."

The other three *adin* stepped away, looking at her in amazement. Bebez grabbed onto Elia's arm. Boris felt a cold shiver crawl up his spine that had nothing to do with the temperature of Mars. Flickers of memory brought him fuzzy glimpses of this woman, dressed in a white uniform, bustling down cold tile halls. "How do you know all this?"

The woman's response was a short laugh. She seemed genuinely amused. "I selected the final *adin* candidates myself. I performed some of the surgery. I *made* you, Boris Tiban. You have survived here because of the augmentations I added to your body. You should be grateful to me with every breath you take of Martian air." She turned around, flexing her arm. The suit made crinkling noises.

"I do not remember these others as clearly," she continued. "There were so many candidates in the first phase."

Boris felt the fury boil within him. It all came back to him now. "Doctor . . . Dycek—is that your name, or have I remembered it wrong?" She was provoking him, taunting him—perhaps she did not know him as well as she thought. Stroganov gawked at her, then at him; yes, he remembered her too, the smell of chemicals, the slice of pain, the promises of freedom, the exile on this planet.

Boris brought the metal staff up. "Maybe I should just smash open your helmet."

"Do what you will. I never intended to return anyway."

Boris stared into her dark eyes distorted by the transparent polymer. He could not say anything. She had made him helpless.

"Tell me why you are so angry," she continued. "We set you free of your labor camp. You signed all the papers. We gave you a world to tame and all the freedom to do it. Better to rule in hell than to serve in heaven, is that not correct?"

All the clever words tumbled in his throat, clambering over each other to come out. Where was the tough, charismatic leader who had conquered Mars? He had made his speeches over and over to the surviving *adin*; but now he had the proper target in front of him, and he was speechless. He clenched his hand so tightly that he actually felt the nails against his thick, numb palm.

The anger finally burst out, and Boris shouted in a way that overrode all his training for shallow breaths and conservation of exhaled moisture. "You created us for Mars—and then you took Mars away!"

He gestured out beyond the cave walls. In his mind he held a picture of the growing lichen, the tracings of frost on the lava rock, the thickening air. Dr. Dycek looked at him through the faceplate. He saw a weary patience in her eyes, which made him even angrier. She did not understand.

"Why is she here?" Elia asked him. "Find out why she is here."

Boris looked down at Dr. Dycek. "Yes, why?"

"I am being replaced. I have no more work on Mars, and I am to be shuttled back to Earth."

Boris tightened his grip on her thin metallic suit. "So now you know what it feels to be obsolete yourself. We watch our world slipping away with each new *dva* establishment, with each water-recovery station, with every normal human setting foot on our planet! The time has come to send them a message they cannot ignore."

Dr. Dycek put her gloved hands on her hips. "I came up here to be swept away in the dust storm. They will never find my body. If you kill me it makes no difference."

"We could dump your body just outside of the flimsy inflatable base. They would find you then."

"Then someone would have to hunt you down," Dr. Dycek said. "Why bloody your hands? No need to add murder to your conscience."

Boris laughed at that. He felt easier now, more in control. "Murder? It is murder only when a human kills another human. *Mars* will be killing you, Dr. Dycek. Not me." He hefted the metal staff over his head, ready to swing it down upon the curved face-plate. She tilted her head up while Boris spoke. "It is the way with all creatures: those who cannot adapt to their environment must die. So here, breathe the clear, cold air of Mars. It will be a grand gesture for the *adin!*"

"Oh Boris, stop!" It was Cora's voice, sounding annoyed. She made her way out of the shadows from the back of the cave. "I once admired your ways, but now I am tired of how you must make a grand gesture of everything. Tearing up our transmitter, sabotaging the *dva* pumping station, even blowing up the Baku oil refinery."

"That was all justified!" Boris snapped. But he watched Dr. Dycek's attention flick away from him as soon as Cora stepped into the light. Cora panted, then grimaced with the internal pain.

"She's pregnant!" Dr. Dycek said. "How? That's impossible!"

For a moment, Boris thought her comment so ludicrous that he stifled a chuckle. How? Does a doctor not know how a woman gets pregnant?

"Even the best Russian sterilization procedures must not be one hundred percent effective," Cora answered.

Dr. Dycek's entire attitude altered. "Your baby will die if it is born up here! It will have none of your adaptations. Just a normal, human child."

"We know that!" Boris shouted.

"This changes everything. An *adin* having a child! The first human born on Mars!" Her voice rose with command as if they were her slaves—just as she had sounded in the *adin* training and therapy sessions back on Earth. "We will have to take you in the crawler vehicle back down," she said to Cora. "I can pressurize the cabin slowly so you will acclimate and then be able to tolerate the atmosphere below for a short time."

Boris felt his control of the other *adin* slipping like red dust through his fingertips. Stroganov and Bebez nodded, looking at the suited figure and ignoring him. Cora stepped forward, so intent with new hope and excitement that she did not try to hide her swollen appearance. "You can save my baby?"

"Perhaps. If we get you back to the base."

"This is good news, Boris!" Elia said. "We thought the baby would die for certain."

Boris released his hold on Dr. Dycek's arm and turned to face his four companions in the cave. "Yes, save the child! And then what? Then everything will be perfect? Then all our problems will be solved? No! Then the Earthers will know where we are. They will come here and watch us die off, one by one. They will make a documentary program about us, the failed experiment. Maybe it will be on worldwide *National Geographic?*"

He moved toward the cave opening to the deepening dusk outside. It was difficult for him to stomp his feet in anger in the low gravity. "You are all fools! I can have more intelligent conversations with the rocks."

Boris Tiban stalked out into the air to stare at the brightening stars, at Phobos rising again in the east and the pinprick of Deimos suspended partway up the sky. He felt like the king of all Mars, a king who had just been overthrown.

Not even Boris's tantrum could disturb Rachel's concentration as she stared at the rounded abdomen of the *adin* woman. The survival of these augmented humans impressed her, but the simple miracle of this pregnancy that should never have happened amazed her much more. A pregnancy, the type of thing men and women had been doing for millions of years—but never before on this planet.

She and her medical team had seen no need to sterilize the female *adin*, a much more difficult operation than a vasectomy. Though Rachel had heard of men siring children years after they had had vasectomies, she and her team considered that possibility to be an acceptable risk. Russian medicine had somewhat low standards for "acceptable risks." Rachel could hardly believe it herself.

But the tight skin stretched over Cora's belly spoke otherwise. The thick *adin* fur wisped up and curled over, showing white patches where toughened skin had been stretched to its limits. Rachel reached out with a gloved hand to touch the bulge, but she could feel little through the protective material.

Cora seemed more preoccupied with excusing Boris's temper.

"He is not always like this. He is strong and has kept us alive by our own wits for ten years now, but everything is running through his fingers. He lost our companion Nicholas two nights ago in a raid." She drew a deep breath. Her words carried a rich Siberian accent that evoked thoughts of wild lands and simple people. "These grand gestures of his always backfire."

Suddenly Cora's mouth clamped shut and she let out a hiss. She squeezed her eyelids together. The skin on her abdomen tightened until it had a waxy texture and was as hard as the rind of a melon. Her hands groped for something to grab onto, finally seizing a lump of lava. She squeezed the sharp edges until blood oozed from shallow cuts in her palms, freezing into a sparkling smear on the rock.

Rachel knelt beside Cora while the other *adin* came closer, showing their concern. Rachel had never had a child of her own; she had been too preoccupied with her work, too driven, too dedicated. She had never regretted it, though. Had she not done something far more important by preparing the first humans to set foot on Mars?

Cora gasped out her next words after the spasm passed. "It's all right. For now. This has been happening for days. I can bear the pain, but I can concentrate on little else."

"You must not have the child here," Rachel repeated. She didn't know if the baby would be getting enough oxygen through the mother's bloodstream even now, but it certainly could not survive in the open air. "How frequent are the contractions?"

"I have no idea," Cora snapped in a voice filled more with pain and weariness than anger. "I don't exactly have a chronometer! Boris left all that behind when we came to the highlands."

"They are about every fifteen minutes," said one of the *adin*, Bebez. "You must get her away from here. Give her whatever help you can offer. The baby will surely die up here."

Rachel would have to give up her own pointless gesture of defiance, standing on the volcano top while the dust storm swept her away. But it seemed a ridiculous thing to do now, like something Boris Tiban would attempt. A grand gesture that would impress no one. Instead, she would accomplish something to hold up in front of Jesús Keefer's face.

Cora's infant would focus Earth's attention once again on the *adin* and the *dva*, and on Rachel's own efforts. She might even get a reprieve, be allowed to stay on Mars to study the remaining altered humans and how they adapted to their changing planet. But she knew she was doing this for something else as well. Better to save a life than to take her own.

"Let us go and save your child, Cora. My crawler is not far."

Cora stood up and Rachel touched her shoulder. The other three *adin* nodded their agreement, but made no move to help as the two women went to the door opening into the Martian dusk.

Outside, Boris Tiban was nowhere to be seen. The sky's green had turned a muddy ochre. The upthrust rocks were stark against the smooth slope of Olympus Mons.

The crawler was gone.

Leaving Cora to stand against a rock, Rachel ran over to where she had stopped the vehicle. The low gravity made her feel light on her feet. The wind ran groping fingers over her suit.

She found the crawler's tracks, already beginning to blur in the wind; then she came to a sloughed-off portion of the chasm wall where a large object had been toppled over the edge. Pry marks in the lava soil showed how Boris had used his metal staff.

As dread surged inside her, Rachel went to the brink of the gorge. More lava rock lay strewn a hundred meters below. In the gathering shadows of night, she could make out the squared-off form of her vehicle, out of reach far below.

In darkness, they used sturdy cables and harsh white spotlights to reach the bottom of the chasm. The *adin* had taken the equipment from the remaining cache of supplies they had brought with them when they had abandoned the Martian lowlands. Low gravity made the climb easier.

Cora allowed Stroganov and Dr. Dycek to help her over the roughest patches. She had to stop four times during the descent while cramps seized her body, demanding all her attention.

Over the past two days the cramps had clenched her stomach muscles, squeezing and pushing, then gradually loosening again. At first they had been intermittent, several an hour and then giving her a few hours' rest before they started again. But the pain grew worse, more regular, more intense, as her muscles lowered the baby, helped position it, started to open Cora up inside. She knew the baby could come within hours, or she might have to endure this for several more days.

She watched Stroganov jerk the thin cable as his spotlight shone down on the crawler vehicle surrounded by broken scree.

He had never told anyone his first name, but clung to his family identity; he traced his lineage back to the first nobles sent by Peter the Great to conquer the wilds of Siberia.

The crawler had plowed a clean path down the cliff as it fell, and its low center of mass had brought it to a rest upright, though canted against a mound of rubble. As Stroganov played the light over the scratched and dust-smeared hull, Cora looked for the disastrous damage she expected to see.

"It appears to be intact," Dr. Dycek said. She squeezed Cora's shoulder and jumped the last few meters to the bottom of the chasm, landing with deeply bent knees. Her voice sounded thin and far away as she shouted through her faceplate. "This vehicle is tough, built to withstand Mars—as you were."

Dr. Dycek held out her hands for Elia to toss down one of the spotlights. From above, Cora tried to pay attention to the operation. Using the spotlight beam, Dr. Dycek climbed around the vehicle, inspecting the metal plates protecting the trapezoidal windowports. She rapped on one with her gloved hand, then held her fist high in satisfaction.

On her own initiative, Cora began the last part of the descent. Stroganov and Elia helped her until they all stood on the jumbled floor of the chasm. Loose boulders the size of houses lay strewn about. Cora looked up to the top of the cliff wall, a black razor-edge that blocked all view of the stars. Bebez had remained in the caves, and Cora saw no other figure looking down at them.

They had called into the darkness for Boris to come and help them, but he had remained silent and hidden.

Dr. Dycek trudged up to them. "The door-lock mechanism is still functioning. The antenna is smashed, though, so we will not be able to let anyone on the base know we are coming." She paused. "From the dents around the antenna base, it looks to me as if Boris knocked it off himself."

The other *adin* said nothing. Cora nodded to herself. Yes, that was the way Boris would do it. He was so predictable.

Then her knees buckled as a new labor spasm squeezed her like a fist and sucked away thoughts of the outside world. Stroganov caught her and held her upright.

Dr. Dycek grabbed one of Cora's arms and began to stumble-walk her toward the crawler. "Come on. We have at least a day's journey before we get back to the base. Even at that, I cannot be certain this chasm will lead us anywhere but a blind end. But there is no other way. The crawler is down here, and we have no choice of roads. You have no time to waste."

Dr. Dycek hauled her into the tilted opening of the crawler's small airlock. Stroganov and Elia helped, each of the *adin* men squeezing Cora's numb skin in a silent gesture of farewell.

"The storm is coming," Stroganov said, sniffing the air.

"I know," Dr. Dycek answered. She made no other comment about it, but faced Cora instead. "We will get you inside and begin the slow pressurization of the interior. We have to make the atmosphere thick enough so the baby can breathe, in case it is born along the way."

Cora dreaded the thought of air as thick as soup and heavy as bricks on her chest, making an ordeal out of every breath — especially during the most exhausting hours of her life.

She doubted the baby would wait until they reached the Earthers' inflatable base.

The airlock door closed behind them, leaving them in claustrophobic darkness. Already Cora longed for one last breath of the cold air on top of Olympus Mons.

As the southern hemisphere of the planet Mars entered its winter season, the falling temperature caused great portions of the atmosphere to freeze out. Water vapor and carbon dioxide piled up in layers to form a polar icecap. The resulting drop in air pressure sucked wind from the northern hemisphere down across the equator. Gathering force, the wind rushed to fill the invisible hole at the bottom of the world, picking up dust particles in a fist as tall as the sky.

The storm hit them three hours after they had left the *adin* encampment. Rachel could barely see as the roiling murk pounded and shook the crawler from side to side. The brilliant high beams of the vehicle's lights revealed only an opaque haze; the low beams illuminated no more than a shallow puddle of ground directly in front of her. Rachel squinted through the whirlwind, hoping to swerve in time to avoid the largest rocks or another gaping chasm. The walls of the crevasse sheltered them from the worst gusts, but vicious crosscurrents forced her to wrestle with the controls.

Rachel had no idea where the narrow canyon would take her, but she had to follow it. She wound her way along the crevasse floor, hoping it would spill out onto the Tharsis plain or climb back up to the flat surface of Olympus Mons. She did not know where the nearest settlement would be, or if she would have a better chance heading straight for the main base facilities.

As they continued, Rachel increased the air pressure in the crawler, gradually acclimating Cora to the change. The muffled sounds of the scouring gale came through only as distant whispers. Rachel's suit worked doubletime to absorb her perspiration. She no longer felt like someone who wanted to surrender.

A wry smile came to Rachel's face: she had never imagined she would be facing the dust storm in such a manner. Her planned suicide had seemed poignant and dramatic at the time, like a great hero going to meet doom—but now she realized that most people would have shaken their heads sadly and pitied her instead. They would have found her pathetic. They would have reevaluated all of her successes, used her final madness to brush aside the accomplishments, and then forgotten about her.

She kept her mind focused on moving ahead, on the need to return to the main base, where she could show Jesús Keefer how important she still was to the Mars project. Keefer had always been impatient with the slow work of the *adin* and the *dva*, wanting instead to have humans scrape out a direct existence on Mars from the start.

But Rachel and her team had made it possible for the first humans to walk free on another world. No matter how the future changed, no one could alter that. And now her work will result in the birth of the first Martian, a landmark event never before rivalled in human history.

Behind her on one of the passenger benches, Cora Marisov spoke little, gasping as another labor spasm hit. Rachel used the vehicle's chronometer to time them. They occurred about every four and a half minutes. Cora seemed oblivious to the storm outside.

"I think . . . " Cora said, gasping words that Rachel heard muffled through her helmet, "you had better find a place to stop the crawler. Park it. Shelter. I need you now."

Rachel slowed the vehicle and risked a glance backward.

Cora lay on the floor, her back propped against the curved metal wall and her legs spread as far apart as she could manage around the mound of her belly. Between her legs a gush of liquid spilled out, steaming and freezing in the icy air.

Her water has broken! Rachel lurched the crawler over to the canyon wall under what she could dimly see as an overhang. Now what would she do? Rachel was a doctor, no problem. No problem! But she had studied environmental adaptation, worked with cyborg enhancements. The closest she had come to witnessing birth was in staring at cells dividing under a microscope. It had been a long time since her basic training, and she had used none of it in practical situations.

She looked down the treads of the crawler and turned back to Cora. The pregnant *adin* woman looked up at her; Rachel hoped the faceplate hid her uncertainty.

"I may be able to help you now," Cora said, "but when the final part of labor comes, I will not be able to hold your hand through this."

The thought of Cora helping *her* in the emergency made Rachel stifle a raw-edged giggle, but Cora continued. "I helped my grandmother deliver two babies when I was small. Midwives still do much of that work in Siberia."

Rachel fought away her scattered emotions and stared into Cora's dark, slanted eyes. "All right, should I check to see how far you are dilated?"

"Yes. Reach . . . inside me. Then we will know how much time I have."

Rachel looked down at her clumsy gloved hand. She checked the external air pressure monitor; though the suit seemed more flexible now that the differential was not so great, she still could not survive unprotected in the crawler cabin. "I dare not remove my suit yet. There is not enough air for me. And the glove is too big as it is. I would hurt you."

Cora's eyes squeezed shut and her body shook. Rachel watched her body straining, the augmented muscles stretched to a point where they seemed to hum from the tension. Cora's fingers scrabbled on the smooth metal floor, looking for something to grasp. After a minute or two, the spasm passed.

Cora took five deep breaths, then brought her attention back to the problem. "We need to learn how long it will be. If I am not fully dilated, we might have enough time to reach your base. If I am, then the baby could come in as little as an hour."

Rachel drove the panic away and tried her best to dredge up alternatives from the cellar of her imagination. "There are small cutting tools in the repair box, and some metal tape." She looked down at her suit. "I could cut off my glove, seal the sleeve around my arm with the tape. Then I could feel inside you."

Cora looked at her, saying nothing, as Rachel continued. "My hand would get numb in this cold, but I can raise the internal temperature here as much as you can stand."

"If you damage the suit, you will never be able to go outside until we reach your base." Cora closed her eyes in anticipation of another labor pain. "Perhaps you should keep driving. Hope we will find help within another hour or so."

Instead, Rachel made up her mind and went to the crawler's tool locker. In this storm, and with the distance yet to travel, they would never get to a safe haven in an hour. She had spent most of a day maneuvering the crawler up the smooth slope of Olympus Mons, making good time and seeing exactly where she was going. She had now been driving barely four hours, over rough terrain, unable to see for the past hour. They would never make it. Better to prepare here.

First, she wrapped the tape around her forearm as tightly as she could, making a crude tourniquet. Then she pulled up the slick fabric around her wrist and removed one of the small cutting tools from the locker. The tough suit material could resist most severe abrasions, but not intentional sawing. Keeping the metal tape at hand, she pulled in a deep lungful of air and sliced across the fabric.

Her ears popped as air gushed out from the suit opening. She could feel the wind and the cold pushing against her skin. The tourniquet could not make a perfect seal. She cut the gash longer, enough that she could pull her fingers out of the glove and thrust her hand through the ragged opening. With her protected hand, she wrapped more metal tape around her wrist where the suit material met the skin. She taped back the flopping, empty glove, then sealed the seam over and over.

Panting, Rachel tried to catch her breath as the suit reinflated. The chemical oxygen regenerator on her back hissed and burbled, adding to the ringing in her ears. Her head pounded, but her thoughts cleared moment by moment.

Cora squirmed on the floor in her own ordeal. Rachel knelt in front of her. "Cora? Cora, I am ready." She touched the *adin* woman's bristly coating of fur, the waxy texture of her polymerized skin. Rachel's hand felt crisp from the cold, then sensitivity faded as it grew numb. "Tell me what I should expect to feel inside you."

Cora blinked and nodded.

The placental water on the crawler floor had sheeted over with a film of ice, clinging in gummy knots to Cora's inner thighs.

Rachel slowly felt the folds of skin between Cora's legs, dipped her fingers into them, then slid her hand inside.

At first the temperature felt too hot, like melted butter, in startling contrast to the frigid air. She forced herself not to withdraw. Her skin burned.

"Feel the opening deep inside. It is surrounded by a ridge," Cora said, biting off each word as she said it. "Tell me how wide it is."

"A little wider than my hand and thumb."

Cora bit her lip.

Rachel withdrew and grabbed the other woman's arm. The biting cold of the air felt like acid on her wet hand. "Is that good or bad. I can't remember my training."

"Bad. No, good. That means this should be over much sooner. A few hours, perhaps."

The sound of the storm outside suddenly turned into a monster's roar, a grinding, crunching sound that pounded through the walls of the crawler. The rock outcropping above them came crashing down, tossing boulders and blankets of dirt.

Rachel fell on her side, clawing at the air; Cora rolled over and curled into a ball to protect her abdomen. Rocks pummeled the top of the crawler, bouncing and thudding. Reddish smears clogged the view from the main front windowports, blowing away in patches as gusts of wind tore it free of the smooth glass.

Rachel got to her knees. She felt herself shaking. The palm of her bare hand seemed to burn into the frigid metal of the floor. "Are you all right?" she asked Cora. The *adin* woman nodded.

The sounds of the avalanche faded into the roar of the storm, but then another, softer thump sounded on top of the crawler. Cora froze, and her eyes widened.

Rachel got up to go to the crawler's control panel. Luckily none of the falling rocks had smashed through the front windowports.

Then a face and shoulders appeared from above, hands reaching down from the roof of the crawler, brushing the dust aside. The face pressed against the glass, peering inside and grinning.

An *adin*. Boris Tiban.

In shock, Rachel caught herself from crying out. She smacked her hands down on the controls for the protective plates, which slammed over the windowports. The last thing she saw was Boris Tiban leaping aside in surprise, vanishing into the tangled murk of the storm. Then the metal clanged into place, leaving the crawler in dimness. The central illumination automatically stepped up, bathing the interior in a blue-white glow.

Cora stared wide-eyed at the sealed windowports. "Boris!" she muttered. She seemed to have forgotten about her labor. "He caused the avalanche. He must have been working at it ever since we stopped."

"Out in the storm?" Rachel could hardly believe what she had seen. "How could he survive without shelter?"

Cora shook her head; Rachel saw a smile on her lips. "He likes to do that, pit himself against the elements. He is proud of how he can cope with anything Mars throws at him. Tamer of Worlds —that is what he wants to be called. He does not like to see you domesticating this planet. Then he will be obsolete."

"I know what that feels like," Rachel muttered, then stopped. "But if Boris tries to kill me, he will also destroy you, and his baby. Does he not realize he will murder his own child?"

Cora hung her head, then shuddered with another spasm. Rachel adjusted the air compressors to increase the pressure inside the crawler more rapidly. When Cora recovered, she looked Rachel in the eye and kept her voice flat.

"He needs the baby to die. He has always planned on it."

Rachel opened and closed her mouth without words; she knew that behind the faceplate she must look like a dying fish in a bowl. "I don't understand."

Cora let her slanted eyes fall shut beneath the thick lash membranes. "His grandest gesture of all. He has been anticipating it for months. We have always known the baby would die at birth. I should never have gotten pregnant. That loss would be a direct fault of the Earthers. He has found a way to blame all of our troubles on you. He is good at that.

"When the baby dies, he will have all the reason he needs to strike back. It will be a catalyst, an excuse. Everything must be perfectly justified. Those are the rules by which he plays." She sighed. "No one ever thought someone like you would come."

Rachel struggled with the sick logic. "What will he do?"

"He plans to go to your inflatable base and destroy it. With his metal staff, he can tear holes right through the sides of the walls. He can run from one section to the next as fast as his legs will take him, striking and moving. He can do it. The alarms will send everyone into confusion. He can burst every module even after they seal themselves. The people inside will be trapped and he can pick them off one room at a time. The Earthers might repair some of the walls, but Boris can just strike again. He can wait longer than any of them."

"But what about you? He's trying to kill you now, too!"

"That is incidental. He loves me in his own way, but he sees the cause as more important. Just like a great revolutionary."

Rachel felt anger welling up inside of her. "Well then, I must make sure he has no reason to attack the base. Your baby will live." She patted Cora's bulging stomach with her bare hand and turned to look at the heavy metal plates covering the window-ports. "We are safe here, for now."

Surrounded by the muffled whirlwind of the storm, Cora Marisov gave birth to a daughter. The crawler walls creaked and groaned as the wind tried to push in, but the shelter remained secure.

As soon as Cora's final labor began, Rachel had no choice but to begin pressurizing the crawler interior as rapidly as the pumps could bring in more air. Many of the intake vents had been clogged with dust from the storm and the avalanche, but the gauges showed the air pressure increasing.

Cora cried out with the effort of her labor, but also gasped, complaining about how difficult breathing had become. "Like a metal band around my chest! My head!"

"There is nothing we can do for it. The baby must breathe when it comes." *No matter what it does to Cora*, Rachel thought. "You are strong. I made you that way."

"I . . . know!"

When Rachel had pulled the slick baby free, it steamed in the air, glistening with red wetness. "A girl!" she said.

Cora's mouth remained open, gasping to fill her lungs. The baby, too, worked the tiny dark hole of her mouth in a silent agonized cry of new life, but she could not find enough air.

Rachel moved quickly now. As she had planned, she shucked her suit and popped open the faceplate, letting the blessed warm air gush out. The shock stunned her, but she forced herself to keep moving, to plow through the black specks in front of her vision. A bright pain flashed behind her forehead. Moments later, a warm, thick trickle of blood came from her nostrils.

She grasped the loose end of the metal tape sealing her wrist to the suit. The grip slipped twice before her numb fingers clutched it and tore it off. She let out a howl of pain, releasing half the air left in her lungs. She felt as if she had just flayed the skin off her arm.

She had to hurry. Grogginess started to claim her, but she stumbled through the motions.

Shivering already, she stepped out of the empty suit, letting the metallic fabric fall in a rough puddle on the floor. She wore only a light jumpsuit underneath, clammy with sweat that froze in icy needles against her skin.

Rachel clamped shut the empty faceplate and grabbed up the baby. The infant's skin, smeared with red from the birth, took on a bluish tinge as she tried to breathe. The umbilical cord, tied in a crude knot, still oozed some blood.

Cora found the strength to reach over and touch the infant one last time before Rachel slid the girl inside the loose folds of the suit and sealed her whispered cries into silence. She began pressurizing it immediately. The folds began to straighten themselves as air pumped inside.

Heaving huge breaths but still starving for oxygen, Rachel grasped the limp sleeve where she had cut off the glove and knotted it. Suit-warmed air blew from the edge, squirting onto her skin. Rachel clutched the roll of metallic tape and wrapped it around and around the end of the sleeve. The hissing noise stopped, replaced by the ringing in her ears. She crawled over to where regenerated air streamed into the chamber, but that helped only a little.

Cora, though, grew worse. "Can't inhale," she said. "Like stones on my chest. Breathing soup." She was too weak to cope with the increasing difficulty.

Rachel felt all her words go away as she looked at the exhausted new mother, at the mess of blood and amniotic fluid and afterbirth tissue on the crawler floor. This had not been clean and quick like the make-believe births shown in entertainment disks. It looked like some slaughter had occurred here. But not slaughter —new life.

Somehow, Cora got to her knees, wavered as she tried—and failed—to draw a deep breath, then crawled toward the airlock. "You must let me out. Dying. Need to breathe."

Rachel, dizzy from her own lack of air, tried to fight against confusion. "Not in the storm! Not right after the baby. You are too weak." But she knew Cora was right. If the *adin* woman had any chance for surviving, it had to be outside, not in here.

Cora reached the door and rested her head against it, panting. "Strong enough," she said, repeating Rachel's words. "You made us that way."

Rachel watched her open the inner door and haul herself into the airlock. The noise of the storm outside doubled. Cora looked at the sagging environment suit on the floor, focused on the squirming lump that showed the baby's movements, then raised her deep-set eyes to meet Rachel's. She looked intensely human and inhuman at the same time.

"I will tell Boris his daughter is alive. Safe." With great effort, she filled her lungs one more time. "He must face that. Adapt to new conditions—his own words." She raised her hand in a gesture of farewell, then sealed the door behind her.

Somehow, her words about Boris Tiban did not reassure Rachel.

The noise of the storm muffled again, grew louder as Cora opened the outer door, then finally resettled into relative quiet. Rachel found herself alone with the newborn baby.

She had to push the crawler into overdrive to break free of the avalanche rubble. The vehicle groaned and lurched as it heaved over boulders, bucking from side to side. Rachel wished she had strapped herself in. Unsupported on the floor, the baby in the environment suit slid over to one corner and came to rest against a passenger bench. She could not hear the infant's cries over the sound of the storm and the straining engine.

"Come on!" Rachel muttered to herself, pounding the plastic control panel. The effort sent a wash of dizziness over her. Her jaws chattered in the cold. The back of the crawler rose up at an angle over the worst of the obstacles, then she found herself free of the rock slide.

She slid the protective plates aside so she could see her course, though the storm made that nearly impossible. Using less caution now, she increased the crawler's speed, trusting the vehicle to crush medium-sized rocks under its treads so she would not need to pick a path around them.

The chasm walls lowered and the floor widened within half an hour. She felt the urgency slackening as confidence grew; she would be out on the flat slope of Olympus Mons in a few moments, and she could use the guidance gear to choose the most direct course back home. She eased the crawler to greater speed.

She turned around to glance at the baby, to make sure it had not been injured.

Then Boris Tiban sprang out in front of the vehicle again and bounded onto its sloping hood. The dust swirled around him, but he seemed to draw energy from the storm. He hefted his metal staff over his head like a harpoon. The expression on his face made him look like a savage beast from the wilds of Mars.

Instinctively, Rachel ducked back. She did not think quickly enough to slam the protective plates over the windowports.

Boris brought the pointed rod down with a crunch in the center of the trapezoidal glass plate. A white flower of damage burst around the tip, and a high whine of air screamed out as he withdrew the staff. He brought the tip down again even harder, puncturing another, larger hole through the thick glass.

Rachel heard the wind's roar and a distant howl that might have been triumph from the *adin* leader. "Stop!" she shouted, expending precious air. She yanked back on the control levers, bringing the crawler to a sudden halt.

The lurch tossed Boris Tiban from his perch, and he rolled nearly out of sight a few meters away. He staggered to his feet, using the metal staff for support.

She slapped at the control panel. The brilliant high beams on the crawler stabbed out like an explosion of light. Boris froze, blinded. He wrapped a forearm over his eyes.

Rachel could have accelerated the vehicle then and crushed him under the tread. But she could not do it. She stared at him, listening to the scream of escaping air from the puncture holes. She had created Boris Tiban and exiled him here. He had survived everything Mars could throw at him, and *she* could not kill him now.

Still unable to see, Boris staggered toward the crawler, raising his staff to strike again.

Cora appeared out of the whirlwind, stumbling and off balance—but perhaps only due to the wind, for she looked stronger now than when she had departed from the crawler. She kept her back to the bright lights.

Boris seemed to sense her presence and turned. He blinked at her in astonishment. Before he could react, Cora snatched the pointed metal staff out of his hand. Delayed by surprise, he did not grab it back immediately. He gestured, as if shouting something through the storm at her.

Then Cora shoved the staff through his chest. In the low

gravity, her strength was great enough for the thrust to lift him completely off the ground. The spear protruded from his body, puncturing the second set of lungs that rose like a hump on his back. Then she tossed him away from her.

Rachel slapped the palm of her hand against the largest hole in the windowport, picturing herself as the legendary Dutch boy who put his finger in the leaking dike. Instantly she felt the biting cold and the suction tearing at her hand, trying to rip it through the hole. She screamed.

Cora had fallen to the ground outside, but she staggered to her feet and stood in front of the vehicle. She made frantic motions with her arms. Their meaning was clear: Go! Now!

Rachel tore her hand away from the windowport, leaving a chunk of meat behind that dribbled blood and slurped as it was sucked outside. A frosty red smear coated the white cracks in the glass.

Blood dripping from her torn palm, Rachel found the metal tape and pushed several pieces over the punctures in the windowport. The tape dug into the hole, pulled toward the outside. She added a second and then third strip of tape over the punctures, and then began to breathe easier.

Outside, red dust had begun to pile around the body of Boris Tiban. Already Mars hurried to erase all traces of the intruder. Boris had thought himself invincible because he could withstand the rigors of the harsh environment. But Mars had not killed him —a human had, an *adin* human.

Hours later, Rachel continued on a straight downhill course. The slope of the volcano offered a relatively gentle road, scoured clean. The wind continued to hammer at her—such storms rarely let up in less than four days—but it no longer seemed such a difficult thing to withstand.

The layers of metal tape sealed the punctures in the front windowport, but air still hummed out. The compressors kept laboring to fill the crawler with air; the heaters warmed the interior as fast as the Martian cold could suck it away. Rachel hoped she could remain conscious for as long as it might take.

The indicators showed the general direction of travel, though the storm and the iron oxide dust in the air could ruin the accuracy of her onboard compass. Boris had smashed her antenna, so she could not pick up the homing beacons of any nearby settlements, nor could she send out a distress signal.

But if she continued down to the base of Olympus Mons, she might encounter one of the *dva* materials-processing settlements that tapped into leftover volcanic heat, unleashing water from hydrated rock, smelting metals. She had been squinting through the dust for hours—and hoping. She could barely hear the baby crying inside her suit.

Rachel thought her eyes had begun to swim with weariness when she finally saw the yellow lights of a *dva* encampment. The squat, smooth-curved walls made the outbuildings look like hulking giants. Much of the complex would be underground.

Rachel let herself slump back in the driver's chair.

She had made it back with the baby. She had returned to her world, when she had intended to be gone forever. Rachel felt a moment of bittersweet failure, wondering now if she could ever have stood alone and faced the onrushing wall of the storm, to let it carry her away into death.

And what would have been the point? An empty gesture for no one but herself.

There was no use mourning the completion of a job well done. Strong people found new goals to achieve, new challenges to face. Weak people bemoaned the loss of great days. Beside her on the crawler floor, this new baby was trying to be strong, to survive against all odds. Rachel Dycek could be strong, too, stronger than Jesús Keefer or the UN administrative council. *Adapt to the hostile environment, and defeat it,* Boris Tiban would have said. Humanity, in all its forms, would never be obsolete. Rachel would not be obsolete until she surrendered to obsolescence.

Ahead, the dim yellow lights of the *dva* settlement looked as welcoming as a Russian traditional New Year's tree. The cold air of Mars whistled outside the windowport of her vehicle, moaning as it tried to enter through the metal tape. But she would not let it harm her.

She had work to do.

Introduction to
Scientific Romance

George Pal's movie version of The War of the Worlds *inspired me to become a writer when I was five years old. The Martian invasion and the destruction of the cities of Earth carried so much terror and so much pathos that it knocked the fuzzy socks off my little feet. The next day, I stole paper from a scratchpad and drew pictures of scenes I remembered from the movie (since I didn't know how to write real words yet), and would tell the story out loud to anyone who would stop long enough and listen.*

The bug bit me hard. I was hooked on science fiction from that point on.

I have read and reread H. G. Wells's novel The War of the Worlds *countless times. When Martin H. Greenberg asked me to contribute to his UFO Files anthology (DAW 1998), he gave me the freedom to write a story that had "anything to do with aliens." I decided to push the boundaries a bit, to write an imaginary scenario of what might have inspired a young Herbert Wells who was, at the time, a poor college student under the tutelage of the great Darwin-defender, T. H. Huxley.*

Scientific Romance

LATE AFTER DARK ON A CHILL NOVEMBER NIGHT, young Wells followed T. H. Huxley up to the labyrinthine rooftop. The air felt damp, tinged with a clammy mist, yet the sky overhead was dark and clear and sparkling with stars.

The meteors would begin falling soon.

The minarets and gables of London's Normal School of Science provided nooks, crannies, gutters and eaves where students could hold secret meetings, perhaps rendezvous with young girls from the poorer sections of South Kensington. Wells doubted, though, that any of his classmates would climb to the sprawling rooftop for the same purpose as his teacher and mentor led him now.

Huxley's creaking bones and aching limbs forced the old man to move slowly along the precarious shingles. Wells knew better than to offer the professor any assistance. Huxley finally found a spot against a gable and eased himself down. Leaning backward, he propped his head up and stared into the depths of the universe.

"Is this your first meteor shower, Herbert?" Huxley asked. "The Leonids are a good place to start. We should see about twenty per hour."

Wells, at only eighteen and much more limber, struggled to

find his own comfortable observation place. "I've seen shooting stars before, sir," he said, "but I've never actually . . . studied them."

Huxley gave a wheezing laugh. His voice sounded strange to Wells, a private conversational tone instead of the forceful oratory for which he had become famous across England. "From what I can see, young man, you study every facet of life with those quick and darting eyes of yours."

Wells blushed, then ran a hand across his face to hide his embarrassment. His unkempt dark hair fell over his forehead, and his mustache showed gaps where the whiskers hadn't yet filled in enough.

He fidgeted, working himself into an awkward squat, holding onto a gutter for balance. Huxley intended to stay out here for hours, but the conversation interested Wells more than his personal comfort. Ideas made mankind superior to other creatures . . . and superior men had superior ideas.

The flash in his peripheral vision took him completely by surprise. "There!" he shouted, gesturing so rapidly that he nearly lost his precarious balance on the angled roof. A streak of brilliant white light shot overhead then evaporated, so transient it seemed barely an afterimage on his eyes.

"The first meteor of the night," Huxley said with a smile, "and you spotted it, Wells. I'm proud of you. But of course, your eyesight is much better than mine."

"But your eyes have seen more things, sir," Wells said, then hated the reverential tone he had let slip.

"Don't flatter me," Huxley warned. The old man's wit and intellect were as bright as the sun, but his personality remained acerbic and abrasive. Wells would tolerate any number of rebukes, though, for the insights the professor had given him during his biology lectures.

Even now, Huxley fell comfortably into the role of teacher. "Make note of the meteorites we see this evening, and you will be able to envision their radiant point in the constellation Leo."

Wells settled back to continue watching. Bright in the western ecliptic, the ruddy point of Mars hung like a baleful eye, not twinkling, though the other stars around it glittered and flickered.

He shivered from the chill in the air, then tapped his foot, always moving, trying to get warm. Due to his severe financial situation, Wells was underweight and scrawny . . . even cadaverous, if one were to believe his roommate and friend, A. V. Jennings. On Tuesdays, the day before weekly pay for the scholars, Wells occasionally could not afford lunch, and Jennings would take him out to fill up on beefsteak and beer so that they could return replenished to the workbench in Huxley's laboratory.

Wells's wardrobe was meagre, consisting of grubby dark suits and worn celluloid shirt collars. His thin jacket was insufficient against the chill of the November evening, but he had no desire to go back inside the school building.

A second meteor appeared overhead like a line drawn with a pen of fire, eerie in its total silence. "Another!"

Around them the city of London made its own nighttime noises. Horsecarts and black cabs clopped quietly by, while prostitutes flounced into dim alleys or waited under the gas streetlamps. Across the park, in the boarding house at Westbourne Grove where he and Jennings shared a room, Wells knew the other residents would be engaged in their nightly carousing, brawls, singing and drinking. Here, high above it all, though, he enjoyed the peace.

Within moments a third meteor passed overhead, far from the trivial human concerns around him. This shooting star was larger and louder than the others, sputtering. Mentally tracing the fiery line back to its origin, Wells saw that the meteor radiated from a point in the sky not far from Mars itself, almost as if the red planet were launching them like sparks from a grinding wheel.

"Do you ever imagine, Professor Huxley, sir," he said as an intriguing idea formed in his mind, "that perhaps these flaming meteors are signals of a kind, even ships that have crossed the gulf of space?" Wells had had many outrageous ideas since the age of seven, and he often spoke his speculations aloud, sometimes to the entertainment of others, sometimes to their annoyance.

Huxley shifted position, looking over at his student with keen interest. "Ships?" His eyes held a bold challenge, as did his tone. "And from whence would they come, Wells?"

Wells rose to the occasion. "Why not . . . Mars, for instance?" He indicated the orange-red pinpoint of the planet. "According to theory, as the solar system cooled, each planet became hospitable to life in relation to its distance from the Sun. On Mars, therefore, intelligent life could have begun to evolve long before any such spark occurred on Earth."

At the mention of evolution, Huxley perked up—just as Wells had known he would. The professor had spent his life as a proponent of Darwinism, had debated buffoons and ill-educated orators in so many forums that Huxley became infamous as 'Darwin's Bulldog.'

Another shooting star passed overhead, as if to emphasize Wells's point.

"Martians," Huxley said with a wry smile. "Interesting. And what do you suppose a Martian would look like?"

Wells folded one leg over the other, in spite of his precarious rooftop position, and restrained himself from answering instantly. Huxley did not suffer foolish or glib answers. "I would suppose that since the Martians are a much more ancient race, they would have minds immeasurably superior to our own. Their bodies would be composed almost entirely of brain."

Two more faint Leonid meteors danced overhead unnoticed. Wells uncrossed and recrossed his legs.

"And what would such beings look like?"

Wells frowned, letting his thoughts flow. "Natural selection would ultimately shape a superior being into a creature with a huge head and eyes. He would have delicate hands, tentacles perhaps, for manipulating tools—but his mentality would be his greatest tool."

"An interesting exercise, Wells. You have quite an imagination." Huxley leaned forward from his cramped position against the gable, scooting across the roof tiles so that he could speak in a low, hoarse voice to his protégé. "But why would Martians want to come to our green Earth? What is their motive?"

Wells was ready for that one. "Mars is a dry planet, cold and drained of resources. Our world is younger, fresher, more vibrant —filled with all the things they have lost over the course of their evolution. Perhaps even now the Martians are regarding this Earth with envious eyes. They might even be drawing up plans for invasion."

As a boy, Wells had studied military history, staging mock battles in the park and observing the movements of one historical army against another. But an interplanetary war was beyond his comprehension.

"A war of the worlds?" Huxley actually chuckled at this. "And you believe that such superior minds as you propose would engage in an exercise as trivial as military conquest? You must not consider them so evolved after all."

Wells kept his thoughts to himself, for he had suddenly realized that perhaps Thomas H. Huxley was a bit naive himself.

In his life, Wells had seen the gross divisions of the upper and lower classes and how each fought amongst the others for dominance. His hard-working, sweet mother had sent him off to be apprenticed to a draper, where he had labored as a virtual slave. After escaping that fate through his own calculated incompetence, Wells had lived with his mother where she was the head domestic servant in a large manor, and she had commanded the workers beneath her. His angry father had once been a gardener, but for years had found no better employment than occasional cricket playing. . . .

The hierarchy remained, no matter what their social standing, powerful and powerless. It proved to Wells's satisfaction the Darwinian basis that all humans had been predators at some time in the past.

Wells answered his professor carefully. "If the Martians are a dying race," he said, "it would be survival of the fittest. The Martians would see Earth ripe for conquest, humans as inferior cattle."

"Survival of the fittest — I'll concede that point, Wells," Huxley said. "We must hope the Martians do not invade." He shifted back to his former position, where he watched for further Leonids.

The two sat in silence, looking into the clear sky. Wells shivered, partially from the cold, partially from his own thoughts.

They watched the stars fall as the red eye of Mars blinked balefully at them.

The following day, in the bustling laboratory section of Huxley's biology course, Wells felt feverish. He wondered if he had caught a chill from the previous night's vigil.

Nevertheless, the sounds of clacking beakers, the smell of old chemical experiments, and the chatter of students engaged his mind. He soon became totally absorbed in the setting up of microscopes and experimental apparatus for the morning's exercise.

One of Huxley's assistants — a demonstrator who delivered occasional lectures when Huxley himself was too ill to speak — prepared the laboratory activity. As if he were a prize French chef, he presented a pot in which he had prepared an infusion of local weeds and pond water. The resulting murky concoction was infested with numerous fascinating microbes.

Wells's workbench partner, A. V. Jennings, was the son of a doctor. He received a small stipend, which allowed him much greater security than Wells, though they both lived in an unpleasant boarding house an intellectual world away from the high atmosphere of Huxley's lecture hall.

Now, while Jennings set up their shared microscope on a narrow table against the windows, Wells went forward with his microscope slide to receive a drop of the precious infusion, as if it were some scientific communion. He carefully slid a cover slip over the beer-colored droplet and returned to where his partner had finished preparing the apparatus.

Under watery light shining through a veil of gray clouds, Wells focused and refocused the microscope. Jennings had a sketchpad, as did Wells, to record their observations. Wells feverishly sketched the alien-looking creatures he observed: protozoans of all types, alien shapes with whipping flagella, hairlike cilia vibrating in a blur . . . blobby amoebas, various strains of algae.

As Wells scrutinized the exotic creatures swarming and multiplying in the tiny universe of a drop of water, he felt like a titan. His looming presence stared through an eyepiece to observe the tiny struggles of pond microorganisms. . . .

Wells realized that the other students had stopped their conversations and stood at attention, as if a royal presence had entered the room. Professor T. H. Huxley had deigned to visit his laboratory this morning.

The intimidating, acerbic old man strode around the workbenches where his students diligently studied the infinitesimal animals they found on their microscope slides. Huxley nodded approvingly, made quiet sounds but little conversation, and moved from station to station.

When the great man came to where Wells stood proudly beside his microscope, Huxley said in a gruff voice, "Morning, Wells." The professor bent over to study their slide, adjusted the focus ever so slightly as if it were his due. "Lovely euglena you have here under the light." He made another noncommittal sound, then moved on to the other students.

Wells stood looking after his mentor, disappointed. Huxley had made no mention of their shared experience with the meteor shower, their imaginative conversation. He had come here for no purpose other than to scrutinize his insignificant students . . . in the same way that Wells and Jennings had been studying the microbes.

His cheeks flushed, and the cool feverish sweat swept over him. He extended his imagination further, wondering if other powerful beings might even now be scrutinizing *Earth* in the same manner, curious about the buzzing and swarming colony of London.

The hair on the back of his neck prickled, as if he could sense the probing eyes watching him from afar.

He was startled to find Jennings regarding him oddly. "You don't look at all well, Herbert," he said. Jennings reached over with practiced ease and touched Wells's forehead. "In fact you're burning up." He frowned. "I think you should go home and rest before this grows more serious."

The fever caught hold with nightmarish strength, and Wells fell into a labyrinth of delirium fostered by the powerful resources of his own imagination.

He saw meteors falling and falling, huge cylinders accompanied by green fire that blazed across the sky. The interplanetary ships crashed to Earth, pummeling England like quail shot.

In the great impact craters where they settled and cooled, the cylinders opened up to reveal that they were warships from the red planet, carrying hoards of invading Martians—hugely developed brains with tentacled limbs that had evolved under a lower gravity.

Their vast mentalities had turned toward the conquest of Earth. The most insignificant of these extraordinarily developed creatures had a military intellect far superior to the combined genius of Napoleon and Alexander the Great.

Using their whiplike appendages, the Martians built war machines, clanking metal things on tall stiltlike legs that surpassed even the imagination of Leonardo Da Vinci.

The clanking machines strode about the English landscape like industrial contraptions he had seen among the dark factories of the dirty towns where he had worked as a draper's apprentice. But these machines were equipped with weapons, powerful heat rays that burned everything in sight.

Hot like Wells's fever.

And overhead the meteors continued falling, falling. . . .

When the fever finally broke, Wells awoke in his narrow, lumpy bed to find Jennings tending him, laying a cool rag over his forehead. A patch of bright, hot sunlight spilled through the window, warming his skin.

Wells croaked, his voice uncooperative, but he spoke quickly, not wanting his roommate to get the best of him with a first witticism. "What now Jennings?" he said. "Are you practicing to become a doctor like your father?"

Jennings smiled. His eyes were red-rimmed, as if he hadn't gotten much sleep. "You've had quite a time of it, Herbert. Been sick for days, feverish, haven't eaten a thing but a bit of broth I managed to acquire for you."

"Worst of all, you've missed three of my lectures," said another voice.

Weakly, Wells managed to prop himself up enough to see another man standing in the small, stuffy room. T. H. Huxley himself.

"Since you are one of only three students who has so far proved worthy of a first-class passing grade," the old professor said, "I wanted to see why you were so rude as to forsake my class." Huxley's voice was stern but subdued, as if he were restraining his normal booming tone only with great difficulty.

"Not to worry, sir," Wells said. "I'm sure Jennings took good notes."

It embarrassed him that Huxley had to see how lowly his student lived. The room in South Kensington had a crowded, squalid appearance, with too many brutish noises that carried through the walls as other boarders came in drunk at all hours. The air was cold—no one had brought up coal for some time—and smelled rank from unemptied chamberpots sitting out in the hall.

The professor maintained a mock stern expression. "I should have been quite disappointed had you died, Wells. Though you are only eighteen, I see great potential in you."

Huxley paced the room as if searching for something significant to say. Wells waited for him. "Quite humbling, isn't it?" the professor finally said. "A superior creature such as yourself, highly evolved and possessed of a grand intellect—laid low by something as crude and insignificant as an Earthly germ."

Wells gave a wan smile in response. "I'm sorry, sir. I shall try to prove my evolutionary superiority henceforth."

Huxley sighed reticently and paused at the door, ready to leave. "You may wish to know, Wells, that I have decided this will be my last semester teaching. I've spent far too many years trying to show everyone the obvious truth, and I shall give it up and retire out of sheer exhaustion."

Distraught, Wells cried, "But, sir, there's so much more we can learn from you!"

"I have wasted far too much time and energy in debates with

fools over the correctness of Darwinism. I've earned myself a rest. But I will need someone to carry on, eventually."

Huxley opened the door, adjusted his hat, and frowned back at his sick student. "With your imagination, I think you can make something of yourself, Wells," he said. "Don't disappoint me."

Then Huxley left, heading out to far more pleasant surroundings on the other side of the park.

Wells leaned back into his bed while Jennings stared at him in awe. "That was quite a benediction, Herbert."

Wells lay back and closed his eyes, dizzy with residual weakness from the fever. But his mind was already whirling and spinning, filled with a thousand thoughts.

"I think I'll rest for a bit, Jennings," he said.

After all, he had to restore his health before he could begin his life's work.

Introduction to
Canals in the Sand

Another story inspired by War of the Worlds.

One day while hiking among the redwoods of California with two friends in the writing business, Daniel Keys Moran and Heather McConnell, I stopped in my tracks as—for reasons that still remain unclear to me—I suddenly had the idea for an anthology of short stories based around Wells's Martian invasion. These tales would relate what other historical figures or literary geniuses might have written under those circumstances—Mark Twain about the Martians on the Mississippi, or Jules Verne about the Martians in Paris, for instance. The anthology, War of the Worlds: Global Dispatches, *was published by Bantam Books, and several of the stories won, or were nominated for, science fiction's major awards.*

For my own contribution (as editor you get first pick, of course!) I chose a small historical tidbit I had learned about the great astronomer, Percival Lowell, a philanthropist observer who had first misinterpreted and then popularized the idea of canals and a dying civilization on the red planet, Mars. The Italian astronomer Schiaparelli had seen the canals from his telescope, but had merely described them as fissures in the landscape. Such mundane explanations did not sway Percival Lowell, however, and one of his schemes was to use his great fortune to dig huge trenches in the Sahara and light fiery geometrical symbols that distant Martians would be able to see.

And so, in the milieu of Wells's Martian invasion, I wondered what Lowell would think about the actual arrival of cylinders from Mars. . . .

Canals in the Sand

UNDER THE SWELTERING HEAT OF THE SAHARA, PERcival Lowell stood beside his tent at the center of the camp and reveled in the clamor of his vast construction site. The excavations extended beyond the vanishing point of the flat desert horizon. Thousands of sweating laborers — who worked for mere pennies a day — moved like choreographed machinery as they dug monumental trenches aaccording to Lowell's commands, scribing a long line in the sand.

Lowell had seen the same on Mars, long canals, straight lines extending thousands of miles across the rusted desert. His own observations had absolutely convinced him that such markings must be indicative of surface life on a dying world.

Other astronomers claimed not to see the network of canals, that the lines on the disk of Mars were not there. It reminded him of the trial of Galileo, when the high church officials and Pope Paul V had refused to see the moons of Jupiter through the astronomer's "optick glass," denying the evidence of their own eyes. Lowell couldn't decide if his own contemporaries were similarly bull-headed, or just plain blind.

He took a deep breath, ignoring the pounding sun. The fiery heat and dust and petroleum stench practically curled the hairs in his mustache. With recently washed hands, he fished inside the front pocket of his cream jacket and withdrew his special pair of pince-nez, with lenses made of red-stained glass. Through the copper-oxide tint, he could look out at the blistering and dead Sahara, seeing instead the scarlet sands of Mars. *Mars.*

How could one stand out here in the desert and not intuitively understand why the Martians would need to construct an extravagant set of canals to transport precious water from the melting ice caps down to their ancient cities? Water covered sixty percent of the Earth's surface, while Mars remained one vast planetary wasteland. The Martians' magnificent canals had endured as their world grew parched and withered with age, as their civilization mummified. By this time, those once glorious minds must be desperate, ready to grasp at any hope.

Lowell strolled out along the well-packed path from the encampment to the long ditch his army of workers had dug in the shifting sands. Compared to what the Martians had accomplished, it seemed a child's futile effort, and it certainly wouldn't endure long—but then Lowell's canal was not required to.

It must remain only long enough to send a signal.

If Ogilvy's calculations were correct, Lowell had little time. He prayed his Bedouin workers would be fast enough. But he vowed nothing would deter him. After all, he had built his great Arizona observatory in a mere six weeks from groundbreaking to first light. He could certainly handle digging a ditch, even if it was ten miles long out in the middle of the Sahara.

Night on Mars Hill in the Arizona Territory, at an elevation of 7000 feet, with clear skies far from the smoke of men. The big refractor and the observatory dome had been completed just in time to allow observations of the 1894 opposition of Mars.

Lowell spent his every free moment at the telescope.

His fellow Bostonian William H. Pickering, an astronomer for Harvard, and his assistant Andrew Ellicott Douglass both stood inside the chill, echoing dome of the Flagstaff Observatory, waiting for Lowell to relinquish the eyepiece. The wooden-plank walls of the observatory dome exuded a resinous scent. From where he sat in the uncomfortable chair, porkpie hat turned backward on his head and sketchpad in his lap, Lowell could sense their impatience.

"It is *my* telescope, gentlemen, and *I* will do the observing," Lowell said, not removing his eye from the wavering disk of the ruddy world, where fine lines appeared and disappeared as the seeing shifted in the Earth's atmosphere.

"Mister Lowell, sir," Pickering said, clearing his throat, "I understand your eagerness to use the refractor, but *we* are your professional astronomers, with the proper qualifications—"

Lowell finally turned, feeling annoyance heat his skin. "Qualifications, Mr. Pickering? I have exceptionally keen eyesight—and an exceptionally large fortune, which has built this telescope and pays your stipend. Therefore I am fully qualified."

He snorted, looking down from his seat on the padded ladder and adjusting the porkpie hat on his head. "Perhaps if your Harvard had agreed to engage in a joint venture with me, Pickering, rather than calling me 'egoistic and unreasonable,' I would be more inclined to share. But instead, my own alma mater could not be convinced to do more than give you two gentlemen leave to work here, and then lease—*lease!*—me one of their small telescopes."

Douglass took a step back and looked to Pickering for his cue. Pickering, as always, cleared his throat and searched in vain for words.

Lowell's nostrils flared over his mustache. "You gentlemen are welcome to devote your nights to the study of the heavens at any other time, but this is *Mars* and it is at opposition. Please indulge this unworthy amateur." He turned back to the telescope, while the others shuffled their feet uncomfortably, and continued to wait. Within moments, Lowell had become totally engrossed in the view, his universe shrunk down to the tiny circle visible through the eyepiece.

Tact was a commodity that served little purpose when time was short. Lowell had selected Pickering, in part, because of his successful studies of Mars in 1892 at Arequipa in Peru. Pickering, a decent though somewhat stuffy administrator, had spent the winter of '93 in Boston supervising the design and construction of this observatory, which had been shipped out piece by piece to Flagstaff the following spring. Every bit of the project was a rush, because Lowell demanded that the telescope absolutely must be functional by the time of the planetary opposition. Such a close encounter with Mars would not come again for many years.

Lowell drew a deep breath, shifted himself in his seat high above the observatory floor, and craned his neck. He fiddled with the eyepiece, and Mars stared back at him. He had the strangest sensation of being on the opposite end of a microscope, as if some immense being from across the cosmos were watching *him*, as someone with a microscope studied creatures that swarmed and multiplied in a drop of water.

His hands working independently, guided by the information channeled through the refractor tube, Lowell deftly sketched Mars, copying the lines he saw on the face of the planet. He had never been an armchair astronomer and would go blind before he ever allowed himself to be considered one. He and his staff had already recorded some four hundred canals on Mars— canals that other observers preposterously refused to see!

Lowell's outspoken beliefs had earned him much scorn, but no descendant of the great Boston family could remain quiet about deep convictions. In this case, and in many others, Percival Lowell knew he was right and the rest of the world was wrong—and he had proved it.

Well after midnight, his eyes burned. He flipped over the page in his sketchpad to where he had already scribed another perfect circle for a new map. Daylight hours were best used to prepare for the next clear night's observing.

Lowell noted that Douglass and Pickering had left unobtrusively, and he hoped they were at least doing work at the other telescopes, since the seeing was so extraordinary this evening. He blinked, oriented his hand and a newly sharpened pencil on the map pad, then pressed against the eyepiece again.

A brilliant green flash leaped from the surface of Mars.

Lowell barely restrained himself from crying out. The flame had been a vivid emerald, a jet of fire as of a great explosion or some kind of immense cannon shot, a huge mass of luminous gas, trailing a green mist behind it.

Once previously, Lowell had seen the glint of sunlight on the Martian ice caps, which had fooled him into seeing a dazzling message—but it had not been like this. Not so green, so violent, so prominent.

Before long he witnessed another green flash, and quickly noted the exact time on the pad in his lap. His excitement grew as he formulated his own explanation for the phenomenon. . . .

Several days later he received a telegram from Ogilvy, a prominent London astronomer, confirming the green flashes from Mars. Ogilvy himself had counted flashes on ten nights, while Lowell himself had recorded several others, which had occurred during the daylight hours in England.

Lowell knew exactly what the flashes must be, and he exhibited no reluctance whatsoever in telling others about his theories. Obviously, these brilliant flares were indications of stupendous launches, a fleet of ships exploding away from Martian gravity into space.

There could be no other explanation. The Martians were coming!

Work crews toiled day and night to move the sand: some complaining, some happy for the meager pay, some shaking their sweat-dripping heads at the insanity of this loud American and his incomprehensible obsession.

The Bedouins thought he was mad, as did many of Lowell's colleagues. But the superstitious Bedouins understood nothing of the universe . . . nor, for that matter, did most other astronomers.

He allowed no slacking in the construction for any reason. Shovels tossed sand up over the walls of the ditches; half-naked boys ran with ladles and buckets, while camels strained to drag barrels of warm water along the length of the dry canal. Lowell supervised here, and he could only hope that the other two trenches would be completed in time to intersect with this one.

When the teams grew too tired to continue, he hired more. Lowell had spread his funds as far as Cairo and Alexandria. He had bribed port officials, paid for the construction of a new railroad out into the desert, leading nowhere, so that a private train could deliver supplies and workers to Lowell's canals.

The sand hissed in the breeze, glittered in the sun. A drummer pounded a cadence to keep the workers in a steady rhythm, like galley slaves. But they were being paid for this labor, and they had volunteered, so Lowell felt no sympathy for them.

Smoke curled into the air, carrying an acrid, sulfurous stench as brown-skinned men dumped wagonloads of hot bitumen into the newly dug trench. The sticky black mass would hold the sand in place, bind it into a thick, flammable mass. Still the walls shifted, and the bitumen ran black and sticky in the heat of the day.

Grumbling, Lowell doubted the sloping walls of sand would hold if one of the great dust storms of the Sahara swept across the dunes. With one mighty breath, God could erase all of Lowell's handiwork, the fruits of years of labor and a squandered family fortune.

If only luck could hold until he sent his signal. . . .

The great Suez Canal had been completed three decades

earlier. For years the United States had discussed excavating a canal across Central America, as soon as the government found some way to grab the necessary land. Lowell's own project was not impossible. It could not be impossible.

He strutted up and down the edge of the ditch, a dusty bandanna wrapped over his mouth, nose, and mustache. He recalled the ancient Hebrew slaves, erecting immense monuments for the pharaohs. But the pharaohs had had decades, even generations, to complete their enormous projects. Lowell had no such luxury.

The line in the sand stretched into a shimmer of mirage in the wavering air. Just a ditch, many miles long, extending to meet two other ditches in what his surveyors guaranteed would be a perfect equilateral triangle.

Back home in Boston, having left the Flagstaff Observatory in the hands of Pickering and Douglass for the autumn, Lowell had calculated the absolute limit of his financial resources, determining the largest excavation he could complete, since the governments of the world refused to help in what they called his "crackpot scheme."

And still Percival Lowell had accomplished little more than a gnat, compared to Martian accomplishments, even allowing for the fact that their task would have been simpler, given that Martian gravity was only a third of Earth's. He had postulated Martian beings, therefore, three times the size of a human; in their reduced gravity, such Martians could be twenty-one times as efficient and have eighty-one times the effective strength of an Earthbound man. For such a species, the project of planetary canals seemed not unlikely.

Lowell's notebooks lay in the tent, but he had done the mathematics himself, letting the engineers double-check his work. Three trenches, each ten miles long, five yards wide, filled with liquid to a depth of an inch or so, equalled thousands and thousands of gallons of petroleum distillate, naphtha, kerosene. The convoys traveled endlessly across the Sahara: an impossible task, made possible—just barely—through the use of his great fortune.

It was a huge investment, but what better way could Lowell spend his money?

Douglass and Pickering had squawked when he had cut his generous allowance of funding for the Flagstaff Observatory down to a maintenance stipend. "How are we to continue our research?" their plaintive telegram had wailed.

"Come to the Sahara," he had replied, "and I will show you."

If Lowell succeeded in signaling the Martians, here and now, astronomical observatories around the world would never again lack for funding.

But they had to hurry. Hurry.

After spotting the green flashes, then laying plans for his great project to signal back to the Martians, Lowell had allotted himself half a year to travel to Europe and generate support. He had taken a first class cabin on a steamer bound for England. Reaching London, he had sought out Ogilvy and immediately enlisted his aid.

The other astronomer had at first been skeptical that there could be any living thing on that remote, forbidding planet. Lowell, however, had been very persuasive.

Obtaining leave from his observatory, Ogilvy accompanied Lowell on his travels. Ogilvy's friend, a journalist named Wells, also asked to travel with them in hopes of getting a good story for his newspaper, but Lowell would have none of it. The newspapers had resoundingly ridiculed Lowell's theories about the Martian canals, and he wanted nothing further to do with reporters, not in the initial stages of a project of such importance.

The two men proceeded across the Channel and thence to Paris for an excellent dinner and conversation with the well-known French writer and astronomer, Camille Flammarion, who gave Lowell's idea a favorable reception. He beamed with pleasure to hear the Frenchman proclaim that Lowell's own theories about the canals and life on Mars had been "ascertained indubitably."

By train and private carriage, Lowell and a wide-eyed Ogilvy — who had never previously visited the Continent — traveled to Italy to meet with the great Giovanni Schiaparelli in his small villa.

A blustery man, not intimidated by challenge, Lowell nevertheless found himself stuttering in awe when he met in Milan with Schiaparelli — discoverer of asteroids and the original cartographer of the canals of Mars.

Schiaparelli had been director of the Milan Observatory since 1862, where he had discovered the asteroid Hesperia, written a brilliant treatise on comets and meteors, and created his original maps of the Martian *canali* in 1877, only a year after Lowell himself had graduated with honors from Harvard. During that same opposition, the American astronomer Asaph Hall had discovered the two tiny moons of Mars, Phobos and Deimos — Fear and Dread. But using only an eight-inch telescope, Schiaparelli had exposed a more profound cosmic secret.

"When I originally drew my maps," the old astronomer said,

struggling with his English, "I meant to represent the lines merely as channels or cracks in the surface. I understand that *canali* implies a different thing to non-Italian ears, suggesting man-made canals—"

"Not *man*-made," Lowell interrupted, extracting his pipe from its case and tamping a load of sweet tobacco from his pouch, "but made by intelligent beings, whose minds may be immeasurably superior to ours. Extraterrestrial life does not mean extraterrestrial *human* life. Under changed conditions, life itself must take on other forms."

"Yes, yes," Schiaparelli nodded, took a sip of his deep red wine, then a bigger gulp. He blinked his rheumy eyes. "But your subsequent observations have convinced even me, my friend."

Lowell leaned forward intently, lacing his fingers together over his knees. "I wish you could see what I have seen on the red disk of the Great God of War, Schiaparelli. Such wonders."

The old astronomer sighed. His rooms were filled with books, oil lamps, and melted lumps of candles in terra cotta dishes. A pair of spectacles lay on an open tome, while an enormous magnifying glass rested in easy reach on another stack of books.

"I can only imagine them. My own eyesight has grown so poor that I must now occupy my mind and my time with the study of history. Though I can no longer study comets or meteors or planets, even an old man with dim vision can make astute observations of history."

"Tell him about Mars, Lowell, my good man," Ogilvy said, searching for something else to eat, and finally settling on some water crackers and old cheese left out on the sideboard in the Italian's dim rooms.

Lowell opened his mind's eye wide as he spoke in an oddly quiet and reverent voice, totally distinct from his usual booming, commanding tone. Thoughts of Mars still made him breathless with astonishment.

"You drew the canals yourself, Schiaparelli—narrow dark lines of uniform width and intensity, perfectly straight. Some even compose portions of great circles across the globe. As I view them from Flagstaff in my best refractor, they look to be gossamer filaments, cobwebs on the face of the Martian disk, threads to draw your mind after them, across millions of miles of intervening void."

Schiaparelli rubbed his eyes. "In my youth I, myself, never conceived them to be more than blemishes."

Lowell raised his eyebrows dubiously. "Geometrical precision on a planetary scale? What else can it be but the mark of an intelligent race? If we could respond in kind, would we not be morally obligated to do so, in the name of humanity?"

Ogilvy coughed on his cracker and looked about for something to drink, finally settling on a wicker-wrapped bottle of Chianti that Schiaparelli had opened for them. He poured sloppily into a glass on the sideboard, then took a quick swallow, only to renew his coughing fit. Lowell scowled at the British astronomer for shattering his spell of imagination.

He puffed on his pipe and settled back in the fine leatherbound chair. Outside on the open balcony, pigeons fluttered in the sunlight. Schiaparelli still watched him with an intent stare. Ogilvy began to page through one of the open history books.

"Imagine it, Schiaparelli," Lowell continued. "Think of a parched, dying world inhabited by a once marvelous civilization, beings with the science and ingenuity to keep themselves alive at all costs. Why, the very existence of a planetwide system of canals implies a world order that knows no national boundaries, a society that long ago forgot its political disputes and racial animosity, uniting the populace in a desperate quest for water. Water . . ."

"And the dark spots, Lowell?" Ogilvy asked, turning back to the conversation. Schiaparelli drank more of his Chianti, amused and fascinated by the description. "Tell him about the oases."

Lowell stood up to stretch, placed his hands behind his back, and turned to the balcony to watch the pigeons. "Pumping stations, obviously."

The old Italian astronomer stared at where the walls of his villa met the ceiling, but he seemed to see nothing, perhaps only a blur with his used-up eyes. Lowell felt a rare flash of sympathy—losing one's eyesight must be the greatest hell a dedicated astronomer could imagine.

"But if Mars is so arid, Lowell, surely all the water would evaporate from these open canals long before it reaches its destination . . . if the temperature is much above freezing, that is—and it *must* be above freezing in order for the water to be in its liquid state." Schiaparelli's forehead creased in a frown.

Ogilvy piped up, pacing the room. "And don't forget, my good man, the astronomical distances involved. If these canals were simple waterways or aqueducts, we would never be able to see them from Earth. They would be much too narrow. How do you account for that?"

Annoyed, Lowell turned to the Englishman. He and Ogilvy had already had this discussion in earnest several times, and again on the train ride to Milan. But he saw Ogilvy's raised eyebrow and understood that the other man had raised the question just to give Lowell a chance to explain.

"Ah, there is a simple answer for both questions," Lowell said, then paused to draw deeply from his pipe. "Almost certainly the lines we see are aqueducts with lush vegetation growing in irrigated croplands along the borders. The only remaining forests on Mars, towering high in the low gravity, sipping precious water from the fertile soil—much as the Egyptians grow their crops in the plains around the Nile. I estimate the darkened fringes of the aqueducts to be about thirty miles wide. This vegetation would not only emphasize the lines of the canals, but would also shield the open water from rapid evaporation. Simple, you see? It is quite clear."

Ogilvy nodded, and Schiaparelli gave a distant smile. The old astronomer seemed more amused than impassioned by the concepts. Lowell came closer to his host, barely controlling his enthusiasm. "My proposed plan follows a similar principle, Schiaparelli. The project I have conceived will take place on a much smaller scale, naturally, since I am but one man and, alas, our own Earthly civilization has no stomach for such dreams.

"I have already dispatched surveyors and work teams to the Sahara, in the flat desert in western Egypt. I will excavate three canals of my own, each ten miles long, across an otherwise featureless basin, to form a perfect equilateral triangle. A geometrical symbol impossible to explain with random natural processes, and therefore a clear message that intelligent life inhabits this world. To make them more visible, I must emphasize my puny canals with lines of fire, by filling the trenches with petroleum products and igniting them. It will be a brief but dramatic message, blazing into the night." His eyes sparkled, his voice rose in volume.

"But why this tremendous effort, my friend?" Schiaparelli asked. "Why now?"

Promptly, he and Ogilvy described the repeated green flashes, the launches of enormous vehicles, ships sent to Earth. Based on Ogilvy's observations and calculations derived from a careful scrutiny of celestial mechanics, Lowell believed he knew the travel time the Martians required to reach Earth.

Lowell's voice became husky. "As you can see, the Martians are on their way. We must show them where to land, where they will be met with an open-hearted welcome by earthbound admirers of their past triumphs and their current travails."

Lowell took a deep breath and spoke with absolute confidence.

"Gentlemen, I intend to lead that party. I will be the first man to shake hands with a Martian."

Finally.

Finally. Lowell had never been a man of extraordinary patience, but the last week of waiting for the three trenches to join at precise corners had been the most interminable time of his life.

Now, under the starlight and the residual heat that wafted off the baked sands, Lowell stood with his torch in hand, feeling like a tribal shaman, ready to ignite his weapon against the darkness, his symbol of welcome to aliens from another world.

The stench of petroleum distillates stung his eyes and nostrils. The chemical smell had driven off the camels and most of the workers, save those few foremen—mostly Europeans—who intended to watch the spectacle. On high dunes in the distance, the curious Bedouins had gathered by their own tents to observe. This would be an event for their storytellers to repeat for generations.

Working with his reluctant assistants Pickering and Douglass, Lowell had gone to a great deal of trouble to calculate the best time when the Sahara night would face Mars, so that his transient shout into the universe had the best chance of being seen—if not from the inbound Martian emissary ships, then from those survivors who had remained on the red planet.

Lowell turned to the telegraph operator beside him. Miles of overland cable had been run to the other vertices of the great triangle in the sand, so that the teams could communicate with each other. "Signal Pickering and Douglass at the other two intersections. Tell them to light their channels."

The telegraph operator pecked away at his key, sending a brief message. When the clicks fell into silence, Lowell stepped to the brink of his canal in the sand. He stared down into the bitumen-lined trench, the foul-smelling black mass that was now pooled with kerosene and gasoline dumped from enormous tanks that had been hauled across the desert by his private railroad.

Lowell tossed his torch into the fuel, then watched the fire spread like a hungry demon, rushing down the channel. The inferno devoured the dumped petroleum, hot enough to ignite the sticky bitumen liner so that the triangular symbol would burn for a long time.

Across the desert into the night, rifle shots rang out, signaling to other torch-bearers stationed along the ten miles of each canal, who also tossed their burning brands into the ditch, so that the fire could engulf the entire triangle. Martians and fire, Lowell thought—what a strange combination.

Lowell's family had already made its mark on the world. Towns had been named after the Lowells and the Lawrences; his maternal grandfather was Abbott Lawrence, minister to Britain. His father, Augustus Lowell, was descended from the early Massachusetts colonists. His family had amassed its fortune in textiles, in landholdings, in finance. But Percival himself would make the greatest mark—on *two* worlds instead of one.

An unbroken wall of flame roared up into the night. He prayed the Martians were watching. He had so much to say to them.

Lowell found it difficult to sleep even long after the inferno had died down. He lay on his cot in his tent, smelling the dying smoke and harsh fumes, listening to the whisper of settling sand sloughing into the bottom of the trench from the burned walls. Far off in the Bedouin camp a pair of camels belched at each other.

In only a year or two, the shifting desert would erase most of his line in the sand, leaving only a dark scar. But if his intended audience received the message, Earth would be a dramatically changed place in that time, and his effort would not be in vain.

Lowell found his situation incredibly strange: he, a wealthy Boston Brahmin, now resting fitfully in an austere tent in the middle of a vast desert that had been made even more unpleasant by his own construction work.

Summoning images of beauty to his mind, he recalled his experiences in Japan, as much an alien world as this Sahara, perhaps even as alien as Mars. He thought of colors bright as enamel and lacquer, gold filigree and cloisonné, the heady perfumes of peonies and burning incense. He remembered being escorted along narrow avenues of carefully tended trees where an explosion of white petals drifted on the winds for the annual cherry blossom festival. He recalled the delicate ritual of a tea ceremony, or the thin atonal melody plucked out on a *biwa* as spiced morsels sizzled on a small hibachi.

During those years as ambassador to Japan, Lowell had lugged his six-inch refractor with him, staring, staring, seeing the Earth but watching the stars. . . .

He had graduated from Harvard with distinction in mathematics at the age of twenty-one, and he had received the Bowdoin Prize for his essay on "The Rank of England as a European Power

Between the Death of Elizabeth and the Death of Anne." He had traveled the world, studied the classics, experienced numerous foreign cultures, proved his facility in languages, even tried to join the fighting in the Serbo-Turkish War. What did he care that mere astronomers scorned his ideas?

Lowell had sailed for Japan in 1883, where he was asked to serve as Foreign Secretary for a special diplomatic mission from Korea to the United States—though at the time he had never even seen Korea. Returning to Tokyo, he had later been asked to help write Japan's new constitution.

Lying sleepless on his cot, he spoke aloud to the apex of his tent, where the canvas rippled in a faint breeze. "I have experience as an ambassador to foreign cultures. I have diplomatic credentials. How could the Martians be stranger than what I have already seen?"

The cylinder screamed through the air with the wailing of a thousand lost souls, trailing behind it a tongue of fire from atmospheric friction and a bright green mist from outgassing extraterrestrial substances.

Lowell burst out of his shaded tent to see the commotion under the midday sun. A burnt smudge of smoke smoldered like a scar across the ceramic-blue sky. Booms of sound thundered in waves as the gigantic ship/projectile crossed overhead.

"It's the emissaries from Mars!" Lowell shouted, raising his hands in the air. "The Martians!"

Like an exploding warship, the cylinder crashed into the desert with a spewed plume of sand and dust. Lowell felt the tremor of impact in his knees, despite the cushioning desert. He laughed aloud, yelling for Douglass and Pickering to join him.

After the burning of the enormous triangle, most of the workers had returned to their widely scattered lands, leaving only a few team bosses to tidy up the loose ends of the construction. Lowell had sold his now useless railroad for scrap steel, giving the salvagers a decent percent of the profits. The place rapidly turned into a ghost town, which some of the European bosses had quietly begun calling "Lowell's Folly." Pickering and Douglass had returned from the other two base camps to join him here. To wait . . .

Now, as the dust settled in the distance, the other two astronomers ran up, their faces ruddy with sunburn and excitement. "We are vindicated!" Lowell cried. He clapped them each on the shoulder. "The Martians are here!"

The remaining Bedouin helpers fled the camp in panic, thrashing their camels to an awkward gallop across the dunes. *Idiots,* he thought. *Fools.* They did not realize the honor that has been bestowed here.

"The world as we know it is about to change. Come, let us put together an expedition. We must welcome our visitors from space."

The heat from the pit rose up in a tremendous wave, overwhelming even the blistering daytime pounding of the Sahara. Pickering dropped back, coughing, but Lowell plodded forward, hunched over, shielding his watering eyes. On an impulse, he reached into the pocket of his cream-colored suit jacket and withdrew his bright red spectacles, placing them over his eyes, seeing the world as a Martian would, the better to understand them.

Because of the residual heat, he could not get close to the crash site, and he felt a terrible dread that the Martian ship had exploded when it struck the ground, that all the interplanetary ambassadors had been obliterated by fire.

But then he heard faint pounding sounds within the metal-walled cylinder, mechanical noises, a soft unscrewing. . . .

Finally, Douglass dragged him back. "It's too hot, Mister Lowell! We must wait."

With savage disappointment, Lowell stumbled away, keeping his head turned to stare at the smoldering crater through his red-lensed spectacles. "I have waited years for this moment. I can tolerate a few more hours—but not much longer than that."

His eyes stinging from tears not entirely caused by the blistering heat, he followed the other two men back to the main camp.

Douglass fetched some water, toiletries, and fresh clothes after sweaty hours spent in the dim shelter of their tents. He and Pickering ate ravenously of a quickly prepared meal, though Lowell himself felt no hunger. His stomach tied itself in knots as he felt his life's work coming to its climax.

Lowell used some of the tepid water to shave, leaning over a small mirror. Then he changed into a fine new suit, and straightened his collar, keeping his gaze intent on the still-glowing pit visible through the propped-open tent flap. Finally, in the cool of the desert night, he told his two companions to wait behind.

"You can't go alone, man," Pickering said, after clearing his throat again.

"Nonsense." Lowell brushed the other astronomer's grasp from his arm. "It was my money that brought the Martians to this landing site, and I claim the right."

"That's the same argument you used with your damned telescope," Pickering muttered, but did not pursue the discussion. Douglass hunkered down, looking forlorn.

Lowell strode across the surrounding dunes in his black leather shoes, mulling over an appropriate speech, wondering if by some miracle the Martians might speak English. No matter, he thought. He had a knack for languages, and would manage to communicate somehow.

Looking dapper, he approached the edge of the pit. He noted with fascination that the heat of the impact had been great enough to fuse some of the sand grains into lumps of glass. If the Martians could survive that, they must be prime specimens indeed.

He stood on the brink, looking down into the glow that lit up the crater as if it were day. A long shiny lid had been unscrewed from the large pitted cylinder and lay on the blasted sands. Below, he saw clanking machines stirring, odd tentacled creatures moving about, exhibiting an industriousness no doubt born by their dire circumstances on Mars. Most remarkable, he saw, was a tall, newly assembled construction rising up on stiltlike tripod legs. The heat was still incredible.

Magnificent! Lowell felt proud and overwhelmed to be mankind's emissary. Now that they had reached Earth, though, the poor Martians could be saved.

Lowell hurried forward to greet the Martians. The wonders of the universe awaited him.

Introduction to
Dune: A Whisper of Caladan Seas

Brian Herbert and I have written close to a million words in the Dune universe, but this short piece is connected to none of them. "A Whisper of Caladan Seas" is actually a footnote to Frank Herbert's magnificent novel, a slight detour of characters barely mentioned during the Harkonnen attack on the city of Arrakeen.

Brian and I began our Dune projects many years ago, when we were brought together by Ed Kramer who, with Brian, had proposed an anthology of Dune short stories. After Brian and I had begun working on the prequel novels, we thought about what we would have written for our story, and this was the piece we developed. It was published shortly before the release of House Atreides, and thus became the first new work of Dune fiction to be published in twenty-two years.

One reviewer liked the story, but added the baffling comment (as reviewers so often do) that he didn't know where we had gotten the mystical aspects of this story, since he recalled no mysticism whatsoever in Frank Herbert's six Dune books (!!!). I still haven't stopped scratching my head over that one.

Frank Herbert also left several fragments from his Dune novels, omitted chapters or notes for other storylines that he never pursued. Eventually, we may put these together. Since Frank never wrote short fiction in the Dune universe, this is the only Dune story in existence, so far.

Dune: A Whisper of Caladan Seas

with Brian Herbert

Arrakis, in the year 10,191 of the Imperial calendar.
Arrakis . . . forever known as Dune. . . .

*T*HE CAVE IN THE MASSIVE SHIELD WALL WAS DARK and dry, sealed by an avalanche. The air tasted like rock dust. The surviving Atreides soldiers huddled in blackness to conserve energy, letting their glowglobe powerpacks recycle.

Outside, the Harkonnen shelling hammered against the bolthole where they had fled for safety. Artillery? What a surprise to be attacked by such seemingly obsolete technology . . . and yet, it was effective. *Damned effective.*

In pockets of silence that lasted only seconds, the young recruit Elto Vitt lay in pain listening to the wheezing of wounded, terrified men. The stale, oppressive air pressed heavy on him, increasing the broken-glass agony in his lungs. He tasted blood in his mouth, an unwelcome moisture in the absolute dryness.

His uncle, Sergeant Hoh Vitt, had not honestly told him how severe his injuries were, emphasizing Elto's "youthful resilience and stamina." Elto suspected he must be dying, and he wasn't alone in that predicament. These last soldiers were all dying, if not from their injuries, then from hunger or thirst.

Thirst.

A man's voice cut the darkness, a gunner named Deegan. "I wonder if Duke Leto got away. I hope he's safe."

A reassuring grunt. "Thufir Hawat would slit his own throat before he'd let the Baron touch our Duke, or young Paul." It was the signalman Scovich, fiddling with the flexible hip cages that held two captive distrans bats, creatures whose nervous systems could carry message imprints.

"Bloody Harkonnens!" Then Deegan's sigh became a sob. "I wish we were back home on Caladan."

Supply sergeant Vitt was no more than a disembodied voice in the darkness, comfortingly close to his injured young nephew. "Do *you* hear a whisper of Caladan seas, Elto? Do you hear the waves, the tides?"

The boy concentrated hard. Indeed, the relentless artillery shelling sounded like the booming of breakers against the glistening black rocks below the cliff-perch of Castle Caladan.

"Maybe," he said. But he didn't, not really. The similarity was only slight, and his uncle, a Master Jongleur . . . a storyteller extraordinaire . . . wasn't up to his capabilities, though here he couldn't have asked for a more attentive audience. Instead the sergeant seemed stunned by events, and uncharacteristically quiet, not his usual gregarious self.

Elto remembered running barefoot along the beaches on Caladan, the Atreides home planet far, far from this barren repository of dunes, sandworms, and precious spice. As a child, he had tiptoed in the foamy residue of waves, avoiding the tiny pincers of crabfish so numerous that he could net enough for a fine meal in only a few minutes.

Those memories were much more vivid than what had just happened. . . .

The alarms had rung in the middle of the night, ironically during the first deep sleep Elto Vitt had managed in the Atreides barracks at Arrakeen. Only a month earlier, he and other recruits had been assigned to this desolate planet, saying their farewells to lush Caladan. Duke Leto Atreides had received the governorship of Arrakis, the only known source of the spice melange, as a boon from the Padishah Emperor Shaddam IV.

To many of the loyal Atreides soldiers, it had seemed a great financial coup—they had known nothing of politics . . . or of danger. Apparently Duke Leto had not been aware of the peril here either, because he'd brought along his concubine Lady Jessica and their fifteen-year-old son, Paul.

When the warning bells shrieked, Elto snapped awake and

rolled from his bunk bed. His uncle, Hoh Vitt, already in full sergeant's regalia, shouted for everyone to hurry, *hurry!* The Atreides house guard grabbed their uniforms, kits, and weapons. Elto recalled allowing himself a groan, annoyed at another apparent drill . . . and yet hoping it was only that.

The burly, disfigured weapons master Gurney Halleck burst into the barracks, his voice booming commands. He was flushed with anger, and the beet-colored inkvine scar stood out like a lightning bolt on his face. "House shields are down! We're vulnerable!" Security teams had supposedly rooted out all the booby traps, spy-eyes, and assassination devices left behind by the hated Harkonnen predecessors. Now the lumpish Halleck became a frenzy of barked orders.

Explosions sounded outside, shaking the barracks and rattling armor-plaz windows. Enemy assault 'thopters swooped in over the Shield Wall, probably coming from a Harkonnen base in the city of Carthag.

"Prepare your weapons!" Halleck bellowed. The buzzing of lasguns played across the stone walls of Arrakeen, incinerating buildings. Orange eruptions shattered plaz windows, decapitated observation towers. "We must defend House Atreides."

"For the Duke!" Uncle Hoh cried.

Elto yanked on the sleeve of his black uniform, tugging the trim into place, adjusting the red Atreides hawk crest and red cap of the corps. Everyone else had already jammed feet into boots, slapped charge packs into lasgun rifles. Elto scrambled to catch up, his mind awhirl. His uncle had pulled strings to get him assigned here as part of the elite corps. The other men were lean and whipcord strong, the finest hand-picked Atreides troops. He didn't *belong* with them.

Young Elto had been excited to leave Caladan for Arrakis, so far away. He had never ridden on a Guild Heighliner before, had never been close to a mutated Navigator who could fold space with his mind. Before leaving his ocean home, Elto had spent only a few months watching the men train, eating with them, sleeping in the barracks, listening to their colorful, bawdy tales of great battles past and duties performed in the service of the Atreides dukes.

Elto had never felt in danger on Caladan, but after only a short time on Arrakis, all the men had grown grim and uneasy. There had been unsettling rumors and suspicious events. Earlier that night, as the troops had bunked down, they'd been agitated, but unwilling to speak of it, either because of their commander's sharp orders or because the soldiers didn't know enough details. Or maybe they were just giving Elto, the untried and unproven new comrade, a cold shoulder. . . .

Because of the circumstances of his recruitment, a few men of the elite corps hadn't taken to Elto. Instead, they'd openly grumbled about his amateur skills, wondering why Duke Leto had permitted such a novice to join them. A signalman and communications specialist named Forrie Scovich, pretending to be friendly, had filled the boy with false information as an ill-conceived joke. Uncle Hoh had put a stop to that, for with his Jongleur's talent for the quick, whispered story—always told without witnesses because of the ancient prohibition—he could have given any of the men terrible nightmares for weeks . . . and they all knew it.

The men in the Atreides elite corps feared and respected their supply sergeant, but even the most accommodating of them gave his nephew no preferential treatment. Anyone could see that Elto Vitt was not one of them, not one of their rough-and-tumble, hard-fighting breed. . . .

By the time the Atreides house guard rushed out of the barracks, they were naked to aerial attack from the lack of house shields. The men knew the vulnerability couldn't possibly be from a mere equipment failure, not after what they'd been hearing, what they'd been feeling. How could Duke Leto Atreides, with all of his proven abilities, have permitted this to happen?

Enraged, Gurney Halleck grumbled loudly, "Aye, we have a traitor in our midst."

Illuminated in floodlights, Harkonnen troops in blue uniforms swarmed over the compound. More enemy transports disgorged assault teams.

Elto held his lasgun rifle, trying to remember the drills and training sessions. Someday, if he survived, his uncle would compose a vivid story about this battle, conjuring up images of smoke, sounds, and fires, as well as Atreides valor and loyalty to the Duke.

Atreides soldiers raced through the streets, dodging explosions, fighting hard to defend. Lasguns sliced vivid blue arcs across the night. The elite corps joined the fray, howling—but Elto could already see they were vastly outnumbered by this massive surprise assault. Without shields, Arrakeen had already been struck a mortal blow.

Elto blinked his eyes in the cave, saw light. A flicker of hope dissipated as he realized it was only a recharged glowglobe floating in the air over his head. Not daylight.

Still trapped in their tomb of rock, the Atreides soldiers listened to the continued thuds of artillery. Dust and debris trickled from the shuddering ceiling. Elto tried to keep his spirits high, but knew House Atreides must have fallen by now.

His uncle sat nearby, staring into space. A long red scratch jagged across one cheek.

During brief inspection drills while settling in, Elto had met the other important men in Duke Leto's security staff besides Gurney Halleck, especially the renowned Swordmaster Duncan Idaho and the old Mentat assassin Thufir Hawat. The black-haired Duke inspired such loyalty in his men, exuded such supreme confidence, that Elto had never imagined this mighty man could fall.

One of the security experts had been trapped here with the rest of the detachment. Now Scovich confronted him, his voice gruff and challenging. "How did the house shields get shut off? It must have been a traitor, someone you overlooked." The distrans bats seemed agitated in their cages at Scovich's waist.

"We spared no effort checking the palace," the man said, more tired than defensive. "There were dozens of traps, mechanical and human. When the hunter-seeker almost killed Master Paul, Thufir Hawat offered his resignation, but the Duke refused to accept it."

"Well, you didn't find all the traps," Scovich groused, probing for an excuse to fight. "You were supposed to keep the Harkonnens out."

Sergeant Hoh Vitt stepped between the two men before they could come to blows. "We can't afford to be at each other's throats. We need to work together to get out of this."

But Elto saw on the faces of the men that they all knew otherwise: they would never escape this death trap.

The unit's muscular battlefield engineer, Avram Fultz, paced about in the faint light, using a jury-rigged instrument to measure the thickness of rock and dirt around them. "Three meters of solid stone." He turned toward the fallen boulders that had covered the cave entrance. "Down to two and a half here, but it's dangerously unstable."

"If we went out the front, we'd run headlong into Harkonnen shelling anyway," the gunner Deegan said. His voice trembled with tension, like a too-tight baliset string about to break.

Uncle Hoh activated a second glowglobe, which floated in the air behind him as he went to a bend in the tunnel. "If I remember

the arrangement of the tunnels, on the other side of this wall there's a supply cache. Food, medical supplies . . . water."
Fultz ran his scanner over the thick stone. Elto, unable to move on his makeshift bed and fuzzed with painkillers, stared at the process, realizing how much it reminded him of Caladan fishermen using depth sounders in the reef fishing grounds.

"You picked a good, secure spot for those supplies, Sergeant," Fultz said. "Four meters of solid rock. The cave-ins have cut us off."

Deegan, his voice edged with hysteria, groaned. "That food and water might as well be in the Imperial Palace on Kaitain. This place . . . Arrakis . . . isn't right for us Atreides!"

The gunner was right, Elto thought. Atreides soldiers were tough, but like fish out of water in this hostile environment.

"I was never comfortable here," Deegan wailed.

"So who asked you to be *comfortable?*" Fultz snapped, setting aside his apparatus. "You're a soldier, not a pampered prince."

Deegan's raw emotions turned his words into a rant. "I wish the Duke had never accepted Shaddam's offer to come here. He must have known it was a trap! We can never live in a place like this!" He stood up, making exaggerated, scarecrowlike gestures.

"We need water, the ocean," Elto said, overcoming pain to lift his voice. "Does anybody else remember *rain?*"

"I do," Deegan said, his voice a pitiful whine.

Elto thought of his first view of the sweeping wastelands of open desert beyond the Shield Wall. His initial impression had been nostalgic, already homesick. The undulating panorama of sand dunes had been so similar to the even patterns of waves on the sea . . . but without any drop of water.

Issuing a strange cry, Deegan rushed to the nearest wall and clawed at the stone, kicking and trying to dig his way out with bare hands. He tore his nails and pounded with his fists, leaving bloody patterns on the unforgiving rock, until two of the other soldiers dragged him away and wrestled him to the ground. One man, a hand-to-hand combat specialist who had trained at the famous Swordmaster School on Ginaz, ripped open one of their remaining medpaks and dosed Deegan with a strong sedative.

The pounding artillery continued. *Won't they ever stop?* He felt an odd, pain-wracked sensation that he might be sealed in this hellhole for eternity, trapped in a blip of time from which there was no escape. Then he heard his uncle's voice. . . .

Kneeling beside the claustrophobic gunner, Uncle Hoh leaned

close, whispering, "Listen. Let me tell you a story." It was a private tale intended only for Deegan's ears, though the intensity in the Jongleur's voice seemed to shimmer in the thick air. Elto caught a few words about a sleeping princess, a hidden and magical city, a lost hero from the Butlerian Jihad who would slumber in oblivion until he rose again to save the Imperium. By the time Hoh Vitt completed his tale, Deegan had fallen into a stupor.

Elto suspected what his uncle had done, that he had disregarded the ancient prohibition against using the forbidden powers of planet Jongleur, ancestral home of the Vitt family. In the low light their gazes met, and Uncle Hoh's eyes were bright and fearful. As he'd been conditioned to do since childhood, Elto tried not to think about it, for he too was a Vitt.

Instead, he visualized the events that had occurred only hours before. . . .

On the streets of Arrakeen, some of the Harkonnen soldiers had been fighting in an odd manner. The Atreides elite corps had shouldered lasguns to lay down suppressing fire. The buzzing weapons had filled the air with crackling power, contrasted with much more primal noises of screams and the percussive explosions of old-fashioned artillery fire.

The battle-scarred weapons master ran at the vanguard, bellowing in a strong voice that was rich and accustomed to command. "Watch yourselves—and don't underestimate *them.*" Halleck lowered his voice, growling; Elto wouldn't have heard the words if he hadn't been running close to the commander. "They're in formations like Sardaukar."

Elto shuddered at the thought of the Emperor's crack terror troops, said to be invincible. *Have the Harkonnens learned Sardaukar methods?* It was confusing.

Sergeant Hoh Vitt grabbed his nephew's shoulder and turned him to join another running detachment. Everyone seemed more astonished by the unexpected and primitive mortar bombardment than by the strafing attacks of the assault 'thopters.

"Why would they use artillery, Uncle?" Elto shouted. He still hadn't fired a single shot from his lasgun. "Those weapons haven't been used effectively for centuries." Though the young recruit might not be well practiced in battle maneuvers, he had at least read his military history.

"Harkonnen devils," Hoh Vitt said. "Always scheming, always coming up with some trick. Damn them!"

One entire wing of the Arrakeen palace glowed orange, consumed by inner flames. Elto hoped the Atreides family had gotten away. . . Duke Leto, Lady Jessica, young Paul. He could still see their faces, their proud but not unkind manners; he could still hear their voices.

As the street battle continued, blue-uniformed Harkonnen invaders ran across an intersection, and Halleck's men roared in challenge. Impulsively, Elto fired his own weapon at the massed enemies, and the air shimmered with a crisscross web of blue-white lines. He fumbled, firing the lasgun again.

Scovich snapped at him. "Point that damn thing away from me! You're supposed to hit *Harkonnens!*" Without a word, Uncle Hoh grasped Elto's rifle, placed the young man's hands in proper positions, reset the calibration, then slapped him on the back. Elto fired again, and hit a blue-uniformed invader.

Agonized cries of injured men throbbed around him, mingled with frantic calls of medics and squad leaders. Above it all, the weapons master yelled orders and curses through twisted lips. Gurney Halleck already looked defeated, as if he had personally betrayed his Duke. He had escaped from a Harkonnen slave pit years before, had lived with smugglers on Salusa Secundus, and had sworn revenge on his enemies. Now, though, the troubadour warrior could not salvage the situation.

Under attack, Halleck waved his hands to command the entire detachment. "Sergeant Vitt, take men into the Shield Wall tunnels and guard our supply storehouses. Secure defensive positions and lay down a suppressing fire to take out those artillery weapons."

Never doubting that his orders would be obeyed, Halleck turned to the remainder of his elite corps, reassessing the strategic situation. Elto saw that the weapons master had picked his best fighters to remain with him. In his heart, Elto had known at that moment, as he did now thinking back on it, that if this were ever to be told as one of his uncle's vivid stories, the tale would be cast as a tragedy.

In the heat of battle, Sergeant Hoh Vitt had shouted for them to trot double-time up the cliffside road. His detachment had taken their weapons and left the walls of Arrakeen. Glowlamps and portable illuminators showed firefly chains of other civilian evacuees trying to find safety in the mountainous barrier.

Panting, refusing to slacken their pace, they had gained altitude, and Elto looked down on the burning garrison city. The

Harkonnens wanted the desert planet back, and they wanted to eradicate House Atreides. The blood-feud between the two noble families dated all the way back to the Butlerian Jihad.

Sergeant Vitt reached a camouflaged opening and entered his code to allow them access. Down below, the gunfire continued. An assault 'thopter swooped along the side of the mountain, sketching black streaks of slagged rock; Scovich, Fultz, and Deegan opened fire, but the 'thopter retreated—after marking their position.

As the rest of the detachment raced inside the caves, Elto took a moment at the threshold to note the nearest artillery weapons. He saw five of the huge, old-style guns pounding indiscriminately at Arrakeen—the Harkonnens didn't care how much damage they caused. Then two of the mighty barrels rotated to face the Shield Wall. Flames belched out, followed by far-off thunder, and explosive shells rained down upon the cave openings.

"Get inside!" Sergeant Vitt shouted. The others moved to obey, but Elto remained fixated. In a single stroke, a long line of fleeing civilians vanished from the cliffside paths, as if a cosmic artist with a giant paintbrush had decided to erase his work. The artillery guns continued to fire and fire, and soon centered on the position of the soldiers.

The range of Elto's full-power lasgun was at least as long as the conventional shells. He aimed and fired, pulsing out an unbroken stream but expecting little in the way of results. However, the dissipating heat struck the old-fashioned explosives in the loaded artillery shells, and the ragged detonation ripped out the breech of the mammoth cannon.

He turned around, grinning, trying to shout his triumph to his uncle—then a shell from the second massive gun struck squarely above the entrance to the cave. The explosion knocked Elto farther into the tunnel as tons of rock showered down, striking him. The avalanche sent shock waves through an entire section of the Shield Wall. The contingent was sealed inside. . . .

After days in the tomblike cave, one of the glowglobes gave out and could not be recharged; the remaining two managed only a flickering light in the main room. Elto lay wounded, tended by the junior medic and his dwindling supplies of medicinals. Elto's pain had dulled from that of broken glass to a cold, cold blackness that seemed easier to endure. . . but how he longed for a sip of water!

Uncle Hoh shared his concern, but was unable to do anything else.

Squatting on the stone floor off to his left, two sullen soldiers had used their fingertips to trace a grid in the dust; with light and dark stones they played a makeshift game of Go, a carryover from ancient Terra.

Everyone waited and waited—not for rescue, but for the serenity of death, for escape.

The shelling outside had finally stopped. Elto knew with a sick certainty that the Atreides had lost. Gurney Halleck and his elite corps would be dead by now, the Duke and his family either killed or captured; none of the loyal Atreides soldiers dared to hope that Leto or Paul or Jessica had escaped.

The signalman Scovich paced the perimeter, peering into darkened cracks and crumbling walls. Finally, after carefully imprinting a distress message into the voice patterns of his captive distrans bats, he released them. The small creatures circled the dusty enclosure, seeking a way out. Their high-pitched cries echoed from the porous stone as they searched for any tiny niche. After frantic flapping and swooping, at last the pair disappeared through a fissure in the ceiling.

"We'll see if this works," Scovich said. His voice held little optimism.

In a weak but valiant voice, Elto called his uncle nearer. Using most of his remaining strength, he propped himself on an elbow. "Tell me a story, about the good times we had on our fishing trips."

Hoh Vitt's eyes brightened, but for only a second before fear set in. He spoke slowly. "On Caladan. . . Yes, the old days."

"Not so long ago, Uncle."

"Oh, but it seems like it."

"You're right," Elto said. He and Hoh Vitt had taken a coracle along the shore, past the lush pundi rice paddies and out into open water, beyond the seaweed colonies. They had spent days anchored in the foamy breakwaters of dark coral reefs, where they dove for shells, using small knives to pry free the flammable nodules called coral gems. In those magical waters they caught fan-fish—one of the great delicacies of the Imperium—and ate them raw.

"Caladan. . ." the gunner Deegan said groggily, as he emerged from his stupor. "Remember how *vast* the ocean was? It seemed to cover the whole world."

Hoh Vitt had always been so good at telling stories, supernaturally good. He could make the most outrageous things real for his listeners. Friends or family made a game of throwing an idea at Hoh, and he would make up a story using it. Blood mixed with melange . . . a great Heighliner race across uncharted foldspace . . . the wrist-wrestling championship of the universe, between two dwarf sisters who were the finalists . . . a talking slig.

"No, no more stories, Elto," the sergeant said in a fearful voice. "Rest now."

"You're a Master Jongleur, aren't you? You always said so."

"I don't talk about that much." Hoh Vitt turned away.

His ancestral family had once been proud members of an ancient school of storytelling on the planet Jongleur. Men and women from that world used to be the primary troubadours of the Imperium; they traveled between royal houses, telling stories and singing songs to entertain the great families. But House Jongleur fell into disgrace when a number of the itinerant storytellers were proven to be double agents in inter-House feuds, and no one trusted them any longer. When the nobles dropped their services, House Jongleur forfeited its status in the Landsraad, losing its fortunes. Guild Heighliners stopped going to their planet; the buildings and infrastructure, once highly advanced, fell into disrepair. Largely due to the Jongleur's demise, many entertainment innovations were developed, including holo projections, filmbooks and shigawire recorders.

"*Now* is the time, Uncle. Take me back to Caladan. I don't want to be here."

"I can't do that, boy," he responded in a sad voice. "We're all stuck here."

"Make me *think* I'm there, like only you can do. I don't want to die in this hellish place."

With a piercing squeak, the two distrans bats returned. Confused and frustrated, they fluttered around the chamber while Scovich tried to recapture them. Even they had been unable to escape. . . .

Though the trapped men had held out little hope, the failure of the bats still made them groan in dismay. Uncle Hoh looked at them, then down to Elto as his expression hardened into grim determination.

"Quiet! All of you." He knelt beside his injured nephew. Hoh's eyes became glazed with tears . . . or something more. "The boy needs to hear what I have to say."

Elto lay back, letting his eyes fall half-closed as he readied himself for the words that would paint memory pictures on the insides of his eyelids. Sergeant Vitt sat rigid, taking deep breaths to compose himself, to center his uncanny skill and stoke the fires of imagination. To tell the type of story these men needed, a Master Jongleur must calm himself; he moved his hands and fingers in the ancient way, going through the motions he'd been taught by generations of storytellers, ritualistic preparations to make the story good and pure.

Fultz and Scovich shifted uneasily, and then moved closer, anxious to listen as well. Hoh Vitt looked at them with glazed eyes, barely seeing them, but his voice carried a gruff warning. "There is danger."

"Danger?" Fultz laughed and raised his grimy hands to the dim ceiling and surrounding rock walls. "Tell us something we don't know."

"Very well." Hoh was deeply saddened, wishing he hadn't pulled strings to get Elto assigned to the prestigious corps. The young man still thought of himself as an outsider, but ironically— by staying in the line of fire and destroying one of the artillery weapons—he had shown more courage than any of the proven soldiers.

Now Hoh Vitt felt a tremendous sense of impending loss. This wonderful young man, filled not only with his own hopes and dreams but also with those of his parents and uncle, was going to die without ever achieving his bright promise. He looked around, at the faces of the other soldiers, and seeing how they looked at him with such anticipation and admiration, he felt a moment of pride.

In the hinterlands of Jongleur, a hilly rural region where Hoh Vitt had grown up, dwelled a special type of storyteller. Even the natives suspected these "Master Jongleurs" of sorcery and dangerous ways. They could spin stories like deadly spiderwebs, and in order to protect their secrets, they allowed themselves to be shunned, hiding behind a cloak of mystique.

"Hurry, Uncle," Elto said, his voice quiet and thready.

With intensity in his words, Sergeant Vitt leaned closer. "You remember how my stories always start, don't you?" He touched the young man's pulse.

"You warn us not to believe too deeply, to always remember that it's only a story . . . or it could be dangerous. We could lose our minds."

"I'm saying that again to you, boy." He scanned the close-pressed faces around him. "And to everyone listening."

Scovich made a scoffing noise, but the others remained silent and intent. Perhaps they thought his warning was only part of the storytelling process, part of an illusion a Master Jongleur needed to create.

After a moment's hush, Hoh employed the enhanced memorization techniques of the Jongleurs, a method of transferring large amounts of information and retaining it for future generations. In this manner he brought to mind the planet Caladan, summoning it in every intricate detail.

"I used to have a wingboat," he said with a gentle smile, and then he began to describe sailing on the seas of Caladan. He used his voice like a paintbrush, selecting words carefully, like pigments precisely mixed by an artist. He spoke to Elto, but his story spread hypnotically, wrapping around the circle of listeners like the wispy smoke of a fire.

"You and your father went with me on week-long fishing trips. Oh, those days! Up at sunrise and casting nets until sunset, with the golden tone of the sun framing each day. I must say we enjoyed our time alone on the water even more than the fish we caught. The companionship, the adventures and hilarious mishaps."

And hidden in his words were subliminal signals: *Smell the salt water, the iodine of drying seaweed . . . Hear the whisper of waves, the splash of a distant fish too large to bring aboard whole.*

"At night, when we sat at anchor alone in the middle of the seaweed islands, we'd stay up late, the three of us, playing a fast game of tri-chess on a board made of flatpearls and abalone shells. The pieces themselves were carved from the translucent ivory tusks of South Caladan walruses. Do you remember?"

"Yes, Uncle. I remember."

All the men murmured their agreement; the Jongleur's haunting words were as real to them as to the young man who had actually experienced the memories.

Listen to the hypnotic, throbbing songs of unseen murmons hiding in a fog bank that ripples across the calm waters.

The shroud of pain grew fuzzy around Elto, and he could feel himself going to that other place and time, being carried away from this hellish place. The parched, dusty air at first smelled dank, then cool and moist. As he closed his eyes, he could sense the loving touch of Caladan breezes on his cheek. He smelled the mists of his native world, spring rain on his face, sea waves lapping at his feet as he stood on the rocky beach below the Atreides castle.

"When you were young, you would splash in the water, laughing and swimming naked with your friends. Do you remember?"

"I . . . " And Elto felt his voice merge with the others, becoming one with them. "We remember," the men mumbled reverently. All around them the air had grown close and stifling, most of the oxygen used up. Another one of the glowglobes died. But the men didn't know this. They were anesthetized from their pain.

See the wingboat cruising like a razorfin under dazzling sunlight, then through a warm squall under cloudy skies.

"I used to body surf in the waves," Elto said with a faint smile of wonder.

Fultz coughed, then added his own reminiscences. "I spent a summer on a small farm overlooking the sea, where we harvested paradan melons. Have you ever had one fresh out of the water? Sweetest fruit in the universe."

Even Deegan, still somewhat dazed, leaned forward. "I saw an elecran once, late at night and far away — oh, they're rare, but they do exist. It's more than just a sailor's story. Looked like an electrical storm on the water, but alive. Luckily, the monster never came close." Though the gunner had been hysterical not long before, his words held such an awed solemnity that no one thought to disbelieve him.

Swim through the water, feel its caress on your body. Imagine being totally wet, immersed in the sea. The waves surround you, holding and protecting you like a mother's arms. . . .

The two distrans bats, still loose from the signalman's cages, had clung to the ceiling for hours, but now they swayed and dropped to the floor. All the air was disappearing in their tomb.

Elto remembered the old days in Cala City, the stories his uncle used to tell to an entranced audience of his family. At several points in each of those tales, Uncle Hoh would force himself to break away. He had always taken great care to remind his listeners that it was *only a story.*

This time, however, Hoh Vitt took no breaks.

Realizing this, Elto felt a moment of fear, like a dreamer unable to awaken from a nightmare. But then he allowed himself to succumb. Though he could barely breathe, he forced himself to say, "I'm going into the water . . . I'm diving . . . I'm going deeper . . ."

Then all the trapped soldiers could hear the waves, smell the water, and remember the whisper of Caladan seas. . . .

The whisper became a roar.

*   *   *

In the velvet shadows of a crisp night on Dune, Fremen scavengers dropped over the ridge of the Shield Wall, into the rubble. Stillsuits softened their silhouettes, allowing them to vanish like beetles into crevices.

Below, most of the fires in Arrakeen had been put out, but the damage remained untended. The new Harkonnen rulers had returned to their traditional seat of government in Carthag; they would leave the scarred Atreides city as a blackened wound for a few months . . . as a reminder to the people.

The feud between House Atreides and House Harkonnen meant nothing to the Fremen—the noble families were all unwelcome interlopers on their sacred desert planet, which the Fremen had claimed as their own thousands of years earlier, after the Wandering. For millennia these people had carried the wisdom of their ancestors, including an ancient Terran saying about each cloud having a silver lining. The Fremen would use the bloodshed of these royal houses to their own advantage: the deathstills back at the sietch would drink deeply from the casualties of war.

Harkonnen patrols swept the area, but the soldiers cared little for the bands of furtive Fremen, pursuing and killing them only out of sport rather than in a focused program of genocide. The Harkonnens paid no heed to the Atreides trapped in the Shield Wall either, thinking none of them could have survived; so they left the bodies trapped in the rubble.

From the Fremen perspective, the Harkonnens did not value their resources.

Working together, using bare callused hands and metal digging tools, the scavengers began their excavation, opening a narrow tunnel between the rocks. Only a few dim glowglobes hovered close to the diggers, providing faint light.

Through soundings and careful observations on the night of the attack, the Fremen knew where the victims would be. They had uncovered a dozen already, as well as a precious cache of supplies, but now they were after something much more valuable, the tomb of an entire detachment of Atreides soldiers. The desert men toiled for hours, sweating into the absorbent layers of their stillsuits, taking only a few sipped drops of recovered moisture. Many water rings would be earned for the moisture recovered from these corpses, making these Fremen scavengers wealthy.

When they broke into the cave enclosure, though, they stepped into a clammy stone coffin filled with the redolence of death. Some of the Fremen cried out or muttered superstitious prayers to Shai-Hulud, but others probed forward, increasing the light from the glowglobes now that they were out of sight of the nighttime patrols.

The Atreides soldiers all lay dead together, as if struck down in a strange suicide ceremony. One man sat in the center of their group, and when the Fremen leader moved him, his body fell to one side and a gush of water spewed out of his mouth. The Fremen tasted it. Salt water.

The scavengers backed away, even more frightened now.

Carefully, two young men inspected the bodies, finding that the uniforms of the Atreides were warm and wet, stinking of mildew and damp rot. Their dead eyes were open wide and staring, but with contentment instead of the expected horror, as if they had shared a religious experience. All of the dead Atreides soldiers had clammy skin . . . and something even more peculiar, revealed when the Fremen cut them open.

The lungs of these dead men were entirely filled with water.

The Fremen fled, leaving their spoils behind, and resealed the cave. Thereafter, it became a forbidden place of legend, drawing wonder from anyone hearing the story as it was passed on by Fremen from generation to generation.

Somehow, sealed inside a lightless cave in the driest desert, all of the Atreides soldiers had *drowned.* . . .

Introduction to
Prisoner of War

According to unofficial military policy, the U.S. Air Force knows exactly what it takes to make the best fighter pilot: balls the size of grapefruits, and brains the size of a pea.

Some might say that it requires all the good qualities of a fighter pilot to walk in Harlan Ellison's footsteps. Harlan is always a hard act to follow, and it's daunting even to try.

When I first talked with Harlan about doing a sequel to his classic Outer Limits *teleplay, "Soldier," he was very skeptical. Given the sheer number of abysmal sequels and bad spinoffs that have graced bookstore racks and theater screens, I suppose he had good reason. "I've never done a sequel to a single one of my stories," he told me. "I never felt the need. If I got it right the first time, I've said all I needed to say."*

In the course of my writing career I have gathered a rather impressive (if that's the word) collection of rejection slips — something like 750 at last count — and I never learned to give up when common sense dictated that I should. So, I went back to Harlan. "You've developed a sprawling scenario of a devastating future war, where soldiers are bred and trained to do nothing but fight from birth to death. Are you telling me that there's only one story to be told in that whole world?"

So, I got to play with Harlan Ellison's toys.

"Prisoner of War" is my tap dance on Harlan's stage, set in the devastating world of "Soldier." It is a story about another set of warriors in a never-ending war, men bred for nothing but the battleground — and how they cope with the horrors of . . . peace.

As a final note, this story was written on the road during the most grueling book-signing tour I ever hope to do — a nationwide blitz of twenty-seven cities in twenty-eight days for my humorous spy thriller, Ai! Pedrito!, based on an old L. Ron Hubbard movie script. I dictated "Prisoner of War" in an unknown number of hotel rooms, wandering down sidewalks, or at whatever park happened to be closest, before the day's work of interviews and autograph sessions began. The chance to do something creative and emotionally engaging gave me something to look forward to during that long, long month.

Prisoner of War

*T*HE FIRST ENEMY LASER-LANCES BLAZED ACROSS the battlefield at an unknown time of day. No one paid attention to the *hour* during a firefight anyway. Neither Barto nor any of his squad-mates could see the sun or moon overhead: too much smoke and haze and blast debris filled the air, along with the smell of blood and burning.

A soldier had to be ready at any time or place. A soldier would fight until the fight was over. An endless *Now* filled their existence, a razor-edged flow of life-for-the-moment, and the slightest distraction or daydream could end the *Now* . . . forever.

With a clatter of dusty armor and a hum of returned weapons-fire, the defenders charged forward, Barto among them. They had no terrain maps or battle plans, only unseen commanders bellowing instructions into their helmet earpieces.

Greasy fires guttered and smoked from explosions, but as long as a soldier could draw breath, the air always smelled sweet enough. Somehow, the flames still found organic material to burn, though only a few skeletal trees remained standing. The horizon was like broken, jagged teeth. No discernible structures remained, only blistered destruction and the endless bedlam of combat.

163

To a man who had known no other life, Barto found the landscape familiar and comforting.

"Down!" his point man Arviq screamed loudly enough so that Barto could hear it through the armored helmet. A bolt of white-hot energy seared the ground in front of them, turning the blasted soil into glass. The ricochet stitched a broken-windshield pattern of lethal cuts across the armored chest of one comrade five meters away.

The victim was in a different part of the squad; Barto knew him only by serial number instead of a more personal, chosen name. Now the man was a casualty of war; his serial number would be displayed in fine print on the memorial lists back at the crèche—for two days. And then it would be erased forever.

Barto and Arviq both dove to the bottom of the trench as more well-aimed laser-lances embroidered the ground and the slumping walls of the ditch. As he hunched over to shield himself, the helmet's speakers continued to pound commands: "KILL . . . KILL . . . KILL . . ."

The Enemy assault ended with a brief hesitation, like an indrawn breath. The soldiers around Barto paused, regrouped, then scrambled to their feet, leaving the fallen comrade behind. Later, regardless of the battle's outcome, trained bloodhounds would retrieve the body parts and drag them back to HQ in their jaws. After the proper casualty statistics had been recorded, the KIA corpses would be efficiently incinerated.

In the middle of a firefight, Barto and Arviq could not be bothered by such things. They had been trained never to think of fallen comrades; it was beyond the purview of their mission. The voice in the helmet speakers changed, took on a different note: "RETALIATE . . . RETALIATE . . . RETALIATE . . ."

With a howl and a roar enhanced by adrenaline injections from inside the armor suits, Barto and his squad moved as a unit. Programmed endorphins poured into their bloodstreams at the moment of battle frenzy, and they surged out of the trench. The Enemy encampment could not be far, and they silently swore to unleash a slaughter that would outmatch anything their opponents had ever done . . . though this most recent attack was assuredly a response to their own previous day's offensive.

Moving as a unit, the squad clambered over debris, around craters, and out into the open. They ran beyond monofilament barricades that would slice the limb off an unwary soldier, then into a sonic minefield whose layout shone on the eye-visor screen inside each helmet.

With a self-assured gait across the no-man's land, the soldiers moved like a pack of killer rats, laser-lances slung in their arms. They bellowed and snarled, pumping each other up. As he ran, Barto studied the sonic minefield grid in his visor, sidestepping instinctively.

From their embankment, the Enemy began to fire again. The smoky air became a lattice of deadly lines in all directions. Barto continued running. Beside him, Arviq pressed the stock of his weapon against his armored breastplate, pumping blast after blast toward the unseen Enemy.

Then a laser-lance seared close to Barto's helmet, blistering the top layer of semi-reflective silver. Static blasted across his eye visor, and he couldn't see. He made one false sidestep and yelled. He could no longer find the grid display, could no longer even see the actual ground.

Just as his foot came down in the wrong place, Arviq grabbed his arm and yanked him aside, using their combined momentum. The sonic mine exploded, vomiting debris and shrapnel with pounding sound waves that fractured the plates of Barto's armor, pulverizing the bones in his leg. But he fell out of the mine's focused kill radius and lay biting back the pain.

He propped himself up and ripped off his slagged helmet, blinking with naked eyes at the real sky. Arviq had saved his life — just as Barto would have done for his squad-mate had their situations been reversed.

Always trust your comrades. Your life is theirs. That was how it had always been.

And even if he did fall to Enemy attack, the bloodhounds would haul his body to HQ, and he would receive an appropriate military farewell before he returned to the earth — mission accomplished. A soldier's duty was to fight, and Barto had been performing that duty for all of his conscious life.

As he activated his rescue transmitter and fumbled for the medpak, the rest of the soldiers charged forward, leaving him behind. Arviq didn't even spare him a backward glance.

Some said the war had gone on forever — and since no one kept track of history anymore, the statement could not be proved false.

Barto knew only the military life. He had emerged from a tank in the soldiers' crèche with the programming wired into his brain, fully aware, fully grown, and knowing his assignment. If ever he had any questions or doubts, the command voices in his helmet would answer them.

Barto knew primarily that he had to kill the Enemy. He knew that he had to protect his comrades, that the squad was the sum of his existence. No good soldier could rest until every last Enemy had been eradicated, down to their feline spies, down to the bloodhounds that dragged away Enemy KIAs.

Winning this war might well take an eternity, but Barto was willing to fight for that long. Every moment of his life had encompassed either fighting, or learning new techniques to kill and to survive, or resting so that he could fight again the next day.

There was no time for anything else. There was no need for anything else.

Barto remembered when he'd been younger, not long out of the tank. His muscles were wiry, his body flexible without the stiffness of constant abuse. His skin had been smooth, free of the intaglio of scars from a thousand close dances with death. Barto and his squad-mates—apprentices all—had fought hand-to-hand in the crèche gymnasium, occasionally breaking each other's bones or knocking each other unconscious. None of them had yet earned their armor, their protection, or their weapons. They couldn't even call themselves soldiers. . . .

Now consigned to the HQ infirmary and repair shop, as he drifted in a soup of pain and unconsciousness, Barto revisited the long-ago moment he had first grasped a specialized piece of equipment designed to maim and kill. The soldier trainees had learned early on in their drill that any object was a potential weapon—but this was a *spear*, a long rough bar of old steel with a sharpened point that gleamed white and silver in the unforgiving lights. A *weapon*, his own weapon.

He spun it around in his hand, feeling its weight—a deadly impaling device that could be used against the oncoming Enemy.

Later, his advanced training would of course include hand-to-hand combat against other soldiers, human opponents . . . but not at first. All trainees were expendable, but if the young men could be salvaged, then the military programming services would turn them into killers.

For months, Barto received somatic instruction and physical drilling by one of the rare old veterans who had survived years of combat. The veteran had a wealth of experience and survival instincts that could not be matched even by the most sophisticated computers. He made sure that Barto fought to the limit of his abilities.

Swinging the spear against nothing, feeling his body move, Barto reacted to the barked commands of the veteran instructor.

Response without thought. He learned how to make the weapon into a part of him, an extension of his reflexes. *He* was the weapon: the spear was just an augmentation.

Then they gave him a taste of blood, real blood. They wanted him to get in the habit of killing.

The small metal-walled arena was like an echo chamber, a large underground room with simulated rock outcroppings, a fallen tree, and other sharp obstacles. Barto didn't question the reality of the scenario. The environment itself was a tool to be used.

During that exercise, the veteran instructor let him wear his helmet . . . but nothing else. Stripped naked, he gripped the spear in his hand and glared through the visor. The helmet earphones gave him reassuring commands in his ears, directions, suggestions. Otherwise, Barto felt helpless—but no *soldier* was ever helpless, because a helpless man could not become a soldier.

Underground, the arena door groaned open, and barricade bars moved away. Barto tensed. He gripped the metal shaft of the spear despite the sweat on his palms.

Suddenly, a whirlwind of bristles and scales, sharp hooves and long tusks launched itself like a projectile. An enhanced boar with scarlet eyes snarled and plowed forward, searching for a target, something against which to vent its anger.

And Barto was the only other creature in the room.

On high pedestals in the gallery above, three enhanced cats watched, blinking their gold-green eyes. The feline spy commanders observed for the invisible overlords who wanted to see how the freshly detanked soldiers reacted in their first real life-or-death test.

The boar charged. Barto jabbed with the spear, but he was too tentative. Before, he had only thrust at imaginary opponents and an occasional hologram projected inside his visor. Now, though, the boar came on like a locomotive. The spear glanced off, opening a mere stinging scratch in the creature's skin. Barto had not imagined its hide could be so tough, its bones so hard. He had made the first, terrible mistake in this duel.

The trivial wound enraged the beast.

Barto dove to one side over a synthetic rock, and the boar rammed into the artificial tree trunk. It spun around, shaking its head, tusks gleaming. The ivory spears in its mouth looked much more deadly than Barto's primitive weapon. The boar attacked again.

A moment of panic rose up like an illusion, but he pounded

it back, and the fear evaporated, bringing a rush of adrenaline. The chemical and electronic components in his body released the substance, making Barto see red rage of his own.

The enhanced boar recovered itself and snorted. Barto knew he had a better chance of striking the target in motion if he didn't use a tiny pinpoint thrust; instead, he swung the heavy metal bar sideways like a cudgel. The sturdy steel bashed the creature's thick skull. The sound of the impact rang out in the hollow room.

The cats watched from their pedestals.

The boar squealed and thrashed. Barto saw that its eyes held an increased intelligence, like that found in the feline spies and in the daredevil bloodhounds that retrieved bodies from the battlefield. The boar responded with a calculated counterattack, trying to outthink this naked human opponent, this would-be soldier. Barto smiled: the boar was the Enemy.

In the frenzy of battle, Barto no longer thought like an intelligent human being. Instead, he relied only on instinct and unbearable bloodlust. He rushed in without forethought, without care, without any sense of self-preservation. After all . . . he had a spear.

The boar tried to feint, to react, but Barto gave the Enemy no chance. He swung again with the staff, drawing a bright red line of blood and putting out one of the beast's eyes. Crimson and yellow body fluids oozed through smashed skin on the boar's snout. It leapt forward, driven by insanity and pain.

Now, Barto used the spear with finesse.

A great calm flowed through him, as if the rest of the world had slowed down, and he saw exactly what to do, exactly where to hold the spear. The sharpened point neatly plunged through the ribcage of the beast and skewered its lungs and heart. Showering a wet-iron smell in the air, the creature lay quivering, trembling . . . dying.

When Barto came back to his senses, he saw that his legs had been slashed open by the boar's tusks. The deep gouges left him bleeding, but oddly without any sense of pain or injury. He looked down and studied the corpse of his opponent, the Enemy. Now he had killed. Barto had fresh blood on his hands, real blood from a vanquished opponent.

He liked the sensation.

He knew that this had been no simple exercise. He knew the boar could well have killed him, and that other trainees who had vanished from the barracks must have failed this part of their instruction.

But Barto had succeeded. He was a *killer* now, and he was one step closer to becoming a soldier.

Time didn't matter. For a soldier, time never mattered. He awoke hours, or days, later back in the HQ infirmary and repair shop — patched up, drugged, but fully aware. A hairless chimpanzee tended him, leaning over in a cloud of disinfectant scents and bad breath. The chimp medical techs knew how to bandage and fix battlefield wounds. They could do no surgery that required finesse, but the soldiers required nothing that needed delicacy for cosmetic effect.

Once injured, if a soldier could be fixed, he would be sent back to the battlefield. If his wounds caused the chimp med-techs too much trouble, he would be eliminated. Every surviving member of the squad bore his share of scars, burns, scabs, and calluses. No one paid attention to these trophies of war; they were part of a soldier's life, not a badge of honor or bravery.

Since Barto hadn't been eliminated, he assumed he must have been fixed.

He sat up on the infirmary cot, and the hairless chimpanzees hurried over, uttering quiet reassurances, a few English words, a few soothing grunts. Triggered by his awakening, a signal was automatically sent back to his squad commander.

Barto listened to an assessment of his repaired leg, his stitched muscles and skin, and his bruises and contusions. *Not too bad,* he thought. He'd suffered worse, sometimes even in training with other soldiers (especially during the initial few months, when they'd first been given their own sets of armor). He remembered that back then his comrade Arviq had thought himself invincible. . . .

During downtime before the soldiers crawled into their assigned sleeping bins, the other squad members were required to file through the infirmary to see their injured comrades. Some came only because of orders to do so; most of them would rather have been sleeping.

But the invisible commanders planted instructions to go to the infirmary simply so that other soldiers could see the wounded, could see what could happen to them if they weren't careful . . . but also so they could see that they just might survive.

Recovering, Barto sat up in the uncomfortable infirmary bed and watched the other soldiers come in. His pain went away with another automatic rush of endorphins to deaden his unpleasant sensations . . . or perhaps his own determination was enough to quell the nerve-fire of agony.

The fighters filed by. He recognized few of them, all strangers without armor and helmets, though he could have identified each one by the serial numbers displayed on their fatigues. These were soldiers, cogs in a fighting machine. They didn't have time to be individuals.

When Arviq came up at the end of the line, he stood brusque, nodding gruffly. "You'll mend," he said.

"Thank you for saving me," Barto answered. It was the closest thing they'd had to a conversation in a long time.

"It's my duty. I await the day when you can fight with us again." He marched out, and the others followed him. Barto lay back and attempted to sleep, to regain his strength. Through sheer force of will, he growled at his cells and tissues to work harder, to knit the injuries and restore him to full health. . . .

Day after day, lying in the infirmary and *waiting* proved far more difficult than any combat situation Barto had ever encountered. Finally, after a maddening week of intensive recuperation, directed therapy aided by medical technology and powerful drugs, he was released from his hospital prison and sent back to the front.

Where he belonged.

The battlefield screamed with pain and destruction, explosions, fire, and death—but to Barto, after being so long in the sheltered quiet of the infirmary, the tumult was a shout of exuberance. He was glad to be here.

The soldiers raced across the ground, each in his own squad position, weapons drawn. They had already driven back the Enemy, and now the fire of laser-lances grew even thicker around them as the others became desperate. They pressed ahead, deeper into Enemy territory than they had ever gone before.

Their helmet locators for sonic mines and shrapnel grenades buzzed constantly, but the reptilian part of Barto's brain reacted without volition, hardwired into fighting and killing. He dodged and weaved, keeping himself alive.

His point man, Arviq, jogged close beside him, and Barto extended his peripheral vision behind the dark visor to enfold his comrade into an invisible protective sphere. He would assist his partner if he got into trouble—not out of any sense of payback or obligation, but because it was an automatic response, his own assignment. He would have done the same for any other soldier, any member of his squad—anyone but the Enemy.

Precision-guided mortars scribed parabolas through the air and exploded close to any concentration of soldiers who did not display the proper transponders. Amidst screams and thunder, a massive triple detonation wiped out over half of Barto's squad, but the others did not fall back, did not even pause. They drove onward, continued the push. The fallen comrades would be taken care of somehow, though no one knew how the bloodhounds would ever make it so deep into Enemy-held territory.

This far behind the main battle lines, the Enemy numbers themselves were dwindling, and Barto fired and fired again. The laser-lance thrummed in his gauntleted hands, skewering a distant man's chestplate and leaving a smoking hole.

But it wasn't really a man, after all. It was the Enemy.

The chase continued, and the survivors of Barto's squad ran in the direction of what must have been Enemy HQ. In his dry, dusty mouth he could taste the sweet honey of victory.

But suddenly, unexpectedly, they triggered a row of booby traps that did not appear on their helmet sensors. Camouflaged catapults popped up, spraying nearly invisible clouds of netting, monofilament webs as insubstantial as smoke but sharper than the most deadly razor.

The flying webwork engulfed four soldiers near him, and they fell into neatly butchered pieces. But oddly enough, so did three of the Enemy soldiers rushing in retreat, as if they themselves hadn't known of these defenses. But their own visor sensors *must* have been keyed to booby traps they themselves had planted. . . .

Though the questions astonished him, Barto did not pause. His job was not to analyze. Paraplegic computer tacticians and the invisible battlefield commanders did all that work. The voices in his helmet told him to push forward, and so he pushed forward.

Arviq ran beside him, still firing his laser-lance — and numbly Barto realized that most of the other soldiers were dead. His squad had been decimated . . . but the Enemy was nearly eradicated as well.

War often required sacrifices, and many soldiers died. But a victory now would pay the bloody cost ten times over.

The thrill of seeing the Enemy nearly exterminated gave Barto all the motivation he needed, even without an adrenaline rush augmented by injectors in his armor. With a shared glance behind opaque visors, he and Arviq both had the same thought, and ran forward with their four remaining companions. They couldn't stop now.

Then large gun emplacements popped out of the ground, more massive than anything he had ever seen before. Barto reeled in unaccustomed confusion. The Enemy had never exhibited technology like this! Automated fire rained down on them, super powerful laser-lances far more devastating than any of the hand-held rifles.

Soldiers screamed. The blasts were like belts of incinerating flame, vaporizing armor and leaving not even bones for the blood-hounds to retrieve. The firepower pummeled anyone who came close, whether friend or Enemy. They had no chance, no chance at all.

An explosion ripped out a deep crater ten meters from them. Someone screamed, but Barto had no voice. The automated super-lasers continued to track across the ground, pinpointing armor, crushing any movement. Barto watched the beams sweep closer, vaporizing everything in the vicinity. The four other squad members died in a puff of blood-smoke and molten armorplate.

On impulse he grabbed Arviq and shoved him hard toward the fresh crater. Together, the two dove into the raw trench just as the splash of disintegration passed over them. The voices in his helmet turned to a rainstorm of incomprehensible static.

Within moments the battle stopped. Everyone else was dead.

All of the laser fire and explosions ceased. All the Enemy, all of the squad, every living thing had been annihilated.

Without saying a word, Arviq hauled himself to his hands and knees and reached over to shake Barto, who also recovered his balance. The two of them sat panting for a moment, stunned but still determined. Neither of them—in fact, no one they knew—had ever been so far behind Enemy lines.

They rose up slowly and carefully into the crackling silence, afraid of other targeted automated systems. Clods of dry dirt fell from their armor. Dust and crackling ash roiled through the air . . . but nothing else moved.

"We won?" Barto asked. "Is the war over?"

"I hope not." Arviq turned to him, his mouth a grim line beneath the opaque visor of the helmet. "The war will never be over. But we may have won this battle."

Barto raised his helmet over the rim of the blasted crater. No weapons responded to the motion. The battlefield remained eerily quiet with only the faint sound of coughing fires and settling dust.

"Must be the Enemy encampment," Arviq said with a grunt. "Increased defenses—maybe even HQ." He grinned. "Success!"

But Barto wasn't so sure. Moving with tense caution, he climbed away from the crater. "No, not HQ. The defenses killed as many of them as us. ID transponders useless."

Arviq joined him, sole survivors on the sprawling battlefield. Barto could see where the huge gun emplacements had raised up from below the surface of the ground. Adjusting his visor filters, he spotted different infrared signatures, metallic traces, solid structures and hollow passages beneath the scarred ground.

Amazed, Barto crept forward. "We've discovered something. We're required to investigate."

"No, back to HQ," Arviq said. "We must report. Our squad was wiped out."

But Barto shook him off. He stood determined, looking ahead across the scabbed landscape. "Not until we have hard reconnaissance. This could be important."

Arviq hesitated only a moment. Neither outranked the other, and they had no time for argument, but the other soldier quickly came to his own decision. "Yes. Reconnaissance is part of our mission."

Most of the time, sly intelligent cats would creep through the darkness, observing Enemy strongholds and reporting back to HQ. But the squad had gone farther into Enemy territory than any known advance, and they might have new information. That was the most important thing. They weren't doing it for the glory or for a possible promotion, or for any sort of reward. Barto and Arviq would take the risk because it was their duty.

"My head, my thoughts . . . are empty," Arviq said, tapping his helmet.

Barto adjusted his earphones, but still received no transmission and no commands. An uneasy silence echoed in his head. The speakers growled no more repetitive commands to attack and kill.

"How can you stand it?" Arviq looked at him.

Barto took a deep breath. "No choice. Tolerate it."

Crouched low, they cautiously advanced toward the automated gun emplacements, but the motion sensors did not reactivate. The weapons had gone through their program and wiped out the threat. Somehow, the two comrades had slipped through the cracks. They could move forward.

Barto and Arviq found a metal hatch-plate in the half-hidden superstructure of the enormous laser-lances. Barto sat down and pressed his helmet against the hatch, carefully listening for any vibration, fully alert. Any moment now he expected the destructive fire to rain out again.

He tugged on the hatch, looking for access controls. "We can infiltrate," he said. "It's an underground bunker. Maybe weapons storage. We can bring supplies or power packs back to HQ."

Together they wiped off dust and blasted dirt from the plate, used tools from their armor belts to crack open the seals, and finally they lifted the heavy hatch.

Still no voices came to their heads, no instructions. The two soldiers were on their own. Barto didn't like it one bit.

They dropped down into the opening, where a steel ladder led into a maw of shadows. They descended, gripping rung after rung with gauntleted hands. *If this was Enemy HQ, Barto thought, it was a much larger complex than anything he and his squad had ever lived in.*

Finally the ladder ended in an underground tunnel with the hatch cover high above them. Barto paused for a moment to scan the surroundings, then they walked forward into dim silence. The tunnels seemed empty, barely used, abandoned for a long time. Barto realized the Enemy soldiers could not have emerged from this place. No one had walked down these access tunnels in a long, long time.

As point man, Arviq led the way. He strode forward, hands on his weapon, ready for anything. A soldier had to be flexible and determined. The small tunnel lights gave little illumination, but their helmet visors augmented the ambient photons.

Cameras in their helmets recorded everything as reconnaissance files to be downloaded back in HQ. They continued for what seemed like miles, trudging deeper and deeper into the Earth. This place was an important facility, possibly a central complex . . . but Barto couldn't begin to understand it.

From up ahead came a faint throbbing from generators and heavy machinery. Finally, they saw brighter light, thick windows, rectangular plates that shone through to another world, a subterranean complex that seemed like a mythical land. Inside huge grottoes, pale ethereal people moved about wearing bright colors. Plants of a shockingly lush green, garish hues that Barto had never seen before, drew the two of them forward like magnets.

"What is this place?" Arviq asked. "Some kind of trick?"

"Paradise."

As the soldiers approached, unable to believe what they were seeing, they crossed an unseen threshold, a booby trap. They heard a brief hum, a crackle of power-surge. Barto reacted just in time to feel a sinking despair — but not fast enough to get out of the way.

A pressing white light engulfed both of them, swallowing them up. In an instant, Barto's visor turned black, then so did his eyes.

When he awoke, the assault on his senses nearly knocked him back into protective unconsciousness. Sounds, smells, colors bombarded him like weapons fire. His armor and helmet had been stripped away, leaving him vulnerable; without it, he felt helpless, soft-skinned, like a worm.

The bed beneath him was warm and soft, disorienting. A gentle and cozy light surrounded him instead of the familiar garish white to which he was accustomed back in his own barracks. Each breath of the humid air was perfumed with a sweet, flowery scent that nauseated him.

Was this an infirmary? Barto turned his head gently, and a raging pain clamored inside his skull. The place reminded him oddly of the time he had been helpless and healing from his previous injury . . . but he saw no hairless chimpanzees, no robotic medical attendants. The sheets were soft and slick, vastly different from the other rough, sterile coverings.

Grogginess smothered his mind and body. Barto tried to return to full awareness . . . but something was wrong. His body remained sluggish and unresponsive, as if the accustomed chemical stimulants were not being released according to program. He needed adrenaline; he needed endorphins.

Arviq lay on another bed beside him, similarly prone, similarly stripped of his armor. When Barto turned his head and directed his gaze in the opposite direction, he was astonished to find another person by his shoulder. Not one of the enhanced animals bred to attend the regiment . . . but a *woman,* a lovely creature with short, honey-brown hair and a shimmering purple garment so brilliant and dazzling that it made his eyes ache.

Responding with combat readiness, he sat up with a lurch — but the woman rushed over and shushed him with a gentle touch. "Quiet now. Everything's all right. You are safe here." Her voice sounded like sweet syrup. *Alien.*

Arviq stirred beside him, groaning in confusion and growing rage.

Then Barto remembered a legend, a story told on the field during the quiet times between battles when some soldiers were more frightened than others. It was a hopeful myth of what happened to brave and dedicated fighters after a death in battle. *Was this . . . Valhalla?*

He glanced over at Arviq, his face contorted with confusion. His eyes glimmered with dark fires. "Are we dead?"

The woman laughed like tinkling crystal. "No, soldier. We are people like yourselves, human beings."

She didn't look like him, though, or any other person he had ever seen. Barto shook his head, refusing to acknowledge the pain left over inside. He'd had enough experience with pain. "You're not . . . soldiers."

The woman smiled and leaned closer to him. A warmth radiated from her scrubbed and lotioned skin. He had never noticed a person's physical features before, never paid attention . . . and he'd never seen anything so beautiful in his life.

"Everyone is a soldier," he said, "either for our side, or the Enemy."

The woman continued to give him a slightly superior smile. "You are soldiers, my friends . . . but we are not. Not here." She gave a gesture to indicate her entire underground world. "After all, it's a war. You're fighting and dying." Her thin, dark eyebrows rose up in graceful arches on her forehead. "Did it never occur to you to ask exactly what you're fighting . . . *for?*"

With a sudden burst of energy and an outcry of rage, Arviq lunged up from his bed, reaching out with clawlike hands, his face full of fury. Even without armor or weapons, any soldier knew how to kill with his bare hands. Somehow he found the energy to lash out, to propel himself into a combat frame of mind.

The woman staggered back from the infirmary beds, startled. Barto saw shadows, more people moving behind observation windows, automatic devices activating. There was another flash of white light, and again he lost consciousness.

When Barto awoke once more, he was alone in a room, clad in soft pajamas with more slick sheets wrapped around him. He found his bed too pliant, too yielding, as if it meant to be comfortable with a vengeance.

The gentle sound of running water trickled from speakers embedded in the wall. The white noise had a soothing effect, the opposite of the perpetual, pressuring commands that had droned into his ears from helmet speakers. Now, the image of a soporific, bubbling brook made him want to lie motionless in a stupor.

He no longer even seemed alive.

This room was smaller, the walls painted pastel colors instead of clean white. The illumination was muted and warm, like sunlight through amber. It made his head fuzzy.

Stiffly, Barto rolled over and found that Arviq wasn't with him this time. His comrade had been taken elsewhere. Was this some sort of insidious Enemy plan? Divide and conquer, separate the squad members.

Had he fallen into some new kind of warfare that went beyond violence and destruction to this personality-destroying brainwashing technique? Barto snarled and tried to find a way to escape — a captured soldier's duty was to escape at all costs.

He didn't hear a door open, felt no movement of the air — but suddenly the beautiful woman stood there with him, setting a platter down on a ledge formed out of the substance of the wall. She leaned over his bed, her entire body smelling of gentle flowers and perfumes. She smiled down at him, parting soft lips to reveal even white teeth. Barto started, ready to fight with hand-to-hand techniques even without his armor or his weapons — but she made no threatening move.

"My name is Juliette," she said, then waited as if he was supposed to recognize some significance to the name.

He answered as he had been drilled. "Barto. Corporal. E21TFDN." He rolled off the serial number in a singsong chant, "Eetoowun teeyeff deeyenn." He had spoken it more than any other word in his lifetime. Then he formed his mouth into a grim line. That was all he had been trained to say. The Enemy rarely, if ever, took prisoners. Everyone died on the battlefield.

"I brought food for you . . . Barto." Juliette picked up a steaming, spicy-smelling bowl from the tray on the ledge. It contained some kind of broth laced with vegetables, even a little meat.

Though he could withstand long periods of fasting, Barto realized how hungry he was. He'd been trained to shut off the hunger pangs and nerve twinges in his digestive system. But he also knew to take nourishment whenever possible, to maintain his strength.

She extended a spoon, and Barto raised his head to accept a mouthful. The spoon was metal with rounded edges. Even such a crude and innocuous weapon could be used in many different ways as a killing instrument. He could have snatched it from her — but he did not, taking the mouthful instead.

The flavors exploded around his tongue, and Barto nearly

choked. It was too intense, too spiced, too fresh—experiences his mouth had never had. Back in the barracks all soldiers ate a common meal, a protein-rich gruel that served as sustenance and nothing else. He'd never before dined on a preparation in which someone had cared about its flavors. He didn't find it at all pleasant.

Juliette gave him another mouthful, and he forced himself to eat it. But he did not let down his guard for an instant.

"The stun-field should have no residual effect on you, Barto," she said. "You'll regain your strength in no time." Her voice sounded odd in his ears, pitched with a higher timbre, musical rather than the implacable instructions that had poured into his ears from the helmet's speakers.

"I'm strong enough," Barto said. "Where is my comrade?"

"He's safe and being tended—but we thought it best to separate you." She took the bowl away, then stood back to appraise him. "I'm curious about you, Barto, Corporal, E21TFDN. I want to be your friend—so let's just use our first names, all right?" She brushed her hand along his arm, and he recoiled at her touch; it felt like warm feathers tickling across the skin. "Can you stand up? I'd like to take you for a walk to show you where you are."

Barto did not argue with her. Regardless of her intentions, Juliette's offer would allow him to continue his reconnaissance. She could show him whatever she wished, and he would gather information. Without the helmet visor and its implanted cameras, he would have to observe with his own eyes, and remember details. But it could be done.

As he swung off the bed, the loose-fitting pajamas felt strange on him, not hard enough, not safe. He walked on the balls of his bare feet, every muscle tense, searching for mysterious threats as Juliette led him out of the room. She took him down underground corridors into even richer light. They passed beautiful images of scenery, forgotten forests and lost mountains . . . waterfalls and lakes unlike anything he had ever seen on the battle-scarred combat fields.

"Who are you people?" Barto said. "What is this place?"

"We're civilians. We went underground centuries ago to escape the fighting, while our armies defended us against the invasion."

Barto tried to assess the information, to fit it like puzzle pieces into the sparse information in his mind. "My squad is . . . part of the defenders? We fight against the invaders?"

She looked at him with a curious, placid expression. Her pale skin, delicate bone structure, and pointed chin gave her an ethereal, elfin appearance. "No one knows which side is which anymore."

Other people, similarly pale-skinned and soft-looking, observed the pair as they walked by. Some smiled, some drew back in fear. Many regarded him with cold, fishlike interest. Juliette seemed to enjoy the attention she received just by being with him.

Barto scanned his surroundings for a way to escape and return to his squad. But then he remembered that, except for Arviq, all of his comrades were dead, annihilated by the immense gun emplacements that protected this underground shelter. Back at his own HQ, the databases must have already recorded him and his point man as casualties of war.

Juliette talked as they continued, her voice a pleasant melange of words. She told him of their days of peace and shelter down below, how the survivors had made an entire world down here by excavating tunnel after tunnel. Here, the civilians did what she called "the great work of humanity"—composing music, dabbling in art, writing poetry and literature . . . though, if they remained isolated down here without experiencing the hard edge of life, Barto didn't know how they found any material to incorporate into their creations.

Though she turned at intersections, descended to different levels, walked in circles, Barto never lost his bearings. He imprinted a map of everything they encountered, knowing he might need to use it later. On his own.

Juliette took him to a greenhouse where the smells nearly stifled him: humid air, the odors of vegetation and mulch, flowers bursting forth like explosions from mortar-fire. Pollinating insects flitted from blossom to blossom, and brilliantly ripe vegetables and fruits made his eyes hurt.

He heard the drip of irrigation systems, saw colorful birds hopping from plant to plant, and a shiver went up his spine. Everything was so quiet here, so gentle. It made him feel too full of energy, too restless.

Barto remembered when he'd been forced to recuperate in the HQ infirmary as the hairless chimpanzees tended to him. He had been bored and frustrated . . . but with a goal—to *heal*, so he could go back and fight. He had managed to wait until his body returned to its optimal condition, when he could go out and serve his purpose in life.

Here, though, these people had a quiet calmness about them, an air of superiority . . . with nothing else to do. Juliette seemed to enjoy it, seemed proud of being a civilian.

Barto had never experienced such vibrant beauty, the smells, the music . . . the sense of *peace*. His body rebelled at the thought, but as the hours went by in the beautiful woman's company he began to feel his resistance crumbling. This was all new to him.

As she showed him their underground "paradise," Barto followed her and listened. Finally, in exasperation, he turned to Juliette and asked, "So there's no war here?" He couldn't believe it. Such a concept had never occurred to him. "No battles?"

"Oh, we have a little." Juliette smiled, then gestured him forward. "Here, let me show you. Maybe you'll find it comforting."

She led him down smooth passages where the temperature grew cooler, the smell more metallic. They walked down glass-walled hallways until they reached a control center.

Battle-plans. Tactical maps. Troop movement displays.

"This is how we maintain our edge, Barto, and our window on the outside world." Juliette's people sat at stations in front of the shifting screens, their fingers raised across control panels. Terrain grids spread out in front of them in bristling colors.

High-resolution panels showed other soldiers, people in familiar armor and helmets, jittery point-of-view images transmitted from visor cameras. Civilian men and women leaned over, punching in commands and speaking into microphones.

"Move left. Open fire."

Another man with a deep voice droned, "Kill the Enemy. Kill the Enemy. Kill the Enemy." He sounded bored. The others looked very relaxed in their positions.

Barto stared with shock as he realized that *these* were the voices he'd heard in his helmet all his life: directing him, helping him plan his attack. *These* were his ultimate commanders in the war.

Astonished, Barto looked over to see Arviq standing inside the control room, chaperoned by a civilian man, also dressed in a loose jumpsuit. His point man's chaperone demonstrated the workings of the controls. Arviq's eyes were wide as he watched the battle.

Sensing the new arrivals, Arviq looked up to see Barto. Their eyes met, and hot understanding flashed between them. *This* was the ultimate headquarters of their army. Arviq reeled from the revelation, but Barto felt a nagging question in the back of his mind. He wondered if other civilians in this control room might be directing the *Enemy* troops in a similar fashion.

Safe in their protected bunkers, these isolated civilians played the deadly war like a game, an exercise. They'd lived here for so long, so comfortably, they seemed uninterested in winning the conflict or ending the crisis . . . merely in maintaining what they already had.

"So you see, Barto," Juliette said, touching his arm again; this time he did not withdraw so quickly, "we understand what you go through. We're familiar with the war, we're there with you inside your head during even the most terrible missions. We know how difficult it is for the soldiers." She smiled. "That's why I'm very glad to offer you asylum here. Stay with us." Now she sounded coy. "I'd be . . . very interested in getting to know you better."

Arviq glowered, out of his element. The chaperone next to him nodded toward Juliette, and she said, "You see, Gunnar is also taking good care of your comrade. Stay here. Consider it well-deserved R&R."

Barto looked around, saw the controllers, heard the familiar command voices. He answered gruffly, "I'm a soldier. I follow orders." Even if it meant he must stop fighting for a while.

Once the two prisoners had resigned themselves to their situation, they were allowed to speak with each other, though neither Barto nor Arviq had ever had much use for conversation. For a week they had made no violent gestures and learned to "behave themselves"—as Juliette described it. As a reward, Barto and Arviq were allowed to sit next to each other in the dining hall.

The room was a large chamber with plush seats and long tables. Lights sparkled from prisms overhead, and the air was redolent with the rich smells of exotic dishes. Various salads and broiled fishes and interesting soups were spread before them. The hall echoed with a murmur of voices.

In his training sessions, Barto learned about the horrors of being a POW, should such a fate ever befall him. But he was now confused, not sure which orders to follow, what was the proper course of action. Juliette had insisted he was their honored guest, not a prisoner. Should he still try to escape? These civilians had given him food and shelter, and a soft bed, though he desperately wanted his narrow basket-bunk back. He longed for the decisive voice in his ears that commanded him to do his duty—but Barto no longer knew exactly what his duty was.

Arviq looked at his plate and poked at the gaudy, frilly dishes that had been served to him. Other soft-skinned civilians walked by, staring at them, whispering to each other. One reached out to touch Arviq on the shoulder, as if on a dare; the soldier lashed out like a python, and the two observers scampered away giggling, as if titillated by the thrill they'd just received.

Barto felt as if he and his point man were on display, specimens for a zoo . . . or humiliated members of a captured Enemy force, dragged before the public as trophies. Shrouded in silence, Arviq seemed to be doing a slow burn as he sat staring at his food, glaring at the other people.

Barto tried to calm himself. His own emotions seemed so much *flatter* since he'd been brought underground, his mind dulled—as if the adrenaline pump, endorphin enhancers, even his root survival instincts had been neutralized. Listening to the muted drone of conversation and music around them, he thought back longingly to the cacophony in the mess hall at his old barracks.

He remembered the clatter of metal trays, the crash of armorplates as soldiers jostled each other. With wordless camaraderie, the squad members sat on hard benches, grabbed their utensils, and gobbled their tasteless food. Together, they recharged their batteries and stoked the fires that they would need for combat in their next mission.

While none of the soldiers knew each other very well, each knew his place in life, his purpose . . . and his Enemy. These underground civilians had nothing to compare with that.

Juliette sauntered up to them, her elfin features positively glowing, as if Barto's presence had increased her own standing among her people. She walked with her tall friend, Gunnar, who had spent days escorting Arviq. She looked down at the food on Barto's plate, and clucked in a mock scolding tone that he should eat more.

Barto felt a strange sensation in his stomach and heart, as if he were basking in the sunlight of her presence. How could Juliette make him feel proud that she had chosen *him* for her special attentions? He had never been singled out for anything before.

On the days when Juliette brought him to the breakfast hall, Barto was glad to see her, eager to hear her voice, just to look upon her face. As his senses became accustomed to his environment, his tongue relished the taste of fresh fruits and breads. The flower scents in the air smelled sweet, and he didn't flinch when Juliette touched him this time, taking him by the elbow. He liked the softness of her fingertips, the way they moved up and down his arm. He felt that he wanted to be even closer to her, to allow her into the walled fortress of himself.

"Do you like it with us here?" Juliette said with a hopeful, even plaintive, lilt to her voice. Ignoring Arviq, she touched the lumpy intaglio of scars on his forearm, tracing patterns and imagining his terrible wounds, as if she had never seen such marks before. "I'd like for you to stay with us, Barto . . . with me." She reached across the table to clasp his hand, and he felt the urge to withdraw. What was she doing?

Gunnar's narrow face seemed drawn and concerned. He shook his head gravely. "You know how he's been trained. You know what this man has been through. He's not a toy for you, Juliette."

"I know exactly what he is," she answered. They both talked as if Barto wasn't even there. "And that doesn't change my wishes one bit."

With intent, flicking eyes, Barto followed the conversation, the conflict. If Juliette wanted him to stay here — and he vehemently wished that she did — then he would stay.

He'd seen the control chambers, the computer screens. He knew that these were the ultimate commanders of the war, the people who issued the instructions through his helmet speakers. His job had been to defend these civilians, to protect them . . . and if Juliette should happen to give him leave to stop the fighting and stay here, with her, then he would follow orders.

Moving around behind him at the dining table, Juliette held out a large purple flower, its petals like a soft starburst. With particular care, she slid it into the close-cropped dark hair behind his right ear. Then she clapped at her audacity and at the spectacle she had made. He flushed.

Barto did not remove the flower, knowing it was somehow special to Juliette. The other civilians in the dining hall spoke to each other, pleased and entertained. Then Juliette danced away with tall Gunnar beside her, leaving the two soldiers to continue eating under the scrutiny of the curious observers.

Arviq looked across the table at him, scowling at his comrade's behavior. He narrowed his flinty eyes at the flower in Barto's hair. "You look like a fool," he growled, and snatched it away.

Back in his too-peaceful quarters with the door sealed and locked from the outside, Barto lay on his too-comfortable bed and then finally curled up on the hard floor. He would sleep better that way. . . .

He dreamed of other times, when there hadn't been so much peace, when he had felt alive and useful and necessary. Where he had known his place in the world.

After one particularly furious foray, he, Arviq, and five other squad members crept ahead, continuing to approach the blasted Enemy territory even after the main conflict was over. They followed trails of blood and footprints, drag marks left by the bloodhounds that had come to retrieve the bodies of Enemy soldiers.

In the dream Barto increased his visor's sensitivity to search for infrared traces of organic waste or warm blood droplets. The enhanced bloodhounds were not trained to cover their trails, and with their heavy, mangled burdens, they left a path that was easy to follow, even across the blistered landscape.

The squad followed the trail back to a shielded Enemy encampment. Barto and his comrades prided themselves in their bravery (or foolhardiness), and they charged into the bunkers with their weapons drawn, their adrenaline packs tuned to full output. Their laser-lances blasted the hinges off the doors and made short work of the plasrock bricks that shored up the damaged buildings.

Within moments, Barto's squad had breached the outer defenses and came in firing. *No mercy.* Many Enemy soldiers were still in their armor, but their weapons were locked in recharging racks. Others fought hand-to-hand, never giving up.

Barto's team suffered heavy losses, but during the fight he was dizzy with exhilaration. By himself, he vanquished fifteen of the Enemy soldiers; altogether, his squad destroyed the entire outpost. *Total victory.*

Throughout the combat, during the screams and explosions, the violence and death, Barto had felt a sure camaraderie between his fellow soldiers. He never let doubt enter his mind, never a question. He knew exactly what he was doing here.

The Enemy bloodhounds, locked in their small home-kennels, bayed until Arviq cut them all down. The dogs seemed to know they had been responsible for betraying their masters' location.

With a resounding cheer of triumph, the survivors of Barto's team gave a shout to celebrate the defeat of the Enemy. Then, as part of a ritual for such infrequent but absolute victories, the men reached down to tear the helmets off the Enemy corpses, taking them for souvenirs.

Barto removed the helmet from the soldier he had just killed, then looked down to see the visage of the Enemy.

In his dream, the face belonged to Juliette.

*   *   *

As days of contained rage and frustration built within him, Arviq found that he didn't even need the supplemental adrenaline pump from his dismantled armor. This was all *wrong!* His blood boiled, his anger rose into a thunderstorm of fury—and he unleashed it upon the walls, the bed, anything in his room. *His cell.*

Arviq didn't want to be a prisoner of war. He wanted to fight, to kill the Enemy. He had been bred and trained for nothing else.

The quiet stillness of this underground civilian world, the soft fabrics, the perfumes, and the too-tasteful food . . . all pushed him into a frenzy. He tore the coverings off his bed and thrashed about, ripping the sheets to shreds. He howled and screamed without words, a bestial cry of damnation. He pounded on the door, but it only rattled in its grooves. Then he threw himself upon the bedframe itself, yanking and pulling, until finally he uprooted it from the floor and walls.

He didn't know if anyone was watching him, nor did he care.

Arviq hurled himself against the metal wall, battering his shoulders, bruising his muscles, but feeling no pain. His body was accustomed to running on the ragged edge of energy, and he had been resting here for days, storing up power in his muscles. Now he released it all in his frenzy.

His attack made marks on the wall, left some smears of his own blood. His fists caused dents. The sealed door rattled again in its tracks; it seemed looser now. He pounded and pounded, receiving no answer.

Finally, Arviq returned to the ruined bedframe, wrenching free a strip of metal that he could use as a crowbar. He had to escape. He had to get back. He didn't belong here.

He wedged the ragged end of torn metal into the door track and *pushed,* prying . . . bending. The door began to buckle, and Arviq worked even harder.

After his nightmares had left him like exorcised demons, Barto fell into a deep slumber and awoke incredibly refreshed. Sometime in the middle of the night he had crawled back into his bed and rested peacefully.

A soldier had to be flexible, had to adapt to new circumstances. At last, he had begun to do just that.

When Gunnar and Juliette came to fetch him, he sensed their tension. The other civilians continued to stare at him, as they had done for days, but now they held a greater glint of fear in their eyes, a more uncertain look on their faces. Barto couldn't understand it, because for the first time since he'd come to this place of sanctuary, he felt more relaxed, more at ease, as if his life had indeed been renewed.

Seeing how the underground people had changed, how their attitude toward him had shifted, Barto knew something must have occurred. He could sense it. "What has happened?" he said.

Gunnar looked at him and answered crisply, "Your friend Arviq has gone on a rampage. He broke out of his room, and he's escaped."

Barto bolted to his feet. He understood Arviq's impulses. He had felt them himself, and now alarm bells rang out in his head. "What has he done?"

Juliette took a deep breath and momentarily closed her eyes, as if the subject itself made her uncomfortable. "He broke his way out of the room. He smashed some windows in the corridors, destroyed one of our greenhouses. That was an hour or so ago. No one has seen him since."

Barto pushed his half-finished breakfast away and stood tall and strong. *Called back to active duty.* He didn't need any more sustenance, no more food to distract him. His mind became focused again, delving into the old hunter/survival mentality.

"I know how he thinks, and I know what he's doing," Barto said. "You cannot let him get away."

"We can't stop him," Gunnar said. "He'd kill all of us if we tried."

Barto shook his head. "You don't understand what Arviq can do, or what will happen if he gets away from this place. You can't just ignore him." Then he looked over at Juliette again. He finally admitted to himself that she was beautiful.

"Can *you* stop him?" Juliette said. "It would be to protect us."

"I will need my armor and my helmet if I'm going to do this."

At first the armor felt rough and strange, but rapidly Barto adopted it as a second skin. The protective covering *belonged,* as much a part of him as his bones and muscles.

Looking at her soldier, Juliette wore a concerned expression, as if he had too easily stepped over the brink. Barto saw something unreadable deep within her brown eyes, a flush on her elfin face, as he picked up the helmet. He looked at her uncertainly one last time, then seated it firmly on his head. He pressed the side speakers against his ears, lowering the visor in place so that he looked at her through filters and scanning devices instead of his own eyes.

Barto drew a deep breath, stretching his chest against the armored breastplate. He flexed his arms against the hard bicep plates, the forearm protections, the gauntlets. His torso was solid and impenetrable. His legs and back, shoulders, hips, everything could withstand the worst that Arviq threw against him.

Barto was invincible.

"I must stop him before he leaves," he said. "He'll report the location of this place to HQ."

Juliette hesitated, moved forward and then stopped, as if she wanted to embrace him but was afraid to. Barto was glad she didn't. He didn't want to get close to her, like this.

The tall chaperone Gunnar stood beside her, his face grim, and he drew her back. "Let him go now, Juliette. He has a mission."

Barto turned and marched out of the room, summoning up his mental map of the underground civilian sanctuary. He would begin in Arviq's quarters, where the point man had smashed his own room and broken loose. It would not be too difficult to pick up his former comrade's trail. Barto knew how to track down a quarry.

Leaving the other inhabitants behind, he followed the tunnels. Most of the civilians reacted with fear when they saw him now. They hid within their own quarters or clustered together in the communal halls, though only one unarmed soldier had gone on a rampage. It was all beyond their experience.

All of these people cowered down here, helpless. And Barto was the only one who could protect them.

Though Arviq had not been able to retrieve his armor or his weapons, Barto did not underestimate him. A properly trained soldier could fashion defensive materials out of just about anything.

At the pried-open door, he stood motionless, assessing Arviq's damaged room, saw how his comrade had wrenched open the barricade using a piece of the bedframe as a lever, how he had battered the walls with his bare hands. Barto saw blood, but knew that Arviq would pay no attention to such minor cuts and bruises. Not Arviq.

Barto had seen him through much worse.

One time on a recon-and-destroy mission, Barto and his point man had ventured into the crumbling ruins of what must have been an impossibly large building, now scarred, empty, and blasted. The structure had fallen into rubble with haphazard girders and broken glass protruding from poured stone walls.

They had chased several Enemies into the wreckage. Their senses screamed that it was probably an ambush, but still the two soldiers had followed, weapons drawn, confident that they could defeat their opponents. He and Arviq separated and traveled along different passageways, using their scanners to pick up infrared footprint traces.

Barto had proceeded cautiously, but Arviq, incensed and determined, charged through the darkened halls, knocking wreckage aside. Finally he had crashed down a rickety iron staircase that shattered into rust as he stepped on it. And he dropped through to the underlevels. . . .

When Barto had found him later, he saw that Arviq had broken his left leg in two places and had sprained his right ankle. His helmet visor was cracked and damaged—yet still Arviq had pulled himself along to find the Enemy. Though severely injured and at an extreme disadvantage, he had slaughtered both of the Enemy soldiers.

From their missions together, Barto knew that his comrade was utterly relentless, feeling no pain and no fatigue. Nothing would stop him from escaping the underground enclave. He would never give up.

And neither would Barto give up. He was the only thing that could keep this civilian paradise protected and intact.

He strode out and moved briskly along the corridors. His bootsteps ricocheted off the metal walls. Arviq had smashed windows and thrown loose objects from side to side, leaving a painfully clear trail—until he had learned better and sensibly stopped his rampage.

Then tracking him became more of a challenge. Barto called up a detailed implanted map of all the underground corridors, which Juliette had added to the information systems in his helmet.

Arviq was running blind, by instinct, just trying to escape, but his movements displayed a pattern. On the map gleaming inside his visor, Barto could see the best paths, learn where to go . . . where to intercede.

Arviq didn't have a chance against a fully armed, fully outfitted soldier, like Barto.

He marched along, his senses tuned to a high pitch. He moved carefully in case the other soldier had set up some kind of booby trap or ambush. That was to be expected. Arviq must know Barto would come after him.

Because Arviq was without his armor, his bare feet left a trail of infrared images on the clean floorplates. The marks were old and fading, but still identifiable with Arviq's genetic signature: droplets of sweat, skin particles, even stride length gave evidence of his passage. The soldier was still bleeding from one of the cuts he'd inflicted upon himself in escaping from the room; occasionally a telltale crimson droplet reinforced Barto's tracking.

The control voice returned, insistent and self-confident. It comforted Barto, who had lived his conscious life hearing the words: "KILL THE ENEMY! KILL THE ENEMY! KILL THE ENEMY!" He no longer felt so alone.

According to the map display, Arviq had made it to within several hundred meters of the long access ladder that led up the shaft to the outside—the battleground where their squad had been killed.

But Barto also knew he had cornered his quarry.

At an intersection of the dimly lit corridors, a framework of girders and support beams held up the ceiling. The place had been long-abandoned by the underground civilians.

Barto's visor-sensors detected a large smear of blood at floor level in a corner, as if Arviq had rested there . . . or as if he had encountered an Enemy, and they had struggled, hand-to-hand. The blood was fresh, wet, warm in IR—like a sign emblazoned there to draw his attention.

Too late, he realized the ambush. From the shadowed support girders above, Arviq let out a loud cry and dropped on top of him. Though he had no armor and no. weapons, the other soldier crashed down upon him with brute force. Barto might have found the conflict absurd if Arviq hadn't been so determined, so passionate—if the other man hadn't been his own comrade for so long.—

Arviq wrapped his left arm in a vice-lock around Barto's neck, trying to wrench the helmet off his head. With his other hand he tried to grab one of the ID-locked weapons sealed in armored holsters on Barto's hips.

Barto rose up like a tank, as if his armor gave him stimulus and energy, though Juliette had told him his artificial adrenaline pumps were disconnected from the suit.

Inside his ears, the helmet commanders shouted, "KILL THE ENEMY! KILL THE ENEMY! DON'T LET HIM ESCAPE!" With a weird disorientation, Barto thought the voice sounded like Gunnar's.

Without letting go, Arviq fought like a wild thing, clamping his knees on either side of Barto's armored chest, trying to tear the helmet off. When Barto staggered backward, slamming his comrade against the metal wall, Arviq let out an explosive exhale of pain and surprise. Barto recovered his balance and slammed him against the wall a second time.

Arviq struggled, but would not let go. He continued pounding with naked fists against the impenetrable armor.

"Come with me!" Arviq shouted loudly enough to penetrate the heavy ear coverings, to break through the harsh command voice. "Let's go back to HQ. Back to our lives, Barto! We don't belong here."

Barto bent over and butted him against the wall, hearing ribs crack this time. Arviq's grip finally loosened. He wheezed in pain, coughed blood. "Let me go then. Just let me run from here. I'll leave." Arviq slumped to one side and scrambled to his feet. Blood from his raw wounds smeared Barto's scuffed armor.

"Can't let you do that," Barto answered. "You must stay here. The commanders gave their orders. Defy them, and you're a traitor."

Arviq stood up, glaring at him. His face was uncovered, his emotions unmasked. "This isn't what we were made for. We are soldiers. War is our life. Not this . . . where we're pets on display." Barto had never really studied his comrade's face before. "What happens when they get bored with us?"

Barto pressed his gloved palm against the hilt of his ID-coded blaster weapon. The device detected its proper owner and released its grip in the holster. Barto yanked the weapon free, held it in his hand.

Not far down the corridor, he could see the tarnished rungs that rose up the dark shaft. It would take so little for Arviq to scramble up the ladder, pop the heavy hatch—and be out, all alone on the blasted battlefield. Without armor or weapons, he didn't have much chance of survival—but Arviq seemed desperate enough to take that option.

Arviq gathered himself up, glared at his former comrade and stepped away. "I know what I am, and what to do." With the back of his hand, he wiped a smear of blood from his mouth. "Which one of us is the traitor, truly?" He turned and, moving slowly, not threateningly, took a step toward the ladder, the escape.

Barto raised the weapon. "Halt."

Arviq turned to look at him with flinty, determined eyes. "I'm dead down here anyway. If I can't get back onto the battlefield, then you may as well blast me now."

Barto powered up his weapon.

The other soldier took two more steps down the corridor.

Inside the helmet, Gunnar's voice shouted, "KILL THE ENEMY! DON'T LET HIM ESCAPE. YOU MUST PROTECT US. KILL HIM!" Barto leveled the blaster at the target.

Then he heard another voice—Juliette's—muffled and distant, but coming closer. She cried out, running down the long-abandoned corridors toward him. "Don't shoot, Barto. You must learn not to kill if you're going to stay here."

"KILL! KILL!" Gunnar's voice bellowed.

Arviq turned as Juliette appeared, all alone, her elfin face distraught. Then he used the moment of distraction to dash toward the rungs.

"KILL!" shouted the voice in Barto's ears again. And he did.

Depressing the firing stud, he blasted his former comrade in the back as he ran. Arviq had no armor, no protection whatsoever. The bolt flared out and incinerated him, turning the other man into a smoking pile of burned bones and cooked flesh that fell in a heap on the floor, as if still trying to run.

"No!" Juliette cried out, but it sounded like a pout. Barto turned to see her standing there. Her expression was stricken, and then even more terrified as he faced her, the charged weapon still in his hand. "I wanted you to stay here with me," she said. "It's a better life, but you've got to learn not to kill. Stay away from violence. You've earned it. You could live here with me in peace and enjoy your life, escape the horrors of war."

"They're not horrors," Barto said in a flat voice. He refused to take off his helmet. He was a soldier now, fully armed, ready to fight. "It's the only thing I know." He holstered the warm blaster. "I can't stay here as a prisoner of war."

"But you're a free man among us," Juliette pleaded, refusing to come closer. She seemed as much confused as saddened. She couldn't understand why he would make this choice.

"I am still a prisoner," he said. "War holds me prisoner." He stood at attention, as if the feline spies were watching him from the shadows. "I must live by fighting, and I must die by fighting. I have no way to escape that."

He understood now that this place, despite its comforts and its new experiences, could not possibly be for him. Not for a soldier.

He didn't begrudge Juliette her civilian life, her pampered existence—and if these people were indeed the commanders in the war, if he was a soldier charged with protecting them, then he must go back and do his duty until death inevitably claimed him on the battlefield. And if he should happen to survive, then he would grow old and train other soldiers until the war was won and the Enemy completely vanquished.

There was nothing else for him to do.

Juliette watched him with despair, then a flash of anger in her brown eyes. Finally, her slender shoulders drooped in defeat. She said nothing else, just watched him with a flush in her cheeks.

Barto didn't know what he had really meant to her . . . if he had merely been a trophy from the battlefield, something that increased her prestige among her people — or if she had really cared for him, in a way.

At the moment it didn't matter. It was irrelevant information.

Leaving his dead comrade behind, sad that the bloodhounds could never retrieve Arviq and take him back to where he could be buried with full military honors, Barto climbed the rungs of the ladder.

It was a long way to the surface, but when he released the hatch and climbed out under the open, bruised sky, he stared for a long moment. He breathed the burnt air, studied the roiling dust from distant explosions.

He lifted his visor to stare out across the stricken field with his own eyes, then he shut the hatch behind him, sealing Juliette and her world underground, keeping her secret safe. And then he strode off, heading in the direction of his HQ.

It would feel good to get back to the business of fighting once again.

Introduction to
Much at Stake

Of all the Dracula stories and movies and books I have seen, not many focus on the historical Prince Vlad the Impaler, a horrific figure in his own right, a genuine folkhero in the Balkans. For the anthology The Ultimate Dracula, *I considered the grave contrasts between Bela Lugosi's classic portrayal of the Count and the legendary basis of Vlad Tepes. After learning that Lugosi himself was a heroin addict and possibly strung out during the filming of Tod Browning's* Dracula, *I realized this gave me the fantastic hook to bring these two men together for a story.*

Normally, it's simply not cost-effective to spend four or five months doing research on what will ultimately be just a short story. But I am very pleased with "Much at Stake," and it has since been reprinted at least five times in various languages. Sometimes the investment is worth it.

Much at Stake

BELA LUGOSI STEPPED OFF THE MOVIE SET, LISTEN-
ing to his shoes thump on the papier-mâché flagstones of
Castle Dracula. He swept his cape behind him, practicing the
liquid, spectral movement that always evoked shrieks from his live
audiences.

The film's director, Tod Browning, had called an end to shooting for the day after yet another bitter argument with Karl
Freund, the cinematographer. The egos of both director and
cameraman made for frequent clashes during the intense seven
weeks that Universal had allotted for the filming of *Dracula*. They
seemed to forget that Lugosi was the star, and he could bring fear
to the screen no matter what camera angles Karl Freund used.

With all the klieg lights shut down, the enormous set for Castle
Dracula loomed dark and imposing. Universal Studios had never
been known for its lavish productions, but they had outdone
themselves here. Propmen had found exotic old furniture around
Hollywood, and masons built a spooky fireplace big enough for a
man to stand in. One of the most creative technicians had spun
an eighteen-foot rubber-cement spiderweb from a rotary gun. It
now dangled like a net in the dim light of the closed-down set.

On aching legs, Lugosi walked toward his private dressing

room. He never spoke much to the others, not his costars, not the director, not the technicians. He had too much difficulty with his English to enjoy chitchat, and he had too many troubling thoughts on his mind to seek out company.

Even during his years of portraying Dracula in the stage play, he had never socialized with the others. Perhaps they were afraid of him, seeing what a frightening monster he could become in his role. After 261 sell-out performances on Broadway, then years on the road with the show, he had sequestered himself each time, maintaining the intensity he had built up as Dracula, the Prince of Evil, drawing on the pain in his own life, the fear he had seen with his own eyes. He projected that fear to the audiences. The men would shiver; the women would cry out and faint, and then write him thrilling and suggestive letters. Lugosi embodied fear and danger for them, and he reveled in it. Now he would do the same on the big screen.

He closed the door of the dressing room. All of the others would be going home, or to the studio cafeteria, or to a bar. Only Dwight Frye remained late some nights, practicing his Renfield insanity. Lugosi thought about going home himself, where his third wife would be waiting for him, but the pain in his legs felt like rusty nails, twisting beneath his kneecaps, reminding him of the old injury. The one that had taught him fear.

He sat down on the folding wooden chair — Universal provided nothing better for the actors, not even for the film's star — but Lugosi turned from the mirror and the lights. Somehow, he couldn't bear to look at himself every time he did this.

He reached to the back of his personal makeup drawer, fumbling with clumsy fingers until he found the secret hypodermic needle and his vial of morphine taped out of sight.

The filming of *Dracula* had been long and hard, and he had needed the drug nearly every night. He would have to acquire more soon.

Outside on the set, echoing through the thin walls of his dressing room, Lugosi could hear Dwight Frye practicing his Renfield cackle. Frye thought his portrayal of the madman would make him a star in front of the American audiences.

But though they screamed and shivered, none of them understood anything about fear. Lugosi had found that he could mumble his lines, wiggle his fingers, and leer once or twice, and the audiences still trembled. They enjoyed it. It was so easy to frighten them.

Before Universal decided to film *Dracula*, the script readers had been very negative, crying that the censors would never pass the movie, that it was too frightening, too horrifying. "This story certainly passes beyond the point of what the average person can stand or cares to stand," one had written.

As if they knew anything about fear! He stared at the needle, sharp and silver, with a flare of yellow reflected from the makeup lights—and van Helsing thought a wooden stake would be Lugosi's bane! He filled the syringe with morphine. His legs tingled, trembled, aching for the relief the drug would give him. It always did, like Count Dracula consuming fresh blood.

Lugosi pushed the needle into his skin, finding the artery, homing in on the silver point of pain . . . and release. He closed his eyes. . . .

In the darkness behind his thoughts, he saw himself as a young lieutenant in the 43rd Royal Hungarian Infantry, fighting in the trenches in the Carpathian Mountains during the Great War. Lugosi had been a young man, frightened, hiding from the bullets but risking his life for his homeland—he had called himself Bela Blasko then, from the Hungarian town of Lugos.

The bullets sang around him in the air, mixed with the explosions, the screams. The air smelled thick with blood and sweat and terror. The mountain peaks, backlit at night by orange explosions, looked like the castle spires of some ancient Hungarian fortress, more frightening by far than the crumbling stones and cobwebs the set builders had erected on the studio lot.

Then the enemy bullets had crashed into his thigh, his knee, shattering bone, sending blood spraying into the darkness. He had screamed and fallen, thinking himself dead. The enemy soldiers approached, ready to kill him . . . but one of his comrades had dragged him away during the retreat.

Young Lugosi had awakened from his long, warm slumber in the army hospital. The nurses there gave him morphine, day after day, long after the doctors required it—one of the nurses had recognized him from the Hungarian stage, his portrayal of Jesus Christ in the "Passion Play." She had given Lugosi all the morphine he wanted. And outside, in a haze of sparkling painlessness, the Great War had continued. . . .

Now he winced in the dressing room, snapping his eyes open and waiting for the effects of the drug to slide into his mind. Through the thin walls of the dressing room, he could hear Dwight Frye doing Renfield again, "Heh hee hee hee HEEEEE!"

Lugosi's mind grew muddy; flares of color appeared at the edges.

When the rush from the morphine kicked in, the pleasure detached his mind from the chains of his body. A liquid chill ran down his spine, and he felt suddenly cold.

The makeup lights in his dressing room winked out, plunging him into claustrophobic darkness. He drew a sharp breath that echoed in his head.

Outside, Dwight Frye's laugh changed into the sound of distant, agonized screams.

Blinking and disoriented, he tried to comprehend exactly what had altered around him. As if walking through gelatin, Lugosi shuffled toward the dressing room door and opened it. The morphine made fright and uneasiness drift away from him. He experienced only a melting curiosity to know what had happened, and in his mind he questioned nothing. His Dracula costume felt alive on him, as if it had become more than just an outfit.

The set for Castle Dracula appeared even more elaborate now, more solid, dirtier. And he saw no end to it, no border where the illusion stopped and the cameras set up, where Karl Freund and Tod Browning would argue over the best way to photograph the action. No booms, no klieg lights, no catwalks.

The fire in the enormous hearth had burned low, showing only orange embers; sharp smoke drifted into the greatroom. He smelled old feasts, dampness and mildew in the corners, the leavings of animals in the scattered straw on the floor. Torches burned in iron holders on the wall. The cold air raised goosebumps on his morphine-numbed flesh.

The moans and screams continued from outside.

Moving with a careful, driven gait, Lugosi climbed the wide stone staircase, much like the one on which he met Renfield in the film. His shoes made clicking sounds on the flagstones, solid stones now, not mere papier-mâché. He listened to the screams. He followed them.

He knew he was no longer in Hollywood.

Reaching the upper level, Lugosi trailed a cold draft to an open balcony that looked down onto a night-shrouded hillside. Stars shone through wisps of high clouds in an otherwise clear sky. Four bonfires raged near clusters of soldiers and drab tents erected at the base of the knoll. Though the stench of rotting flesh reached him at once, it took Lugosi's eyes a moment to adjust from the brightness of the fires to see the figures spread out on the slope.

At first, he thought it was a vineyard, with hundreds of stakes arranged in rows, radiating from concentric circles of other stakes. But one of the "vines" moved, a flailing arm, and the chorus of the moans increased. Suddenly, like a camera coming into focus, Lugosi recognized that the stakes contained human forms impaled on the sharp points. Some of the points were smeared with blood that looked oily black in the darkness; other stakes still shone wicked and white, as if they had been trimmed once again after the victims had been thrust down upon them.

Lugosi gasped, and even the morphine could not numb him to this. Many of the human shapes stirred, waving their arms, clutching the wounds where the stakes protruded through their bodies. They had not been allowed to die quickly.

Dim winged shapes fluttered about the bodies—vultures feasting even at night, so gorged they could barely fly, ignoring the soldiers by the tents and bonfires, ignoring the fact that many of the victims were not even dead. Ravens, nearly invisible in the blackness, walked along the bloodstained ground, pecking at dangling limbs. A group of the soldiers broke out in laughter from some game they played.

Lugosi squeezed his eyes shut and shivered. Revulsion, confusion, and fear warred within his mind. This must all be some illusion, a twisted nightmare. The morphine had never affected him like this before!

Some of the victims had been skewered head down, others sideways, others feet down. The stakes rose to various heights, high and low, as if in a morbid caste system of death. A rushing wail of pain swept along the garden of bloody stakes, sounding like a choir.

From the corridor behind Lugosi, a quiet voice murmured. "Listen to them—like children of the night. Do you enjoy the music they make?" Lugosi whirled and stumbled, slumping against the stone wall; the numbness seemed to put his legs at a greater distance from his body.

Behind him stood a man with huge black eyes that reflected tears in the torchlight. His face appeared beautiful, yet seemed to hide a deep agony, like a doe staring into a broken mirror. Rich brown locks hung curling to his shoulders. He wore a purple embroidered robe lined with spotted fur; some of the spots were long smears of brown, like dried spots of blood wiped from wet blades. His full lips trembled below a long, dark mustache.

"What is this place?" Lugosi croaked, then realized that he had answered automatically in the stranger's own tongue, a language as familiar to Lugosi as his childhood, as most of his life. "You are speaking Hungarian!"

The stranger widened his eyes in indignation. Outside, the chorus of moans grew louder, then quiet, like the swell of the wind. "I speak Hungarian now that I am no longer a prisoner of the Turks. We will obliterate their scourge. I will strike such fear in their hearts that the sultan himself will run cowering back to Constantinople!"

One of the vultures swooped close to the open balcony, and then flew back toward its feeding ground. Startled, Lugosi turned around, then back to face the stranger who had frightened him. "Who are you?" he asked.

The Hungarian words fit so naturally in his mouth again. Lugosi had forced his native language aside to learn English, phonetically at first, delivering his lines with power and menace to American audiences, though he could not understand a word of what he was saying. Understanding came much later.

The haunted stranger took a hesitant step toward Lugosi. "I am . . . Vlad Dracula. I bid you welcome. I have waited for you a long time."

Lugosi lurched back and held his hand up in a warding gesture, as if reenacting the scene when van Helsing shows him a box containing wolfsbane. From childhood Lugosi had heard horrible stories of Vlad the Impaler, the real Dracula, rumored to be a vampire himself, known to be a bloodthirsty butcher who had slaughtered hundreds of thousands of Turks—and as many of his own people.

In the torchlit shadows, Vlad Dracula paid no attention to Lugosi's reaction. He walked up beside him and stood on the balcony, curling his hands on the stone half-wall. Gaudy rings adorned each of his fingers.

"I knew you would come," Dracula said. "I have been smoking the opium pipe, a trick I learned during my decade of Turkish captivity. The drug makes my soul rest easier. It makes me open for peace and eases the pain. I thought at such a time you might be more likely to appear."

Vlad Dracula turned and locked eyes with Bela Lugosi. The dark, piercing stare seemed more powerful, more menacing than anything Lugosi had mimed in hundreds of performances as the vampire. He could not shirk away. He knew now how the Mina character must feel when he said "Look into my eyes . . ."

"What do you want from me?" Lugosi whispered.

Vlad Dracula did not try to touch him, but turned away, speaking toward the countless victims writhing below. "Absolution," he said.

"Absolution!" Lugosi cried. "For this? Who do you think I am?"

"How are you called?" Dracula asked.

Lugosi, disoriented yet accustomed to having his name impress guests, answered, "Bela Lugos—no, I am Bela Blasko of the town of Lugos." He drew himself up, trying to feel imposing in his own Dracula costume, but the enormity of Vlad the Impaler's presence seemed to dwarf any imaginary impressiveness Lugosi could command.

Vlad Dracula appeared troubled. "Bela Blasko—that is an odd name for an angel. Are you perhaps one of my fallen countrymen?"

"An angel?" Lugosi blinked. "I am no angel. I cannot grant you forgiveness. I do not even believe in God." He wished the morphine would wear off. This was growing too strange for him, but as he held his hand on the cold stone of the balcony it felt real to him. Too real. The sharp stakes below would be just as solid, and just as sharp.

He looked down at the ranks of tortured people covering the hillside, and he knew from the legends about the Impaler that this was but a tiny fraction of all the atrocities Vlad Dracula had already done. "Even if I could, I would not grant you absolution for all of this."

Vlad Dracula's eyes became wide, but he shrank away from Lugosi. "But I have built monasteries and churches, restored shrines and made offerings. I have surrounded myself with priests and abbots and bishops and confessors. I have done everything I know how." He gazed at the bloodied stakes, but seemed not to see them.

"You killed all these people, and many many more! What do you expect?" Lugosi felt the fear grow in him again, real fear, as he had experienced that war-torn night in the Carpathian Mountains. What would Vlad Dracula do to him?

Some of those victims below were Lugosi's own countrymen —the simple peasants and farmers, the bakers and bankers, craftsmen—just like those Lugosi had fought with in the Great War, just like those who had rescued him after he had been shot in the legs, who had dragged him off to safety, where the nurses tended him, gave him morphine. Vlad Dracula had killed them all.

"There are far worse things awaiting man . . . than death," the Impaler said. "I did all this for God, and for my country."

Lugosi felt the words catch in his throat. For his country! His own mind felt like a puzzle, with large pieces of memory breaking loose and fitting together in new ways. Lugosi himself had done things for his country, for Hungary, that others had called atrocities.

Back in 1918 he had embraced Communism and the revolution. Proudly, he had bragged about his short apprenticeship as a locksmith, then had formed a union of theater workers, fighting and propagandizing for the revolution that thrust Bela Kun into power. But Kun's dictatorship lasted only a few months, during which Romania attacked the weakened country, and Kun was ousted by the counterrevolution. All supporters of Bela Kun were hunted down and thrown into prison or executed. Lugosi had fled for his life to Vienna with his first wife, and from there, penniless, he had traveled to Berlin seeking acting jobs.

Lugosi had scorned his faint-hearted American audiences because they proved too weak to withstand anything but safe, insignificant frights — yet now he didn't believe he could stomach what he saw of the Impaler. But Vlad Dracula thought he was doing this for his people, to free Wallachia and the towns that would become great Hungarian cities.

"I fight the Turks and use their own atrocities against them. They have taught me all this!" Vlad Dracula wrung his hands, then snatched a torch free from its holder on the wall. He pushed it toward Lugosi, letting the fire crackle. Lugosi flinched, but he felt none of the heat. It seemed important for Dracula to speak to Lugosi, to justify everything.

"Can you not *hear* me? I care not if you are not the angel I expected. You have come to me for a reason. The Turks held me hostage from the time I was a boy. To save his own life, my father Dracul the Dragon willingly delivered me to the sultan, along with my youngest brother Radu. Radu turned traitor, became a Turk in his heart. He grew fat from harem women, and rich banquets, and too much opium. My father then went about attacking the sultan's forces, knowing that his own sons were bound to be executed for it!"

Vlad Dracula held his hands over the torch flame; the heat licked his fingers, but he seemed not to notice. "Day after day, the sultan promised to cut me into small pieces. He promised to have horses pull my legs apart while he inserted a dull stake through my body the long way! Several times he even went so far as to tie me to the horses, just to frighten me. Day after day, Bela of Lugos!" He lowered his voice. "Yes, the Turks taught me much about the extremes one can do to an enemy!"

Vlad Dracula hurled the torch out the window. Lugosi watched it whirl and blaze as it dropped through the air to the ground, rolled, then came to rest against a rock. Without the torch, the balcony alcove seemed smothered with shadows, lit only by the starlight and distant fires from the slaughter on the hillside.

"After I escaped, I learned that my father and my brother, Mircea, had been ambushed and murdered by John Hunyadi, a Hungarian who should have shared their loyalty! Hunyadi captured my father and brother so he could gain lordship over the principalities my father controlled. He struck my father with seventy-three sword strokes before he dealt the mortal blow. He claimed that he had tortured my brother Mircea to death and buried him in the public burial grounds." Dracula shook his head, and Lugosi saw real tears hovering there.

"Mircea had fought beside John Hunyadi for three years, and had saved his life a dozen times. When I was but a boy, Mircea taught me how to fish and ride a horse. He showed me the constellations in the stars that the Greeks had taught him." Dracula scraped one of his rings down the stone wall, leaving a white mark.

"When I became Prince again, I ordered his coffin to be opened so that I could give him a proper burial, with priests and candles and hymns. We found his head twisted around, his hands had scraped long gouges on the top of his coffin. John Hunyadi had buried him alive!"

Vlad Dracula glanced behind him, as if to make certain no one else wandered the castle halls so late at night, and then he allowed himself to sob. He mumbled his brother's name.

"Just a few months ago, in my castle on the Arges River in Transylvania, the Turks laid siege to me and fired upon the battlements with their cherrywood cannons. One Turkish slave forewarned me, and I was able to escape by picking my way along the ice and snow of a terrible pass. My own son fell off his horse during the flight, and I have never seen him again. My wife could not come with us, and so rather than being captured by the Turks, she climbed the stairs of our tallest tower overlooking the sheer gorge, and she cast herself out of the window. She was my wife, Bela of Lugos. Do you know what it is like to lose a wife like that?"

Lugosi felt cold from the breeze licking over the edge of the balcony. "Not . . . like that. But I can understand the loss."

In exile from Hungary back in 1920, Lugosi had left his wife Ilona in Vienna, while he tried to find work in Berlin in German cinema or on the stage. He had written to her every other day, but she had never replied. He learned later that her father, the executive secretary of a Budapest bank, had convinced her to divorce him, to flee back to Hungary and to avoid her husband at all costs because of the awful things he had done against his own country. Dracula's wife had chosen a different way out.

Outside, Lugosi heard distant shouts and the jingling of horses approaching at a gallop. He saw the soldiers break away from their tents, scattering the bonfires and snatching up their weapons. The Impaler seemed not to notice.

"I do not know who you are, or why you have come," Vlad Dracula said. "I prayed for an angel, a voice who could remove these demons of guilt from within me." He snatched out at Lugosi's vampire costume, but his hand passed directly through the actor's chest.

Lugosi shrank back, feeling the icy claw of a spectral hand sweep through his heart. Vlad Dracula widened his enormous dark eyes with superstitious terror. "You truly must be a spirit come to torment me, since you refuse to grant me absolution."

Lugosi did not know how to answer. He delivered his answer with a stuttering, uncertain cadence. "I . . . I am neither of those things. I am only a traveler, a dream to you perhaps, from a time and place far from here. I have not lived my life yet. I will be born many centuries from now."

"You come not to judge me, then? Or punish me?" Vlad Dracula looked truly terrified. He looked down at the hand that had passed through Lugosi's body.

"No, I am just an actor—an entertainer. I perform for other people. I try to make them afraid." He shook his head. "But I was wrong. What I do has no bearing on real fear. The acting I do, the frights I give to my audience, are a sham. That fear has no consequences." He leaned out over the balcony, then squeezed his eyes shut at the scores of maimed corpses, and those victims not fortunate enough to have died yet. "Seeing this convinces me I know nothing about real fear."

In the courtyard directly below, shouting erupted. Marching men hurried out into the night. Someone blasted a horn. Lugosi heard the sounds of a fight, swords clashing. Vlad Dracula glanced

at it, dismissed the commotion for a moment, then locked his hypnotic gaze with Lugosi's again. The anguish behind the Impaler's
eyes made Lugosi want to squirm.

"That is all? I have prayed repeatedly for an apparition, and
you claim to have learned something from *me*? About fear? All is
lost. I have been abandoned. God is making a joke with me." His
shoulders hunched into the fur-lined robe, and he reddened with
anger.

Lugosi had the crawling feeling that if he had been corporeal
to the Impaler, Vlad Dracula would have thrust him upon a
vacant stake on the hillside. "I do not know what to tell you, Vlad
Dracula. I am not your conscience. I have destroyed enough
things in my own life by trying to do what I thought was right and
best. But I can tell you what I think."

Vlad Dracula cocked an eyebrow. Below, a clattering sound
signaled a portcullis opening. Booted feet charged across the
flagstone floor as someone hurried into the receiving hall. "My
Lord Prince!"

Lugosi spoke rapidly. "The Turks have taught you well, as your
atrocities show. But you have perhaps gone too far. You cannot
undo the things you have already done, the thousands already
slain. But you can change how you act from now on. Your brutal,
bloodthirsty reputation is already well-earned. Mothers will
frighten their children with stories of Vlad the Impaler for five
hundred years! Now perhaps you have built enough terror that
you no longer need the slaughter. The mere mention of your
name and the terror it evokes may be enough to accomplish your
aims, to save Hungary from the Turks. If this is how you must be,
try to govern with *fear*, not with death. Then your God may give
your conscience some rest."

Vlad Dracula made a puzzled frown. "Perhaps we are together
because I needed to learn something about fear as well." The
Impaler laughed with a sound like breaking glass. "For one who
has not lived even a single lifetime, you are a wise man, Bela of
Lugos."

They both turned at the sound of a running man hurrying up
the stone steps to the upper level where Lugosi and Vlad Dracula
stood side by side. The messenger scraped his sword against the
stone wall, clattering. He swept his cloak back, looking from side
to side until he spotted Dracula in the shadowy alcove. Sweat and
blood smeared his face.

"My Lord Prince! You did not respond!" the man cried. A crimson badge on his shoulder identified him as a retainer from one of the boyars serving Vlad Dracula.

"I have been in conversation with an important representative," Dracula said, nodding to Lugosi. Surprised, but falling back on his training, Lugosi sketched a formal bow to the messenger. But the retainer looked toward where Lugosi stood, blinked, and frowned.

"I see nothing, my Lord Prince."

In a rage, Vlad Dracula snatched out a dagger from his fur-lined robe. The messenger blanched and stumbled backward, warding off the death from the knife, but also showing a kind of sick relief that his end would be quick, not moaning and bleeding for days on a stake as the vultures circled about.

"Dracula!" Lugosi snapped, bringing to bear all the power and command he had used during his very best performances as the vampire. Vlad Dracula stopped, holding the knife poised for its strike. The retainer trembled, staring with wide blank eyes, but afraid to flee.

"Look at how terrified you have made this man. The fear you create is a powerful thing. You need not kill him to accomplish your purpose."

Vlad Dracula heard Lugosi, but kept staring at the retainer, making his eyes blaze brighter, his leer more vicious. The retainer began to sob.

"I need not explain my actions to you," he said to the man. "Your soul is mine to crush whenever I wish. Now tell me your news!"

"The sultan's army has arrived: It appears to be but a small vanguard attacking under cover of darkness, but the remaining Turks will be here by tomorrow. We can stand strong against this vanguard—many of them have already fled upon seeing their comrades impaled on this hillside, my Lord Prince. They will report back. It will enrage the sultan's army."

Vlad Dracula pinched his full lips between his fingers. He looked at Lugosi, who stood watching and waiting. The messenger seemed confused at what the Impaler thought he saw.

"Or it will strike *fear* into the sultan's army. We can use this. Go out to the victims on the stakes. Cut off the heads of those dead or mortally wounded—and be quick about it!—and catapult the heads into the Turkish vanguard. They will see the faces of their comrades and know that this will happen to them if they fight me. Find those whose injuries may still allow them to live and set them free of the stakes. Send them back to the sultan to tell how monstrous I am. Then he will think twice about his aggression against me and against my land."

The retainer blinked in astonishment, still trembling from having his life returned to him, curious about these new tactics Vlad Dracula was attempting. "Yes, my Lord Prince!" He scrambled backward and ran to the stone steps.

Lugosi felt the walls around him growing softer, shimmering. His knees felt watery. His body felt empty. The morphine was wearing off.

Dracula tugged at his dark mustache. "This is interesting. The sultan will think it just as horrible, but God will know how merciful I have been. Perhaps next time I smoke the opium pipe, He will send me a true angel."

Lugosi stumbled, feeling sick and dizzy. Warm flecks of light roared through his head. Dracula seemed to loom larger and stronger.

"I cannot see you as clearly, my friend. You grow dim, and I can barely feel the effects of the opium pipe. Our time together is at an end. Now that we have learned what we have learned, it would be best for you to return to your own country.

"But I must dress for battle! If we are to fight the sultan's vanguard, I want them to see exactly who has brought them such fear! Farewell, Bela of Lugos. I will try to do as you suggest."

Lugosi tried to shake the thickening cobwebs from his eyes. "Farewell, Vlad Dracula," he said, raising his hand. It passed through the solid stone of the balcony wall. . . .

The lights flickered around his makeup mirror, dazzling his eyes. Lugosi drew in a deep breath and stared around his tiny dressing room. A shiver ran through him, and he pulled the black cape close around him, seeking some warmth.

Outside, Dwight Frye attempted his long Renfield laugh one more time, but sneezed at the end. Frye's dressing room door opened, and Lugosi heard him walking away across the set.

On the small table in front of him, Lugosi saw the empty hypodermic needle and the remaining vial of morphine. Fear. The silver point looked like a tiny stake to impale himself on. Morphine had always given him solace, a warm and comfortable feeling that made him forget pain, forget trouble, forget his fears.

But he had used it too much. Now it transported him to a place where he could see only the thousands of bloodied stakes and moaning victims, vultures circling, ravens pecking at living flesh. And the mad, tormented eyes of Vlad the Impaler.

He did not want to think where the morphine might take him next—the night in the Carpathians during the Great War? Or his secret flight across the Hungarian border after the overthrow of Bela Kun, knowing that his life was forfeit if he stopped? Or just the pain of learning that Ilona had abandoned him while he worked in Berlin? The possibilities filled him with fear—not the fear without consequences that sent shivers through his audiences, but a real fear that would put his sanity at risk. He had brought the fear upon himself, cultivated it by his own actions.

Bela Lugosi dropped the syringe and the small vial of morphine onto the hard floor of his dressing room. Slowly, with great care, he ground them both to shards under the heel of his Count Dracula shoes.

His legs ached again from the old injury, but it made him feel solid and alive. The pain wasn't so bad that he needed to hide from it. What he found in his drug-induced hiding place might be worse than the pain itself.

Lugosi opened his dressing room and saw Dwight Frye just leaving through the large doors. He called out for the other actor to wait, remembering to use English again, though the foreign tongue seemed cumbersome to him.

"Mr. Frye, would you care to join me for a bit of dinner? I know it is late, but I would enjoy your company."

Frye stopped, and his eyes widened to show how startled he was. For a moment he looked like the madman Renfield again, but when he chuckled the laugh carried delight, not feigned insanity.

"Yes, I would sure like that, Mr. Lugosi. It's good to see you're not going to keep to yourself again. The rest of us don't bite, you know. Nothing to be afraid of."

Lugosi smiled sardonically and stepped toward him. The pain in his legs faded into the background. "You're right, Mr. Frye. There is nothing to fear."

Introduction to
New Recuits

I never much liked history in high school because of the uninspired manner in which the subject matter was taught . . . but then I entered college and discovered professors who had a genuine passion for ancient times and places.

Though I was a Physics/Astronomy major, I became so interested in history courses that I ended up with a minor in Russian History. In one of my classes, I discovered a few off-hand references to the horrific work camps established during the time of the Napoleonic Wars. These camps were run by the brutal General Arakcheev, with the blessing of the normally gentle Tsar Alexander I. Immediately I sensed material for a very creepy story, and when the professor handed out a term paper assignment, I decided to use that as an excuse to do my research.

Unfortunately, Arakcheev's workcamps were so obscure that virtually no books had been published on the subject, and few scholarly articles had been written, even in Russian (much less translated into English). Nevertheless, I found enough details and all the material for a dark fantasy plot. When I delivered the term paper, the professor was quite pleased; he said he had learned a great deal about the concentration camps and that he had never read such details before.

I smiled and said, "Then I should make up my information more often."

He was not in the least amused.

In any event, as accurate as I could make it, here is my story of what might have happened in those obscure Russian encampments. . . .

New Recruits

April 28, 1825

MY DEAREST TANIA,

In the military colonies of our beloved Tsar Alexander I, circumstances do not often grant me an opportunity to write you a personal letter—a truly *personal* letter which none of them have read beforehand. Things are still in a state of confused shock here after the tragedy—some of the buildings are still smoldering, and Lieutenant Goliepin has assumed temporary command; but he has not had us drill for two days now—and I am taking these precious moments of solitude to write you what I fear will be a rather lengthy letter.

Perhaps you may understand the reason for my prolonged silence once you realize the daily routine we undergo here. General Ursov, who was our commanding officer, believed that perfect discipline is the highest achievement any man can hope to accomplish in his lifetime. Thus we spend three days a week in intense military drill from 6 A.M. to 11 A.M. and then again from 2 P.M. to 10 P.M. But then, Tania, you are not accustomed to the slavery of clocks, so these numbers probably mean nothing to you. On alternate days we erect new buildings since Ursov insists that "building is the best means of ensuring that one's name will be remembered after one is dead"—we also drain the land, dig ditches and clear the stumps and stones . . . and we attempt to reclaim the swamp near which our colony is situated, which turns into a death-trap mire every spring when the snow melts.

I believe the peasants, though, have it even worse than we soldiers do. They must rise two hours before us to care for the cattle, wash down the sidewalks, sweep the streets, sand the paths, or clean the latrines. And they must also drill with us in the morning, before going out into the fields to till the soil, *in uniform*. Even their six-year-old boys are required to drill. If only the Tsar knew what it was like—surely he'd change things.

Tsar Alexander said that he wanted these colonies to be places where we soldiers could settle down in times of peace, grow our own food, and live with our families. All I know is that I have been here almost a year—and you, dear sister, and the rest of my family are still not with me. It almost brings tears to my eyes when I think of the day I was conscripted. How you and Mother wept, how the rest of the village already mourned me as dead. Twenty-five years of military service! I might as well be dead. I remember how Father and I drank too much vodka, for it was expected that I overindulge on the last night of my freedom. And then the next morning, riding in the lurching wagon along the muddy, pitted road, my head throbbing and my insides churning, and adding my own groans to those of the other new recruits riding in the crowded back of the wagon. I remember it rained that day—a light, misty rain . . . a gray rain. . . . That was over a year ago.

I am writing this letter myself, Tania, for I have perfected my knowledge of how to read and write here. I am hoping you will know to take this to Father Paniskii—how is he? Is he still alive? —and he will read it to you. Father Paniskii always liked me—he was always so kind. I first learned from him how to read, remember? He was going to send me to one of the church schools, but I was taken into the army before I had finished my lessons from him—barely enough time for me to learn to manage by myself. Old Endovik says that I am lucky to have a priest that I love, for he says the only priest he remembers from his village was a mean, unfriendly man. Endovik has been in the army so long.

Endovik is the man I live with—*lived* with; I still cannot believe he is dead. But his death was the means for me to get this letter to you—you shall see. I must tell all this in order, lest I lose my sanity by going off on too many tangents. You know me, Tania, as does Father Paniskii, so you know I am not a liar or a storyteller. And I sincerely hope that you will show this letter to no one else, for they will surely not believe me—especially after the "official statement" of what happened here is released. You must believe me—you will see.

It was spring, and wet, and miserable—perfect for the outbreak of cholera which struck our camp. Over one quarter of our population died from the disease, in throes of vomit and diarrhea which brought about the exhaustion which killed them. The peasants suffered worse than the soldiers did—and while both Endovik and I escaped the sickness, both of our peasant hosts died within hours of each other. They were a childless peasant man and wife, who had been kind to us and looked on their two soldier "lodgers" as the children they had never been blessed with. When we weren't drilling, Endovik and I helped them with their chores. They died, with the last words of each asking how the other had fared. "Regaining strength," we had said. "Coming along nicely."

We were taken to new, hastily erected barracks which were crowded with all the refugees from other cholera-stricken households. Every home which had encountered cholera was abandoned, and due to the strict, almost vicious measures of General Ursov, the epidemic was contained within one section of buildings.

No one can say what Ursov intended to do with the abandoned buildings. In all sensibility he should have burned them to the ground—everything a cholera victim has touched or even gazed upon should be destroyed as a precaution against further spread of the disease. But the General's stubborn . . . one could almost call it *worship* of the things he had accomplished, which would not allow him to destroy the buildings erected under his command.

The houses are symmetrically arranged along the main road— a watchtower stands for observing the fields; the chapel and the fire station are in the center of the village, surrounded by the officers' quarters and other administerial buildings. One entire block of houses along the road stood empty, waiting for new occupants.

General Ursov had ordered new recruits from the Tsar in St. Petersburg, and he worked us survivors harder to make up for the loss of workers—and still he did not relax our military training. "Discipline is more important than rest," Ursov had said. I'll add my curse to all those others who have cursed him at one time or another, for one reason or another.

Even before it seemed possible—only four days after Ursov had sent his request to Tsar Alexander—the new recruits arrived. It was not possible that a message could have reached St. Petersburg, that the Tsar could have arranged for new troops and sent them to our colony in only four days. Yet they were here, and we looked on them as a blessing. A blessing! At the time we did see them as such. I think of them differently now.

The rain had stopped in order to make way for the heavy fog which had rolled in, wet and gray. The soldiers were standing in ranks for our military drill which had already gone on for several hours. We were wet and cold and exhausted—but if we had let any of it show we would have been given an extra part of an hour of practice. Endovik doesn't have to drill much with us—he's a veteran; he had survived his twenty-five years of military service. Endovik was a tough old man. He had been conscripted in 1799, before Tsar Paul I was assassinated, then served under our Tsar Alexander. He had fought against Napoleon at Borodinó in 1812, and he helped erect this military colony in 1818, almost exactly seven years ago to the date. He had survived his term of service— one of the few, for twenty-five years of discipline like Ursov's is not easy to survive—and now the army, by its own promises, was forced to take care of him, begrudgingly. Tsar Alexander doesn't know how bad things are—I am sure of it.

But, I promised I would not digress. We were standing in the fog, drilling monotonously, when we saw someone marching down the main road, spectral figures silhouetted in the fog. Now, these military colonies are isolated, and no one is allowed in—not government officials, not police—without the express permission of the commanding officer. We didn't know what to think of the strange figures in the fog, until they emerged.

A young corporal, dressed in an old, dusty uniform, marched at the head of a column of twenty peasants, all thin and covered with scanty, tattered garments in the cold and wet. Their skin was pale, and their eyes were blank and staring as if they had had their very souls wrenched from them. They made no sound—no speaking, no shuffling of feet, simply quietly stepping as they marched past the troops standing at attention in the midst of our drilling.

Ursov watched as the corporal marched up to him. The General frowned, as if he vaguely recognized the other man but could not place him. Ursov seemed troubled.

The corporal halted in front of the General, saluted, and presented himself and his column of peasants. "General Ursov," he said, "I am Corporal Belidaev. I have brought you these new recruits, as you requested, to replace some of the colonists who fell in your tragic epidemic." Belidaev gestured to the vacant-faced peasants, allowing his words to sink in. Then he spoke again. "They are from the village of Vendeévna."

Ursov's eyebrows shot up, and it seemed to me that he paled rapidly. The General fidgeted, and the expression on his face seemed not to be able to decide which final form to take, as if he could not enforce the discipline on his own emotions which he demanded of his troops.

Belidaev stood placidly, matching his stare with those of the peasants. Ursov endured it uncomfortably until he turned to Lieutenant Goliepin. Goliepin is Ursov's little servant who does everything the General tells him to. Goliepin isn't very bright and that's why the General likes him. In fact, I think I have a sharper mind than the Lieutenant—and it is very shocking, believe me, the first time you realize that you are truly more intelligent than your superiors are!

Ursov snapped to Goliepin, "Lieutenant, see to it that these new recruits are placed in the empty buildings."

"The *empty* buildings, sir?"

"You are standing right next to me, Goliepin—has the fog gotten into your ears?"

Goliepin dug a finger into his left ear, seeming to take the General's question seriously. "No, sir. But the empty buildings are—"

Ursov's temper was rising. "I know full well which buildings I am talking about! If I didn't know about them, I could hardly *suggest* them, now could I?"

"But—"

"Goliepin!" Ursov roared, his face livid, all traces of his former pallor gone. "Am I not the commanding officer here? Do I not give the orders? And are you not to follow them? Without question! I leave this matter in your hands—I trust the new recruits will be settled adequately."

Ursov turned and stormed away toward his private quarters. He was very upset and did not look at Goliepin standing confused in his wake, nor at Belidaev and his peasants. We soldiers were all very mystified. Belidaev was grinning to himself.

The atmosphere of the barracks in the evening always contains a mixture of different emotions. After a long session of drilling, which encompasses most of the afternoon and all of the evening, the prevailing mood is exhaustion. And the next day we would labor in the fields, or out in the swamp trying to "reclaim" it.

We were crowded in the hastily erected barracks, and the noises of many men drifted through the air, mingled with the odors of sweat and dirt. Some of the newer soldiers could be heard whimpering in their sleep, dreaming of wives or families or villages left behind for the next twenty-five years. Endovik says that the ones who whimper never survive the term of service. I wonder if I whimper in my sleep. A dim lantern stood in the center of a small wooden table, surrounded by four soldiers attempting to play a game about which no one could remember the rules precisely, but that didn't seem to bother them much. They couldn't cheat if no one knew the rules anyway.

Endovik's bunk was next to mine—technically he was a farmer-colonist now that he had retired, free to till his land and be self-sufficient. But many things had been changed in the crisis of the epidemic. Many of the men lay wide awake in their bunks, staring and trying to find whatever they wished for. That's the funny thing about exhaustion—it is harder to sleep if you're completely exhausted than it is if you aren't tired at all. By the time your muscles and nerves relax enough to permit sleep, it is time to wake up anyway. Oh well, not even the Tsar can change that.

Endovik usually stayed awake to talk with me, since he knew I wouldn't be able to sleep for some time. Those were the times when I missed you the most, and also the times when life in the military colonies was the most bearable. Endovik and I became great friends during those quiet conversations. Poor Endovik.

I told him about the new recruits, and Corporal Belidaev, and Ursov's reaction to the name of Vendeévna.

"Vendeévna?" Endovik said, and I looked at him to see that he was frowning, searching his memories. "Vendeévna was the name of the village that was here—before the colony. General Ursov had us tear it down to erect the colony. . . ."

"Why would Belidaev say his peasants were from Vendeévna then? Could there be another village with that name near here?"

Endovik pursed his lips and scratched his cheek by the mole under his ear. "Maybe you should know more about our General Ursov, Alexis," he said to me.

I lay on my back and listened—Endovik was good at telling stories.

"Ursov was the fifth son of a nobleman, and entered the army in the hope that his family name might bring him more success than the family fortunes would have. He fought against Napoleon at Borodinó under Field Marshall Kutuzov—and was the only survivor of his company because he hid in the dark corner of a ruined peasant home as soon as the heavy shooting started. Instead of being hung for cowardice as he should have been, Ursov was promoted. He had noble blood in his veins. I fought at Borodinó too—I was even shot in the arm."

Endovik fumbled with his shirt, but it was dark, and I had seen the scar before anyway. "If only the Tsar knew. . . . " We both sighed. Endovik continued.

"That was the time when I was half-finished with my term of service. The memories of my family were just numb spots in my mind, and the anticipation of getting out of the army was a dream, endlessly far away.

"After the wars, Ursov was given a soft administerial position in the military, right where he could embezzle money which was supposed to buy better food and uniforms for the soldiers. Then the Tsar started his program of military colonies, and transferred Ursov out of his easy desk job and dropped him here in the wilderness to establish a new colony!" Endovik allowed himself a small chuckle. I was beginning to suspect that he was making much of this up, but I didn't know how much, nor did I really care.

"Tsar Alexander had selected this piece of land to be the site of Ursov's colony—out in a muddy swamp—where stood a generations-old peasant village named Vendeévna. It was common practice in erecting a military colony to raze the existing village, level it to the ground, and build a new military colony on the site, each building constructed according to a master plan. However, the peasants of Vendeévna had lived in their traditional village for as far as their memories stretched into the past—and they realized that Ursov was a lazy desk-man who had gone to fat in the previous few years.

"The peasants of Vendeévna rose up and refused to allow the construction of the colony, saying that the document of authorization from the Tsar had been forged—even though none of them could read—because the Tsar would never do such a thing.

"Then Ursov changed into a completely different person. He was like a raving, bloodthirsty general. He resented being here even more than the soldiers did and decided to make things even more miserable for the rest of us. Perhaps he saw a chance to make up for his cowardice at Borodinó—although he would probably make me run the gauntlet if he knew I had suggested he has a conscience—maybe there were other reasons. The General had us soldiers take out our weapons, fit the bayonets. We were to put the peasants in their places by violence.

"I remember one of our soldiers . . . I can't remember his name . . . was originally from Vendeévna, and he refused to fight against his own townspeople. Ursov shot him dead right in front of all of us and ordered the rest of us to attack—our muskets and bayonets against sticks and pitchforks . . . we had seen what would have happened had we disobeyed the General's orders. What could we do? The soldiers had been worn thin from Ursov's discipline—and he unleashed them to burn and pillage. I don't know how many peasants were killed before Vendeévna surrendered. Ursov sent the survivors out into the steppe, without provisions, with orders to travel to the nearest military colony, which was about a hundred *versts* away, with no villages in between." Endovik sighed, "We never received word if any of them reached their destination. . . ."

The old man drew a heavy breath. Many of the other soldiers had already gone to sleep. I was startled by the sudden darkness as the gameplayers extinguished their lantern and got up from their table, groping in shadows to find their bunks.

"But why would anyone claim to be from Vendeévna seven years after that village was leveled?"

Endovik was silent for a short while, then spoke. "I just tell the stories—don't ask me to explain them."

Three days a week we practiced our military drill. On alternate days we worked. Hard. Since it was springtime, most of the soldiers and peasants were out working in the fields, plowing and planting. Lt. Goliepin had taken Corporal Belidaev and his twenty peasants out into the swamp to try to "drain" it. Nobody really knew what they were doing out in the swamp—Goliepin least of all—but they were kept busy sloshing in the mud, skirting the deep and treacherous muddy pools, and digging random trenches that led nowhere.

I had been assigned to sweep the streets and sidewalks, due to the cholera-inflicted shortage of peasants. This was the first time I had done this job, but I found it much more tolerable than working in the swamp, or even in the fields. Ursov is very imaginative, I must admit, for he can find tasks which absolutely *must* be done that no one else would even think of doing. Such as sweeping the trunks of trees. . . .

It was midmorning, and I had been working for five hours. I had swept most of the main street clean, and I was working on the walk in front of General Ursov's headquarters. I was tired, but I dared not rest so close to the General's watchful eye. I kept working, and it was very quiet.

But peace doesn't last very long in the colony. I heard a horse coming, and looked up to see Goliepin galloping down the street toward the General's headquarters. Goliepin looked agitated, and his horse, covered up to its belly with globs of mud, looked angry at him for being so stupid as to bring a horse into the treacherous swamp. I watched the lumps of mud the horse left in its wake to mark its hoofprints, standing out in a bold trail down the center of the street I had just spent five hours sweeping.

"General! General!" Goliepin cried as he charged up the walk. I had to leap out of the way or be trampled. "There's been an accident!"

Ursov burst out of his office, a half-crumpled piece of paper in his hand. Goliepin tried to catch his breath, but Ursov would have none of it. "Well, what's happened? Have you—"

"One of the peasants is drowned! He fell into a deep pool of mud in the swamp and sank under! We tried to get him out, but ... the mud must be softer than I thought—we couldn't find him! Not even his body! And the other peasants just . . . just stood there!"

Ursov reacted strangely to the news of the death. He appeared almost happy for a moment, or relieved may be a better word. Then he suddenly turned angry and snapped at Goliepin. "You shouldn't have left them alone out in the swamp just to tell me about the death of a peasant, you fool! They're under your *command!* You aren't a messenger boy, Goliepin! Now make the rest of them work harder for their carelessness!"

Goliepin looked confused for a moment, then seemed to think better of being confused; he saluted, turned his horse and rode back down the clean street, laying down another set of hoofprints. I looked at the mud and sighed. One doesn't complain.

We stood rigidly in our ranks, enforcing absolute discipline on ourselves. Our faces betrayed no emotion, our bodies allowed no movement whatsoever, not even a shiver in the cold night. It was time for the final roll call before retiring to our barracks; Ursov seemed to find it helpful to our sleep that we each get a good chill before turning in. Our uniforms were old and thin, and did little to keep out the cold wind.

All the colonists stood in neat lines, facing the General who stalked back and forth in front of the ranks, hands clasped behind his back. Goliepin went carefully down each column, counting with his fingers, and losing track more than once so that we had to stand in the cold longer while the Lieutenant corrected his error.

Goliepin went to the single line of the twenty silent peasants under the supervision of Corporal Belidaev. Belidaev stood serenely as Goliepin counted his charges. Once again, the Lieutenant's voice broke out in a half-whine of surprise. "General!"

Ursov had been watching Belidaev intently, and strode over as Goliepin shouted again, abruptly lowering his voice as he realized the General had stepped closer. "The new peasants are all here!"

Ursov frowned, "And should they not be? They were under your command."

"No, sir, General! I mean they're *all* here! Even the one who drowned! Well, he didn't drown if he's here—I mean the one we *thought* had drowned! The one *I* thought—"

Ursov pushed past the babbling Lieutenant and moved slowly down the column of peasants, glaring at each one of them. He came to the man, an old man, caked with mud, his clothes, his hair—mud dried even on his eyes and lips, in his mouth and teeth. He stared at the General with unblinking eyes, and made no sign that he saw anything.

It took a supreme effort for the rest of us soldiers not to break discipline and turn our heads to watch the silent conflict. We could feel the tension crawling in the air, and we were certain that much more was here than we were aware of.

"Excuse me, General." The voice startled Ursov in the silence, and he snapped his head up. Belidaev had spoken. "I did not mention this before, but I believe you knew my sister?"

It appeared as if someone had physically struck the General. Ursov stormed up to Belidaev, and his face was terrible to see, yet he also appeared helpless at the same time.

"Surely you must remember her, General?" Belidaev continued, his voice mildly taunting. "She had long brown hair in braids. And a mole on her left cheek?"

Ursov seethed, and Belidaev raised his voice, almost shouting into the General's face: "A *mole on her left cheek!*"

Something snapped in Ursov, and he let out a cry of rage as he struck Belidaev a blow across the face which would have toppled a horse. Belidaev stood firmly.

"Tomorrow morning you shall endure the *knut!*" Ursov roared, and he stormed off to his private quarters, but it seemed almost as if he fled.

Belidaev smiled.

When we finally retired to the barracks, generally with more noise than was necessary (but then we needed some release from the amount of control Ursov's discipline forced on us), I found Endovik already in his bunk. I spoke to him, but he didn't answer. I frowned, knowing he couldn't be asleep with all the commotion the soldiers were causing, and upon bending closer to him I saw that he had a strange pallor. He was shivering.

"Endovik?"

His face had a tight expression of pain and discomfort, and when I touched him, his skin had a clammy feeling. Tears swam in front of my vision.

"Endovik?" I asked again.

He opened his eyes and sighed heavily. "I know. . . ."

We both had seen enough of the epidemic in the past weeks that neither of us could have any doubt. We had watched the same thing happen to our peasant hosts. I wanted to run away, but I couldn't. Not from Endovik.

"Could you help me to the infirmary, please, Alexis?" Endovik looked up at me; and I helped him out of his bed.

That was the bravest thing I have ever done in my life — it required more courage than any battlefield would have. I remember stumbling across the compound, together in the darkness, Endovik leaning heavily on me, his steps uncertain. At any moment I waited for the fatal germ to cling to my clothes, to be inhaled in each breath, wondering if I had already contracted cholera, if I was already doomed. Endovik was shivering all the way, or was it me?

When I finally returned to my own bed, I lay shaking for a long time, listening to the silence which Endovik's breathing normally filled. . . .

A heavy feeling of tension, uneasiness, filled the air as we filed out of the barracks early the next morning to witness the punishment of Belidaev. The sun had just risen, and the air was still chill as we marched to the plaza where we normally drilled at the center of the colony.

Ursov sent a group of soldiers with bayoneted muskets to the cholera houses to bring forth Belidaev and the peasants. The General's face was bright and smiling in anticipation of the event. Ursov seemed to feel that since he was in a position of importance he was required to strike back viciously at anyone who questioned his authority, to fight back at anyone who fought against him. He knew he had not earned his rank—especially after his cowardice at the battle of Borodinó—and perhaps he felt he had to struggle harder to keep it, as he had against the insurrection of the original peasants of Vendeévna. And now Belidaev and his peasants were frustrating the General because they seemed to be taking care to do nothing Ursov could fight against. They were like ghosts from his past who had come—not to haunt the General—but to let him haunt himself.

Two of the soldiers reappeared, stiffly resting their guns on their shoulders, flanking Belidaev as he marched toward the General. Behind them came the column of twenty peasants, also closely guarded. I could see no reason for this and I am certain I wasn't the only one mystified, since neither the peasants nor Corporal Belidaev had ever shown any form of resistance whatsoever.

Belidaev, however, did not seem to be disturbed in the least when he walked up to Ursov, even pulling slightly ahead of his guards (which we found to be one of his strangest actions yet, since each of the other colonists lives in mortal terror of the *knut*).

"Good morning, General!" he said.

Ursov's face went livid with rage, and he angrily barked orders for Belidaev's two escorts to strip the Corporal of his shirt and to bind him to a sloped wooden post sticking out of the ground at an angle. Dried blood stained the post and the ground around it, for we were forbidden to scrub this reminder of past punishments while we were forced to keep the rest of the colony so meticulously clean.

Belidaev rested against the post and did not struggle as the soldiers lashed his wrists together—more tightly than they had to, but they had no wish to incur the General's rage. The peasants of Vendeévna stood silently, looking on with their staring eyes.

Ursov removed a long rawhide lash from his belt, holding the sweat-polished handle in one hand and caressing the braided leather thongs with his other. For the occasion he had added several sharp metal barbs to the end—I had not seen him do this for any other's punishment.

"Before you whip me, General, aren't you going to announce my *crime?*" Belidaev called, his voice pitched to draw the greatest irritation from Ursov. "You do remember my *crime*, don't you, General?"

This evoked a brief murmur from the onlookers, almost a murmur, before they caught themselves and remained silent. Indeed, none of us understood exactly what Belidaev was being punished for.

Ursov responded with a violent crack of the whip, striking across the Corporal's back. Belidaev didn't wince, or show any outward sign of pain; but a thin red line of blood appeared on his back.

"Hah! So you do bleed!" the General cried out, as if this were some odd sort of victory.

"You sound as if you expected otherwise, General?" Belidaev spoke calmly. Ursov whipped him again, and again.

And again, for a full hour. The pattern of interlaced red lines on Belidaev's back had been obliterated by the flow of blood—but still the Corporal showed no pain, nor did he ask for any release from his punishment. He seemed to be drawing strength from the very ground his feet were touching, from the air he breathed, from the place that was Vendeévna.

The General too was drawing strength from his own reservoir of anger and bitterness, from some wellspring within himself which poured forth hatred for this Belidaev with a greater intensity than I have ever before seen, in any man!

At last Ursov, exhausted, had to pause for a moment. He wiped sweat off his forehead and his upper lip, reaching inside his coat for a silver flask of vodka. He filled a capful, took a small sip, then downed the rest in a gulp. The General replaced the flask and wiped his sweaty palm on his pant leg before gripping the whip handle again.

Ursov continued the beating for another hour, leaving us to wait and watch when we would normally be practicing military drill. The peasants of Vendeévna remained silent, looking on with their staring eyes. The General was trembling and seemed incapable of continuing.

Belidaev himself finally looked weakened; his eyes were closed, his back was shredded, and the flesh hung in bloody strips. As Ursov watched, the Corporal slowly slid down the post slippery with his own blood, and fell to his knees.

Ursov seemed to draw strength from this and shouted for the doctor to bring smelling salts. The doctor seemed to have been waiting for this, and passed the smelling salts in front of Belidaev's face, reviving him. The doctor was a particularly uncaring man, with rough patches of stubble always scattered on his chin, as if he never shaved but could not grow a beard. His eyes were dull and tired. As Belidaev struggled to get to his feet, Ursov continued the beating again until the Corporal collapsed once more.

Like a wolf pouncing on his fallen prey, the General removed some small metal spikes from his pocket and savagely branded Belidaev on the forehead and both cheeks, leaving ugly, raw wounds. Smiling, he rubbed gunpowder into the bleeding facial wounds so that the scars would be permanent; then Ursov stepped back to inspect his work.

Belidaev was silent, huddled against the post. Ursov turned smartly to glare at the peasants, as if to find some signs of despair or compassion for the Corporal. The General seemed furious when he failed to find any. He strode up to the peasants, glaring at them, slowly pacing before each one of them, gloating.

"You see, filth, I command here! My word is power in this colony, and your resistance has no effect. Belidaev is weak — you are all *nothing!* My command comes directly from the Tsar —" The General stopped before the old man who had vanished into the swamp mire; the peasant was still caked with dried mud which clung to his hair, his lips, his eyes. "And my every action is sanctioned by him!"

Abruptly, the mud-covered peasant spat full in Ursov's face. The General looked as if his throat would burst as his roar tried to charge out of his mouth.

"Soldiers! I want every person in this colony to form two columns! Goliepin! See that *every* man has a rod or whip! Every one of these accursed peasants will run the gauntlet! With a full thousand men on a side! I will see their blood run on the ground!"

"Haven't you seen that already, General?" A hoarse voice — Belidaev struggling against the ropes that bound him to the post. Ursov stormed over to him and kicked him savagely in the left kidney.

"You seem not to care about your own pain, Belidaev; I hope you find the punishment of your peasants more enjoyable!"

The gauntlet was formed rapidly. Ursov clapped his hand on certain soldiers as he passed, indicating that they were to lead the peasants between the two lines of soldiers armed with sticks and whips. Each soldier, when chosen, went up to a peasant, bared the peasant's back, and pointed the bayonet of his musket at the other's chest, lashing the peasant's hands to the barrel of the gun. The peasants offered no resistance whatsoever.

A long stick like a broom handle was thrust into my hands, and I knew what I had to do. I stood uneasily in line, waiting for the peasants to be led past. I saw the doctor kneeling by Belidaev, and I was angry for a moment, wondering why he had left Endovik. And then the peasants began to march between the two columns of soldiers.

It is a strange thing to have to beat someone you hold nothing against, someone you don't even know. Yet with Ursov watching us, we had to strike the peasants with all the strength we could manage — or we would end up running the gauntlet ourselves. As the peasants filed by, the soldiers holding their muskets were crouched and wary, lest they be struck themselves as they moved slowly backwards.

The blows fell, and the peasants didn't seem to mind. They uttered not one sound, and I struck with all my might, for Ursov stood near me. An old peasant woman was led past me, but she did not flinch when I tried to crack her skull with my wooden rod. My arm was numb from the force of the blow, yet an *old woman* did not feel it!

The peasants were taken through the gauntlet, and none of them fell. Not one, not even the oldest and frailest among them. They waited at the end, and Ursov was livid. He stormed forward and grabbed the man who stood next to me. "*You!* You weren't striking hard enough! Send them through the gauntlet again!" the General shouted, "And you will follow them through as punishment for your laxness!"

Then Ursov pointed at me, and my blood froze in my veins as I thought I would be forced to run the gauntlet myself. But then I realized I was to lead my companion through. His hands were stiff and trembling as I lashed them to my musket, pointing the bayonet at his chest. His eyes were wide, and I could not tell if he hated me for doing this. I didn't even know his name — that made things easier.

We followed the peasants of Vendeévna through the two columns of throbbing sticks and whips. The man I led winced and cried out and stumbled as each blow fell — but the peasants made no sound. About halfway through the long column, my companion collapsed and would not get up again as his blood oozed through bruises and smashed skin. Ursov ordered for a flat sled to be brought, then made me slide the almost unconscious man on it. I then continued to drag the man through the lines as the other soldiers beat his motionless form.

I was drenched with sweat, both from exertion and anxiety, as

I emerged from the end of the lines; the other soldiers who had led the peasants looked in a similar condition, far more distraught than the peasants themselves were. The peasants were unscathed. The doctor nonchalantly shuffled forward to look at the bloody man on the sled as Ursov bellowed for the peasants to run the gauntlet again.

The soldiers all groaned—not aloud, of course, as they were too afraid of the General for that—but I could sense their dismay. "Not this one, General," the doctor said, indicating the man I had led. "He won't survive it."

Ursov scowled. "Take him to the infirmary, then." He glared at the peasants, as if to say 'How dare you emerge without a scratch while one of my men undergoes half what you have and almost dies.' That look was so filled with hatred that I know I would have shriveled up right there if it had been directed at me.

"Belidaev, too?" the doctor mumbled, breaking Ursov's silent anger.

"No! He can stay in the barracks!" Then the General, at the peak of his frustration, dismissed the troops. He turned his back to all of us and strode off toward his office, looking for all the world like a mighty man who had just had his own impotence held out before him.

It was dark and silent in the barracks; most of us were asleep, and even the sounds of the men were muted as they went deeper into their dreams, or their nightmares, or the day's strange events. I was thinking about Endovik.

The door burst open, striking the wall to which it was hinged with a flat *crack*, waking us in an instant. Ursov stood alone, framed in the doorway, silhouetting himself with the glow from the lantern he held in his left hand. The General entered the barracks, his boots making his footsteps loud on the wooden floor. He was fully uniformed, carrying a pistol in his belt and his whip in his right hand.

"Up! *Up!*" he shouted hoarsely. Ursov strode among the bunks, rapping them with the wooden handle of his whip as the soldiers struggled to their feet. "Up, scum! You have a task to perform! Dress yourselves as quickly as you can! Hurry!"

We did so, at first muttering among ourselves in our weariness; and then, remembering our fear of the General, we pulled our clothes on in silence, hastily buttoning enough buttons to make us look dressed. Then Ursov ordered us out of the barracks and into three lines.

We were marched across the compound to the three buildings where Belidaev and the peasants of Vendeévna were housed, standing next to the other cholera-emptied buildings.

"Another case of the cholera sickness has been reported," the General spoke to us. "To prevent another epidemic, the doctor has placed the victim in the strictest isolation, and will not allow even the medical staff to tend him, lest they pass along the disease." Rage filled me, and I almost flung myself at Ursov. Endovik! They weren't even tending him!

"We must burn these plague buildings and everything in them to prevent another epidemic!"

Ursov ordered us to gather straw and pile it up around the buildings, so that we could set them on fire. We worked uneasily, and the General became increasingly impatient.

Finally, one of the soldiers spoke up. "General, sir, shouldn't we . . . shouldn't we get the peasants out first?"

Ursov snarled and cracked his whip across the soldier's back. "You will follow my orders! Without question! I command! Do I not control this colony and everything in it? By the order of the Tsar!" The soldier was cowed and went back to work; the General turned and muttered quietly, almost to himself, "We will see if they are demons or not."

Next we were ordered to gather up hammers, nails, and pieces of wood with which to board up the doors and windows of the three occupied buildings. Each of us worked rapidly, afraid, and the three buildings were quickly secured. The strangest thing, to me, about the entire business was that the occupants of the buildings never stirred, never shouted, never tried to break out, not with all our sounds of hammering, and Ursov's shouting. An eerie, unnatural sensation filled all of us. Perhaps the General was right —maybe the peasants of Vendeévna *were* unholy demons. Enough had happened since the new recruits had arrived that none of us was certain what to think any more.

Ursov's voice was laced with fear as he ordered the straw set on fire, as if he knew he finally had to confront Belidaev in an unearthly duel, but did not know what the outcome would be. The fires were set first on one of the buildings, then the next, and finally the third building where the bleeding form of Belidaev had been taken earlier that day.

The wood burned quickly, as if eager to cleanse itself, hungry to be purged of the cholera and of the spirits within. Each of us waited, fascinated by the flames, waiting with dread to hear the first screams of the peasants within. But they never came. The wood cracked and spat as it was consumed, and the fires began to climb the walls.

Belidaev's building was in flames—and the door was suddenly flung open, the boards barricading the door shattered as if they did not exist. Belidaev stood in the doorway, framed in flames—all his lashes and bruises were healed, even the brands on his cheek and forehead had vanished. He stepped out of the burning building and turned to face Ursov, glaring at him with eyes made of shattered pain and ice.

"Good evening, General," Belidaev said.

Ah, Tania, the horror as I write this!

Ursov used a mask of rage to cover his fear, and he lashed out at Belidaev with his whip. The General gasped in pain of his own and let the whip fall, looking in astonishment at the line of torn cloth across his chest, as if he himself had been whipped. Belidaev was untouched. Ursov fingered the sticky blood on his chest.

"You see, General, you continue to bring about your own punishment." Ursov stood speechless, his fear forming its own discipline.

Belidaev crossed his arms over his chest. "Do you know what night this is, General? This is our anniversary. Do you remember what happened seven years ago, General?"

Ursov clenched his fists into tight balls, but he seemed too much afraid to take any direct action.

"The peasants of Vendeévna rose up against you and your military colony—but you had them put down with your muskets and bayonets. You *ordered* your soldiers to pillage and burn— Vendeévna had to be razed anyway, you said, to establish the military colony here. One of your soldiers, a Corporal Belidaev, had been born and raised in Vendeévna before being drafted into the Tsar's army. When he tried to speak out to protect the people of his village, you shot him in front of the other soldiers to show them what would happen if they disobeyed the *great* General Ursov who had fought so *bravely* at the battle of Borodinó. Do you remember shooting poor Corporal Belidaev, General?"

"You are lying!" Ursov shouted.

"And after you had turned your soldiers loose on the village to rampage, you went through the people yourself like a wolf. You raped my sister Marta, General—do you even remember? She had long brown hair, braided—and a mole on her left cheek. You told her you would shoot our parents if she did not submit—and even though in her fear she cooperated with you in every way, still you rammed your bayonet into her throat when you had finished with her! Do you remember? You thought you had no conscience, General—I am here."

"You can't know! You were dead!"

"The village of Vendeévna was here for generations, General. The peasants farmed here, sweated and died here—for *generations*. You don't think you can remove all that by tearing down the buildings and erecting your own? Your military colony, General, is like a thorn in the skin of the earth, which is being pushed outward. The time has come, General—the splinter will be removed."

Ursov turned to us with a strange, wild expression in his eyes. "Lies! They are not true!"

The building roared in flames behind Belidaev, but he didn't seem bothered by the heat. He beckoned to Ursov. "Would you care to enter the fires of Hell a few moments sooner, General?"

Ursov grabbed the pistol from his belt and pointed it at Belidaev. "You will die, demon!"

"Yes!" Belidaev hissed. "The demon will die!"

The General fired—and fell to the ground with a bullet hole in his chest, and shock on his face. His blood soaked into the soil of Vendeévna to mingle with the peasant blood he had spilled there so many years ago.

Belidaev laughed and turned to step inside the burning building, vanishing in the flames.

Just this morning, when some of the soldiers ventured into the still-smoldering wreckage of the cholera buildings—under direct orders, since no one had willingly ventured into them since the night of the fires—they found no bones or any other remains of Belidaev or the peasants of Vendeévna. Somehow I wasn't surprised.

I went to visit Endovik this morning, but he had already died. The doctor wouldn't even let me say goodbye to the body of my friend. It was too risky, he said. However, Endovik's death is allowing me to send you this letter. Lieutenant Goliepin has the command now, and he is very confused with all the new duties thrust upon him. I have told him that Endovik had a sister, and I asked him if I could write her a letter of consolation. Goliepin was happy to have one small duty taken from him and he quickly waved me away. He won't have time to read this letter either, and so I will trust that it reaches you uncensored.

I believe that the "official" story states something to the effect that Ursov died of cholera, and the buildings were routinely burned to remove the threat of pestilence. Officially, we never received any new recruits from Vendeévna.

Give my love and greetings to Father, and I will write you again if I can, but it may not be possible for a while. Know that you are with me and that you are my strength to endure twenty-five years of military service. I love you all, and God's blessing upon you.

Alexis

Introduction to
Final Performance

When I learned that Shakespeare's famous Globe Theatre had burned down during the initial performance of his play, "Henry VIII," I began to sense the possibility for a story. When I discovered that the theater itself had been torn down and rebuilt using the same wood, and that some players may or may not have been murdered there . . . well, I decided it just had to be a ghost story.

After having my short fiction appear for years in numerous small press magazines, "Final Performance" became my first professional sale to The Magazine of Fantasy and Science Fiction.

With the popularity of the Academy Award-winning film Shakespeare in Love, *the Globe Theatre has since become familiar to many people.*

This story, though, is a bit darker.· . . .

Final Performance

SCENE I

London, this last day of June, 1613. No longer since than
yesterday, while Burbages' Company were acting at the
Globe the play of Henry VIII, and there shooting off certain
(cannons) in way of triumph, the fire catched and fastened
upon the thatch of the house, and there burned so furiously
as it consumed the whole house, all in less than two hours,
the people having enough to do to save themselves.

— Thomas Lorkins, eyewitness
to the burning of the Globe Theatre

Setting — London. *Night. The charred ruins of the Globe Theatre.
Little remains of Shakespeare's playhouse: skeletal, blackened beams,
the stone foundations. It is late November 1613 — a light dusting of
snow covers the ground.*

Enter Cuthbert Burbage, *half-owner of the Globe, brother of
Richard Burbage, who is the famous actor of the Lord Chamberlain's
Men, Shakespeare's company.*

230

STRANGE HOW SILENT LONDON WAS SO LATE AT night. The houses surrounding him were dark, all candles extinguished for the night as sleeping townspeople huddled under deep piles of blankets. It was a cold November.

His breath congealed into thick plumes of steam as he walked, looking upward at the stars—intensely bright in the cold, crisp air. His left hand was kept warm from the rising heat of the lantern he carried, spilling out a small pool of dirty orange light on the snow ahead of him. The numb fingers of his right hand groped among the folds of his coat pocket, searching for warmth.

Burbage's cheeks were flushed, and his ears hummed in the silence; his belly felt warm and full from the several tankards of beer he had drunk at the inn. The loud voices and forced laughter still rang in his ears. But everything else was silent now: the night air with barely a breeze, the thin covering of snow which seemed to muffle his footsteps. He had so little to do now—and it would remain the same all winter—with only his trips to the inn, until spring. In spring he and Richard were going to rebuild.

His footsteps impressed black marks on the new snow in Maiden Lane, and he stood before the ruins of the Globe. Only a few charred beams stood upright, painted white with a thin coating of snow—like the skeletal remains of some mythical beast. It was dark, and he could see little by the light of his feeble lantern: a pile of burned timbers and blackened foundation stone blocked his view of the stage.

A sadness filled him—perhaps the beer made him more susceptible—but it was an eerie, powerful, almost tangible emotion. This, the greatest theatre in London, which once had seated fifteen hundred people, now stood a pile of cinders and lonely ash.

No one had died in the fire, even though they had had a full house that last day. Well, one *had* died . . . but not from the flames. Burbage had carefully covered that up: the brothers planned to rebuild the Globe, and superstition would drive people away from a playhouse where it was known a murder had been committed.

The external feeling of sadness strengthened, and waves of despair and pain buffeted him, seeming to emanate from the ruins, like the cries of a mortally wounded animal in its death throes. Burbage frowned: he hadn't realized how much beer he had drunk. Now, perhaps, he understood the way Richard felt every time he came near this place.

But then Richard had always been the sensitive one, the one

so filled with passion. At times, Burbage envied his brother, who was so sure of himself always, totally devoted to his profession as an actor. Richard's one desire was to perform on stage, and he did such a tremendous job. He lived for the Globe—Shakespeare himself had written many parts specifically for him to portray. Cuthbert Burbage had also acted on stage, only occasionally; but to him it was nothing more than repeating the lines he had memorized, picturing himself as a tool to move the play along. For Richard the characters were *real*.

It was not a hating envy he had for his brother, but a gentle one. Richard had no doubt as to his calling in life. The other Burbage was still waiting for his own calling. He had acted at times, when it was necessary; he also managed the Globe Theatre, because his father had bequeathed it to Richard and him—and because he did a good job at it. His brother was a superb actor, and he himself a shrewd businessman. The combination worked well, the previous success of the Globe had proved that.

But he wasn't sure that the loss of the Globe was the only reason for Richard's recent moody behavior, his anxiety. Being as popular as he was, Richard had little trouble acting in some of the other theatres in London. But he had seen something that night, when the Globe had burned, something that had shaken him badly. Burbage had waited for his brother to tell him, waited; but it had been five months, time enough for Richard's wound to heal . . . or fester.

Perhaps things would be better come spring, when they could rebuild the theatre. Smiling vaguely, he remembered when they had first built the Globe, fifteen years before. Their father had built his own playhouse, The Theatre, in 1576—the first playhouse in all of London—in all of Europe, Burbage had heard (but who could possibly know all of Europe?). And on their father's death over twenty years later, The Theatre had passed on to Richard and Cuthbert Burbage—just as its lease ran out.

The landlord, one Giles Allen, was a singularly uncooperative man, despite Richard's impassioned speeches about an actor's need to have a playhouse in which to dissipate his creative energy, despite Cuthbert's tedious, patient negotiations. Allen had it in his mind to tear down the original playhouse because of "the greate and greevous abuses that grewe by The Theatre."

But the Burbages had turned the tables on him, tearing down The Theatre themselves and using the old wood, taking it to the south side of the Thames where they had erected the new Globe

Theatre. Burbage chuckled aloud as he remembered Giles Allen, his face splotchy, almost exploding with anger, cheated out of destroying the playhouse himself.

His low chuckle seemed alarmingly loud in the deep silence. Around him, the snow seemed to muffle all other sound; even the wind had stopped. He tensed as his ears, numb from the cold, picked up a low sound, a strange sound. The thin blanket of snow had been left undisturbed since the last snowfall early the previous morning—only his own footprints left a trail to the ruins. He was the only one around—he had to be. The effects of the beer buzzed in his ears—perhaps they were playing tricks on him. He took another step into the ruins, stopping beside a blackened beam fallen at an odd angle. He rested his hand on the charred wood; melted snow ran along his fingers, carrying black particles of soot. He listened again, and he was sure. He looked at the snow around him—no one had entered the ruins in the past day.

Yet inside, unmistakably, he heard voices.

SCENE II

On December 28, 1598, Richard and Cuthbert Burbage "and divers other persons, to the number of twelve . . . armed themselves . . . and throwing down the sayd Theatre in verye outrageous, violent and riotous sort . . . did then also in most forcible and ryotous manner take and carry away from thence all the Wood and timber thereof unto the Banckside . . . and there erected a newe playhowse with the sayd timber and woode."

—Giles Allen, in a lawsuit
against the Burbages in Middlesex Court

Setting—London. *The Globe Theatre, intact, before the burning. Morning. In the basement under the stage is* Thomas Radclyffe, *a young actor, rehearsing his lines, making sure he is satisfied with their delivery. He has been cast as Henry VIII in Shakespeare's new play, "All is True," which will be performed for the first time at the Globe this afternoon.*

The basement is dim and shadowy, lit only by the light shining through the open trapdoor of the stage. It is cluttered with old props, a discarded mask of a ghost from an old play, costumes hung from sharp garment hooks on the wall beams.

Radclyffe closed his eyes tightly. He *was* Henry VIII. He filled his chest, thrusting it forward in a kinglike manner; he propped one hand on his hip. He imagined himself to be dressed in the garments King Henry wore in the portraits he had seen. His personality was putty, changing, fitting into a new mold, as an actor was required to do. He was almost ready.

His master, Havermont, had shown him this technique to *know* his characters, to *be* the people he was to portray. Radclyffe had been attached to Master Havermont almost seven years, lodging and boarding with the experienced actor since he had been ten years old. Thomas Radclyffe had been an extremely apt pupil—a bit impulsive, a bit impatient, his master had said, but Radclyffe wasn't sure now if the impressions he had given hadn't also been mostly an act.

After sending him through the typical women's roles—the bane of all apprentices before they started to sprout whiskers—Havermont had prepared him for the veteran actor's own particular types of parts so that Radclyffe could take his place at the time of his master's death.

And now Radclyffe had had the role of Henry VIII pressed upon him. Havermont had died suddenly; Radclyffe was not yet quite prepared, and perhaps he had let it go to his head a bit—his first salaried role, and it was *almost* the leading man. But Radclyffe took it seriously—he always took his acting seriously—spending much of his free time down here, in the musty peacefulness of the basement of the Globe, where he could be totally alone, and let his dialogue fall into the quiet psyche of the theatre.

The lines came into his head—he was ready for them. He took up where he had left off the day before, trying to set his mind in the same mood. King Henry has just been informed that the people are outraged over a new tax, levied by the evil Cardinal Wolsey—no, not "evil," not yet, for the King still considers him a trusted friend. Wolsey, played by Richard Burbage, is the *real* star of the play, in a part written by Shakespeare especially for Burbage. But the audience would go from the play remembering *him*, Thomas Radclyffe, Henry VIII.

He lowered his voice, taking on a forgiving, almost condescending tone, placing himself into the reality of the play. He is a King, he told himself, about to remove a tax he considers unjust, a tax which he has known nothing about, which Wolsey has placed upon the people but has just denied doing so. The King holds Wolsey as friend, and believes him.

" 'Things done well and with a care exempt themselves from fear; things done without example, in their issue are to be fear'd.' "

"*Louder.*"

Radclyffe reacted instinctively, raising his voice. " 'Have you a precedent of this commission? I believe, not any.' "

"*More regal—more pride! With rising anger!*"

" 'We must not—' " He paused, looking around the shadows of the basement, frowning. "Who is there? Who has spoken?"

"*With rising anger! What is the next line? 'We must not rend our subjects from their laws, and stick them in our will.' This must be spoken angrily—not in a condescending tone.*"

Radclyffe became distressed, looking around the cluttered, cobwebbed shadows of the Globe's basement, but saw no one. He listened to the voice, trying to pinpoint it—but it was a whisper, an echoing melange of voices.

"Where are you?" Then his eyes centered on something, propped up against the wall, a mask used once for the part of the ghost of Hamlet's father. He felt an eerie chill crawling in the skin of his back. "*What* are you?"

Radclyffe moved toward the mask slowly, afraid, but intrigued.

"*A part of your profession. A muse? No, not quite so . . . quaint. We ARE the Globe Theatre.*"

Radclyffe picked up the mask, his fingers trembling. He looked to see if anything hid behind it—nothing. The frozen, empty mouth of the mask continued to pour forth its words.

"*Thirty-seven years ago James Burbage built The Theatre—the first playhouse in all of Europe. And then his sons Richard and Cuthbert Burbage tore it down and used the same wood to build this, the Globe Theatre. Can you think that all those performances, year after year, all those actors pouring their souls into these walls, could have no effect on the wood of this place? A part of it remains here. We are the soul of this playhouse—and you shall perform as we direct you when you perform on our stage, in our walls.*"

"No!" Radclyffe cast the mask back to the ground. The eye-holes continued to stare back at him. Anger and pride sprang from his years of training. "I would be *no* actor if I did only as you tell me. My Master Havermont has taught me to be a great performer. He has shown me that I am to interpret the characters as *I* choose; I am to say the lines as *I* decide. The acting must come wholly from *me*, or else I am just repeating words. Master Havermont is right, and I will not listen to you."

He had never doubted the existence of ghosts—nobody in

London did. But he knew that ghosts were probably evil—and probably dangerous.

The voice paused, taking on a more sinister tone. *"You hold your dead master in high esteem, then?"*

" 'The gentleman is learned, and a most rare speaker; to nature none more bound; his training such that he may furnish and instruct great teachers, and never seek for aid out of himself.' Indeed, I hold him in esteem."

"Then do you not think a part of him abides with us?" The voice was different now, familiar . . . Havermont's voice.

"Be silent! I will believe that part of him abides with you—if you are truly the leavings of great actors—but it is a *bad* part, much like the scum on top of a beautiful pond. My master would never counsel me to listen to every whim of a spectator! I will speak *my* lines, with *my* voice, and *my* mind!"

Radclyffe turned, anger on his face, perhaps to cover his fear, and stormed toward the basement steps. Suddenly he was slammed against the wall by unseen hands and held there by a force he could not define. His eyes began to show fear. The voice came at him from every beam, every shadow.

"We have more power here than you think! You would be safer if you did not resist!"

Radclyffe used his anger again to push off the paralyzing fear. " 'Be advis'd; heat not a furnace for your foe so hot that it do singe yourself!' "

Radclyffe flailed his hands in the air as if to fend off the unseen enemy, and he broke away, running quickly up the stairs.

SCENE III

Yea, truly for I am persuaded that Satan hath not a more speedy way and fitter school to work and teach his desire to bring men and women into his snare than these . . . plays and theatres are, and therefore necessary that these places and plays should be forbidden and dissolved and put down by authority.

—John Northbroke, a clergyman,
*A Treatise against Dicing, Dancing and Interludes
with other idle pastimes* (1577)

Setting—The uppermost floor of the Globe Theatre, just under the thatched roof. Raw beams cast odd shadows. Cuthbert Burbage is loading gunpowder into one of three cannons, props, which he is preparing as a stage effect for the afternoon's first performance of "All is True."

Enter Thomas Radclyffe, *moving tentatively, looking nervous, a little shaken.*

Burbage kept his eye on the stream of black powder, pouring slowly so as to spill none of it. He heard the young actor approach. "One moment, Thomas . . ." he said aloud, and thought he saw Radclyffe jump, startled, from the corner of his eye. Burbage inspected his work and looked at the other two cannons for a moment, then turned to face Thomas Radclyffe.

The young actor fumbled with his words for a moment, and found it easiest to say, "What are those for?"

"They are cannons, Thomas! Stage effects! You know, in the first act, when you, King Henry, and your party enter Cardinal Wolsey's palace all cloaked and hidden? Well, when the King enters, we shall fire these cannons—armed with only paper wadding, of course—to let the *audience* know that the royal presence has just arrived—and also give them a little start!"

Burbage smiled, rubbing his hands together, then looked at Radclyffe, dissolving his expression into a frown. The young actor was pale and gaunt, obviously frightened. "And where is the bold, proud young actor who drives us all nearly mad with his outbursts of eagerness?"

Radclyffe seemed to fumble for words; he found different ways for his fingers to interlock with each other. "Well, Mister Burbage, sir, it is difficult to—"

"Speak!" Burbage snapped, not angrily, but with a tone of get-down-to-business that stopped all further stuttering from the young actor.

"Down in the basement—this theatre—Mister Burbage, there are *ghosts!*"

"Hissst!" Burbage turned him away, then looked worriedly down to the stage where some of the other actors were rehearsing. None of them seemed to be paying any attention. "King's death-bed, man! Hush when you speak of such things! Ghosts? If that rumor were to be unleashed, it would ruin us as surely as if we were to burn the place down ourselves!"

Burbage shook his head, concerned, then looked hard at Radclyffe. "Now, these ghosts—you have seen them? Where?"

"In the basement—I didn't *see* them, but rather heard them."

Burbage let out an audible sigh of relief. "The basement! Thomas, any man can get the jitters when he's alone down there among all the old props and shadows. The wood creaks a little, a few rats rustle about here and there. And your imagination makes the rest—"

"No! It wasn't like that, Mister Burbage! Not just odd sounds, but *words!* I had a conversation with the ghosts!"

"And what did these ghosts have to say?"

"They tried to force me to say my lines in different ways, making me act in their manner, and not my own. They tried to twist my talent, taking the . . . the *life* out of my portrayal."

Burbage almost laughed, but contained himself. "Most ghosts try to murder people, Thomas—but your ghosts want to be your acting coaches!" He saw the expression on Radclyffe's face, became serious. "Maybe it's Havermont come back to help you?"

"No!" Radclyffe looked angry, upset, downcast. "You don't understand! They are *evil!* They try to twist my acting talent to their own ends! I cannot perform that way!"

The young actor stopped and changed his emotions abruptly, saddened, almost accusing. "You can't understand—you're not an actor. You don't know what it means to me." He drew in a deep breath. "You don't believe me."

Burbage didn't. But he had enough tact to pause a moment, considering the best way to handle the young actor. He reached up to put a hand on Radclyffe's shoulder. "I know you, Thomas. I know that your temper is a little short, and that you are inclined to act without thinking sometimes. But I have never known you to have a wild imagination, and I have never known you to lie. Seeing this change in your mood, now, it is obvious to me that *you* believe what you say. But I ask you this, Thomas—say no word of this matter to anyone. If you must speak further on it, come to me, and only me. Surely you realize how this could ruin us if handled improperly. Any demon a man might find at the bottom of a bottle of ale would be seen as a ghost of the Globe—and people would flock away from this 'haunted theatre' as if it were a plague house! No, we must keep silent about this."

"But the ghosts will still be here!"

Burbage sighed. "Thomas, what would you have me do? I cannot get two strongmen and have them evicted as we would any other troublemakers!"

"Bring a bishop! Someone, anyone from the Church! To exorcise the ghosts!"

Burbage widened his eyes almost in shock. "A priest? King's deathbed, Thomas! Do you spend no time out in the city, or are you always sheltered here in the theatre? Have you not heard the Puritans' outcry against all places of amusement, theatres in particular? Did you not know that my father was forced to build the original Theatre outside the city of London because of the public outcry? And even then he was brought before the London Lord Mayor in the Middlesex Court more times than you can count on your hands. No priest would come near the Globe, unless he wanted to burn it down. The Puritans would like nothing more than to hear that Satan has haunted our playhouse."

Radclyffe seemed to hear, but not believe. He lowered his voice, almost glaring at Burbage. "You and your brother should never have used the old wood from The Theatre." Radclyffe's face was angry, and he turned to walk away.

"Thomas!" Burbage called, worried. The young actor didn't turn. "Don't do anything rash!"

Radclyffe didn't answer as he disappeared down the ladder leading from the loft. Burbage looked after him for a long moment, forming his lips into a troubled frown, then he began to load gunpowder into the other two cannons.

SCENE IV

Things done well and with a care exempt themselves from fear.
—William Shakespeare, *Henry VIII*,
first performed at the Globe Theatre, June 29, 1613

Setting—the basement of the Globe Theatre. It is mid-afternoon on the day of the first performance of "All is True." Upstairs, offstage, noises can be heard as people file in to fill the theatre. The play will begin soon.

Enter Thomas Radclyffe, afraid, but moving with determination. He carries a torch he has made, naked fire pouring light into the darkness.

He paused, swallowing hard, forcing his mouth into a grim, determined line, while holding the torch in front of him like a weapon. He filled his mind with anger and obsession. Martyr—like Buckingham in the play. If need be.

"Hear me, ghosts!" Radclyffe's voice trembled, then gained in strength. "You are evil! You are oppressive! You stifle the creative expression of all actors—I must destroy you to save my profession. 'Ye blew the fire that burns ye!' "

He picked up the mask from the floor. "What? Are you silent? Have you fled?"

Radclyffe dropped the mask and crushed it under his feet, finding a small, inadequate outlet for his anger and fear. He heard the people above, waiting for the play to begin. Someone would probably be looking for him.

"You are brave, young actor—are you not afraid?"

" 'Things done well and with a care exempt themselves from fear.' " Radclyffe looked up to find the source of the voice—and saw another mask, a new one he hadn't seen before, propped in the corner of one of the beams. The mask was finely painted and detailed enough to look lifelike. Almost lifelike. It was Henry VIII, but subtly, hauntingly familiar, with definite traces of Radclyffe's own face embedded within the features.

The young actor shuddered briefly, then steeled himself. "I will burn this theatre down and destroy the cursed wood which you inhabit. You will not harm me—I have chosen this time with care—for if you do, you will expose yourselves to all of London!"

He waited for a reply, hearing only the crackle of his torch in the silence, until the voice spoke again.

"Ah, but you forget, young actor, that we ARE this theatre . . . and when we are filled with an audience—" Radclyffe's torch was suddenly snuffed out, plunging him into darkness. *"We are strongest of all!"*

And he felt a cold, icy grip, not quite like hands, around his throat. . . .

SCENE V

Will not a filthy play with a blast of trumpet sooner call thither a thousand than an hour's tolling of bell bring to a sermon a hundred?

—Stockton, a preacher,
in a sermon against The Theatre, 1578

Setting—the ground level of the Globe Theatre; the yard is filled with people, trying to get a clear view of the stage, which is raised

*above the crowd. At the entrance stands a placard announcing the
day's play. Similar leaflets are scattered throughout London, tacked
onto wooden posts, competing with many other announcements.*

*As people file through the single, narrow entrance, a man stands
with a small box in hand, collecting one penny from all who enter.
Those who are content to stand continue into the yard; those who
wish a seat or a private box are required to pay an extra sum.*

Cuthbert Burbage *sits among others in a Twelvepenny Room, one
of the best seats in the playhouse, with his guest,* Lady Dalton. *She
is older than he, dressed in gaudy finery, decked with jewels. Burbage
looks at the activity around him; he is impatient.*

"If they don't start soon, we won't finish the play before sunset,"
he muttered to himself. "Can't have a performance without daylight, you know."

"Cuthbert, this is so exciting!" Lady Dalton peered eagerly into
the crowd, as if to find out which of her social acquaintances had
failed to attend the play, and how many had failed to get seats as
exquisite as her own.

Burbage looked at her, scowling slightly. The Lady Dalton was
rather rich . . . and rather old, and rather dim. Damn his business
sense.

"Is Shakespeare *himself* here today, Cuthbert?"

"Of course he is—" Burbage snapped, "You don't think he'd
miss the first performance of his new play?" He caught himself,
placing some sweetness into his voice. "There he is, just across the
yard from us . . . see, in one of the other Twelvepenny Rooms."

"Sooo!" she cooed.

Burbage looked around uncomfortably; he wondered if Radclyffe had been found yet. The play had to start soon—he was
afraid the young actor was going to ruin his first important role
by chasing after ghosts in his imagination. *Radclyffe—don't be a
fool!*

The noises of the audience waned like a dying fire after one
of the Lord Chamberlain's Men stepped out onto the stage, speaking the Prologue. People smothered their random sounds, focusing on the words being spoken, waiting to be taken away to
another reality.

And the play began.

Burbage leaned back in his seat, relaxing slightly, or at least
seeming to. They wouldn't have started the play without Rad-

clyffe, even though he didn't make an appearance until the second scene.

Lady Dalton seemed to be more interested in the audience than in the play. Burbage watched his brother Richard perform, strutting around as Cardinal Wolsey in all his evil glory—Richard enjoyed the villain parts at times, but then Burbage could never tell what his brother really enjoyed and what was just an act.

(Wolsey accuses the innocent Buckingham, the martyr, of treason, and has him arrested, to be brought before the King's court.)

The first scene ended, and Burbage grew tense again. He sat up, waiting the unbearable few moments. Why was he uneasy? The performance was of prime importance—Radclyffe knew that—he imagined himself to be a devoted actor, and he would never miss his first important role.

The audience background noise rose up quickly for a few moments, but was dampened again as Scene II began. King Henry entered with pomp and glory—and Burbage finally felt at ease. After all, he should never have been worried. He knew Thomas Radclyffe—the young actor had been so proud of himself after receiving this part that he wouldn't have forfeited this performance for anything.

Yet Burbage squinted—and thought he saw something strange about Radclyffe's face. Of course, the makeup would have changed it somewhat—but he thought he saw sharp edges, shadows, almost as if Radclyffe were wearing a very detailed mask . . . but no, he could see the mouth move.

Still, he felt uneasy again. Lady Dalton probably couldn't even see that far.

"What is happening, Cuthbert?" she whispered.

Burbage almost imperceptibly rolled his eyes heavenward. "This is the trial of Buckingham at the King's court. Queen Katherine has just entered to beg the King to withdraw an unfair tax that takes one-sixth of every man's possessions—"

Lady Dalton seemed to be barely listening. "Who's Buckingham?"

Burbage sighed.

The scene progressed. Radclyffe's voice was the same, but Burbage seemed to notice some special quality, a lilt, an intonation, which made the young actor's voice stand out. Burbage had never considered himself a theatrical critic—he heard the lines, saw which ones were delivered more masterfully than others. And people paid to see the performances—he drew his livelihood from that. But he hadn't felt any special drive, any special presence about acting. Until now, in Radclyffe's voice, he felt the very embodiment of a performance, the life, the calling—yet he couldn't pin it down. He couldn't say why, but he was somehow aware that Radclyffe was giving the best performance he had ever seen.

Richard, though, seemed to be acting strangely. There—he had just stumbled over a line. Richard had never stumbled over a line before, not in all of Burbage's recollection. Was it jealousy? No, it was almost as if he were . . . scared of something. But what would Richard ever be so afraid of that he couldn't successfully cover it up?

The scene continued; Burbage felt a low buzz in the audience as the people remarked on how outstanding, how superb the young actor was. What would have seemed an almost interminably long scene any other time, now held them enthralled.

And at last the scene was over.

He felt a tap on his shoulder. Burbage was startled and turned to find the man next to him pointing out into the corridor where stood a young boy, one of the apprentice actors of the Lord Chamberlain's Men. The boy looked agitated, pale and sweating. He seemed unable to speak, but gestured desperately for Burbage to come to him.

"Excuse me, Lady Dalton," he whispered in her ear. She smiled. "One of my actors wishes to speak with me."

"Oh, of course, Cuthbert—please hurry back."

Burbage went to the boy as the third scene began. They spoke in quiet voices. "What is it?"

The boy was trembling. "I've found him, Mister Burbage!"

"What? *Who?*"

"Come! Quickly!" The boy took his arm and drew him down the corridor through the curtains behind the tiring room, backstage, and to the narrow basement steps.

"What could possibly be down here, boy?"

"He is dead, sir! *Murdered!*"

"Who?"

"Thomas Radclyffe, sir! He's hung up on the wall, by his neck —on one of the clothes hooks!"

"You're *mad*, boy! He's just been—"

They entered the dimness of the basement, surrounded by the muffled echoes of the performance overhead. Burbage didn't need to look very closely to see a burned-out torch on the floor, and a shadowy figure hung on the wall with its feet dangling off the floor. And the face was that of Thomas Radclyffe.

"King's deathbed!" Burbage gaped a moment, realized what he

was doing, then composed himself almost immediately, thinking fast. The boy stood next to him. Burbage made his face firm and expressionless, but he felt cold.

"This . . . could ruin us. A murder! At the Globe Theatre!" He looked quickly at the boy. "You have told no one?"

"No, sir! I thought it wisest to speak only to you!"

"Good! You are intelligent, boy. I have a gold piece for you if you tell no one. Not one word. If you *do* speak of this, I will find it very easy to destroy your acting career for the rest of your life."

"Oh, not one word, sir. Please don't feel you need to use threats, Mister Burbage."

"No . . . no. I know. I have to think of what to do. Keep quiet and be sure no one else comes down here. Calm. I must be calm. *We* must remain calm." He sighed. "I'd best be back to the Lady Dalton before she says anything. Until I can talk to Richard." He heaved a long breath, then muttered, "Oh, deathbeds for the entire royal family! How are we ever going to patch *this* up?"

They walked up the stairs. "But, Mister Burbage—if Thomas Radclyffe is dead down here . . . then *who* is on the stage?"

Burbage paused, gripping the rail. "I don't know . . . and I am afraid to know."

He walked slowly back and seated himself beside Lady Dalton as Scene IV was just beginning. He gripped the arms of the chair to stop his hands from trembling. Burbage was surprised to find her watching the play.

She pointed to the action on the stage. "What are they having a party for, Cuthbert?"

Burbage tried to get his mind back on the play, to focus on something other than his cold fear. "Uh . . . Cardinal Wolsey, my brother Richard, is having a great dinner at his palace, with many lords and ladies. See . . . they're all sitting around having idle dinner conversation, until—" He waited: it would have been gleeful and childlike anticipation in other circumstances. Trumpets sounded; drums rolled; and the cannons blasted, thundering in his ears.

And as his ears rung, Burbage thought he heard Thomas Radclyffe's voice, somehow—the real voice, not the false acting voice on the stage: this was different, a whisper running through his head, though not intended for his own ears.

"Now, we fight on equal terms."

Unseen, some of the burning paper wadding from the cannons settled on the thatched roof, smoldering, kindling itself, setting fire to the roof.

The Lady Dalton squealed in terror at the cannon sound, then in delight. The audience, half-deafened, murmured in confusion.

On the stage, a company of cloaked and hooded strangers entered, hiding their faces. Burbage continued to explain. "The cardinal's guests think these are some foreign ambassadors — but they are really the King and his party in disguise. There . . . that one is the King." *Or is it something that I will never understand?* he thought to himself. *There are more things in heaven and earth, Cuthbert Burbage, then are dreamt of in your philosophy.*

"How do you know that's the King?" Lady Dalton asked.

"From the *cannons* — we wouldn't blast cannons for anyone but the royal presence, now would we?"

"Oh."

They watched as the hooded company made its slow procession across the stage.

"There, now Cardinal Wolsey suspects that one of the masquers is the king . . . he says as much . . . and he decides to unmask him. . . ."

Burbage watched his brother walk on the stage toward one of the hooded figures, reaching up tentatively — more tentative than he actually should have been. He gripped the folds of the hood and began to draw it back.

"FIRE!" someone shouted.

Suddenly all hands were pointed toward the thatched roof which was in flames. Others took up the cry; tumult erupted. People fled toward the single narrow entrance.

On the stage, Richard Burbage cried out wildly; his face was white as a sculpture. The hooded figure was gone, the false Thomas Radclyffe, vanished. Unnoticed in the uproar.

And flames began to devour the Globe.

> . . . some of the Paper or other stuff wherewith (the cannons) were stopped, did light on the Thatch, where being thought at first but an idle smoak, and their eyes more attentive to the show, it kindled inwardly and ran round like a train, consuming within less than an hour the whole House to the very ground . . . yet nothing did perish but Wood and straw and a few forsaken cloakes. Only one man had his breeches set on fire, that would perhaps have broyled him if he had not by the benefit of provident will put it out with bottle ale.
>
> — Sir Henry Wotton, eyewitness
> to the burning of the Globe Theatre

> . . . while Burbages' Company were acting at the Globe the play of Henry VIII, and there shooting off certain (cannons) in way of triumph, the fire catched and fastened upon the thatch of the house, and there burned so furiously as it consumed the whole house, all in less than two hours, the people having enough to do to save themselves.
>
> — Thomas Lorkins, eyewitness
> to the burning of the Globe Theatre

Cuthbert Burbage found his brother Richard, much more shaken than he should have been from the fire, standing in the churning crowd around the flaming wreckage. Night was falling. A heavy beam collapsed in a shower of sparks.

Silently, together, they watched their Globe Theatre burn. . . .

SCENE VI

— Epilogue —

Setting — London. *Darkness.* Cuthbert Burbage *has entered the cold, snow-covered wreckage. Voices.*

He listened, creeping closer — the voices were strange and scattered, speaking a pastiche of lines from old Shakespeare plays. They didn't sound like children's voices; in fact, they seemed to carry a great deal of emotion, sadness, loss.

He stepped around some fallen timbers and came in view of the burned-out remnants of the stage. In the shadows he saw strange figures, masked and costumed.

"What are you doing there? Who are you?" Burbage shouted, his anger rising before he had time to think. He expected them to scatter and run like frightened children, but instead the figures turned to look at him.

Burbage stepped out from behind the wreckage and moved toward them. "Where did you get those masks?" he demanded, trying to place a tone of angry command in his voice.

The central figure turned toward him; he wore an old mask of the ghost of Hamlet's father, smashed-in but painstakingly repaired, blackened a little in the fire. He spoke in a deep, eerie voice, like many voices all in one.

"*We are the Globe Theatre, and we are almost dead. Do not disturb our final performance.*"

Burbage halted a moment, then stepped forward. "You are trespassing," he said coldly, standing directly before the figure, glaring at the mask. He saw nothing behind the eyeholes. Nothing.

They confronted each other in silence. Unexpectedly, Burbage reached up to pull the mask off, and beheld the face of a leering skull, desiccated and fire-blackened.

Before Burbage could cry out, the mask was snatched away from his numb fingers and placed back on the figure's head.

Burbage felt cold, and his eyes misted over with terror and confusion. "*What* are you?" The words slid through his clenched teeth like a cold wind.

"*A truly talented actor leaves a part of himself, part of his soul, within the theatre in which he performs. This wood, these timbers, are from the very first playhouse in all of Europe, which has absorbed countless performances. . . . We are what is left.*"

Burbage first began to tremble. "*You!* Ghosts! You are what Richard saw! You killed Thomas Radclyffe! Murdered him!"

"*We acted only to protect ourselves. In vain.*"

Burbage stood motionless, only his thoughts whirling—fear, anger, confusion—and he could not function until he accepted his inability to accept. "I do not understand . . . I cannot believe this."

"*You are not an actor. You will not understand.*" The central figure continued to stare at him with the frozen expression of the mask. "*Tell your brother Richard—he will understand. It will comfort him. He knows us, but he does not realize it. Tell him not to fear us.*"

Burbage found he had taken one step backward, and another.

The masked figure raised his voice. "*Leave us! To complete our performance!*"

Burbage felt his fear taking precedence over all his other emotions, and he took another step backward, staring at the troupe of spectral figures one final time. Then he turned to flee from the ruins of the Globe Theatre.

> The wreckage of the Globe lay in Maiden Lane, covered with snow, until the winter of 1614 passed. "And the next spring it was new builded in a far finer manner than before."
>
> —Master John Stow, *General Chronicle of England*

With a tile roof, and new timber.

Introduction to
The Old Man and the Cherry Tree

Another college history course, Medieval Japanese this time—and another term paper. I had been intrigued by the structure and archetypes in Japanese folktales, which struck me as quite different from the Western conventions I'd been brought up reading. For months, I immersed myself in hundreds of Japanese folktales until I felt I had a good flavor for the stories that had entertained the ancient Samurai and Japanese peasants.

This short piece was a "thunderbolt" story: when I was quite literally at the typewriter pounding out my term paper, I was inspired to write this story. I yanked out the paper, stuck in a clean piece, and wrote "The Old Man and the Cherry Tree" in one sitting with very little editing.

The major magazines didn't quite know what to do with this story, but I eventually placed it with a small press magazine, Grue; it was later selected to be reprinted in the Year's Best Fantasy Stories *(DAW).*

And who says term papers never benefit a student?

The Old Man and the Cherry Tree

H E HAD LIVED ALMOST HIS ENTIRE LIFE WITHIN the walls of the Buddhist monastery. The priests there told him the Shōgun would cut off his head if he ventured outside ever again.

Many years before, his father had been a powerful lord, a *daimyo*. But the Shōgun had gone to war with the *daimyo*, ordering that all the lord's family be executed. On the final night, while the father sat bemoaning the imminent loss of his life, the boy's mother had managed to steal away to the nearby monastery with her dearest son. She begged the head priest to save him, to secretly give her some other boy to be executed in her son's stead. The man told her it would be improper for a priest to undertake such a task; but after she offered large sums of money, the priest admitted that the monastery was sorely in need of a second golden image of Amida for the altar. Besides, the boy he had in mind for the exchange was a mere foundling anyway, given over to the care of the monastery however the priests saw fit.

They struck the bargain. The mother kissed her son, then gave him to the priest as he emerged from the monastery with a second boy who somewhat resembled the *daimyo*'s son.

Before the priest could take her son into the monastery walls forever, she reached into her robes and carefully withdrew a package wrapped in fine silk. Upon seeing the silk, the priest's eyes opened eagerly. "This is for my son," she said, handing it to the child. "Your father's blade—the sword of a great *daimyo*." She unwrapped the silk to reveal a lovely jewel-encrusted short sword. Gold covered the grip, and fine characters danced on the blade. "You must keep it always by you because it will bring you good luck. When all else has been forgotten, still it will tell you the name of your father—see, it is engraved on the blade. You will learn to read it after the good priest has taught you the characters." The priest's eyes reflected the gold of the sword, and he fervently promised to care for the boy. The mother bowed and disappeared with her false son into the night shadows from which she had come.

The boy grew up in the monastery. The priests soon stopped trying to take his father's sword from him when they realized they would never be able to sell it, not with the name of the rebellious *daimyo* engraved on the blade. And they never made the effort to teach him to read, considering themselves safer if the boy was not constantly reminded of his true identity.

The boy took his pleasure in gardening, caring for the plants and trees in the monastery's beautiful garden. He was especially captivated by a single cherry tree which had been planted by three novices the very morning the Shōgun had cut the heads off the rest of the boy's family. The small cherry tree had stood so frail and frightened in the garden, reminding the boy of how he must appear to the other monks.

As the boy grew older, he never shaved his head, or took the vows, nor studied the sutras as did the other novices. He planted and tended his flowers and trees and shrubs in the garden, until the monastery became known for the beauty harbored within its walls. But above all, the boy—now a young man, actually—tended the single cherry tree with all the love he possessed, until it became the glory of the entire garden. In spring the cherry tree would explode with pure white flowers, as if a sweet-scented winter had dropped gently into the monastery garden. At the time, it was said that the blossoms lingered longer on this cherry tree than on any other in all of Japan, and people traveled great distances to gather up some of the fallen petals, which they used for curing the sick and for making love potions.

Sometimes, in secret, the *daimyo*'s son would climb up into the tree and look out over the monastery walls which kept him imprisoned. None of the priests had bothered to tell him that the old Shōgun had died, nor that the new one did not care about the young man's family name. Instead, he sat up in the boughs under the silver moonlight and looked out to see the wide world he would never be able to explore, listening to the wind in the leaves of his tree and the faint sounds of snoring from the monks' sleeping quarters.

In time, he came to consider the cherry tree his closest and dearest friend. He talked to it as he tended the rest of his garden, and the other novices began to snicker and laugh among themselves about the strange gardener who talked to trees.

So the years passed. The tree continued to grow, and the gardener continued to grow older. Year after year the white blossoms came, and the *daimyo*'s son — now an old man — took no greater joy than in watching the petals drift in the wind. He wept for those that caught like kites on an updraft and escaped, floating down on the other side of the monastery wall.

Each spring many people came to see the blossoms, some even making grand processions all the way from Kyoto. The pilgrims talked among themselves about the exquisite beauty of the delicate white flowers, and of the glowing, honest satisfaction in the face of the old gardener who stood so proudly beside his tree.

And then one year the tree did not blossom.

The other plants in the old man's garden launched forth their leaves and flowers as always, but day after day the cherry tree remained barren, as motionless as a stillborn babe. The people who came to see the tree departed in disappointment — it had once been magnificent, they said sadly, but the old cherry tree had died, and they would have to go elsewhere from now on.

The monks began to talk that they would soon cut down the marvelous tree, and burn its wood in the fire.

The old man could not bear to hear this and, recalling the days of his youth, he somehow managed to climb into the tree, searching the branches for buds, any small flickering of life. But the branches were as dry and as barren as the paper on which the monks copied their sutras. The old man saw other cherry trees in the distance, gleaming with their white flowers and scattering petals into the wind. Then his heart knew for certain that the old cherry tree had died, and he threw his arms around the lifeless bole of his only friend, weeping until the curious monks came out and called for him to come down. His legs were weak, but he managed to descend the tree and stood shaking. The monks left him, whispering among themselves, and went back to their work.

As he looked long and hard at the lifeless branches of the cherry tree, the old man decided what he must do. That night, when all the monks slept, he crept out into the darkness of the garden and lifted up one of the flat rocks he had long ago placed around the cherry tree. Under the rock rested his father's jeweled sword, glinting in the light of the dying moon—the colorful silk wrappings had rotted, but the sword was untarnished and as sharp as ever. The old man looked grimly at the blade.

There was one way to show one's utmost devotion, to remove grief and end this life of confinement and pain. Brave warriors followed their lords to death, committing *seppuku* to show their absolute loyalty no matter how their lord had died. And if the warriors could slit their bellies in an ecstasy of pain and honor, couldn't the old man do the same at the death of his dearest companion, his cherry tree? His father's sword was a special sword, the sword of a great *daimyo*, perhaps even containing a little magic. This act would be his final gift to the tree he had loved for so many years.

The old man loosened his robe and squatted down as near as he could to the dead cherry tree. He held the sharp point of the *daimyo*'s sword against his stomach, looking down at the engraved characters signifying his father's name—but he still could not read them. The night was cold and crisp, probably the last such night in spring. The noise of the rustling barren branches above sounded to him like a death rattle.

Done properly, *seppuku* would have been a grand occasion—with many priests and faithful companions by his side. But the old man did not have even so much as a white cloth to sit upon. Tradition required that once he had slit his belly, once he had proven his devotion and bravery, his closest friend was then permitted to strike off his head to end the pain. But the old man had no best friend, so after he made the deep thrust and long sideways cut, he was forced to bear the pain as best he could, until he could bear it no longer . . . and then it made no difference. His blood spilled onto the earth.

The next morning the monks came out into the garden for their tea and found him there. They shook their heads, muttering at how the lonely old man had finally ended his life, but that he had not even done *seppuku* properly. The old gardener had become well known and many people—bringing their donations—would have come to see the death ceremony. The old man had been very inconsiderate not to let them know of his intentions. Some of the monks came to carry him away, and marveled at the beautiful sword they found upon him. No one knew where he had gotten it, and none of them recognized the name of the long-forgotten *daimyo* written on the blade. The monks cleaned the sword, and placed it in their treasury.

But that morning, when the sun rose high enough that its rays struck the old cherry tree, something wondrous happened. The wind picked up. A shiver ran through the ground as a silence descended on the garden. Some of the monks dropped their tea, burning their fingers, scowling at each other. Then they all looked at the dead cherry tree.

The barren branches trembled, as if the old tree were straining with all its might . . . and suddenly every branch, even the smallest twigs, brought forth a deep red flower, as scarlet as fresh blood. As the monks watched, gaping in amazement, the tree covered itself with flowers, more than it had ever borne before.

One brash novice crept up to the new flowers in wonder and touched them. He cried that the petals felt wet, then yelped in pain. "It burns! My fingers!" He tried to wipe the moisture off on his robe, then ran to hide inside the monastery.

Word spread quickly throughout the land, and people flocked to see the Blood Tree, as it had been named. The Shōgun himself came to see the miracle. When the monks told him the story of the old man who had tended the tree, and of the mysterious sword he had used to commit *seppuku,* another old man from the vicinity recalled the name of the rebellious *daimyo* and how a previous Shōgun had executed the entire family. The others remembered how at the same time the monastery had received a generous donation from the wife of the *daimyo* . . . and although they could not be certain, many guessed the identity of the gardener.

The Shōgun commanded that the monks bring him the ashes of the old man, and they carried out a simple clay urn, bowing their heads in embarrassment that they had not given the ashes a more ornate resting place. The Shōgun spoke in his most respectful voice so that all could hear. "If this old man was truly the son of a rebellious *daimyo,* trapped for all his life in the sanctuary of the monastery walls for his own protection, long after it was necessary, I . . . I, the Shōgun, now pardon him. I set him free so that he need no longer remain inside these walls."

So saying, the Shōgun reached into the urn and flung the

ashes high in the air, watching as they drifted out to explore the world on their own.

The Blood Tree shuddered, and, with a cracking sound, collapsed into a heap of charred splinters, burned from the inside out. The people gasped, and even the Shōgun was amazed.

Many years later, wandering peddlers could sometimes be seen at night, keeping to the shadows and entering houses where the seeds of dissent had already been sown, secretly offering to sell splinters of the Blood Tree which would cause almost-instant bad fortune and possibly even death to one's enemies.

The Shōgun caught several of these peddlers, and executed them.

Introduction to
Sea Dreams

This story certainly shows the influence of a collaborator, because "Sea Dreams" is unlike any short fiction I would have written alone. This is much more atmospheric, poetic, and ethereal.

The prose gained all those qualities from my wife, Rebecca Moesta, who had written several drafts of this story, originally inspired by the Beatles' song, "Julia," off the "White Album." She tried numerous approaches, but could not make the story work to her satisfaction. She finally gave the manuscript to me and asked if we could tear it down to the basics and start it all over again.

"Sea Dreams" was written for the anthology, The Immortal Unicorn (HarperCollins), edited by Peter S. Beagle, Janet Berliner and Martin H. Greenberg. You won't find any horses with horns in this story, though, just a thematic connection to the unicorn myth.

Sea Dreams

with Rebecca Moesta

*J*ULIA CALLED ME TONIGHT AS SHE HAS SO MANY times before. Not on the telephone, but in that eerie, undeniable way she used since we met as little girls, strangers and best friends at once. It usually meant she needed me, had something urgent or personal to say.

But this time I needed her, in a desperate, throw-common-sense-to-the-wind way . . . and she knew it. Julia always knew.

And she had something to tell me, too.

Alone in the tiny bedroom of my comfortably conservative Florida apartment, I felt it as surely as I felt the cool sheets beneath me, and the humid, moon-warm September air that flowed through my half-opened window. At such times, common sense goes completely to sleep, leaving imagination wide awake and open to possibilities. And she called out to me.

Julia had been gone for five years, gone to the sea. Others might have said "drowned," might have used "gone" as a euphemism for "dead." I never did. The only thing I knew—that anyone *could* know for certain—was this: Julia was gone.

It had begun when we were eleven. That year, my parents and I left our Wisconsin home behind to spend our vacation at my grandmother's oceanside cottage in Cocoa Beach, Florida.

I had grown up in the Midwest, familiar with green hills and sprawling fields, but nothing had prepared me for my first sight of the Atlantic: an infinite force of blue-green mystery, its churning waves a magnet for my sensibilities, a sleeping power I had never suspected might exist.

Excited by the journey and the strange place, I was unable to sleep that first night in Grandmother's cottage. The rumble of the waves, the insistent shushing whisper of the surf muttering a white-noise of secrets, vibrated even through the glass . . . and grew louder still when I got up and nudged open the window to smell the salt air.

There, in the moonlight, a young girl stood on the beach—someone other than Grandmother, her friends, and my parents, talking about grown-up things while I patiently played the role of well-behaved daughter. Another girl unable to sleep.

I put on a bikini (my first) and a pair of jeans, tiptoed down the stairs, and let myself out the sliding glass door onto the sand. As I walked toward the ocean, reprimanding myself for the foolhardiness of going out alone at night, I saw her still standing there, staring out into the waves.

She seemed statuesque in the moonlight, fragile, ethereal. She had waist-length hair the color of sun-washed sand, wide green eyes—I couldn't see them in the dark, but still I *knew* they were green—and a smile that matched the warmth and gentleness of the evening breeze.

"Thank you for coming," she said. She paused for a few moments, perhaps waiting for a response. As I carefully weighed the advisability of speaking to a stranger, even one who looked as delicate as a princess from a fairy tale, she added, "My name is Julia."

"I'm Elizabeth," I replied after another ten seconds of agonized deliberation. I shook her outstretched hand as gravely as she had extended it, thinking what an odd gesture this was for someone who had probably just completed the sixth grade. Which, I discovered once we started to talk, was exactly the case—as it was for me.

We spoke to each other as if I had lived there all along and often came out for a chat, not like strangers who had just met on the beach after midnight. Within half an hour, we were sitting and talking like old friends, laughing at spontaneous jokes, sharing confidences, even finishing each other's sentences as though we somehow knew what the other meant to say.

"Do you like secrets? And stories?" Julia asked during a brief lull in our conversation. When I hastened to assure her that I did—though I had never given it much thought—she fell silent for a long moment and then began to weave me a tale as she looked out upon the waves, like an astronomer gazing toward a distant galaxy.

"I have seen the Princes of the Seven Seas," she said in a soft, dreamy voice, "and each of their kingdoms is filled with more magic and wonder than the next. . . . The two mightiest princes are the handsome twins, Ammeron and Ariston, who rule the kingdoms of the North."

She had found a large seashell on the beach and held it up to her ear, as if listening. "They tell me secrets. They tell me stories. Listen."

Julia half closed her green eyes and talked in a whispery, hypnotic voice, as if reciting from memory—or repeating words she somehow heard in the convolutions of the seashell.

"They have exquisite underwater homes, soaring castles made of coral, whose spires reach so close to the water's surface that they can climb to the topmost turrets when the waves are calm and catch a glimpse of the sky. . . ."

I giggled. Julia's voice was so earnest, so breathless. She frowned at me for my moment of disrespect, and I fell silent, listening with growing wonder as her story caught us both in a web of fantasy and carried us to a land of blues and greens, lights and shadows, beneath the shushing waves.

"Each kingdom is enchanted, filled with light and warmth, and the princes rarely stay long in their castles. They prefer instead to ride across the brilliant landscapes of the underwater world, watching over their realms.

"Their loyal steeds are sleek narwhals that carry Ammeron and Ariston to all—"

"What's a narwhal?" I asked, betraying my Midwestern ignorance of the sea and its mysteries.

Julia blinked at me. "They're a sort of whale—like unicorns of the sea—strong swimmers with a single horn. Ancient sailors used to think they were monsters capable of sinking ships. . . ."

She cocked her head, listening to the shell. Her face fell into deep sadness for the next part of her story, and I wondered how she could make it all up so fast.

"The sea princes enjoy a charmed existence, full of adventure —they live forever, you know. One of their favorite quests is to hunt the kraken, hideous creatures that ruled the oceans in the time before the Seven Princes, but the defeated monsters hide now, brooding over their lost empires. They hate Ammeron and Ariston most of all, and lurk in dark sea caves, dreaming of their chance to murder the princes and take back what they believe is rightfully theirs.

"On one such hunt, when Ammeron and Ariston rode their beloved narwhal steeds into a deep cavern, armed with abalone-tipped spears, they flushed out the king of the kraken, an enormous tentacled beast twice the size of any monster the two brothers had fought before.

"Their battle churned the waves for days—we called it a hurricane here above the surface—until finally, in one terrible moment, the kraken managed to capture Ammeron with a tentacle and drew the prince toward its sharp beak, to slice him to pieces!"

I let out an unwilling gasp, but Julia didn't seem to notice.

"But at the last moment, Ammeron's brave narwhal—seeing his beloved prince about to die—charged in without regard for his own safety, and gouged out the kraken's eye with his single long horn! In agony, the monster released Ammeron and, thrashing about in the throes of death, caught the faithful narwhal in its powerful tentacles and crushed the noble steed an instant before the kraken, too, died."

A single tear crept down Julia's cheek.

"And though the prince now rides a new steed, his loyal narwhal companion is lost forever. He realizes how lonely he is, despite the friendship of his brother. Very lonely. Ammeron longs for another companion to ease the pain, a princess he can love forever.

"Ariston also yearns for a mate—but the princes are wise and powerful. They will accept none other than the perfect partner . . . and they can wait. They live forever. They can wait."

We watched the moon disappear behind us and gradually the darkness over the ocean blossomed into petals of peach and pink and gold. I was awed by the swollen red sphere of the sun as it first bulged over the flat horizon, then rose higher, raining dawn across the waves like a firestorm. I had never seen a sunrise before, and I would never see one as beautiful again.

But with the dawn came the realization that I had been up all night, talking with Julia. My parents never got up early, especially not while on vacation. Still, I was anxious to get back to my grandmother's house, partly to snatch an hour or two of sleep, but mostly to avoid any chance of being caught.

I knew exactly what my parents would say if they discovered

I had gone out alone, spent the quiet, dark hours of the night talking to a total stranger—and I wouldn't be able to argue with them. It *did* sound crazy, completely unlike anything I had ever done before. *Irresponsible.* Even thinking the terrible word brought a hot flush of embarrassment to my cheeks.

But I wouldn't have traded that night for anything. Though I resisted such silliness for most of my life, that was the first time I ever experienced magic.

The vacation to Cocoa Beach became an annual event. Even when I went back to Wisconsin, Julia and I were rarely out of touch. My parents taught me to be practical and realistic, to think of the future and set long-term goals. Julia, however, remained carefree and unconcerned, as comfortable with her fantasies as with her real life.

We wrote long letters filled with plans for the future, and the hopes and hurts of growing up. We weren't allowed to call each other often, but whenever something important happened to me, the phone would ring and I would know it was Julia. She knew, somehow. Julia always knew.

During our summer weeks together, Julia spent endless hours telling me her daydreams about life in the enchanted realms beneath the sea. She had taught herself to sketch, and she drew marvelous, sweeping pictures of the undersea kingdoms. After listening to her for so long, I gradually learned to tell a passable story myself, though never with the ring of truth that she could give to her imaginings.

From Julia, I learned about the color of sunlight shining down from above, filtered through layers of rippling water. In my mind, I saw plankton blooms that made a stained-glass effect, especially at sunset. I learned how storms churned the surface of the sea, while the depths remained calm, though with a "mistiness" caused by the foamy wavetops above.

I learned about hidden canyons filled with huge mollusks, shells as big and as old as the giant redwood trees, which patiently collected all the information brought to them by the fish.

Julia told me about secret meeting places in kelp forests, where Ammeron and Ariston went to spend carefree hours in their unending lives playing hide-and-seek with porpoises. But the lush green kelp groves now seemed empty to them, empty as the places in their hearts that waited for true love. . . .

One day we found a short chain of round metal links at the

water's edge. What its original purpose was or who had left it there, I could not fathom. Julia picked it up with a look that was even more unfathomable. She touched each of the loops again and again, moving them through her fingers as if saying some magical rosary. We kept walking, splashing up to our ankles in the low waves, until Julia gave a small cry. One of the links had come loose in her hand. She stared at it for a moment in consternation, then gave a delighted laugh. She slid the circlet from one finger to the next until it came to rest on the ring finger of her right hand, a perfect fit.

"There. I always knew he'd ask." Julia sent me a sidelong glance, a twinkle lurking in the green of her irises. She loosened another link and slipped it quickly into my hand.

"All right," I sighed, feeling suddenly apprehensive, but knowing that it was no use trying to ignore her once she got started. "Who is 'he,' and what did he ask?"

"I am betrothed to Ammeron, heir to the Kingdom of the Seventh Sea," she said proudly.

"Sure, and I'm betrothed to his brother Ariston." I held up the cheap metal ring on my finger. "Aren't we a bit young to get engaged, Jule?"

Julia was unruffled. "Time means nothing in the kingdoms beneath the sea. When a year passes here, it's no more than a day to them. Time is infinite there. Our princes will wait for us."

"You really think we're worth it? Besides, how do they know whether or not we accept?" I challenged, always adding a completely out-of-place practicality to Julia's fairy tales. But my sarcasm sailed as far over Julia's head as a shooting star.

"Wait," she said, grasping my arm as she swept the ocean with her intense gaze. Suddenly, she drew in a sharp breath. "Look!" Her eyes lit up as a dolphin leapt twice, not far from where we stood on the shore. "There," she sighed, "do we need any more proof than that?"

Even in the face of her excitement, I couldn't keep the slight edge out of my voice. "I'll admit that I've never seen dolphins leap so close to shore, but what does that have to do with—"

"Dolphins are the messengers of the royal families beneath the sea," she replied in her patient way. Always patient. "One leap is a greeting. Two leaps ask a question. Three leaps give an answer." She flashed a smile at me. There was certainty in her voice that sent a shiver down my back. "And now they're waiting for us to respond!"

I struggled for a moment with impatience but couldn't bring myself to answer with more of my cynicism. I tried my most soothing voice. "Well, I'm sure Ammeron will understand that you—"

But she wasn't listening. Before I could finish my thought, she was running at top speed along the damp, packed sand. I looked after her, and as I watched in amazement, she executed three of the most graceful leaps I had ever seen, strong and clean and confident. I knew I would look foolish if I even tried something like that. I'd probably fall flat on my face in the sand.

By the time I caught up to her, Julia was looking seaward, ankle-deep in waves, with tears sparkling on her lashes—or perhaps it was only the sea spray.

In her hand she held two more of the metal links from the chain she had found. Silently she handed me one of the links, then closed her eyes and threw the remaining one as far into the water as she could. I did the same, imitating her gesture but without the same conviction.

"Elizabeth," Julia said after a long moment, startling me with her quiet voice, "you are a very sensible person." It sounded like an accusation—and coming from Julia, it probably was.

We moved to dryer sand and sat for a long time watching the waves, letting the bright sun dazzle our eyes. Perhaps too long. But Julia's hand on my arm let me know that she saw it, too.

Far out in the water a dolphin leapt. Three times.

Our lives were divided each year into reality and imagination, north and south, school and vacation, rationality and magic, until we finished high school.

I planned my life as carefully and sensibly as I could. My parents had taught me that a woman had to be practical—and I believed it. I chose my college courses with an eye toward the job market, avoiding "frivolous" art and history classes (no matter how much fun they sounded). After all, what good would they do me later in life?

My one concession to the lifelong pull the ocean had exerted on me, was that I chose to go to school at Florida State. Luckily, it was a perfectly acceptable school for the business management and accounting classes I intended to take, so I wasn't forced to define my reasons more precisely.

And it allowed me to see Julia more often.

Julia, on the other hand, always lived on the edge of reality. My parents disapproved of her, and I grew tired of defending her choices, so we came to the unspoken agreement that we would avoid the subject entirely . . . though even I couldn't help being a bit disappointed in my friend. To me, it seemed Julia was wasting her life away at the seaside.

I tried to help her make some sensible choices as well. She wasn't interested in college, preferring to spend her days hanging out near the ocean, making sketches that she sold for a pittance in local gift shops, doing odd jobs.

I convinced her to learn scuba diving. With her love of the sea, I knew she would be a natural, and in less than a year she was a certified instructor with a small, steady business. I even took lessons from her, as did one of my boyfriends, though that relationship ended in disaster.

As for romance, I occasionally went out on dates with men I met in classes, since I felt that our mutual interests should form a solid basis for long-term partnership, but my dating resulted only in passionless short-term relationships that usually ended with an agreement to be "just friends." I never let on how much these breakups really hurt me, except to Julia.

After each one, I would call Julia and she would meet me at The Original Fat Boy's Bar-B-Que, waiting patiently while I drowned my sorrows in beer and barbecued beef. Then we would drive to the beach, where I'd cry for a while, tell her the whole miserable tale, and vow never to make the same mistake again. Sometimes she drew tiny caricatures of my stories, forming them into comical melodramas as I spoke, until I was forced to acknowledge how silly or inconsequential each romance seemed as I dissolved into laughter and tears.

Julia dated often, drifting through each relationship with little thought for the future, until the inevitable stormy end—usually (I suspected) sparked by Julia's spur-of-the-moment nature and consequent unreliability that frequently frustrated men. Somehow on those nights, she would call to me and, no matter where I was, I would feel the need to go walking on our beach. And she would be there.

Once, feeling particularly burned at the end of a tempestuous relationship, she asked what she was doing wrong—a rhetorical question, perhaps, but I answered her (as if I had had a better track record in love than she had). "You're spending too much time in a fairy tale, Jule. I used to really love your stories about the princes and the sea kingdoms, but we're not kids any more. Be a little more practical."

The ocean breeze lifted her pale hair in waves about her face as her sea-green eyes widened. "Practical? I could say you're living in just as much of a fairy tale, Elizabeth. The American Dream . . . following all the rules, taking the right classes, expecting to find treasure in your career and a prince in some accountant or lawyer or doctor. Doesn't sound any more realistic to me."

I felt stung, but she just sighed and looked out to sea, getting that lost expression on her face again. "I'm sorry. I didn't mean to dump on you like that. Don't worry. I guess I shouldn't be so upset either. It doesn't really matter, you know. After all, I'm betrothed to the Prince of the Seventh Sea."

And I managed to laugh, which made me feel better. But Julia had a disturbing . . . *certainty* in her voice.

The last time I ever saw Julia, her call was very strong. I was studying late on campus preparing for a final exam when for no apparent reason I felt an overpowering need to get away from my books, to talk to Julia. It had been months since I'd seen her.

No—she needed to talk to *me*.

Even though there was a storm warning in effect, I ran out the door without even stopping to pick up a jacket, got into my car, and sped all the way to Cocoa Beach. As I sprinted down to the beach behind Julia's house, I saw her standing on the sand. Dimly silhouetted against the cloudy sky, she wore only a white bathing suit, and her long hair blew wildly in the wind as she stared out to sea. It reminded me of the first time I had seen Julia as a little girl, standing in the moonlight.

When I approached her and saw her startled expression, I abruptly realized that something was very wrong: Julia hadn't expected me.

"You called me, Jule," I said. "What's going on?"

"I . . . didn't mean to." She seemed to hesitate. "I'm going diving."

Then I noticed the pile of scuba gear close by, near the water's edge. I understood Julia's subtle stubbornness enough to realize that she placed more weight on her feelings than on simple common sense, so I stifled the impulse to launch into an anxious safety lecture and kept my voice neutral. "I know you have plenty of night diving experience, but you shouldn't dive alone. Not tonight. The weather's not good. Look at the surf."

For a while, I thought she wouldn't answer. At last she said softly, "David's gone."

"The artist?" I asked, momentarily at a loss before successfully placing the name of the current man in her life.

She nodded. "It doesn't really matter, you know. He fell head-over-heels for a pharmacist. It hit him so hard, I almost felt sorry for him. Don't worry; I don't feel hurt. After all . . . " Her voice trailed off. Her fingers toyed with the plain metal ring that hung from a silver chain around her neck. She had kept it all these years.

Her face was calm, but the storm in her sea-swept eyes rivaled the one brewing over the ocean. "After all," she finished with an enigmatic quirk of her lips, "I think tonight is my wedding night."

Uneasy, I tried for humor, hoping to stall her. "Don't you need a bridesmaid, then? I'll just go get my formal scuba tanks and my dress fins and meet you back here, okay?"

After a minute or so she looked straight at me, clear-eyed and smiling. "Thank you for coming. I really did need to see you again, but right now I think I need to be alone for a while."

"I'm not so sure I should leave," I said, stalling, reluctant to let her go, unable to force her to stay. "Friends don't let friends dive alone, you know?"

"Don't worry, Elizabeth," she said, barely above a whisper. "Remember, no matter what happens . . . I'll call you." She put on her diving gear, letting me help her adjust the tanks, kissed me on the cheek, and waded into the turbulent water. "I'll call you in a week—probably less. I promise."

I watched intently as Julia swam away from the beach, toward the deep water; I watched until I saw her head disappear beneath the waves.

Later, Julia's tanks and her buoyancy compensator vest were found in perfect condition on the shore a few miles away. And a plain silver neck chain. That was all.

That was five years ago. And tonight, when I needed her the most, I heard her call again.

Now, sitting on the damp sand, I listen to the hushed purr of the waves and stare at the Atlantic Ocean under the moonlight.

At times like this, here on the beach where Julia and I used to sit together, I wonder if I really was the sensible one. Yes, I made all the "right" choices, earned my degree, found a suitable job, got a comfortable apartment—though no dashing prince (accountant, lawyer, or otherwise) seemed to notice. I had been supremely confident that it would only be a matter of time.

But then, with a simple blood test, I ran out of time. Next came more tests, then a biopsy and a brief stay in the hospital. And behind it all loomed the specter of more and more time spent among the other hopeless cancer patients — walking cadavers — with the ticking of the deathwatch growing louder and louder inside their heads.

I would rather listen to the ocean.

It wasn't fair!

I raged at the universe. Hadn't I done everything right? Then why had I fallen under a medical curse, with no prince to kiss my cold lips and dislodge the bit of poisoned apple from my throat?

I needed to hear Julia's stories again. I longed to know more about the princes and their sea-unicorns, the defeated kraken, the tall spires of coral castles, in that enchanted undersea world where everyone lived forever.

I found a seashell on the shore, washed up by the tide, as if deposited there for me alone. I picked it up, brushing loose grains of sand from the edge, held it to my ear . . . and listened.

Far out in the water, I saw a dolphin make a double jump, two graceful silver arcs under the bright light of the moon.

My heart leapt with it, and I stood, blinking for a moment in disbelief. Then, feeling surprisingly restless and full of energy, I decided to go for a run along the beach.

And if I happened to leap once, twice, or three times . . . who was there to know?

Introduction to
The Ghost of Christmas Always

It was an annual tradition for me, Kristine Kathryn Rusch, Dean Wesley Smith, Nina Kiriki Hoffman, Jerry and Kathy Oltion, and other writers to gather in Oregon on Christmas Eve, and to each read a newly written Christmas story. Similar to how I wrote my story, "Scientific Romance," I began to read biographies of Charles Dickens, and to dig into his background: what he had done, and how perhaps he might have been inspired to write A Christmas Carol.

I was intrigued to discover that Dickens himself had suffered family tragedies and may even have had a ghost or two in his own past. That provided the right springboard for this Christmas story, which is also about a writer's career and choices.

The Ghost of Christmas Always

After she died I dreamed of her every night for many
months, sometimes as a spirit, sometimes as a living
creature, never with any of the bitterness of my real sorrow,
but always with a kind of quiet happiness, which became so
pleasant to me that I never lay down at night without a
hope of the vision coming back . . . And so it did.

— Charles Dickens, in a letter
to the mother of Mary Hogarth, 1842

Stave One

MARY WAS DEAD, TO BEGIN WITH. AND YET EACH
Christmas Eve her ghost came to haunt Charles Dickens.
He waited the year round for the one night he could see her again,
if only for a brief time.

Dickens gripped the arms of his chair, then let his eyelids fall
half closed. Across from him, aromatic smoke came from a fire in
the sitting-room hearth. On the mantelpiece sat a scrolled ivory-
and-gold clock with slim hands reaching toward midnight, when
Mary would come.

Wind rattled the windowpanes, pushing winter cold into the

great house on Devonshire Terrace. The Dickenses had added mahogany doors, marble mantels, and carpets to their new home —such extravagance was expected from the author of *Nicholas Nickleby, Oliver Twist,* and, of course, *Pickwick Papers.*

But on the silent night before Christmas, the house felt like a deserted stage in the theatre, filled with props and costumes but no actors. Mary had never lived here with them. His young sister-in-law had died before the unparalleled success swept over Dickens's life.

He stood up from the chair, brushed at his robe, and walked to the mantel. Dickens had urged the four children, his wife Kate, and the maid to retire early this night. None of them would suspect why he wanted them fast asleep.

Beside the clock stood Mary's portrait, painted by Phiz, the artist who illustrated so many of Dickens's installments. After Mary's death had devastated him, Dickens begged Phiz to do the portrait from memory, as a special favor. Now Dickens touched the lines of her face, the soft eyes gazing at something unseen but wondrous, the curves of her dark hair. Sweet Mary Hogarth, the delightful sister of his moody and shallow-minded wife.

Kate would be snoring upstairs, grossly pregnant with their fifth child. She would carry out the same chores on Christmas day as she did every day. She had no broader imagination, doing only what she felt her wifely obligations demanded. Not like young Mary, who was always so bright, so fascinated. . . .

"Can't you gaze at that portrait any time, Charles Dickens? I have only a short while here with you."

Dickens turned, smiling. He felt a rush of happiness. Mary Hogarth stood there, spectral and unchanged since her death six years before. She wore a shimmering white gown that reflected a light not from the fireplace and blew in a breeze that Dickens himself could not feel.

"I was waiting for you," he said.

"Just as I wait for this one night when I'm allowed to see you again." She took a step forward but did not touch him. She made no sound as she moved. "This year I have a present for you, Charles, a gift I hope you will treasure as much as I treasure giving it to you."

He could not think of what to say. He, Charles Dickens, who spoke in front of great audiences, who performed in the theatre, who read his own sketches aloud to crowds from the streets, found himself unable to utter a simple sentence to the wavering image of a sixteen-year-old girl. He finally said, "Merely seeing you again is enough to make me glad for the next twelve months."

Mary smiled and, keeping her gaze on his, reached forward to touch the clock. "But this is better. I give you Time."

"Time?" he asked, not comprehending but feeling his heart filled with wonder. "I do need more of it, with all my commitments."

"No," she said with a lilt in her voice that reminded him of the times that they laughed, Charles and Kate and Mary, when they went on outings to the theatre. "I give you *your* time, Charles. Your past, your present, and what is yet to come."

Before he could say more, Mary turned the hour hand backward from midnight in a full circle until it reached eleven o'clock. As the hand touched the top of the dial, the chimes rang out.

Mary extended her fingers to him. "Take my hand, Charles. Let me show you."

Eagerly he wrapped his fingers around her cold flesh, insubstantial but as strong and insistent as the wind. Mary led him to the window and drew back the curtains. The distant lights of London sprawled out below, making him think of the crowded streets, tall buildings leaning out over alleys, small fires and candlelit windows.

"Step with me into the past," she said.

Fighting back the tremors of fear in his voice, Dickens asked, "Long past?"

"No. Your past." And she stepped partway through the window, through the sash as if it were no more than a bit of fog.

"Wait!" he cried, "I am mortal! I cannot pass through brick and stone and glass."

"Bear but a touch of my hand, Charles." As Mary said this, she gave a tug. Dickens walked forward clad only in slippers and dressing gown, blinking as he stepped through and out into a clear winter night. But he felt no cold, no wind, only astonishment, for he found himself many miles from his home on Devonshire Terrace.

Stave Two

Though it was dark, Dickens could make out the three-storey house before him, with glowing orange lights in several of the windows. By day he would be able to see the nearby Kentish countryside, Chatham, and the Medway Valley.

"Good Heaven!" Dickens cried, "I was a boy here! My father worked in the naval dockyard."

Mary just smiled at him and raised her hand. Dickens found that they floated off the ground, rising along the terraces and shingles, to one of the upstairs windows where a single light still burned.

"That was my room!" Dickens said, keeping his voice to a whisper.

"And here is someone you'll like to see, no doubt."

They pressed their faces close to the window, and Dickens noted that, though the winter air must be very cold, neither his breath nor Mary's left any frost upon the window.

Inside the room he saw a plump woman with grayish-brown hair tied neatly behind her head. She sat in a chair pulled near to a pair of beds in which lay a boy and a girl. Both children had eyes wide and mouths slack with rapt fascination and terror. The woman leaned forward to talk; her eyes squinted and her face contorted as she spoke, waving her hands.

"Why it's old Mary Weller, our maid! Bless her heart—Mary Weller alive again!"

The maid lurched out in the middle of her story, splaying her fingers like claws. Both children squirmed backward in their beds, defending themselves with nervous giggling.

Dickens, delighted, turned to the spirit beside him. "She used to tell us horrible stories about Captain Murderer! And how he'd indulge his taste in wives by killing them off and baking them into pies! Ugh—my sister Fanny and I used to lie awake shivering in terror every time she told us one of those stories. But I loved them. I used to make up my own."

Mary patted him with her cold hand. "You've been a writer since the time you were a little boy. Come with me, around the corner."

They descended to the ground again, but when they turned the corner, Dickens found that they had reached an alley far distant from the old house. The light had changed to a gray wintry afternoon. People crowded the street, women wrapped in dark clothes tugging children alongside them on the frozen mud. Thawed patches of slush surrounded steaming piles of fresh horse manure. Dogs ran about, harrying burly men who carried packages and crates. Off to one side a man hauled a narrow pauper's coffin on his back, passing unnoticed through the streets. Signboards protruded out over doors proclaiming lodging houses, barbers, poulterers, a tripe shop, a sausage-maker.

"This is the Strand!" Dickens said, nearly letting go of Mary's hand in his excitement. "I got lost here one day when I was a boy."

"In fact, there you are right now." Mary indicated a small child gawking at the crowds, stumbling along with wonder-filled eyes. The boy looked as if he had been crying, but the tears dried to streaks in the cold air.

"I had a shilling and fourpence in my pocket," Dickens said. "My godfather gave it to me. I knew I would be rescued somehow. And I was very hungry."

They followed the boy, observing yet unseen by the pedestrians. Little Charles Dickens walked along, dressed in a warm jacket, bumping into unshaven men who ignored him. He stared from window to window in food shops, shuffling his feet, looking around. He kept walking.

Finally he stopped in front of a pile of cooked sausages in a window. A paper sign in front read "Small Germans, a Penny." The boy stared at the sausages, shivering. He licked his lips. He took a deep breath, mustering courage, and strode in. The shopkeeper squinted at him with an amused grin, but the boy seemed confident now that he knew what to ask for.

"If you please, would you sell me one of those sausages?" His voice sounded tiny as Dickens listened. The boy reached into his pocket and took out a single penny. The shopkeeper used his fingers to pick up one of the sausages from the back of the pile and plucked the penny from the boy's hand at the exact moment he surrendered the sausage.

Charles Dickens felt his cheeks flushing with the delight of the memory. "The sausage wasn't very warm," he told Mary, "but it was one of the most delicious things ever to pass my lips. Of course part of it was that I had bought it myself."

The boy wandered the streets again, in and out of yards and little squares, chased off by cooks he gawked at, bullied by a gang of young toughs who wanted the rest of the money in his pockets. The boy broke into a run, pushing through the crowds, splashing in the slush, until he lost the boys in a dark alley lined with dim counting houses where misers changed their gold.

The boy stood in the growing dark, looking unspeakably forlorn.

"Can we not help him?" Dickens said.

Mary shook her head. "No, Charles, we are here only to observe. You pity this boy now, but would you have traded that single day in your life for anything you can imagine?"

"No, never. It astonishes me even now to think of how much

I used from that day in *Oliver Twist*, and in *Nicholas Nickleby*, and in half a dozen of my sketches for the periodicals."

"And you will continue to find ways to use it. You're a writer, Charles, heart and soul. Everything you experience is fodder for the tales that delight so many people."

As Mary spoke, Dickens heard a loud cough and saw a middle-aged man come up to the wretched boy and ask what was wrong. The man's clothes were drab and worn, but the brass buttons on his coat had been polished with care.

"That watchman took me home," Dickens said in a whisper. "I remember his cough, how he wheezed all the way. I was afraid I was going to catch the plague from him."

Mary strolled ahead, turning her back on the departing boy and the coughing watchman. "Why don't you come around the corner with me? We'll pass another decade."

Still astounded, Dickens followed her as the scene once again changed. He found himself in a dark court, narrow but clean. Clouds the color of ice on a deep pond covered the sky.

In front of a dark office, a young man strode by with a polished walking stick. He looked like a twenty-year-old dandy, with gleaming shoes, black waistcoat and vest. His gray felt trousers were new and unwrinkled, his green cravat impeccably tied. The brim of a brushed top hat shaded his face. The young man moved with a nervous manner as he stopped in front of the dark office—and then Dickens recognized the mail slot and the stencilled letters above it that read EDITOR'S BOX.

"This is Fleet Street! That's me, posting my very first contribution for the *Monthly Magazine*."

The young man pulled out a long envelope and, trying to appear nonchalant, slipped it into the black hole of the mail slot before striding away. He rapped his walking stick on the cobblestones, swaggering but hurrying, as if afraid to be caught at what he had done.

"I paid half a crown for the next issue of that magazine, and there it was in print! One of my sketches, 'A Dinner at Poplar Walk,' I think it was. I remember how it felt to see my words in print for the very first time."

Mary's voice took on a tone of chiding. "And you didn't even receive payment for the piece."

Dickens laughed. "What did it matter then? I was speaking to a whole world of readers! People were reading what I had written. I walked up and down Westminster Hall for half an hour. My eyes could hardly see, I was so excited!"

"Yet now you grow angry at anyone who prints even a bit of your correspondence without offering you royalties."

Dickens stiffened. "They make enormous amounts of money off me just by placing my name on their masthead! Pirates have made me lose thousands of pounds by flaunting the copyright law."

She had touched a sore spot, but he did not want to ruin their short time together by arguing. He softened his voice to change the subject. "These memories are delightful, Mary. Show me more!"

Her expression remained solemn. "Do not thank me until you have seen them all. Some of them may not be so precious, though they are as important."

Dickens felt a chill from inside. "What do you mean?" His tone spoke plainly that he did not want to hear the answer.

"Our time grows short," she said. "Quick! You must see one last memory of your past."

As she led him down the street, the sky darkened into night, growing blacker with each step they took. Greenish-white glows from gas streetlights made the scene shift with a harsh mixture of glares and shadows. As Mary hurried him along, Dickens saw the buildings again, recognizing the brick façade, the wrought-iron fence, the decorative lintels and arches of Mecklenburgh Square.

As they approached, Dickens saw a tall man open the wrought-iron gate in front of a three-storey brick home. He was accompanied by two women, one larger and hanging on the man's arm, the other thin and delicate with dark hair pinned up under a bonnet. The man gestured for them both to precede him through the gate, then caught up with them under the rounded arch of the doorway. They all seemed to be laughing and enjoying themselves.

Dickens stood trembling, refusing to go another step. Mary pulled at him, but he closed his eyes. "No, Mary! Oh no, no!"

But she was insistent and drew him stumbling toward the door. "Was I not always a good friend to you, Charles? Without this visit, you cannot hope to receive everything I bring to you."

She led him through the half-open door into the rented home where young Charles Dickens lived with his new wife Kate and her sixteen-year-old sister Mary.

"We had just gone to the theatre, do you remember?" Mary said in a distant voice, as if she barely remembered herself. "It was late when we got home, about one o'clock in the morning. I had gone up to bed—"

"Stop!" he said. He had spent years with every detail of that evening pounding in his head, haunting his nightmares. There, in front of him, in the old house he and Kate and the children had left only a short time ago, he watched a younger, carefree version of himself removing his coat and handing it to the maid. He set his walking stick against the rail of the stairs, tossed his top hat behind him in a cocky gesture to hit the hat rack, but of course he missed and was just bending over to pick it up when he heard a choking cry from upstairs. Mary's voice.

It echoed in his ears, in his memory.

Sweating and shivering at the same time, Dickens watched himself, running up the steep staircase, grabbing the rail and launching himself upward with every step. "Mary!" his younger self cried in concerned surprise.

Watching the scene unfold again, the elder Dickens could not stop himself from shouting the same as he dashed up to the second floor bedrooms. His footfalls made no sound on the steps.

Just inside the door of her room, Mary lay on the floor gasping, begging for help. Young Dickens sent for a doctor. His face was drawn and horrified.

As he watched from his invisible vantage, the elder Dickens shook his head. "The doctor will not be able to do anything. They said you had a diseased heart, Mary. And now I have a broken one, all over again."

He turned to the spectral form of Mary, who watched without emotion the image of herself writhing on the floor. Young Dickens and Kate helped her onto the bed. She would die there the following day.

"This scene has haunted me more than any other," Dickens said. "Every letter I wrote for a year bore a black border in remembrance of you."

He sighed, but it came out more like a moan. "When I was writing *The Old Curiosity Shop* and the time came when Little Nell had to die, I trembled for days beforehand, recalling your death. It cast the most horrible shadow upon me, and it was all I could do to keep moving at all."

Mary sighed, and he felt her spectral hand squeeze his. "Sometimes you are too sentimental, Charles."

Dickens saw that time had changed again. Mary Hogarth lay on her bed, but sunlight streamed through the windows, and the younger Charles Dickens held her in his arms, pulling the bedclothes over to keep her warm. He stroked her tangled hair . . . and felt her die in his arms.

Dickens watched himself take her cooling hand between his palms and slip one of the rings off her finger. "I will wear this ring of yours until the day I might join you," he said.

Dickens the observer stared at the ring on his own finger, still there after six years. To crush away the tears he rubbed his knuckles against his eyes. His head rang from the memory.

Then the ringing sound became the chiming of the clock, and he and Mary's ghost returned to the warm sitting room in Devonshire Terrace. After all this time and all the years observed, the hour of midnight was just striking.

Stave Three

Dickens drew a deep breath to drive back all the memories he had thought tucked away safe and sound. He warmed his hands over the fire, then, exhausted, he shuffled back to his chair. Before he could turn 'round and sink into the cushions, before the clock finished striking the hour of twelve, Mary stopped him.

"We have no time to rest, Charles. This is a busy night for both of us."

He blinked at her, but now the delight of his reunion with Mary had been blunted by watching her death all over again. "I can't bear any more memories just now. I'm afraid of what else you might dredge from the mud of my past."

He squeezed his eyes shut, but Mary's voice grew lighter. "Not your past, Charles. Now we will go and see who you are right now. Until the clock strikes one, let us observe your present."

This baffled him, and he made sure to let her see it on his face. "What do you mean? I know who I am."

"Are you quite certain?"

"How can I not?"

In answer, Mary narrowed her eyes and looked at him with a penetrating gaze that made her seem centuries older than her sixteen-year-old form suggested.

"All right then, Spirit," he said. "Conduct me where you will."

Mary went to the door of the sitting room and beckoned him. "Shall we go upstairs, then?"

The hall was dim and orange, lit by candles Kate had left burning for him after she went to bed. The flickering illumination set off sparks from Mary's flowing white dress.

As they went up the stairs, Dickens felt light on his feet, and he wondered if he was really moving himself. When the fourth stair failed to creak under his step, he knew that this would be another shadow-show of visions, a theatre performance Mary staged for him.

She turned down the upstairs hall and opened the door to the master bedroom. By the sunlight in the window Dickens saw it was morning again, that very morning. Kate sat back in a rocking chair, working on another embroidered pillowcase; their maid Anne had drawn the pattern for it, as usual. Draped along the scrolled arm of the rocker hung limp bundles of bright threads. Kate shifted and tried to be comfortable, but her pregnancy made her look awkward no matter what she did. Her eyes, her cheeks, everything about her looked bloated, especially in contrast to the shining spirit of her sister. Kate's face looked like a poor reproduction of Mary's, carved out of a potato.

Three of the four children sat in the room with her. Little Katie and Mamie peered at a book showing sketches of knights in shining armor; baby Walter lay on the bed making sounds like the water draining out of a wash basin.

"Kate sits here all day and does nothing," Dickens said. "Not at all like you, Mary. She takes no interest in my activities—"

"What would you have her do?" Mary asked. "The baby is due in less than a month. She watches the children, makes certain they refrain from bothering you, though many times they bother *her* to no end. Do you even notice?"

Interrupting her, the door burst open and five-year-old Charley ran in with tears brimming in his eyes. The boy made hiccoughing noises and brushed past Dickens, missing him by no more than an inch, but Charley did not even see his father. In his small hand the boy held a little white note and a pincushion.

Kate looked up from her embroidery, saw the note, and allowed a brief and surprising expression of anger flicker behind her eyes. Dickens remembered writing the reprimand note himself and placing it on Charley's bed after he had completed his daily inspection of the household.

"What is it, Charley?" Kate asked. Her voice sounded soothing. Mamie and Katie turned the pages of their book, pretending to ignore their brother's anguish, while the baby kept gurgling.

The boy had to snuffle twice before he could hand her the note. His mother had no chance to read it before he burst out, "He says he's angry because I forgot to put my brown shoes in their box. I just left 'em by my bed." He drew a shaking breath and tried to fend off his tears long enough to speak what disturbed him the most. "And tomorrow's Christmas!"

Kate shook her head. "Don't expect mere Christmas to make

your father an easier man. What reason has he to be merry?" She smiled at the boy. "We'll have to make twice as merry ourselves!"

Dickens remained at the door, stung, as Kate heaved herself out of the rocking chair. She set her embroidery aside, unable to catch a packet of green thread that unraveled and spilled onto the floor. She paid it no heed and gave the boy a gentle hug.

"Look at this, Charles," Mary's spirit said from across the room. She ran her translucent fingers over the frame of a small watercolor portrait showing the four children at play. "Do you remember it?"

Indeed he did — it was the going-away gift from a painter friend when he and Kate had departed for six months to tour America. Dickens insisted on leaving the four children behind, claiming that the stress of travel and the inconvenience of having them along would be detrimental to his own activities.

Kate had mourned the thought of being separated from her children for half a year and begged not to go, but Dickens went ahead with the plans, the arrangements, the packing. Finally, Dickens sent his ebullient actor friend, William Macready, to speak to Kate; as instructed, Macready told Mrs. Dickens that a wife's duty was to accompany her husband wherever he wished to go, and to be happy doing it. Kate took only the watercolor portrait of the children to keep her company; she propped it up in their room every night during the journey.

"You dragged my sister against her will to a foreign land she had no wish to see. You never asked her if perhaps she would like to include something in your plans. Instead you took her to see *you* speak, to see *you* read aloud and give performances on the stage. You travelled to visit Washington Irving and Edgar Allan Poe and Henry Longfellow, and what did she profit from it all? The chance to hear you quietly insult your hosts and America in general, to complain about conditions there?"

Dickens backed toward the hall, and Mary's spirit whisked across the floor, moving through Katie and Mamie by their picture book. The anger in her eyes frightened him.

"Can we not see something else, Mary? I beg you!"

"Of course," she said, passing him and flowing down the stairs. "Let's go watch the great Charles Dickens at work."

He dashed after her as Mary went to his writing study. Inside, he saw the fire licking at fresh logs in the large fireplace. It was the first blaze of the morning, and he had added enough logs to keep it burning for a long time; he knew he would become immersed in his writing and pay it no attention.

Dickens saw himself sitting at the desk, bent over a sheet of paper with pen in hand and inkwell nearby. A jumbled stack of papers lay at his left elbow, with one page nearly falling to the floor. A smudged thumbprint from a spilled drop of ink obscured a word in the margin. The only sounds in the room were the scratching of pen against paper, frequent clinks into the inkwell, the sizzling sound of the fire, and his own rapid breathing.

But as Dickens stood and watched the scene, he heard a rustle and saw little Mamie bundled in a blanket on the sofa. Her face had the rubbed-raw blush of one recovering from a fever. She propped a book on her bent knees. Keeping both eyes on her father at his desk, Mamie very carefully turned the page, as if terrified she might make a sound.

"I remember this day! A week ago—Mamie was sick, and I told her she could rest in my study while I worked." He turned and looked to Mary for reassurance.

"You don't appear to be paying much attention to your daughter." Mary's voice remained cold.

The Dickens at the desk sprang to his feet and ran to a small mirror on the wall. He pushed his face to the reflection, opened his mouth, made bizarre contortions of his lips and eyebrows, then ran back to the desk. Picking up his pen, he scribbled down an entire paragraph without stopping, tilting the pen at an extreme angle to keep the words flowing without interrupting the sentence to dip into the ink again.

A moment later he stood up, went to the mirror once more, and proceeded to have a stop-and-start conversation with himself.

"It's nothing unusual," Dickens said to Mary. "Sometimes I get rather involved with my characters." But he felt his cheeks burning at this intrusion into a private moment. "It helps me stage some of my scenes."

But Mary seemed not at all concerned about that, looking instead at the girl on the sofa. Mamie watched her father's actions, bewildered and frightened, but she made no sound.

"Your children are afraid of you, Charles. They see you as a whirlwind, always busy, never to be disturbed. You're a great mystery to them."

"Nonsense, they love me. I am their father!"

"You are a stranger."

Dickens returned to the hall, turning his back on the scene in the study. "I presume you have some design with these pantomimes, Mary. Get on with it."

She took his hand, and this time hers felt colder than ever.

"Follow me, then. We'll walk outside." She opened the front door to a sunny winter afternoon, and they set foot on a street deep in the heart of London. The great house on Devonshire Terrace vanished behind them as they stepped into the bustle of activity. Dickens saw that they left no footprints in the snow.

They moved unhindered through the constant stream of passersby, the businessmen, the beggars. Dickens recognized the man stumping along at a furious, distracted pace. He was dressed in a fur greatcoat over a brown frock coat, then a red waistcoat from which a gold watch chain dangled. Two linked diamond pins fastened an extravagant cravat poking up around his Adam's apple. Mary hurried up beside the man, dragging her companion along.

"What are you trying to show me here, Mary? I know I like to walk, sometimes as much as thirty miles in a single day. It helps me plan my stories, to converse with my characters. And I know very well what I look like."

"*Do* you know what you look like?" Mary asked, pulling him around to face the image of himself. The man kept walking ahead, eyes cast down, his exhalations in the cold air visible from his nose. "Look closely. See yourself not posing for the mirror."

Dickens inspected the familiar clean-shaven boyish face, with wide nose and thick lips, long brown hair curling around his ears. But then he saw the shadows under the eyes, the sagging weariness in his defiant stride, the hunch of the shoulders, the tight frown heavy on his lips.

"I thought you said this would be visions of the present," Dickens said. "Surely this must be me some years in the future."

Mary shook her head. "That is how you appear to others even now. You appear harried, overworked, with never enough time. Constantly pushing yourself toward goals no man could meet."

"With good reason!" he said, turning toward her. "Is it so quiet in the grave that you can't hear them shouting how Charles Dickens has lost his popularity? The last installments of *The Old Curiosity Shop* were selling a hundred thousand copies a week, but now *Barnaby Rudge* barely sells a third of that, even at its best!"

He stopped. Mary faced him, as the other image of Dickens continued his lonely walk along the streets, muttering to himself.

"I took a year away from writing to travel in America, and when I returned I thought the public would be hungry for my work, waiting to snap up anything I might do. But my *American Notes* received nothing but a cool reception from my readers.

They used to snap up every tidbit so eagerly—are they all tired of it now? This week's installment of *Martin Chuzzlewit* is selling only twenty thousand copies. Am I finished as a writer?"

Mary's face grew stern, an alien expression on the girl he had cherished for so long in his dreams. "And how much time do you waste giving speeches, attending gaudy social events? And that's only when you're not losing your temper with your friends or shouting at your publisher, or carrying on your endless fight for a reformed copyright law."

"The pirates are stealing me blind with bastard copies of my stories!"

"You don't seem to be doing much good work with the money you already possess. What would you do with more of it?"

Dickens made no answer, but Mary had not finished taunting him. "You write weekly sketches, you work on two novels at a time, you write one-act farces and you star in them as well. No wonder your children don't know their father; no wonder dear Kate ignores you in simple defense against how you ignore her."

"But writing is my business!" Dickens said, crossing his arms over the gaps in his robe.

"Business!" cried Mary. "Mankind is your business. Don't you realize that a single story from you could do more good work than the House of Commons can manage in a year? In your constant challenge to produce more and more, you've forgotten what stories mean. Don't you remember your passion for a story that *demands* to be told? Or are you more interested in instant projects to increase your fame—if only for the moment?"

He stammered, "But, but that is not how I think of it at all."

Mary turned and pointed to the figure still striding away. "Look at him, walking as fast as he can but with his eyes to the ground. He'll reach his destination and go right past it without even knowing. You are a writer, Charles. Surely you can appreciate such a metaphor?"

Dickens, feeling a heavy weight inside his chest, turned away. "I want to go back inside now."

Mary stopped in front of a leatherworker's shop and grasped the handle of the door. Behind the glass, Dickens could see only shadows of the proprietor and customers moving about. Before she opened the door, Mary's expression softened.

"Think of your children," she said, "and the story that Kate tells them of the three little pigs. Is it better to build a hundred huts of straw, or one or two fortresses of stone?"

She opened the door. "Stop writing books of straw."

He followed her inside, into his own sitting room again. The single chime rang out into the room as the clock struck one.

Stave Four

"I have only one more thing to show you, Charles," Mary said to him. "A glimpse of things yet to come."

Dickens wanted to go nearer the fire, but found he could not move. "I think I fear that more than the other images." He realized his voice sounded thin. "But I know you must have good intentions in your heart."

Mary's eyes twinkled, and she flashed a smile at him. Once again she looked the playful sixteen-year-old, and his heart began to ache. "Stop your worrying. You may even enjoy this."

With a lilt in her step, Mary crossed the sitting room to a door Dickens had never seen before. It looked dark and narrow, perhaps a place where Captain Murderer would keep his blades for trimming wives into bite-sized pieces.

Mary drew the door open without a creak. The firelight sparkled on the brasswork of the knob, which was different from any of the ornate latches Dickens had installed on the other mahogany doors.

Inside, he could see a shadowy passage, lit by white glow along the ceiling, as harsh as gaslight but not the same. Mary snatched his hand and drew him inside. He tried to resist, but his feet felt like leaden weights hooked to puppet strings.

The warm light of the sitting room hearth dwindled into nothing and vanished as they stepped forward. The air felt cool and smelled musty. The room was too dark to be observed with any accuracy, but Dickens glanced around, anxious to know what kind of room it was.

As his eyes adjusted he saw that the narrow walls were not walls at all, but shelves. Book shelves, filled with row upon row of bound volumes. "What is this place, Mary? A library perhaps?"

She stopped in front of a long shelf and raised her hand. Around them the light grew brighter, and he could distinguish all the books of different heights and sizes, with cloth or leather bindings of black, blue, brown.

"Have a look at this one, Charles." With a crook of her finger, she tugged the first volume on the shelf a little way out. He squinted down at the gold-stamped letters on the spine.

"Why, that's my *Pickwick!* In an edition I have never seen." He made a small groan. "Someone else has pirated it then!"

Mary's gentle laughter sounded like a bird in the forest. "Have you forgotten that we stepped into your future? Things yet to come."

Dickens ran his fingers over the spines. "And here's *Oliver Twist,* and *The Old Curiosity Shop!*" But as he continued down the line he stopped.

"Hard Times? A Tale of Two Cities? Great Expectations? Bleak House? The Mystery of Edwin Drood? David Copperfield?" He looked at her, dazed. "Who are all these people? Where are these places? Did I write so many books?"

Mary seemed entranced by the delight she saw on his face. "Of course."

He reached out to pull one of the books from the shelves, but Mary stopped him. Sliding the volume back into place, she shook her head. "That is forbidden. If you'd like to learn these characters and know these stories, then you must write them yourself. Only that way can you, and the world, have these books."

He continued to stare at his own name engraved on the spines as if on a monument, CHARLES DICKENS. The thought of all those novels whirled in his imagination; he felt his fingers itching to get back to his pen and paper. Then he remembered the other things Mary had shown him that evening.

"Here is something you will enjoy even more," Mary said as she turned to the opposite shelf, and he saw more books, so many that they were stacked on top of each other, piled up out of sight, causing the shelves to bow in the middle. His name appeared on many of those spines, often in the titles.

"Biographies of you, critical treatises, textbooks. The scholars have had as much enjoyment chronicling your life as studying your novels."

Dickens could only gape in astonishment. He felt his vision going dim with euphoria. He had never imagined this, not even in his most pretentious fantasies.

Mary took down one of the tomes and flipped to a page, then began to read in the flickering light. " 'Charles Dickens was a great English novelist and one of the most popular writers of all time. A keen observer of life, Dickens had a great understanding of people. He showed sympathy for the poor and helpless, and mocked and criticized the selfish, the greedy, the cruel.' "

She closed the book with a slam and a smile. "What you will

find even more remarkable, I think, is that the passage I just read will be written *more than a century after your death.* Your own fame will outshine that of Walter Scott, and Poe and Irving and Longfellow, all those you so admire."

Dickens had to grasp at one of the shelves to keep from falling backward. By the stiffness he felt on his face, he knew he must be grinning like an idiot. But then a suspicion of her own words cast a cloud across his thoughts.

"Answer me one question, Mary—are these the images of things that *will* be, or are they the images of things that *may* be only?"

Mary began to walk back down the long corridor of shelves toward the sitting room.

"Mary! Tell me!" His slippers made skittering noises on the hard floor as he ran to catch up with her.

She stood at the door that led into the firelit room. "Perhaps. But you must remember that your writing is not about *writing,* but about people. As is your life. It won't matter how clever you are, how many projects you can juggle at once, how many instances your name appears in the newspapers. You have a power to move the world if you choose to do so. But will you make the effort?"

Dickens pushed back into the sitting room. "Yes, I will! I won't forget the lessons you taught me."

He felt like dancing. The hands on the clock had somehow returned to midnight, and as he looked the hour began to chime once more.

Mary stood alone in the center of the room, and her white gown took on a grayish tinge, as if shadows seeped into the fabric. Her skin seemed paler than before, with a shimmering quality like cheap candlewax running into puddles.

"Now I must leave you, Charles. My time here is finished. Look to see me no more. And look that, for your own sake, you remember what has passed between us!"

She stepped backward toward the window, fading as she went. Dickens reached for her, but the euphoria made him numb to the thought of never seeing her again.

"Wait!" he called. "You've given me a gift beyond measure. Isn't there something I can do for you? Some way I can repay you?"

Mary continued to dissolve into the air, but at the last moment she turned her gaze full upon him. "Write me a Christmas story," she said.

And when the last stroke of twelve had chimed, her ghost vanished completely.

Charles Dickens remained before the glowing hearth for a full hour, watching the logs slump into embers, before he finally turned and left the sitting room, going to the stairs that led to his bed. Kate would be long asleep, but he would do his best not to disturb her. As his foot fell on the fourth step, the creaking wood reminded him that he was whole and substantial, and alive. As were his family and his friends.

A *Christmas story?* he thought. His head pounded with the dizzying memories of the evening, and he knew sleep would be a long time coming. He wondered if he would get any ideas.

Introduction to
Drumbeats

For those of you who don't recognize the name of the coauthor on this story, Neil Peart is the drummer and lyricist for the rock group Rush. The Rush album, Grace under Pressure, *had inspired my first novel,* Resurrection, Inc., *and I had sent a copy of the published book to the band. I was delighted when Neil Peart wrote me a letter in response. We struck up a correspondence, then eventually met several times, and when I was asked to contribute a story for the second* Shock Rock *(Pocket Books) anthology, working with Neil seemed a natural thing to do.*

Neil himself has bicycled around Africa several times, and has written the most detailed and insightful travel journals that I have ever read. The character in this story is loosely based on him, of course, and large portions of the narrative are taken from these travelogues, with additional work by Neil to make the story fit together.

While writing intelligent and meaningful lyrics to his songs, Neil always had aspirations of being a writer. However, after the story got published and he received his portion of the meager payment, Neil decided that he wouldn't quit his job as a platinum-selling rock drummer any time soon. . . .

Drumbeats

with Neil Peart

*A*FTER NINE MONTHS OF TOURING ACROSS NORTH America — with hotel suites and elaborate dinners and clean sheets every day — it felt good to be hot and dirty, muscles straining not for the benefit of any screaming audience, but just to get to the next village up the dusty road. Here, none of the natives recognized Danny Imbro or even knew his name. To them, he was just another White Man, an exotic object of awe for little children, a target of scorn for drunken soldiers at border checkpoints.

Bicycling through Africa was about the furthest thing from a rock concert tour that Danny could imagine — which was why he did it, after promoting the latest Blitzkrieg album and performing each song until the tracks were worn smooth in his head. This cleared his mind, gave him a sense of balance, perspective.

The other members of Blitzkrieg did their own thing during the group's break months. Phil, whom they called the "music machine" because he couldn't *stop* writing music, spent his relaxation time cranking out film scores for Hollywood; Reggie caught up on his reading, soaking up grocery bags full of political thrillers and mysteries; Shane turned into a vegetable on Maui. But Danny Imbro took his expensive-but-battered bicycle and bummed around West Africa. The others thought it strangely appropriate that the band's drummer would go off hunting for tribal rhythms.

Late in the afternoon on the sixth day of his ride through Cameroon, Danny stopped in a large open market and bus depot in the town of Garoua. The marketplace was a line of mud-brick kiosks and chophouses, the air filled with the smell of baked dust and stones, hot oil and frying *beignets*. Abandoned cars squatted by the roadside, stripped clean but unblemished by corrosion in the dry air. Groups of men and children in long blouses like nightshirts idled their time away on the streetcorners.

Wives and daughters appeared on the road with their buckets, on their way to fetch water from the well on the other side of the marketplace. They wore bright-colored *pagnes* and kerchiefs, covering their traditionally naked breasts with T-shirts or castoff Western blouses, since the government in the capital city of Yaoundé had forbidden women to go topless.

At one kiosk in the shade sat a pan holding several bottles of Coca-Cola, Fanta, and ginger ale, cooling in water. Some vendors sold a thin stew of bony fish chunks over gritty rice; others sold *fufu*, a doughlike paste of pounded yams to be dipped into a sauce of meat and okra. Bread merchants stacked their long baguettes like dry firewood.

Danny used the back of his hand to smear sweat-caked dust off his forehead, then removed the bandanna he wore under his helmet to keep the sweat out of his eyes. With streaks of white skin peeking through the layer of grit around his eyes, he probably looked like some strange lemur.

In halting French, he began haggling with a wiry boy to buy a bottle of water. Hiding behind his kiosk, the boy demanded eight hundred francs for the water, an outrageous price. While Danny attempted to bargain it down, he caught sight of a gaunt, grayish-skinned man walking through the marketplace like a wind-up toy running down.

The man was playing a drum.

The boy cringed and looked away. Danny kept staring. The crowd seemed to shrink away from the strange man as he wandered among them, continuing his incessant beat. He wore his hair long and unruly, which in itself was unusual among the close-cropped Africans. In the equatorial sun, the long stained overcoat he wore must have heated his body like a furnace, but the man did not seem to notice. His eyes were focused on some invisible point in the distance.

"*Huit-cent francs,*" the boy insisted on his price, holding the lukewarm bottle of water just out of Danny's reach.

The staggering man walked closer, tapping a slow monotonous beat on the small cylindrical drum under his arm. He did not change his tempo, but continued to play as if his life depended on it. Danny saw that the man's fingers and wrists were wrapped with scraps of hide; even so, he had beaten his fingertips bloody.

Danny stood transfixed. He had heard tribal musicians play all manner of percussion instruments, from hollowed tree trunks, to rusted metal cans, to beautifully carved *djembe* drums with goat-skin drumheads—but he had never heard a tone so rich and sweet, with such an odd echoey quality as this strange African drum.

In the studio, he had messed around with drum synthesizers and reverbs and the new technology designed to turn computer hackers into musicians. But this drum sounded *different,* solid and pure, and it hooked him through the heart, hypnotizing him. It distracted him entirely from the unpleasant appearance of its bearer.

"What is that?" he asked.

"*Sept-cent francs,*" the boy insisted in a nervous whisper, dropping his price to seven hundred and pushing the water closer.

Danny walked in front of the staggering man, smiling broadly enough to show the grit between his teeth, and listened to the tapping drumbeat. The drummer turned his gaze to Danny and stared through him. The pupils of his eyes were like two gaping bullet wounds through his skull. Danny took a step backward, but found himself moving to the beat. The drummer faced him, finding his audience. Danny tried to place the rhythm, to burn it into his mind—something this mesmerizing simply *had* to be included in a new Blitzkrieg song.

Danny looked at the cylindrical drum, trying to determine what might be causing its odd double-resonance—a thin inner membrane, perhaps? He saw nothing but elaborate carvings on the sweat-polished wood, and a drumhead with a smooth, dark brown coloration. He knew the Africans used all kinds of skin for their drumheads, and he couldn't begin to guess what this was.

He mimed a question to the drummer, then asked, "*Est-ce-que je peux l'essayer?*" May I try it?

The gaunt man said nothing, but held out the drum near enough for Danny to touch it without interrupting his obsessive rhythm. His overcoat flapped open, and the hot stench of decay made Danny stagger backward, but he held his ground, reaching for the drum.

Danny ran his fingers over the smooth drumskin, then tapped with his fingers. The deep sound resonated with a beat of its own, like a heartbeat. It delighted him. "For sale? *Est-ce-que c'est à ven-dre?*" He took out a thousand francs as a starting point, although if water alone cost eight hundred francs here, this drum was worth much, much more.

The man snatched the drum away and clutched it to his chest, shaking his head vigorously. His drumming hand continued its unrelenting beat.

Danny took out two thousand francs, then was disappointed to see not the slightest change of expression on the odd drummer's face. "Okay, then, where was the drum made? Where can I get another one? *Où est-ce qu'on peut trouver un autre comme ça?*" He put most of the money back into his pack, keeping two hundred francs out. Danny stuffed the money into the fist of the drummer; the man's hand seemed to be made of petrified wood. "*Où?*"

The man scowled, then gestured behind him, toward the Mandara Mountains along Cameroon's border with Nigeria. "Kabas."

He turned and staggered away, still tapping on his drum as if to mark his footsteps. Danny watched him go, then returned to the kiosk, unfolding the map from his pack. "Where is this Kabas? Is it a place? *C'est un village?*"

"*Huit-cent francs,*" the boy said, offering the water again at his original price.

Danny bought the water, and the boy gave him directions.

He spent the night in a Garouan hotel that made Motel 6 look like Caesar's Palace. Anxious to be on his way to find his own new drum, Danny roused a local vendor and cajoled him into preparing a quick omelette for breakfast. He took a sip from his eight-hundred-franc bottle of water, saving the rest for the long bike ride, then pedaled off into the stirring sounds of early morning.

As Danny left Garoua on the main road, heading toward the mountains, savanna and thorn trees stretched away under a crystal sky. A pair of doves bathed in the dust of the road ahead, but as he rode toward them, they flew up into the last of the trees with a *chuk-chuk* of alarm and a flash of white tail feathers. Smoke from grass fires on the plains tainted the air.

How different it was to be riding *through* a landscape, he

thought—with no walls or windows between his senses and the world—rather than just riding *by* it. Danny felt the road under his thin wheels, the sun, the wind on his body. It made a strange place less exotic, yet it became infinitely more real.

The road out of Garoua was a wide boulevard that turned into a smaller road heading north. With his bicycle tires humming and crunching on the irregular pavement, Danny passed a few ragged cotton fields, then entered the plains of dry, yellow grass and thorny scrub, everywhere studded with boulders and sculpted anthills. By seven-thirty in the morning, a hot breeze rose, carrying a perfume like honeysuckle. Everything vibrated with heat.

Within an hour the road grew worse, but Danny kept his pace, taking deep breaths in the trancelike state that kept the horizon moving closer. Drums. Kabas. Long rides helped him clear his head, but he found he had to concentrate to steer around the worst ruts and the biggest stones.

Great columns of stone appeared above the hills to the east and west. One was pyramid-shaped, one resembled a huge rounded breast, yet another a great stone phallus. Danny had seen photographs of these inselberg formations caused by volcanoes that had eroded over the eons, leaving behind vertical cores of lava.

The road here, too, was eroded, a heaving washboard, which veered left into a trough between tumbled boulders and up through a gauntlet of thorn trees. Danny stopped for another drink of water, another glance at the map. The water boy at the kiosk had marked the location of Kabas with his fingernail, but it was not printed on the map.

After Danny had climbed uphill for an hour, the beaten path became no more than a worn trail, forcing him to squeeze between walls of thorns and dry millet stalks. The squadrons of hovering dragonflies were harmless, but the hordes of tiny flies circling his face were maddening, and he couldn't pedal fast enough to escape them.

It was nearly noon, the sun reflecting straight up from the dry earth, and the little shade cast by the scattered trees dwindled to a small circle around the trunks. "Where the hell am I going?" he said to the sky.

But in his head he kept hearing the odd, potent beat resonating from the bizarre drum he had seen in the Garoua marketplace. He recalled the grayish, shambling man who had never once stopped tapping on his drum, even though his fingers bled. No matter how bad the road got, Danny thought, he would keep going. He'd never been so intrigued by a drumbeat before, and he never left things half finished.

Danny Imbro was a goal-oriented person. The other members of Blitzkrieg razzed him about it, that once he made up his mind to do something, he plowed ahead, defying all common sense. Back in school, he had made up his mind to be a drummer. He had hammered away at just about every object in sight with his fingertips, pencils, silverware, anything that made noise. He kept at it until he drove everyone else around him nuts, and somewhere along the line he became good.

Now people stood at the chain-link fences behind concert halls and applauded whenever he walked from the backstage dressing rooms out to the tour buses—as if he were somehow doing a better job of *walking* than any of them had ever seen before. . . .

Up ahead, an enormous buttress tree, a gnarled and twisted pair of trunks hung with cable-thick vines, cast a wide patch of shade. Beneath the tree, watching him approach, sat a small boy.

The boy leaped to his feet, as if he had been waiting for Danny. Shirtless and dusty, he held a hooklike withered arm against his chest; but his grin was completely disarming. "*Je suis guide?*" the boy called.

Relief stifled Danny's laugh. He nodded vigorously. "*Oui!*" Yes, he could certainly use a guide right about now. "*Je cherche Kabas—village des tambours.* The village of drums."

The smiling boy danced around like a goat, jumping from rock to rock. He was pleasant-faced and healthy looking, except for the crippled arm; his skin was very dark but his eyes had a slight Asian cast. He chattered in a high voice, a mixture of French and native dialect. Danny caught enough to understand that the boy's name was Anatole.

Before the boy led him on, though, Danny dismounted, leaning his bicycle against a boulder, and unzipped his pack to take out the raisins, peanuts, and the dry remains of a baguette. Anatole watched him with wide eyes, and Danny gave him a handful of raisins, which the boy wolfed down. Small flies whined around their faces as they ate. Danny answered the boy's incessant questions with as few words as possible: did he come from America, did black boys live there, why was he visiting Cameroon?

The short rest sank its soporific claws into him, but Danny decided not to give in. An afternoon siesta made a lot of sense, but now that he had his own personal guide to the village, he made it his goal not to stop again until they reached Kabas. "Okay?" Danny raised his eyebrows and struggled to his feet.

Anatole sprang out from the shade and fetched Danny's bike for him, struggling with one arm to keep it upright. After several trips to Africa, Danny had seen plenty of withered limbs, caused by childhood diseases, accidents, and bungled inoculations. Out here in the wilder areas, such problems were even more prevalent, and he wondered how Anatole managed to survive; acting as a "guide" for the rare travelers would hardly suffice.

Danny pulled out a hundred francs—an eighth of what he had paid for one bottle of water—and handed it to the boy, who looked as if he had just been handed the crown jewels. Danny figured he had probably made a friend for life.

Anatole trotted ahead, gesturing with his good arm. Danny pedaled after him.

The narrow valley captured a smear of greenness in the dry hills, with a cluster of mango trees, guava trees, and strange baobabs with eight-foot-thick trunks. Playing the knowledgeable tour guide, Anatole explained that the local women used the baobab fruits for baby formula if their breast milk failed. The villagers used another tree to manufacture an insect repellent.

The houses of Kabas blended into the landscape, because they were *of* the landscape—stones and branches and grass. The walls were made of dry mud, laid on a handful at a time, and the roofs were thatched into cones. Tiny pink and white stones studded the mud, sparkling like quartz in the sun.

At first the place looked deserted, but then an ancient man emerged from a turret-shaped hut. An enormous cutlass dangled from his waist, although the shrunken man looked as if it might take him an hour just to lift the blade. Anatole shouted something, then gestured for Danny to follow him. The great cutlass swayed against the old man's unsteady knees as he bowed slightly —or stooped—and greeted Danny in formal, unpracticed French. "*Bonsoir!*"

"*Makonya,*" Danny said, remembering the local greeting from Garoua. He walked his bike in among the round and square buildings. A few chickens scratched in the dirt, and a pair of black-and-brown goats nosed between the huts. A sinewy, long-limbed old woman wearing only a loincloth tended a fire. He immediately started looking for the special drums, but saw none.

Within the village, a high-walled courtyard enclosed two round huts. Gravel covered the open area between them, roofed over with a network of serpent-shaped sticks supporting grass mats. This seemed to be the chief's compound. Anatole grasped Danny's arm and dragged him forward.

Inside the wall, a white-robed figure reclined in a canvas chair under an acacia tree. His handsome features had a North African cast, thin lips over white teeth, and a rakish mustache. His aristocratic head was wrapped in a red-and-white-checked scarf, and even in repose he was obviously tall. He looked every bit the romantic desert prince, like Rudolf Valentino in *The Sheik*. After greeting Danny in both French and the local language, the chief gestured for his visitor to sit beside him.

Before Danny could move, two other boys appeared carrying a rolled-up mat of woven grass, which they spread out for him. Anatole scolded them for horning in on his customer, but the two boys cuffed him and ignored his protests. Then the chief shouted at them all for disturbing his peace and drove the boys away. Danny watched them kicking Anatole as they scampered away from the chief, and he felt for his new friend, angry at how tough people picked on weaker ones the world over.

He sat cross-legged on the mat, and it took him only a moment to begin reveling in the moment of relaxation. No cars or trucks disturbed the peace. He was miles from the nearest electricity, or glass window, or airplane. He sat looking up into the leaves of the acacia, listening to the quiet buzz of the villagers, and thought, *I'm living in a* National Geographic *documentary!*

Anatole stole back into the compound, bearing two bottles of warm Mirinda orange soda, which he gave to Danny and the chief. Other boys gathered under the tree, glaring at Anatole, then looking at Danny with ill-concealed awe.

After several moments of polite smiling and nodding, Danny asked the chief if all the boys were his children. Anatole assisted in the unnecessary translation.

"Oui," the chief said, patting his chest proudly. He claimed to have fathered thirty-one sons, which made Danny wonder if the women in the village found it politic to routinely claim the chief as the father of their babies. As with all remote African villages, though, many children died of various sicknesses. Just a week earlier, one of the babies had succumbed to a terrible fever, the chief said.

The chief asked Danny the usual questions about his country, whether any black men lived there, why had he visited Cameroon; then he insisted that Danny eat dinner with them. The women would prepare the village's specialty of chicken in peanut sauce.

Hearing this, the old sentry emerged with his cutlass, smiled widely at Danny, then turned around the side wall. The squawking of a terrified chicken erupted in the sleepy afternoon air, the sounds of a scuffle, and then the squawking stopped.

Finally, Danny asked the question that had brought him to Kabas in the first place. *"Moi, je suis musicien; je cherche les tambours speciaux."* He mimed rapping on a small drum, then turned to Anatole for assistance.

The chief sat up startled, then nodded. He hammered on the air, mimicking drum playing, as if to make sure. Danny nodded. The chief clapped his hands and gestured for Anatole to take Danny somewhere. The boy pulled Danny to his feet and, surrounded by other chattering boys, dragged him back out of the walled courtyard. Danny managed to turn around and bow to the chief.

After trooping up a stairlike terrace of rock, they entered the courtyard of another homestead. The main shelter was built of hand-formed bricks with a flat roof of corrugated metal. Anatole explained that this was the home of the local *sorcier,* or wizard.

Anatole called out, then gestured for Danny to follow through the low doorway. Inside the hut, the walls were hung with evidence of the *sorcier*'s trade—odd bits of metal, small carvings, bundles of fur and feathers, mortars full of powders and herbs, clay urns for water and millet beer, smooth skins curing as they hung from the roof poles. And drums.

"Tambours!" Anatole said, spreading his hands wide.

Judging from the craftsman's tools around the hut, the *sorcier* made the village's drums as as well as stored them. Danny saw several small gourd drums, larger log drums, and hollow cylinders of every size, all intricately carved with serpentine symbols, circles feeding into spirals, lines tangled into knots.

Danny reached out to touch one—then the *sorcier* himself stood up from the shadows near the far wall. Danny bit off a startled cry as the lithe old man glided forward. The *sorcier* was tall and rangy, but his skin was a battleground of wrinkles, as if someone had clumsily fashioned him out of papier-mâché.

"Pardon," Danny said. The wrinkled man had been sitting on a low stool, putting the finishing touches to a new drum.

Fixing his eyes on his visitor, the *sorcier* withdrew a medium-sized drum from a niche in the wall. Closing his eyes, he tapped on it. The mud walls of the hut reverberated with the hollow vibration, an earthy, primal beat that resonated in Danny's bones. Danny grinned with awe. Yes! The gaunt man's drum had not been a fluke. The drums of Kabas had some special construction that caused this hypnotic tone.

Danny reached out tentatively. The wrinkled man gave him an appraising look, then extended the drum enough for Danny to strike it. He tapped a few tentative beats, and laughed out loud when the instrument rewarded him with the same rich sound.

The *sorcier* turned away, taking the drum with him and returning it to its niche in the wall. In two flowing strides, the wrinkled man went to his stool in the shadows, picked up the drum he had been fashioning, and moved it into the crack of light that seeped through the windows. Pointing, he spoke in a staccato dialect, which Anatole translated into pidgin French.

"The *sorcier* is finishing a new drum today," Anatole said. "Perhaps they will play it this evening, an initiation. The chief's baby son would have enjoyed that. From the baby's body, the *sorcier* was able to salvage only enough skin to make this one small drum."

"What?" Danny said, looking down at the deep brown skin covering the top of the drum.

Anatole explained, as if it was the most ordinary thing in the world, that whenever one of the chief's many sons died, the *sorcier* used his skin to make one of Kabas's special drums. It had always been done.

Danny wrestled with that for a moment. On his first trip to Africa five years earlier, he had learned the wrenching truth of how different these cultures were.

"Why?" he finally asked. *"Pourquoi?"*

He had seen other drums made entirely of human skin taken from slain enemies, fashioned in the shape of stunted bodies with gaping mouths; when the drums were tapped, a hollow sound came from the effigies' mouths. He knew that he was wrong for trying to impose his Western moral framework on the inhabitants of an alien land. *I'm sorry, sir, but you'll have to check your preconceptions at the door,* he thought jokingly to himself.

"Magique." Anatole's eyes showed a flash of fear—fear born of respect for great power, rather than paranoia or panic. With the magic drums of Kabas, the chief could conquer any man, steal his heartbeat. It was old magic, a technique the village wizards had

discovered long before the French had come to Cameroon, and before them the Germans. Kabas had been isolated, and at peace for longer than the memories of the oldest people in the village. Because of the drums. Anatole smiled, proud of his story, and Danny restrained an urge to pat him on the head.

Trying not to let his disbelief show, Danny nodded deeply to the *sorcier*. "*Merci*," he said. As Anatole led him back out to the courtyard, the *sorcier* returned to his work on the small drum.

Danny wondered if he should have tried to buy one of the drums from the wrinkled man. Did he believe the story about using human skins? Probably. Why would Anatole lie?

As they left the *sorcier*'s homestead to begin the trek back to the village, he looked westward across the jagged landscape of inselbergs. At sunset, the air filled with hundreds of kites, their wings rigid, circling high on the last thermals. Like leaves before the wind, the birds came spiraling down to disappear into the trees, filling them with the invisible flapping of wings.

When they reached the main village again, Danny saw that the women had returned from their labor in the nearby fields. He was familiar with the African tradition of sending the women and children out for backbreaking labor while the men lounged in the shade and talked "business."

The numerous sons of the chief and various adults gathered inside the courtyard near the fire, which the old sinewy woman had stoked into a larger blaze. Other men emerged, and Danny wondered where they had been all afternoon. Out hunting? If so, they had nothing to show for their efforts. Anatole directed Danny to sit on a mat beside the chief, and everyone smiled vigorously at each other, the villagers exchanging the call-and-response litany of ritual greetings, which could go on for several minutes.

The old woman served the chief first, then the honored guest. She placed a brown yam like a baked potato on the mat in front of him, miming that it was hot. Danny took a cautious bite; the yam was pungent and turned to paste in his mouth. Then the woman reappeared with the promised chicken in peanut sauce. They ate quietly in a circle around the fire, ignoring each other, as red shadows flickered across their faces.

Listening to the sounds of eating, as well as the simmering evening hush of the West African hills, Danny felt the emptiness like a peaceful vacuum, draining away stress and loud noises and hectic schedules. After too many head-pounding tours and adrenaline-crazed performances, Danny was convinced he had forgotten how to sit quietly, how to slow down. After one rough segment of the last Blitzkrieg tour, he had taken a few days to go camping in the mountains; he recalled pacing in vigorous circles around the picnic table, muttering to himself that he was relaxing as fast as he could! Calming down was an acquired skill, he felt, and there was no better teacher than Africa.

After the meal, heads turned in the firelight, and Danny looked up to see the *sorcier* enter the chief's compound. The wrinkled man cradled several of his mystical drums. He placed one of the drums in front of the chief, then set the others on an empty spot on the ground. He squatted behind one drum, thrusting his long, lean legs up and to the side like the wings of a vulture.

Danny perked up. "A concert?" He turned to Anatole, who spoke rapidly to the *sorcier*. The wrinkled man looked skeptically at Danny, then shrugged. He picked up one of the extra drums and ceremoniously extended it to Danny.

Danny couldn't stop smiling. He took the drum and looked at it. The coffee-colored skin felt smooth and velvety as he touched it. A shiver went up his spine as he tapped the drumhead. Making music from human skin. He forced his instinctive revulsion back into the gray static of his mind, the place where he stored things "to think about later." For now, he had the drum in his hands.

The chief thumped out a few beats, then stopped. The *sorcier* mimicked them, and glanced toward Danny. "Jam session!" he muttered under his breath, then repeated the sequence easily and cleanly, but added a quick, complicated flourish to the end.

The chief raised his eyebrows, followed suit with the beat, and made it more complicated still. The *sorcier* flowed into his part, and Danny joined in with another counterpoint. It reminded him of the "Dueling Banjos" sequence from the movie *Deliverance*.

The echoing, rich tone of the drum made his fingers warm and tingly, but he allowed himself to be swallowed up in the mystic rhythms, the primal pounding out in the middle of the African wilderness. The other night noises vanished around him, the smoke from the fire rose straight up, and the light centered into a pinpoint of his concentration.

Using his bare fingers—sticks would only interrupt the magical contact between himself and the drum—Danny continued weaving into their rhythms, trading points and counterpoints. The beat touched a core of past lives deep within him, an atavistic, pagan intensity, as the three drummers reached into the Pulse of the

World. The chief played on; the *sorcier* played on; and Danny let his eyes fade half-closed in a rhythmic trance, as they explored the wordless language and hypnotic interplay of rhythm.

Danny became aware of the other boys standing up and swaying, jabbering excitedly and laughing as they danced around him. He deciphered their words as "White Man drum! White Man drum!" It was a safe bet they'd never seen a white man play a drum before.

Suddenly the *sorcier* stopped, and within a beat the chief also quit playing. Danny felt wrenched out of the experience, but reluctantly played a concluding figure as well, ending with an emphatic flam. His arms burned from the exertion, sweat dripped down the stubble on his chin. His ears buzzed from the noise. Unable to restrain himself, Danny began laughing with delight.

The *sorcier* said something, which Anatole translated. "*Vous avez l'esprit de batteur.*" You have the spirit of a drummer.

With a throbbing hand, Danny squeezed Anatole's bare shoulder and nodded. "*Oui.*"

The chief also congratulated him, thanking him for sharing his White Man's music with the village. Danny found that ironic, since he had come here to pick up a rich African flavor for *his* compositions. But Danny could record his impressions in new songs; the village of Kabas had no way of keeping what he had brought to them.

The withered *sorcier* picked up one of the drums at his side, and Danny recognized it as the small drum the old man had been finishing in the dim hut that afternoon. He fixed his deep gaze on Danny for a moment, then handed it to him.

Anatole sat up, alarmed, but bit off a comment he had intended to make. Danny nodded in reassurance and in delight as he took the new drum. He held it to his chest and inclined his head deeply to show his appreciation. "*Merci!*"

Anatole took Danny's hand to lead him away from the walled courtyard. The chief clapped his hands and barked something to the other boys, who looked at Anatole with glee before they got up and scurried to the huts apparently to sleep. Anatole stared nervously at Danny, but Danny didn't understand what had just occurred.

He repeated his thanks, bowing again to the chief and the *sorcier*, but the two of them just stared at him. He was reminded of an East African scene: a pair of lions sizing up their prey. He shook his head to clear the morbid thought, and followed Anatole.

In the village proper, one of the round thatched huts had been swept for Danny to sleep in. Outside, his bicycle leaned against a tree, no doubt guarded during the day by the little man with the enormous cutlass. Anatole seemed uneasy, wanting to say something, but afraid.

Trying to comfort him, Danny opened his pack and withdrew a stick of chewing gum for the boy. Anatole spoke rapidly, gushing his thanks. Suddenly the other boys materialized from the shadows with childish murder in their eyes. They tried to take the gum from Anatole, but he popped it in his mouth and ran off. "Hey!" Danny shouted, but Anatole bolted into the night with the boys chasing after.

Wondering if Anatole was in any real danger, Danny removed the blanket and sleeping bag from his bike, then carried them inside the guest hut. He decided the boy could take care of himself, that he must have spent his life as the whipping boy for the other sons of the chief. The thought drained some of the exhilaration from the memory of the evening's performance.

His legs ached after the torturous ride upland from Garoua, and he fantasized briefly about sitting in the Jacuzzi in the capital suite of some five-star hotel. He considered how wonderful it would be to sip some cold champagne, or a Scotch on the rocks.

Instead, he lifted the gift drum, inspecting it. He would find some way to use it on the next album, add a rich African tone to the music. Paul Simon and Peter Gabriel had done it, though the style of Blitzkrieg's music was a bit more . . . aggressive.

He would not tell anyone about the human skin, especially the customs officials. He tried without success to decipher the mystical swirling patterns carved into the wood, the interwoven curves, circles, and knots. It made him dizzy.

Danny closed his eyes and began to play the drum, quietly so as not to disturb the other villagers. But as the sound reached his ears, he snapped his eyes open. The tone from the drum was flat and weak, like a cheap tourist tom-tom, plastic over a coffee can.

He frowned at the gift drum. Where was the rich reverberation, the primal pulse of the earth? He tapped again, but heard only an empty and hollow sound, soulless. Danny scowled, wondering if the *sorcier* had ruined the drum by accident, then decided to get rid of it by giving it to the unsuspecting White Man who wouldn't know the difference.

Angry and uneasy, Danny set the African drum next to him; he would try it again in the morning. He could play it for the chief, show him its flat tone. Perhaps they would exchange it. Maybe he would have to buy another one.

He hoped Anatole was all right.

Danny sat down to pull the thorns and prickers from his clothes. The village women had provided him with two plastic basins of water for bathing, one for soaping and scrubbing, the other for rinsing. The warm water felt refreshing on his face, his neck. After stripping off his pungent socks, he rinsed his toes and soles.

The night stillness was hypnotic, and as he spread his sleeping bag and stretched out on it, he felt as if he were seeping into the cloth, into the ground, swallowed up in sleep. . . .

Anatole woke him up only a few moments later, shaking him and whispering harshly in his ear. Dirt, blood, and bruises covered the boy's wiry body, and his clothes had been torn in a scuffle. He didn't seem to care. He kept shaking Danny.

But it was already too late.

Danny sat up, blinking his eyes. Sharp pains like the gash of a bear trap ripped through his chest. He felt as if a giant hand had wrapped around his torso, and would *squeeze* until his ribs popped free of his spine.

He gasped, opening and closing his mouth, but could not give voice to his agony. He grabbed Anatole's withered arm, but the boy struggled away, searching for something. Black spots swam in Danny's eyes. He tried to breathe, but his chest wouldn't let him. He began slipping, sliding down an endless cliff into blackness.

Anatole finally found an object on the floor of the hut. He snatched it up with his good hand, tucked it firmly under his withered arm, and began to thump on it.

The drum!

As the boy rapped out a slow steady beat, Danny felt the iron band loosen around his heart. Blood rushed into his head again, and he drew a deep breath. Dizziness continued to swim around him, but the impossible pain receded. He clutched his chest, rubbing his sternum. He uttered a breathy thanks to Anatole.

Had he just suffered a heart attack? Good God, all the fast living had finally caught up with him while he was out in the middle of nowhere, far from any hope of medical attention!

Then he realized with a chill that the sounds from the gift drum were now rich and echoey, with the unearthly depth he remembered from the other drums. Anatole continued his slow rhythm, and suddenly Danny recognized it. A *heartbeat.*

What was it the boy had told him inside the *sorcier's* hut — that the magical drums could steal a man's heartbeat?

"*Ton coeur c'est dans ici,*" Anatole said, continuing his drumming. Your heartbeat lives in here now.

Danny remembered the gaunt, shambling man in the marketplace of Garoua, obsessively tapping the drum from Kabas as if his life depended on it, until his hide-wrapped fingers were bloodied. Had that man also escaped his fate in the village, and fled south?

"You had the spirit of a drummer," Anatole said in his pidgin French, "and now the drum has your spirit." As if to emphasize his statement, as if he knew a White Man would be skeptical of such magic, Anatole ceased his rhythm on the drum.

The claws returned to Danny's heart, and the vise in his chest clamped back down. His heart had stopped beating. Heartbeats, drumbeats —

The boy stopped only long enough to convince Danny, then started the beat again. Anatole looked at him with pleading eyes in the shadowy light of the hut. "*Je vais avec toi!*" I go with you. Let me be your heartbeat. From now on.

Leaving his sleeping bag behind, Danny staggered out of the guest hut to his bicycle resting against an acacia tree. The rest of the village was dark and silent, and the next morning they would expect to find him dead and cold on his blankets; and the new drum would have the same resonant quality, the same throbbing of a captured spirit, to add to their collection. The sound of White Man's music for Kabas.

"*Allez!*" Anatole whispered as Danny climbed aboard his bike. Go!

What was he supposed to do now? The boy ran in front of him along the narrow track. Danny did not fear navigating the rugged trail by moonlight, with snakes and who-knows-what abroad in the grass, as much as he feared staying in Kabas. In the morning, the chief and the *sorcier* would come to look at his body, no doubt to appraise their pale new drumskin, and Danny planned to be long gone by then.

But how long could Anatole continue his drumming? If the beat stopped for only a moment, Danny would seize up. They would have to take turns sleeping. Would this nightmare continue after he had left the vicinity of the village? Distance had not helped the shambling man in the marketplace in Garoua.

Would this be the rest of his life?

Stricken with panic, Danny nodded to the boy, just wanting to be out of there and not knowing what else to do. *Yes, I'll take you with me. What other choice do I have?* He pedaled his bike away from Kabas, crunching on the rough dirt path. Anatole jogged in front of him, tapping on the drum.

And tapping.

And tapping.

Four thousand copies of this book have been printed by the Maple-Vail Book Manufacturing Group, Binghamton, NY, for Golden Gryphon Press, Urbana, IL. The typeset is Elante, printed on 55# Sebago. The binding cloth is Arrestox B. Typesetting by The Composing Room, Inc., Kimberly, WI.